D1591024

BEC McMASTER

SOULBOUND

THE DARK ARTS SERIES

Soulbound: A Dark Arts Novel
Copyright 2017 (c) Bec McMaster

All rights reserved. No part of this book may be reproduced, scanned or
distributed in any manner whatsoever, without written permission from
the author, except in the case of brief quotation embodied in critical
articles and reviews.

This novel is a work of fiction. The names, characters, places and
incidents are products of the author's imagination, or are used
fictitiously. Any resemblance to persons living or dead, actual events,
locales or organizations are entirely coincidental.

Edited and proofread by: Hot Tree Editing
Print formatting by: Cover Me Darling and Athena Interior Book Design
Cover Art (c) Damonza.com

ALSO AVAILABLE BY BEC MCMASTER

LONDON STEAMPUNK SERIES

Kiss Of Steel

Heart Of Iron

My Lady Quicksilver

Forged By Desire

Of Silk And Steam

Novellas in the same series:

Tarnished Knight

The Curious Case Of The Clockwork Menace

**LONDON STEAMPUNK: THE BLUE BLOOD
CONSPIRACY SERIES**

Mission: Improper

The Mech Who Loved Me

DARK ARTS SERIES

Shadowbound

Hexbound

Soulbound

BURNED LAND SERIES

Nobody's Hero

The Last True Hero

The Hero Within

LEGENDS OF THE STORM

Heart of Fire

Storm of Desire

OTHER

The Many Lives Of Hadley Monroe

*What readers are saying about
Bec's action-packed romances*

"The Mech Who Loved Me has everything I've come to expect from McMaster: compelling characters, **sizzling sexual tension**, mystery, danger, and of course, true love."
- *Let Them Read Books Blog*

'Richly imagined, gritty and dark, and **full of hot heroes and hot sex**... utterly delicious. " – *Smart Bitches, Trashy Books* for *Kiss of Steel*

"Action, adventure...and **blazing hot seduction**...Bec McMaster offers it all." -**Eve Silver, author of** *Sins of the Flesh* for *Kiss of Steel*

"This book was so damn good and surpassed beyond my expectations...I haven't read anything like this before..." – *Dreamy Addictions Blog for Nobody's Hero*

Kiss Of Steel – Georgia RWA Maggies Best Paranormal Romance 2013

Heart Of Iron – One of Library Journal's Best Romances 2013

Forged By Desire – RITA Finalist Paranormal Romance 2015

Of Silk And Steam – RT Reviews Best Steampunk Romance 2016

Mission: Improper – #1 Amazon Steampunk Bestseller, Finalist for 2016 PRISM Award Best Steampunk

Hexbound – Winner of the 2016 PRISM Award for Historical Fantasy

PROLOGUE

Being able to See the future is not always a gift.

— Cleo Montcalm

CLEO MONTCALM WOKE to a dream.

She sat at a small table in a room with no walls, a room that stretched into infinity. The ceiling was the night sky, blossoming to early dawn on the horizon, and a floor of black and white tiles gleamed beneath her. A chessboard reigned on the table in front of her, a game in progress. There was a silence to the place that felt somewhat leaden, and her skin itched as though thousands of invisible eyes watched her.

She was not alone.

She never was, when she found herself at this immortal chessboard.

"You look tired," said a faintly amused voice, a voice that echoed slightly, as if it came from a throat that was somehow hollow. The figure seated opposite her wore a silk cloak and hood of purest ebony, and it could have been male or female—she could never tell.

It was certainly not human, regardless of gender.

"What am I doing here?" she demanded, her heart leaping in her chest. She pushed away from the small table with its chessboard, and turned around, but there was no escape. Not physically. "Why did you pull me into this cursed place again?"

"What did I tell you the last we met?" The voice finally sounded male.

Cleo slowly turned to look at him—it. The last time she'd woken in this plane had been following the incident in which her husband, Sebastian Montcalm, had been gravely wounded. "You said I was here to make the moves," she whispered, and she could no longer avoid the sight of that mocking chessboard. "And I did. I put my bishop into play, and it defeated yours."

"Defeated?"

There were now two white bishops on the chessboard. "Verity Hawkins came to our side," Cleo said, her voice strengthening. "She's one of *my* pieces now. I'm winning."

But even as she said the words, she began to take in the structure of play.

"Are you," said the entity, and it wasn't a question.

The board had changed. The white queen no longer wore her blindfold; a fitting tribute, since Cleo herself had lost the piece of linen that guarded her regular sight, and protected her true Vision. The white king wore her husband's face, and though he still protected her, he'd moved several paces away from her to counter the demon's threat.

Or perhaps the distance indicated the way he'd left her following the demon's previous move.

After all, it was a marriage of convenience between them, not a true alliance.

The black king's carved face had finally revealed itself. Drake de Wynter, Sebastian's father, was now the human vessel for the demon, a blow from which they were struggling to recover. The black king radiated menace as it replaced a square that had previously held one of her heretofore-unseen pawns.

Who had she lost? She couldn't see all the faces on the little pieces, as though some magic obscured them from her.

I don't want to make the moves. I don't want to set the play. Cleo wrapped her arms around her middle. This game had consequences beyond what she was prepared to pay, but the last time they'd played, the demon had been merciless.

"Of course you make the moves. You're the one who can see the future." Those hollow words were branded across her mind from the previous dream it had dragged her into.

But I can't. I can't see the future anymore.

And her pieces were her friends. One wrong move and she'd lose another one.

"Your move," the demon said.

The black queen had advanced with her array of pawns. Cleo couldn't see the trap or what the demon intended with this advance, but she knew it was a threat. Premonition itched along her spine, like icy little prickles. Following the loss of her blindfold, and her Visions along with it, Premonition was virtually all she had left.

"And what if I refuse?" She lifted her gaze.

The demon remained still. "Then you forfeit your turn. And I gain it. If you refuse to play, then I will make *my* move."

Cleo paced in front of the board, rubbing at her mouth. Her eyes kept settling on the black queen. Just what was he planning with that piece? Who was the black queen meant to represent? The face remained blank, but the woman's dress was low-cut and vaguely obscene. The last time they'd played, the black queen wore the face of Sebastian's mother, but there had to be a reason it was blank now. Could he change the importance of players?

"I traded you a player," the demon said. "Drake for Verity. Which do you think is the more powerful piece?"

Drake. Cleo swallowed, and considered the board. He was trying to draw her attention to the black king, but every itch of her Premonition said that the queen was the dangerous one.

"Make your move, Cassandra."

She flinched at her old title, and then waved her hand slowly over the board, trying to "feel" which piece to play. The second she reached the black queen, an image sprang into her mind; a mirror with a hooded figure lifting its hands to the cloak it wore, as if to reveal itself—

"I don't think so," said the demon, shattering the swift pulse of vision before the black queen could be revealed. "Not yet, at any stage."

Instinct shivered as Cleo paused over the white king. *Sebastian.*

But he was gone from her side, trying to recover from the loss of his father, and the part he had played in it. Drake had sacrificed himself for Sebastian, and her husband had taken the blow hard.

Or at least, she presumed he had. All her letters remained unreturned, and he'd shut down the mental link they shared, until she could barely feel him anymore.

"Wake up," she whispered to herself. "Cleo, wake up."

You need to escape this nightmare.

Her hand reached inexorably toward the white king, just as something began sucking at her. Vision hammered through her. A book sat unopened on her bed, and as she looked at it, the book jerked open, its pages rifling in an unseen wind....

What did it mean?

The world swirled around her as she blinked back to reality. The skin on her arm seemed to waver, her skirts shivering in some nonexistent breeze. "I choose Sebastian."

"So be it," said the dark entity opposite her, and Cleo shivered as she heard the amusement in its voice as if she'd just stepped into its trap. It reached out a pale hand and set the black queen into play. "White king meets black queen. I wonder who shall win? Sebastian? Or—"

"Wake up!" some part of her screamed.

And Cleo sat up in bed with a gasping breath as her opponent's laugh echoed in her ears.

CHAPTER ONE

When the red comet rules the skies, the Prime shall fall. A new Prime shall ascend to the head of the Order. Three sons. Three relics. Three sacrifices. Only then can the Prime be torn down.

—Prophecy as spoken by the Order's previous Cassandra

THE PROBLEM WITH being able to see the future was what happened when you no longer owned those abilities.

Cleo Sinclair, no, *Montcalm*—she had to keep reminding herself she was married—stepped inside the Black Horse Pub and gently tugged her gloves off. The scent of the place almost made her eyes water; stale beer, hints of vomit, and the pall of malignant sorcery that coated her tongue like something metallic.

"I really don't think we should be here, ma'am," said her nervous footman, a sorcerer named Jeremy Prior, who was serving his apprenticeship with the Order of the Dawn Star. "This is Balthazar's Labyrinth." His eyes showed their whites as he looked around. "Our sort don't come here. This is where black magic lurks, and those as have been cast out of the Order scurry about. You can find anything occult here—but the price you pay isn't in coin. Or so they say."

"Precisely." *You can find anything.* She was tired of sitting on her thumbs and waiting for word from her reluctant husband. She had a demon to find, and without her visions.... Well, a girl had to do something. She'd been dreaming of a mirror of late, and it had hounded her nights long enough. She needed to find it, and her dreams had brought her here. She didn't know if they meant anything... but then she'd never seen that mirror before in her life. All she knew was she needed it. It had to be a sign of her divination gifts trying to send her a message. "Come along then, and step lively. The sooner I find what I'm looking for, the sooner we can leave."

"But the Prime—"

"Is busy," Cleo interrupted. "We don't need to disturb Lady Rathbourne, and if successful here, then hopefully I shall be able to aid her current cause."

She couldn't simply sit at home anymore, trying to avoid the nightmares that woke her. Cleo needed *to do* something to stay them.

She was the only one who had caught a glimpse of the demon's plans.

A half-dozen residents peered at her from the dim confines of the tavern, then blinked in shock. The bartender almost dropped the glass he'd been polishing, and Cleo swept toward him with a smile, knowing her appearance had set the cat among the pigeons. It wasn't every day a young woman dressed like one of the *haut monde* entered this place.

The bartender was a short man, standing on a stool behind the counter. Part imp, perhaps, judging by the set of his nose and forehead. His sleeves were rolled up, revealing a heavy manacle around his left wrist, and runes burned a bright copper against the brass. A shackle by the look of it, which meant he'd run afoul of the Order at least once.

And considering her status as an Order sorcerer, she doubted he'd be much inclined to help her.

"Good day," Cleo greeted. "I'm interested in passage beyond those doors"—she tipped her head toward the enormous steel bank vault doors at the end of the room—"and I'm willing to pay for it."

"You," said the imp, "don't belong here."

"I've been trying to tell her that the entire carriage ride," Jeremy blurted, "but she won't listen to me."

"Mr.—"

"Cochrane," said the imp, and then spat on the floor beside his stool. He leaned on the counter. "You should listen to your friend here. It ain't my place to warn away pretty little morsels like yourself"—this with a sneer—"but there aren't many rules in the Labyrinth. And if you walk in there, chances are, you won't walk out."

"I'm aware of the risks," she said, forcing herself to smile through her teeth. "My father was Lord Tremayne— you might have heard of him."

Cochrane's face paled, but he recovered quickly. "Heard his lordship's dead."

"Yes." It didn't hurt as much as it once had. Her visions had seen the cause of her father's death, but he'd chosen his own road in the end. He hadn't had to stray down the dark path she'd seen. "My point being... if you think this is the worst I've encountered, then you are very much underestimating me. If you think your Labyrinth dangerous, then I assure you it's a walk in the park. My father dabbled with demons. He tried to undermine the Order, and paid for it with his life. Dion Letchworth dandled me on her lap when I was a child, before she sold her soul to a demon. Madame Firth was my first tutor in the Dark Arts, and let me assure you, she was not a very kind mentor." Cleo frowned. "Sir Alaric Erskine was my godfather, though he died when I was two. Or got sucked into one of the Shadow Dimensions he was dabbling with—Father never really did say. But... you do see my point?"

"Don't say I didn't warn you."

Capitulation. Excellent. "How much will passage cost?"

"Twenty quid." Cochrane snapped.

More than she'd expected. "Well, I'm not carrying a great deal of coin on me. I only have ten pounds. Would you accept a favor?"

"No coin, no passage."

"Perhaps a reading?" Cleo persisted. She reached for Mr. Cochrane's hand. "Brace yourself."

"What the devil are you—"

Then she was touching his manacle, and images exploded into being around his head. Cleo's gaze went distant. She couldn't access her Foresight anymore, but predictions were still within her capability, and several other gifts of the divination arts, such as psychometry—the ability to read an object's history. A woman sprang to being, luring Cochrane into shadows. "There was a woman," Cleo said hollowly. "She trapped you here. Or urged you to do something that put you on the wrong side of the Order. A theft.... I can't see what it is, but you stole something for her. That's why you're bound. There's... a curse hanging over you. She's coming back for you, to break the curse. There's a tattoo on your skin, some sort of rune, and it will flare gold the day she sets foot on these shores again—"

"That's enough!" Cochrane jerked his hand from beneath hers, and nearly fell off the stool. He looked horrified. "No! She can't come back. She was bound. Locked away. *No.*"

Cleo drew her vision back to the here and now, seeing the sweat on Cochrane's temples. "Payment enough?"

He was practically gray now. Staggering off his stool, he turned for the bank doors, waddling across the room. "Go! I want no more of your ilk in here!" Turning the little round wheel, he unlocked the door to the Labyrinth, and swung it open.

Behind the enormous door, another world opened up, raucous sound assaulting them. People bustled past, sparing the doors a curious glimpse, but no more. It looked like some darkened version of the Portobello Road markets outside the Black Horse Pub.

"Go, you cursed bitch!" Mr. Cochrane snarled, gesturing her through.

An enormous stone golem guarded the passageway beyond, and Cleo glanced at it as she stepped into a world she'd barely imagined even existed. "How do we get out?"

"Find your own way out!" Cochrane snarled, and slammed the heavy bank vault door in her face.

"I think you riled him," Jeremy said. "I don't think you should have mentioned that bit about his curse."

"Probably not." People never did like to catch a glimpse of their future. "That wasn't so hard though, was it? We're inside."

Now to find the mirror she needed.

Jeremy peered with sickly fascination at the warren of alleyways hidden from the world by a glass-paned roof above them. Fat tallow candles sat in every crevice, casting plenty of light to see by, and there were dirty puddles in the narrow cobbled streets, though the liquid within looked like ink and not water. "I think that might have been the easy part."

Cleo laughed, and set off along Main Street. "Oh, Mr. Prior. Where's your sense of adventure?"

He staggered past a woman in a hooded cloak, pushing a barrow full of little dolls that gave one an eerie sense. "It is wondering why I ever left the Prime's manor this morning. I mean, my sense of adventure could be studying some of my dusty old grimoires right now. It could be sipping a hot cup of tea in the safety of the Prime's library. It might even extend to some of Cook's ginger biscuits, because I'm fairly certain I feel a little nauseous."

"I didn't ask you to come," she pointed out.

Jeremy stiffened in protest, his Adam's apple bobbing nervously. "I could hardly leave you to venture here alone!"

"You're a gentleman, Mr. Prior. No doubt about that." She looked along the narrow branches of alleys that spiraled out from Main Street. All she'd seen in her dreams had been the inside of a bookstore, and dozens of musty books, a dark mirror calling to her, almost throbbing inside her dream, as if it demanded she pick it up.

Closing her eyes, she splayed her hands wide, feeling the bite of the three rings she wore beneath her gloves. The chips of marble and diamond in them revealed her to be an acolyte of the Light Arts, which had to be hidden here. Each ring represented a different Order level she'd passed, and three was only two more than what an apprentice wore. Her father had never seen much use in educating her outside her divination. No, he wanted what her Visions could bring him: gold, power, allies. But it was moments like these that made her wish she'd had someone to teach her more than divination, healing, and wards.

This way, itched her sense of premonition. At least *it* was finely tuned. Cleo opened her eyes, staring down the alley she faced. Not a creature stirred anywhere along the narrow passage, and the second stories leaned toward each other, creating an almost tunnel effect. Shadows loomed.

"Of course." Jeremy swallowed. "It had to be this one."

She walked slowly into the shadows. The shop windows were grimy here. Ripples of movement within one particular window betrayed a presence watching them.

There was no wind in Balthazar's Labyrinth, but the sign above the next shop made a creaking sound. *Gentian's Baubles and Books*. Premonition shivered through her.

Something was about to happen. She could never quite tell what, as her sense of premonition was vague, at best, but this *might* be the place she'd been searching for. It could also mean three ruffians were about to leap out and assault her and poor Jeremy, but she didn't think so. The itch wasn't screaming beneath her skin. Nothing dangerous lurked.

Or nothing too dangerous.

Cleo pushed open the door. It swung open with a merry tinkle that seemed vastly out of place.

"Welcome, miss...." The shopkeeper's eyes slid over her, his fleshy mouth widening in a smile when he saw her pretty rose-colored skirts, and the elegant sweep of her hat. A pigeon ripe for plucking, said his expression. "What may I do for you? A book, perhaps? Or maybe some occult item?" He picked up a brass idol of a monkey, gesturing to it with a showman's flair. "This statue came all the way from the Balinese islands. They say it can speak a dozen languages, and predict the future if keyed right."

Cleo brushed the monkey's leering face with her gloved finger. Not a single quiver chilled her skin.

"Nonsense. There's not even a hint of sorcerous energy coming off it. If I didn't know better, I'd say you were trying to fleece me." She graced him with her sweetest smile. "But a man like you wouldn't be so foolish, would you?"

Turning on her heel, she swept through the shop, searching for what she wanted—and finding little more than dust and fake relics.

"Ah, of course I'm not trying to fleece you." The shopkeeper scurried after her. "Perhaps I could interest you in an amulet worn by Helen of Troy herself—"

"Very pretty." She stepped around him. "But not what I'm looking for."

"A jade carving of—"

Cleo held her hand up. "No, I'm interested in an Ouroboros Mirror. A colleague of mine told me you might have one on hand." Remington Cross hadn't precisely been speaking to *her* when he'd mentioned it, but that little fact didn't matter so much.

The shopkeeper's face paled. "I'm afraid I don't have one."

Lie. She couldn't always sense when someone was speaking the truth, but the lie jarred along her nerves like a badly sawed violin. Cleo turned her unsettling gaze upon him. "Do you take me for a fool?"

Tugging her lace gloves off, one fingertip at a time, she sauntered through the shop. "While it could be said I'm here unofficially"—she made sure he saw the rings on her fingers that heralded she was from the Order—"I do have a special dispensation."

To find out whatever she could about the demon who'd taken Drake de Wynter's body as a Vessel, and how to defeat it.

"Three rings," said the shopkeeper, folding his arms over his chest, "mark you as a lower-level member of the Order."

Cleo smiled. "One with the ear of Lady Rathbourne. I'm currently residing at her home."

Wariness entered his eyes. "The new Prime."

"There. See." Her smile grew. "I knew you would understand the importance of my presence here."

It was a good thing he couldn't tell whether she was lying or not, though poor Jeremy's bug eyes, and the way he appeared to be holding his breath in disbelief, nearly gave her away. Lady Rathbourne had said nothing about coming here. Indeed, she'd probably have sent someone else if she'd had any idea what Cleo intended.

"Grave matters are afoot in London. I need an Ouroboros Mirror to confirm the truth of my Visions. And I know you have one, and it is potentially available for... three hundred and seventy-five quid, I believe."

The shopkeeper's eyes bulged. "How did—" He sharpened abruptly. "That was a special discount I offered for a regular customer who offers me plenty of repeat business."

"Remington Cross," she mused, "is a friend of mine. He's decided not to purchase it."

"I can't go any lower than four hundred and fifty," he replied mutinously, and she knew she had him.

"I'm afraid I don't have that sort of coin upon me," she replied, reaching inside her reticule, "but what I propose is a trade."

"I don't—" He stopped talking when he saw the amulet she produced. Indeed, he stopped breathing.

"An amulet worn by Nefertiti herself, or so I am told. I always doubted the truth of that, to be honest." She laid the amulet on the counter. "However, Nefertiti or not, the ankh *is* imbued with wards of a certain degree. You may test it, if you care to."

"Where did you get such a thing?"

She felt a touch of sorrow, her smile slipping for a moment. "It was deeded to me along with the rest of my father's estate. The amulet belonged to Lord Tremayne."

After that, there was little to be haggled over. The shopkeeper knew he'd gotten a good deal, and frankly, Cleo no longer cared about the odd pieces she'd inherited. Her father had sealed his own fate the day he formed a pact with a demon. She'd warned him of her Visions. It was his own damned fault he hadn't listened to her.

Or so she told herself.

"The mirror?" Cleo reminded the fellow, as he gently buffed the amulet as if to question whether it was real or not.

"I'll fetch it for you."

"Seems an incongruous trade," Jeremy finally said, the mirror wrapped and settled under his arm, as they headed for the exit of the Labyrinth. "An amulet worn by Nefertiti herself, imbued with Lord Tremayne's best magic.... What does this mirror do?"

"It's the most powerful scrying device ever created. There were three of them, crafted by Angelica Cosson over a century ago. One was lost, one was destroyed, and this"—she gestured to the package under his arm—"is the only one left at large in the world. It can see through any ward, any illusion, any plane or dimension, in fact."

"If it does all that, then why was it only four hundred and fifty quid?"

"Because there is a vast cost to looking into the mirror. One has to be a powerful seer with years of learning in the divination arts behind them to even be able to control it. That limits a significant portion of the Order. Secondly...."

"Secondly?"

"Some say if you don't have the training to control it, or the strength of will, then it can steal your soul. The mirror's connected to the Shadow Dimensions and powered by the Black Arts. A good many sorcerers will have nothing to do with it purely on those terms."

"What do *you* intend to do with it?" he asked, with a frown.

"I thought I might start by sacrificing a few chickens...."

He looked at her sharply.

"Really, Mr. Prior." Cleo rolled her eyes. "What do you think I'm going to do with it? I planned to look in it." Cleo sidestepped an old woman hunched over a barrow filled with dark charms. They were almost back to Main Street, and traffic was growing thicker. "There's a Vision I once had, one concerning a threat to London. I need to be able to see more of the Vision."

And considering her access to Foresight had been destroyed when her father tore her blindfold from her eyes, she needed another way to access the ability.

Desperate times called for desperate measures. Lady Rathbourne didn't think it was necessary. Yet. But she hadn't seen the future. Cleo had, and it haunted her dreams every night.

She simply couldn't wait another day.

Jeremy clearly pondered this as they found Main Street. There was only one official way out of the Labyrinth, which meant crossing Mr. Cochrane again. No doubt there were others, squirrelled away in back rooms and hidden tunnels, but the less they dealt with the denizens of the Labyrinth, the better.

"Has Lady Rathbourne approved of this?" Jeremy finally asked. "It's just... you gave the impression she wanted us to carry out this task, and I thought I was finally helping the Order, but I can't see the new Prime suggesting we turn to the Black Arts. If anyone were to find out...."

"Nobody's going to find out."

"That wasn't an answer."

But Cleo stopped listening. Premonition itched under her skin. And this time it had sharp knives.

Danger, her senses whispered to her. Taking Jeremy by the sleeve, she slowed their pace. The Labyrinth was dangerous by itself—this wasn't the Order, where rules and laws were in place, and the Prime's Sicarii assassins would hunt down any who disobeyed those laws. The sorcerers and creatures that lived in this hidden world deep in the heart of London were already outcasts. Their only rule was: the strong survive.

Nobody looked at them suspiciously. Indeed, more attention seemed to be given to a man and a woman hurling abuse at each other several yards away, something about a cursed amulet not working....

A flash of red caught her eye between the amused onlookers. A woman strode toward them in a velvet walking dress, wearing a broad-brimmed hat with marvelous feathers.

Cleo slammed her back against the brickwork, her breath catching in her chest. *Morgana*. That was Morgana, her husband's mother, and the woman who'd threatened to kill her. Which could only mean the tall man walking beside Morgana was the demon. She hadn't caught too much of a glimpse of him.

"What is it?" Jeremy rasped. Every hint of color had drained from his face.

"Don't move." She looked away as Morgana gathered her skirts and strode around a puddle. The other woman hadn't seen them yet, but she was moving with surprising alacrity. They had to get out of here. "This way."

Shoving him in front of her, she pushed him into an alley. *Premonition, don't fail me now.* Cleo opened her divination instincts up to opportunity. *Find me a way out.*

Behind them, someone cried out. Cleo started running, grabbing a fistful of her skirts.

This way. Something tugged at her.

She turned down the next alley, and her skin started itching furiously.

"Not this way!" Grabbing Jeremy's arm, she hauled him back the way they'd come.

Taking blind turn after blind turn, she relied solely upon her sense of premonition. It had never failed her before, and when they fetched up in front of a small walled garden in a very old section of the Labyrinth, she thought this might be the first.

There was a door ahead of them. Somewhere to hide perhaps, and her instincts were clearly leading her here. Cleo pushed it open, panting under her breath, and found herself in a garden. Snaking vines of ivy crawled up the building beside them, and she was almost certain a few of the strands turned their arrow-shaped leaves toward them as they stepped through into the courtyard. It felt like a hundred eyes watched her.

The garden looked disused. But it wasn't empty.

A man surveyed the statue, his hands clasped behind his back. Cleo froze, and Jeremy crashed into her. What on earth was the fellow wearing? It looked like something out of the Renaissance.

Slowly the man turned. Black curls tumbled over his face. A handsome man, though his neatly trimmed mustache made him appear slightly evil. "Ah, my queen. We meet at last," he said, in a deep baritone.

Cleo glanced behind her. He was definitely referring to her. "I'm afraid you've confused me with someone—"

"Have I?" He stepped down from the ledge around the fountain, looking around. "It's been a long time since I've walked these alleys. Nothing truly changes."

Cleo grabbed Jeremy by the sleeve, and tilted her chin toward the door. The man was mad. Time they got out of here. "We'll just leave you to your own thoughts then—"

"White Queen, your eyes so bright," the stranger almost breathed, "Glowing now you've lost your Sight."

White queen. A shiver of fright edged through her as she took a step in retreat. Was this one of the demon's men? There was no other way he could know that particular name. "What do you want?"

"I have a gift for you." He smiled at her knowingly, then turned and reached for a book that had been resting on the fountain ledge. "It might help with your studies."

Studies?

"Here, now," Jeremy stammered, stepping between them. "You keep that thing in your hands, and keep your hands where we can see them!" His aura began to glow as he drew power from the world around him—even from her—as if he prepared himself for some sorcerous working.

Oh, Jeremy. The boy wore *one* ring. Bravado was all well and good, but this wasn't the sort of place to confront a fellow.

Cleo drew the pistol she was carrying in her reticule. Bullets did little against a warded sorcerer, but these particular bullets were carved with runes that could slice right through any ward. "Stand aside, Jeremy."

He started at the crack of her voice.

"Stand aside," she repeated firmly, and when Jeremy shifted, she lifted the pistol and stared through the sights at the stranger. "You *will* tell me who you are, and what you mean by all this rubbish, and you will tell me *now*."

"My name is Quentin Farshaw."

"Impossible," she retorted. "Quentin Farshaw was one of the first seers in England."

"*The* first."

She eyed his ridiculous brown attire. "Are you trying to tell me you're over three centuries old? If so, you're wearing the wrong era. You should be in something Elizabethan."

"I left it in the Renaissance."

Cleo cocked her head, and then drew the hammer on the pistol back. He smiled at her as if he hadn't a care in the world. "Farshaw died in 1562. He'd just written *Sidestep Through Time*, and he claimed the information within it could destroy the world. He died and the book vanished. Only fragments of it remain."

"Did he?" An eyebrow cocked. "Someone must have forgotten to pass that along to me."

She breathed out a laugh. Her truth senses weren't tingling. Her divination believed him, even if she didn't. This was ridiculous. Perhaps they too were no longer working correctly, along with her Visions. "Even if you *were* Quentin Farshaw, what on earth would possess you to wait for me here? To pass a book along? I assume it's a piece of *the* book?"

"No, it's the entire thing." Farshaw looked down. "And you need it so you can stop what is to come. Or the skies over London will blacken, and this fair city will be destroyed." He looked up, staring directly through her.

"You know what I speak of. I know you do. You've seen it. We've all seen it."

Cleo's blood chilled. London's doom was *her* Vision. The one that had been haunting her for years. "What do you mean we've all seen it?"

"I am part of a collective who watches over England's safety. Every seer, from my bloodline down, sees the same thing. You have to stop it."

Sebastian. Her husband was always at the center of her prophetic doom. The darkness originated with him, weighing down upon his shoulders as the skies above them split open. It was only when she was near there was any sign of hope in her Vision. A stream of light erupted between them, driving away the darkness... but it was never enough. The darkness always overcame the light, and with Sebastian avoiding her these days, it wasn't as if she could try to stop it before it even began. Cleo's breath caught. She'd been hoping she'd have more time.

"How do I stop it?" she whispered.

"With the Blade."

"The Blade of Altarrh was destroyed," she said, though she knew that wasn't true. Morgana had cast an illusion so an innocent kitchen knife took the brunt of the magic that "destroyed" it.

Only an ally of Morgana—or someone who'd been there—would know that.

"And you need to find the black queen."

Cleo's breath exploded out of her. "How?"

"To find the black queen you need to go back to your past. Take the book. Perhaps it will show you how." He pressed it into her hands. "My time with it is done."

She caught a swift glimpse of the cover. There'd been a book in the dream the demon had pulled her into. Was this it? "What do I do with it?"

Farshaw stepped back. "I wouldn't want to spoil the surprise. But you should hurry up and read it. You don't have much time. You need to reach the full potential of your gifts, and quickly. The mirror will help to guide you, but you'll need the book for what is to come."

What's to come—? The mirror? "Sir," she called, taking a step toward him as he retreated. "None of this makes any sense."

He checked his pocket watch, frowning faintly. "Good luck, my queen."

Then he vanished into thin air.

CHAPTER TWO

CLEO WAITED UNTIL night fell over Lady Rathbourne's home. She'd been staying here for the past month, for the simple reason that she'd had nowhere else to go upon her father's death.

The return home had been uneventful, though Jeremy couldn't quite get over the fact "*he disappeared into thin air.*" Cleo herself had been more dubious. People didn't just disappear. Sorcery didn't work like that. The only person who seemed to have the ability to translocate was Verity Hawkins, and she was completely untutored in the laws of sorcery, enough so that her conscious mind didn't *know* it shouldn't be able to teleport. It didn't stop Verity, however, and it hadn't stopped the man she'd encountered.

Unless....

The other possibility was that he was telling the truth. Had she *actually* spoken to Quentin Farshaw? Had he somehow survived whatever had happened to him that night?

He'd be almost... what? Three hundred and fifty years old?

If so... how had he suddenly appeared in Balthazar's Labyrinth, at precisely the right time to meet her? Knowing of the mirror, and her vision?

He'd been the first sorcerer to see through time, but was there more to it than that?

"Concentrate," she growled to herself, flipping the covers off her bed, and slipping from its warm embrace. She needed to be thinking about the mirror, and preparing herself for the next step. Not dwelling on a man who absolutely *could not* have translocated through *time* itself.

Making her way to the cellars with the Ouroboros Mirror under her arm, she locked the enormous iron-bound door behind her, then went around the room of Lady Rathbourne's ritual space, lighting the candles there. Ianthe's workspace was immaculate.

An Ouroboros Mirror was a dangerous device. Cleo put it flat on Ianthe's altar, a scrap of black silk covering the glass. Then she knelt in front of it, gathering her night-robe about her.

London's doom was a storm gathering on the horizon. Drake de Wynter, the previous Prime of the Order—and her husband's father—had been forced to offer his body for the demon to use as a vessel. She needed to know what her vision meant.

And how to stop it.

Cleo dragged the black silk from the mirror's surface. Oval in shape, it seemed harmless enough, if one didn't look directly into the polished black obsidian sheen of the mirror. A pair of bronze snakes twined around each other, circling the edge of the mirror, and she couldn't tell where one snake began and the other finished... or perhaps there truly was only one. Ouroboros. Trepidation filled her, and she began to still her mind, keeping her gaze from the mirror's inky surface until she'd meditated long enough. Anyone who stared into a mirror like this without the ability to master themselves and their divination arts would find themselves trapped within it.

"You're the Cassandra," she told herself sternly.

You were, whispered something dark within her.

I still am. Her father might have stolen her Visions by stealing her blindfold, but Drake had insisted she still had the ability. Only doubt and lack of self-belief held her back from her gift of Foresight.

Her gaze dropped to the carved sigils around the mirror, as she quietly gathered her power. The center of her forehead burned, her Third Eye awakening, and Cleo picked up the knife she'd brought and pressed the sharp tip to her finger. "*Hesharazadh.*"

A simple word of power to clear her mind, and command her Third Eye.

The world vanished into far too many shapes and edges as she opened her Sight. She could see the real world, as well as echoes of others. Feeding her blood to the mirror's runes, she began to chant lightly under her breath.

Black mist curled off the mirror. Taking a deep breath, Cleo rested both hands on the edges of the bronze frame, then leaned over it and looked down.

Her own face stared back, though her cheekbones were shockingly sharp, and there was a darker expression about her face. It looked like a version of her that might have existed if she'd been drawn to the Black Arts her father practiced. A silver Unicursal Hexagram dangled from her ear in the image, and she wore enough black lace to make a widow jealous. The last thing she wanted to see was herself. Or a version of herself that didn't exist. She shook her head, and black mist coalesced into something else. "Show me London's doom."

London sprang out of the shadows, stark and grimy. Little figures began to form. Snow on the ground. A bloody triangle in the pristine white—no, two of them, interlaced in another hexagram. A man stood in the center of it, feeding blood into the star as he cut a woman's throat. She couldn't see who the man was from above. Black hair meant it could be her husband, or perhaps his oldest brother. Or a stranger, though she suspected it was all connected.

"Draw back," she whispered to herself, and the image grew smaller, showing some of the detail around it.

A lush garden by the look of it. Bodies scattered here and there, as if there'd been some great bloody fight between opposing forces.

A hooded figure walked slowly across the snow toward the hexagram, the black velvet of their cloak dragging behind them and leaving a trail. Clouds began to boil above the garden. The air grew static, and there was a flicker in the center of the sky, almost like a seam. Hands lifted to lower the hood, black velvet gloves reaching to the person's elbows, and she held her breath, waiting to see—

"White Queen," something whispered, and she heard the chittering sounds of something inhuman nearby.

Dread began to whisper down her spine. Cleo couldn't tear her gaze from the mirror, but she felt certain there was something in the room with her, something behind her. She'd missed the hooded figure's reveal. The scene focused on the seam in the sky now, and she was right. There *was* something straining behind that invisible scene, the sky bulging as if something fought to push its way through.

She'd never seen *that* before. Always her vision focused on Sebastian, and the darkening clouds above him.

Movement shifted at the edge of her vision. Cleo's heart began to pound and she cried out softly, trying to force her gaze away from the mirror.

"*Black queen,*" whispered something else, behind her. "*Two sides to a coin.*"

What did that mean? Cleo ground her teeth together, sweat dripping down her temples. She needed to control the mirror. Not the other way around. "Show me the black queen," she demanded.

The hooded figure came into view again.

"*An uncertain heart with blood as black as ebony,*" the mirror whispered. "*If she commits to the Black Arts, she will rise and London will fall. The Horde will ride through London streets, bringing blood and death to the world, and it will be your fault, White Queen.*"

A stab of pain went through her temples, and Cleo cried out, losing the image. Fine. The black queen must be strongly warded. Two sides to a coin. Did that mean the black queen was like her? A seer?

"Who is she?"

"*Light or Dark? She hasn't decided yet. The demon has been courting her for years.*"

Maybe that was one way to find her nemesis? All she needed to do was go through the Order's book of registered sorcerers, and find any who were born with the same gift she had.

...your fault....

The mirror began to change. Something pushed beyond its misty surface. A formless face lifted out of the glass, almost as if it were covered in liquid quicksilver. Only the thin surface of the obsidian held it back from her world.

Cleo began to shake. "How do I stop her? How do I find her?"

"The key to defeating the darkness lies with Sebastian," said the face. *"He will tip the balance."*

The driving ache behind her eye grew worse. She couldn't hold the trance much longer. Cleo blinked, and realized she was leaning toward the bloody mirror. Tendrils of black mist curled off the glass, caressing her face.

"Feed me," it whispered. *"More of your sweet, sweet blood, and I'll show you more. I'll show you everything...."*

"How do.... How do I stop London's doom from happening?" she whispered, her eyelids blinking sleepily. She was so tired, and it would be so easy to fall asleep on the mirror.

The black tendrils brushed a strand of hair behind her ear. One looped behind the back of her neck. *"A kiss,"* it whispered. *"A kiss is all I ask. And then I'll tell you everything...."*

Premonition screamed through her.

Cleo fought, forcing her arms straight. The curl of mist in her hair tightened, becoming a noose that dragged her down, the face lifting to meet her, its mouth yawning wide open—

"Begone!" shouted a firm voice. "Let her go!"

Lightning crackled. Cleo felt strange hands catch hold of her, and then they were tearing her away from the mirror's hungry face. It sank back into the black mist of the mirror's surface, like a thwarted whale leaping from the sea and plunging back down.

Little tendrils of mist crept over the edges of the mirror, crawling for her hands and her bloodied finger. Blood dripped from her nose, and Cleo fought to close her Third Eye as the mirror pulled at her.

"Stand back." She recognized the voice now. Lady Rathbourne.

Relief flooded through her, leaving her hiccupping, and then something flashed through her field of vision—

Glass shattered. There was an enormous impact of power hitting the mirror's heart, and it blew Cleo back onto her hands. A shimmering ward enveloped her, protecting her from the shards of black glass. The mist screamed a high-pitched scream, and then it withdrew abruptly within the frame from whence it had come. Cleo slammed her hands over her ears as the mirror died a slow death.

Panting, Lady Rathbourne stepped around her, lowering the staff she wielded. She looked to have come directly from bed, her open robe fluttering around her nightgown, and her black hair tumbling down her back. "Is it destroyed?"

Cleo reached for the frame. Shattered pieces of glass lay strewn around it, but the frame was lifeless now. Inert. The little glowing eyes of the snake had faded. "What was that thing?"

"An Ouroboros sees directly into the Shadow Dimensions, and summons something there to answer your questions. Something that can pierce the veil of time," Ianthe said, kneeling at her side and helping her to sit up. "What were you thinking? It could have killed you."

"Noted." Cleo pressed her hand to her forehead, pushing against her eyes. Everything in her ached. "It was somewhat stronger than I'd anticipated."

Or maybe she was weaker.

Doubt flushed through her again. She'd lost so much. The failure dug sharp claws into her. A year ago she would have wielded the mirror without a concern. A year ago she'd been the mighty Cassandra, the Order's most gifted seer.

"Your fault...," whispered the mirror.

"How did you know?" she murmured, trying not to shake.

Ianthe helped her sit up. "The cellar's warded," she said dryly. "I felt you breach the wards and came to investigate. Learn anything important?"

"Time's running out. I don't know when, but my Vision happens when there is snow on the ground."

They both exchanged a look.

"Winter won't last much longer," Ianthe murmured. "Today was warmer than last week. The snow will melt soon."

"Two weeks at most," Cleo added. "Unless we get another storm."

Ianthe covered the dead mirror with her night-robe, refusing to look at it. "What else?"

The black queen. She hesitated, and then told Ianthe everything, including the sighting of Morgana in the Labyrinth.

"Who is the black queen?" Ianthe asked, when she'd finished.

"Two sides of the same coin," she replied gruffly. "Which I'm taking to mean she has divination talents. She's connected to Sebastian somehow. Perhaps... an old lover. I don't know. I do know the demon's been courting her for a long time. The mirror said she hadn't decided whether she wanted to commit to the Light or to the Black Arts yet."

"The only one who might know is...."

"Sebastian," Cleo whispered, for none of it made any sense.

Her vision had always shown him at the center of the storm. His uncontrollable powers set it off. Didn't they? But if Sebastian was the one who brought London to its knees, then how was he the key to saving it?

Ianthe's dark brow quirked, as she took in the glass all over the room. "I know you two have had your differences for the past month, but I think it's time we summoned your husband here."

Differences? Cleo looked away. He'd practically abandoned her after the loss of his father to the demon. But they didn't have time for hurt feelings. "Agreed."

CHAPTER THREE

'There are three types of bonds a sorcerer can use; a wellspring bond, where one sorcerer can hand over power—and control—to another; the bond between Anchor and Shield, which is somewhat more reciprocal; and a soul-bond, that rare bond that can be created between lovers, allowing them true connection. Forever.'

—Lady Eberhardt's transcription on Soul-bond's

"CONCENTRATE," ADRIAN BISHOP snapped, rapping Sebastian's knuckles with his humming quarterstaff. "You don't have time to be woolgathering. Or your mother will rip your throat out the next time she comes for you."

Sebastian's eyes narrowed, and he shook his fingers as his staff vanished into nothingness between them. Sometimes he could really grow to hate this half brother of his.

"My mother would have to find me first." Gathering his brewing power, he forced himself to visualize the staff of raw energy in order to reform it. "And if you're resorting to using that bitch's name in an attempt to trick me into an emotional reaction, then you're not going to win."

"Oh?" Bishop arched a mocking brow as Sebastian's attempt to reform his own quarterstaff flickered... and failed. "Are you certain of that?"

It wasn't his mother, Morgana, who was plaguing him.

"Certain."

"Where's your head today then? For it's certainly not focused here."

There was no way in hell he was going to answer that.

"My head's in the game," Sebastian said coldly, facing his half brother with empty hands. "There's nothing I want more than to learn to control my sorcery, so I can bring my mother to heel."

"Truly?" Bishop stalked a slow circle around him. "You've been making so much progress in controlling your power. But today.... One would almost think some emotion was plaguing you, making you revert to Expression. You can't even form your staff right now, can you?"

"Like this?" Holding his hands out, Sebastian forced himself to imagine a glowing staff of pure energy in his hands, and breathed out the power word he'd chosen to form raw energy into sorcerous matter. Bishop had been teaching him to harness his will, rather than rely on the emotional energy of Expression.

Expression could be dangerous, especially when you could tear a house into pieces at a single angry thought. It was better this way, learning to rely on repetitive rituals, power words, and meditation to work sorcery. Safer. But he still fell into old habits whenever his temper roused.

Bishop stalked him in a slow circle, a faint smile curling his lips when the glowing staff sprang into being, flickering hazily before Sebastian reinforced it with pure willpower.

"Like that, yes. Now let's see what you can do with it." Twirling his hands, Bishop manipulated his own staff.

Both staves cracked together with an electric hum. Physically, Sebastian was larger than his half brother, and slightly stronger. But Bishop moved like a predatory leopard, with a careful calculating grace. Every move he made seemed to have been carefully mapped out in an advance campaign Sebastian only ever discovered, when it was too late. Sebastian felt Bishop's quarterstaff yield infinitesimally, and took the opportunity it presented.

Crack. A wild swing. Another.

Bishop leaned back, his spine bending to an extraordinary degree as Sebastian's staff swept over him.

Sebastian snarled, and swung his staff back the other way, which his brother ducked again.

"You're getting angry," Bishop pointed out, sidestepping the next blow without even bothering to swing his own staff.

He aimed a final blow at Bishop, putting the full force of his body behind the swing this time—and his brother swept his own staff up, meeting Sebastian's staff in a shower of green and gold sparks.

The impact pushed Sebastian back several inches. He gripped his energy staff as Bishop swung his like a windmill between his fingers, and behind him.

"Want me to show you how it's really done?" Bishop asked.

"You always do enjoy showing off."

"Block me," Bishop replied, with the faintest of smiles, and then that glowing green staff was whirling toward him.

Sweat trickled down his temples as Bishop unleashed a wild flurry of blows upon him that he could barely block.

"You're bigger than I am. Stronger," Bishop told him, right before he smacked Sebastian's hands with the end of his staff. "So how am I beating you?"

Ouch. He shook his fingers in the air, and then clenched his fist several times to try and distract himself from the pain. "Years of experience, perhaps."

Bishop swung another blow at him. Somehow the move was dangerously precise, almost delicate. Sebastian blocked it, his feet forced back a step. Then another.

"The fact you're an assassin," he snapped, starting to feel the rough edge of his temper ride him. "And I don't have your practice in killing someone."

"Experience counts," Bishop agreed. "But control means so much more. The second you get angry, you start swinging wildly." Bishop smashed a blow into Sebastian's ribs, then another to the knee with the other end of the staff. He backed off, twirling it in his hands like a blur of light. "The wilder you swing, the more open you leave yourself."

Wonderful. A lesson in sorcery in the bargain. Sebastian limped forward, holding his staff low. Control. Right. He swung tightly, and Bishop swept the blow aside, returning a fierce set of feints that almost clipped Sebastian about the ears.

Gold sparks rained across the timber floors as their staves met. Again. Sebastian could feel the power humming through his veins as he fought to keep control over his sorcery. There was an exhilaration to this, something purely physical that kept his mind from thinking too much.

"You want to beat her, don't you?"

Morgana. Sebastian countered the next blow, and shoved his brother back with pure strength. *Yes.*

This time the only warning he had was the dark flash of Bishop's black eyes, and then he swept low and nearly took Sebastian's feet out from under him. Sebastian leapt over the staff at the last minute. Definitely working up a sweat now. His shirt clung loosely to his body in patches.

"When she comes at you, she works to make you lose control, doesn't she?" Bishop asked. "Using words, actions, threats... whatever it takes to emotionally compromise you. Your mother knows she can't beat you if it comes to strength of sorcery alone, so she refused to teach you how to control it. And if you face her again—with my training—then she knows what your weaknesses are."

Block. Blow. Block. Sebastian grunted as Bishop's staff disengaged in a brief feint and rapped him under the ribs on the other side.

Sebastian glared at him. *Prick.*

"Learn how to keep your head when all you want to do is take off mine."

This time Sebastian managed to block the next blow. Bishop swung his staff around his head, sidestepping around him, clearly looking for weaknesses.

"Good." Bishop nodded at him. "You're thinking now. Thinking requires control. It requires watching and planning, and using the other person's moves against them. It also requires understanding their weaknesses."

This time he drove the end of his staff straight under Sebastian's defense, and just below his sternum.

With an explosion of air from his lungs, Sebastian landed flat on his back on the floor, and slid at least four feet, fetching up near a set of iron-gray skirts. An explosion of white appeared behind his eyes as the pain drove through him like an iron spike shoved into his lungs.

The staff vanished from his hands. The room vanished. All that remained was the ache in his chest as he curled around himself, and the urge to vomit.

A faint clucking sound echoed in the room. Lady Eberhardt rolled her eyes and stepped over him. "Really, Adrian? A duel?"

"He doesn't have time to be coddled," Bishop shot back, his staff vanishing too. "The next time Morgana comes at him, it's not going to help him if he can knot a rope with his mind. No. He needs protection—and a means to attack. If he can control his will when under pressure, then she just might not kill him."

"Didn't know... you cared," Sebastian gasped. This half brother of his had intended to kill him, before Verity— Bishop's wife—insisted there had to be another way of controlling the threat of his enormous powers.

Bishop offered him a hand.

He never could quite decipher this brother's expressions, but there was a faint twitch of Bishop's brow as he hauled Sebastian to his feet. "You're the key to getting my father back from the demon. Or at least, that's what your wife keeps telling everyone."

Of course.

Sebastian bent over and rested his hands on his thighs. *Hell.* Everything hurt. But most of all, the mention of his wife shattered any gains he'd made that day.

The soul-bond between he and Cleo was growing steadily weaker every day—through lack of consummation, Sebastian guessed. But he could still feel her there, a little heated knot in the back of his mind.

If he focused, he could sometimes see through her eyes, or hear what she was thinking, but for some mysterious reason, today that knot was walled off.

It felt like pressing his hands against a glass pane, and trying to feel her heat through it.

She'd learned to lock him out, the same thing he'd done to her several weeks ago, when he *didn't* want her knowing what was going through his mind. It was somewhat jarring to realize how much he'd come to rely upon the bond with her in such a short time.

"What's going on?" Bishop asked Lady Eberhardt.

Lady E straightened Bishop's collar, an almost maternal gesture that drew Sebastian back into the dark recesses of the past.

He brushed away the memory of his own mother doing that to him as a little boy. Before she betrayed him.

"Ianthe's called a meeting. She has information on how to deal with the demon, and apparently, an old ally who just might be able to help us," Lady Eberhardt said.

The demon. Sebastian flinched and turned around, locking his wrists behind his back in order to stretch. He didn't know his father. All Drake had ever been was a name his mother cursed. He'd been raised to be a weapon against his father, the former Prime of the Order of the Dawn Star—a group of sorcerers who'd cast his mother out of their ranks years ago. He'd spent years poisoned by her lies, certain Drake saw him as only a threat.

And instead the man had sacrificed himself to save Sebastian from a demon's clutches.

It unnerved him. *Why?* Guilt harassed him, but the uncertainty was what kept him awake of nights. *Why* would his father do that? Sebastian was nothing to him. They'd only spoken once or twice, on a mental plane his father created.

And he'd worked with his mother to betray the man; to blackmail his apprentice, kidnap his granddaughter, and force Drake to yield his position as Prime.

Of course, he hadn't had much bloody choice in the matter. Morgana had put a sclavus collar upon him when he was thirteen, and used the control ring that accompanied it to force him to her will.

He was bloody lucky Bishop had decided against killing him—though he knew his brother had spared him only because he needed Sebastian's power to confront the demon that wore Drake's body.

"Finally," Bishop said. "It's about time we had something to work toward. It's been a month since that creature took my father as a vessel, and so far there's been no sign of it. It's up to something. It has to be. But we've found no trace of it."

"It will be out there somewhere." Distaste soured the old woman's voice. Sebastian looked up sharply, and Lady E's lip curled. "But that, I think, is something Ianthe needs to speak to you both about."

"Agatha—"

"Tut, tut." She poked Bishop's sweaty shirt. "You're dripping all over the place. The pair of you need to freshen up, and then we can take the carriage to the Earl of Rathbourne's house. Ianthe's holding the meeting there, and I'm not going to breathe a word about her intentions until then, so you might as well stop wasting your breath."

Bishop exchanged a look with Sebastian that was so long-suffering he *almost* felt a sense of kinship with the bastard.

Almost.

But there was one smile-suffocating fact about the Earl of Rathbourne that Lady Eberhardt hadn't mentioned, though she locked that gimlet gaze upon Sebastian as if she could sense where his thoughts were going.

"Yes," she said, lacing both hands on her cane. "It's time you strapped on your breeches, Sebastian, and confronted your wife."

Cleo. His mouth went dry. He didn't think he was ready for this.

But then, when would he ever be?

Cleo stared out over the gardens of the Earl of Rathbourne's manor, tilting her face to the meager sunshine. It had rained earlier that morning, and the gardens were lightly dewed. Snowdrops poked their heads through some of the half-melted snow, and lush fir needles shed their winter mantle.

Color saturated the world around her.

Sunlight stained her eyelids.

And thank goodness, it no longer hurt her so badly to look upon the gardens, which had always been her one great love.

The first week after she lost the blindfold she'd worn since she was five had been the worst. It had been a month now. The headaches no longer plagued her so badly, and sunlight was no longer a spear through her raw eyes. She couldn't stay out here for very long—she was still growing used to using her neglected eyesight—but every day was a little better.

A shiver trembled over her skin, and Cleo looked down in shock. It felt almost like one of her Foresight visions was forthcoming, but that was impossible. Her first prediction had been that she would lose her Visions the day she gained her sight back, and so far she'd been correct. All she had left were her dreams, and her Premonition, which was marching down her skin like little ants in steel shoes.

It felt like a storm brewing on the horizon.

Like the tickle of a feather down her spine.

What on earth—?

Cleo's breath caught as she finally realized what had been bothering her all along. The tiny little knot in her mind—which she associated as the soul-bond she shared with the husband who refused to have anything to do with her—was pulsing.

Sebastian is coming.

Of course. The meeting wasn't for another two hours, but it was clear Bishop and Sebastian were arriving early.

A thrill ran through her. Cleo hurried into the house, capturing a hint of her reflection in the mirror. Her cheeks were red from the chill, and *oh, heavens,* she was wearing her worst gown, and—

Ianthe lifted her head from where she'd been patiently reading a book to her daughter, Louisa. Her voice trailed off. "What is it?"

"Sebastian." The word came out breathlessly, so Cleo cleared her throat and tried to explain. "I can feel him coming in this direction."

The other occupant of the room, Eleanor Ross, looked up sharply. Eleanor had been Drake's lover before the demon possessed him, and she'd been waiting impatiently for any word of the demon. "Already? The meeting's not for another two hours."

"Sebastian's coming?" Louisa looked up in delight, her dark plaits swinging. "Oh, that's wonderful! We can take tea with him." She seemed to remember where she was now. "I mean, may we, Mother?"

And all of a sudden Cleo realized what this meant.

This would be the first time Sebastian had set foot under the same roof as the woman whose daughter he'd helped kidnap. Louisa had been a pawn Sebastian's mother, Morgana, used to force Ianthe to betray her master. Sebastian had been Louisa's ally at the time, protecting her from his mother's wrath, but Ianthe wouldn't have forgotten her blackmail ordeal.

No, to Ianthe, Sebastian was the reason she'd betrayed the man she loved as a father, and then he'd been the reason that man offered himself up as a vessel to the demon.

Damn him. His imminent arrival set her all at sea. "I could meet him at the gate perhaps, and—"

"It's fine." Ianthe closed the book, her violet-blue eyes shining with a Prime's cool strength of will. "I called for the meeting. I knew I would see him. Besides...." She brushed Louisa's hair, not quite able to keep all her disapproval off her expression. "Lou thinks he's her friend, and that he protected her when his mother kidnapped her. Lou, why don't we sojourn to the garden? I know you would like to see Sebastian, but Cleo's his wife. I'm certain she would like a moment or two alone with him, and perhaps he can come visit you in the garden when he's done?"

Would he even want to see her? Cleo froze. She'd sent him over a dozen letters in the past month and tried to see him twice, but he was either "not at home" or "under the weather."

"Coming, Eleanor?" Ianthe asked.

Cleo was no fool. What he was, was avoiding her. Her heart pounded.

Why could she be so brave when she was facing down a creature from the mirror, but tremble at the thought of seeing him again? She wanted to see him. She'd stared wistfully at her ceiling every day for a month, cursing him under her breath for tying her in knots like this. But now the moment was here....

Eleanor limped toward her, leaning heavily on the cane she now used. "Just remember... the boy's been through a great deal, but that's no excuse to treat you poorly."

"I wouldn't let him anyway," she said crossly.

Eleanor smiled. "Good luck."

Ianthe and Louisa had vanished, and Eleanor followed them out, her cane tapping on the tiles. Cleo hastily tidied her hair in the mirror. Then there came a sharp rapping at the door. She hurried out onto the top of the stairs.

The door opened, and the butler announced his guests in a monotonous drone Cleo ignored, searching for faces, her heart thundering behind her ribs—Mr. Bishop, Lady Eberhardt, and—

And there he was.

Sebastian.

Her husband.

After weeks of not even a letter to ask how she was.

A month in which he'd refused to see her when she tried to call upon him, to help him, to scratch this uncertain itch within her that seemed to be their bond.

Days of Lady Eberhardt patting her hand and telling her to be patient, that Sebastian was learning to master his emotions, and he would come round, and—

Their eyes met.

The shock of his beauty was an instant slap in the face. Black hair the color of a raven's wing was brushed back off his temples, and his eyes were like molten quicksilver. Her gaze strayed to that full mouth, and the masculine cleft in his chin. She'd never seen him before their marriage, though she'd heard the maids whispering about how handsome he was. With her blindfold on, all he'd ever been to her was a voice, a warm body, someone kind, who'd seemed to yearn for her gentle nature.

Someone who'd once stroked her hair in the middle of the night, in the bed they both shared, and whispered that he couldn't touch her. That he did not dare.

That she'd married a monster.

And she'd given her heart to him in that second, only to have him dash it at her feet with a flagrant lack of regard the second he was free of his mother.

Cleo, the girl who'd never feared to face a single dragon in her life, couldn't stand there a single second longer.

Grabbing her skirts, she turned and fled.

CHAPTER FOUR

SEBASTIAN'S BREATH PUNCHED out of him for a second time that day.

Cleo was nothing but a whirl of blue skirts, her long blonde hair braided messily, and her eyes—

Her eyes were pretty and brown and filled with hurt. He couldn't really recall seeing them before. He took a step after her, his hand reached out as if to somehow catch her, before he realized what he was doing.

Two sets of eyes locked on him. Sebastian found it difficult to swallow. He lowered his hand. "My apologies. Perhaps—"

"Get after the gel." Lady Eberhardt snorted. "This can wait. Judging from the expression on her face, your wife won't."

It's better this way. He couldn't hurt her like this—and he knew, from nights spent stroking his psychic senses against that golden knot in his mind, that he had.

Sebastian's weight shifted. No matter what he told himself, the desire to go to her warred with common sense.

He'd forgotten how beautiful she was.

"This is the one time I'm inclined to agree with Agatha," Bishop said, tugging off his gloves. There was a marriage ring on his finger, barely a week old, and seven others to denote his rank in the Order. "Recent experience has taught me never to take your wife's feelings for granted."

"I thought I was supposed to be learning to control my emotions?"

Bishop cocked a brow. "Is your meeting with Cleo going to upset them?"

Seeing her, talking to her was going to do more than that. It was going to obliterate any scrap of control he owned.

"Go," Bishop repeated gently, his dark gaze taking in the answer that was no doubt showing on Sebastian's face. "Bottling up your emotions isn't healthy either."

Sebastian ground his teeth together. "I don't want to disappoint her." That wasn't the entire truth.

I don't want to hurt her.

I don't want... to see her disappointment in me. To see the hopeful way she looks at me fade.

Which it would.

It was only a matter of time.

And yet, putting off this conversation was cowardly. She deserved better.

Sebastian gritted his teeth and strode after her, his heart kicking in his chest like a mule.

Finding her wasn't difficult. Their soul-bond led him straight to her. Though unconsummated, it seemed to have strengthened even in the brief seconds since they'd come face-to-face.

And it had been fading. It had.

Or was he only fooling himself?

Cleo stared at the small duck pond in the gardens out back, her shoulders ramrod straight. She was much smaller than he. Light to his darkness. Hope to his bleakness.

And in that moment he could remember what she'd looked like the night of their marriage, when she'd tended to his bullet wound wearing only a flimsy nightgown, and asked him not to be cruel to her. She could tolerate disinterest or his lack of affection, but not cruelty, she'd claimed.

She'd lied.

A month of forcing himself to stay away from her had hurt her more than he'd imagined.

"Cleo," he began, his voice a stark whisper. Mother of night, a part of him wanted to linger in this moment, to drink her in. But everything else inside him withered and died. He would only destroy her.

"My apologies," she said, clearing her throat and glancing back over her shoulder at him. "If I'd known you were coming, I would have prepared myself better. I didn't.... I meant to...."

"Avoid me?" he asked.

Her soulful gaze locked with his. "I thought that was my line?"

He stared at her, taking in every inch of her heart-shaped face, and the storm of emotions crossing it, hungry in a way he'd not been aware of. A surge of need swept through him. Something he'd never felt before.

He wanted to kiss her.

No, he wanted to do more than that, and the second he thought it, fear and distaste overrode him, and his fingers curled into a fist.

Cleo was the purest young woman he'd ever met. He'd only taint her. She deserved better. And strike him blind, but all he could picture was the day they'd first met, when she'd leaned up on the balustrade of a garden folly, and pointed to the lake behind him and said, "*Look!*"

He'd turned, a second before he realized she couldn't see anything, and then the warmth of her body was pressed against his, her lips sliding like a silken caress over his mouth, and all his senses fled.

It was barely a kiss.

And it was the only thing that had sustained him through the dark nights that followed.

"Are you going to say something?" Cleo demanded, and he realized he'd been lost for words for far too long.

"I've missed you," he admitted, precisely what he hadn't meant to say. Sebastian turned away, the muscles in his abdomen tightening. *Control yourself, damn it.* "I'm sorry if you've felt neglected, but I had a great deal to work through."

Her tone softened. "I could have helped you."

"No." The word came out sharper than he'd intended. *You're the cause of half my problems.* "You're safer here."

"Safer? Pray tell... in what way?"

"Safer from me," he said in the cool tone he used to inure his feelings.

Cleo flung her arms wide. "Everyone wants to keep me bloody safe." She tripped on her basket, and breadcrumbs scattered, sending ducks quacking and squawking at her feet. "'You are precious and pure,' my father used to tell me when he *locked me away* inside his estate, so I never had a chance to even see any of the world—"

"I am not your father—"

"No?" Cleo's skirts swept against his shins as she stepped closer, staring up at him with an obstinate gleam in her dark brown eyes. "You're right, you're my husband. But one could be forgiven for thinking otherwise, couldn't they? Do you think you're the only one who's lost *everything*? Do you think you're the only one who stares at the ruins of their life and wonders where they are going?" She clenched her fists, her dark eyes gleaming. "I can't see the future anymore, Sebastian. My *own father* took that away from me the second he tore my blindfold free. And then he died, and as much of a monster as I realized he'd become, he was still my father. Still the only anchor I had in this world, until you. And you don't want me, and I've barely seen you. And Drake is gone, and I know he was *your* father, and you feel guilty for what happened to him, but he was also the person who promised to help me. I have nothing. I have *no one*. Ianthe and Lucien are kind, but they're not you."

He could stand her anger, but not her tears. "Cleo—"

But she set her palms against his chest as if to hold him at bay, and Sebastian staggered back against the garden arch.

"Don't touch me," she said, a single glossy tear sliding down her cheek as she held herself stiffly. "I am not so desperate as that."

She'd wanted him to touch her.

Once.

He stepped closer. "I can't think when I'm around you. And as much as you doubt it, I'm not good for you, Cleo, especially right now. I gave myself over to the demon, and I can still feel the stain of it upon my soul. Drake promised the demon his body because of me." The words came out a little hoarsely. "I have to help get him back, and destroy that creature. I needed to think, to try and learn whatever Bishop could teach me. And I couldn't do that with you nearby."

Another tear. Her lip trembled. "I could have helped you. I could have supported you."

"And then my mother is still at large, and she knows you're important to me. She will kill you, just to cut at me."

"She promised to kill me, regardless of whether you're in my life or not. I stood against her," Cleo whispered, her anger softening. "She won't forgive that."

"No. She won't forgive that." Sebastian reached up and cupped her soft cheek. "I never meant to hurt you. Don't cry. Please don't cry."

Somehow he wrapped his arms around her. Then she was in his arms, her face pressed against his shoulder as she sobbed. And he could feel her tears wetting his collar, his throat, feel the tremble in her body as her misery wracked her. Cleo. *Cleo.* The one perfect thing in his world. The one thing that could destroy him utterly.

Or no, perhaps it was the other way around.

You destroy everything you ever touch, said his mother's poisonous whisper, in his memories.

And he knew himself well enough to believe it.

Even now, the press of Cleo's body brought uncomfortable memories. He wanted to soften, wanted to melt against her, but her breath whispered against his throat, and suddenly it was another's woman's breath, and he could still feel the choking bite of the sclavus collar, even though he'd melted the fucking thing.

Sebastian sucked in a sharp breath through his nostrils. *Cleo. You're with Cleo. Not someone else.*

But his heart was racing, and he could feel his body cringing away from hers.

This was the best he could do in this moment.

Sebastian squeezed his eyes shut, clinging to the sobbing frame of his wife, feeling as though every sucked-in breath that shook her stabbed him in the heart. "I'm sorry," he said, all knotted up inside, stroking her back, feeling the press of her spine behind the bones of her corset.

And she lifted her face, her mouth tilting toward his in a rush.

Sebastian set her away from him, staggering back in shock. "*No.*" That couldn't happen.

Cleo stared at him, her hand pressed against her lips as if he'd slapped her. Tears ravaged her reddened cheeks. He saw the moment she made a decision, and he reached for her, but it was too late.

"I understand," she whispered, wiping her eyes.

Then she turned and walked away, and this time he did not go after her. For though she didn't understand, he couldn't, in this moment, explain his sudden revulsion.

CHAPTER FIVE

'Demons find it difficult to exist in the mortal plane. Something in this world drains them. They are not created of flesh, as we are, and require a great deal more energy than we do to survive, be it from blood magic, or sex. They much prefer to take a human body as a vessel, to anchor them in the mortal plane, and protect them from whatever natural forces pull at them. This also makes them invulnerable to mortal weapons, for they are... not truly here, in the sense that we know it. The only known way to weaken a demon is to kill its vessel, and trap it in a warded circle, though such a task is not easy.'

—Alaric Godsgrave, *Book of Demonology*

"WHY DON'T YOU tell them why they're here?" Ianthe murmured, holding her hands out to the coals in the grate, as if she was cold.

Cleo bit her lip, looking at the beautiful Prime. Every eye in the room was upon her; Lady Eberhardt; Ianthe's husband, Lucien; Mr. Bishop and his wife, Verity; Sebastian.... Only Ianthe stared into the grate, as if she could almost see the Vision Cleo had seen in the mirror.

"You had a Vision?" Lady Eberhardt prompted.

"Not quite." Cleo took a deep breath. "I bought an Ouroboros mirror in Balthazar's Labyrinth. But I've been having dreams lately. Or nightmares, if I'm to be specific. They feel so real. Almost as though my visions are trying to come back, but my conscious mind is not letting them, and it's only when I sleep they break through."

"And what did you see?" Lady E asked.

Another slow breath. It flashed through her mind again, as if it were painted on the back of her eyelids; blood, death, her friends falling before the demon's wrath... and yet, a single moment of hope. "The demon's been lurking in the depths of the London undergrounds while it gluts itself on blood, and restores its power. It's stronger now, after we cut at it last month. It's about to make its move. I saw it wade through gardens splashed with blood as Order sorcerers try to incarcerate it. They die. We all die. I saw Ianthe's broken body on the snow"—Lucien Devereaux sucked in a sharp breath—"I saw Lady Eberhardt's lifeless eyes staring at a blackened sky. Bishop... it goes after you first, because you're the only one who could kill it. Or the body it wears. But there is one ray of hope. It wants to destroy the Relics Infernal. They're the only thing that could control it, and I suspect they're the only thing that can send the demon back to its realm, and free Drake's body from being its vessel."

"Well." Lady Eberhardt cleared her throat. "That's fairly brutal. Where is it?"

"That's the one thing I can't see," she admitted, and all their searches had turned up nothing.

"Ianthe, you should take Louisa and flee," Lucien said, his lips firming as he stared at his wife.

"What about you?" Ianthe demanded. "I'm not going to leave you here. And running only means I prolong my sentence, I suspect."

Husband and wife stared at each other hopelessly.

Then Lucien turned to Bishop. "He's my father, and yours. I know you want to save him, but I won't risk my wife—"

"We have to try." Bishop murmured, tugging off his gloves. He picked up the box he'd brought with him and set it on the table in the middle of them all. Taking a deep breath, he opened it up, revealing a small golden chalice within.

"I have some small divination gifts. Enough to know Cleo's Visions see only probabilities," Lady Eberhardt said. "There's a chance we can turn the path of fate."

"We have the Chalice," Bishop said. "That's one of the Relics. And we know who has the second Relic."

"Oh, we should ask Morgana if she'd care to hand it over," Sebastian said in a cool, almost bored tone. "I'm sure my mother would be so kind as to do that."

"I wasn't planning on asking her," Bishop said.

"I could steal it," Verity suggested, and Bishop glared at his wife.

"Absolutely not."

Verity Hastings had the ability to translocate. It was an impossible gift, but she'd been raised by the Hex Society in Seven Dials, a bunch of gifted curse workers who refused to join the Order. There were rules of sorcery Verity hadn't learned, and apparently her conscious mind didn't know enough about the laws of energy and sorcery to understand she simply *shouldn't* be able to punch in and out of a room.

But the first rule of sorcery, and the one currently affecting Cleo's Visions, was Mind over Matter.

Verity believed she could do it, and hence she could.

"Morgana wouldn't even know I was there," Verity replied, crossing her arms over her chest.

"Morgana knows your talents," Bishop snapped, "and I daresay she's accounted for them."

"He's right," Sebastian said. "She'll have set traps."

Malice whispered through the room as the Chalice began to smoke and smolder. It was crafted with sorcery from the Grave Arts, which meant it could raise an army of the dead, and had, not so long ago. Cleo glanced down at it. Had nobody else noticed?

"Are you doing that Adrian?" Lady Eberhardt barked.

Bishop glanced down. "No. It senses my power sometimes though, and it starts singing to me."

Singing?

"Can you close that bloody box up," Lady Eberhardt grimaced, rubbing her chest. "It's making my chest ache."

Bishop shut the box, and then seemed to take a deep breath.

"There's more," Cleo announced into the sudden silence. She licked dry lips, turning to Sebastian. "You and I are the key to bringing Drake back. I don't know how. I don't know why. But I saw us. Together. And it was quite clear that if we... if we stray from each other's side... then we'll fall."

She wasn't about to mention Quentin Farshaw, or his ludicrous claim Sebastian was both the cause and the key to overthrowing the black queen. Nobody needed to know about that. His brothers, Lucien and Bishop, had only just begun to accept him and consider him less of a threat than they once had.

Sebastian looked up slowly, his face expressionless. "As you wish."

And she didn't know if he believed her, or if he thought she wanted to somehow keep him by her side.

A knock sounded on the door.

All heads turned, and a handsome gentleman somewhere in his thirties appeared, tugging off his gloves. Taller than most of the others—apart from Sebastian—he stood with a certain belief in himself that was attractive, though the dark hair and eyes certainly helped.

"Am I late?" he asked.

Clearly she had an uncomfortable fondness for dark hair, she thought, her gaze flickering to Sebastian, then back to the stranger. One glimpse of her husband's face, however, broke the spell the newcomer cast. No man was more handsome than her husband, and that wasn't mere pride speaking, but a simple truth. Sometimes she almost thought she was growing used to it. Indeed, it had been easier when she *was* blindfolded, for then she wasn't prone to breaking into blushes whenever she looked at him.

"Remy." Relief broke in Ianthe's voice, and she went to his side, pressing a fond kiss to his cheek. "Thank you for coming."

"Still not going to return to the theatre?" The stranger quirked a dark brow as he stepped inside the room, closing the door behind him.

"She had a better offer," Lucien replied dryly, resting one hand on the mantle.

The two men locked eyes, and the newcomer smiled faintly. "A shame. You always did own the stage, my dear." He examined Ianthe's face. "Though I must admit your new role suits you too. *Prime* of the Order? Aren't we moving up in the world."

"I sometimes wish I hadn't," Ianthe replied sadly, and Cleo knew she was thinking of the loss of her mentor, Drake, who had been the previous Prime.

"We'll get him back," the stranger said. "Now, what's all this I hear about relics?"

Ianthe swiftly introduced him to the group. Cleo had heard her mention Remington Cross, the Great Magician, but she'd thought him merely an old friend of Ianthe's. He wasn't of the Order, though there was a strange aura about the man. Power of some sort. Not sorcery, as she knew it, but he exuded an exotic sort of danger that made her a little wary.

"The Chalice," he noted, sinking into Ianthe's abandoned chair as if he belonged there. "Haven't seen that in an age."

"You've seen it?" This from Bishop.

Lady Eberhardt snorted, and she and Mr. Cross exchanged glances. Cross leaned forward, turning the Chalice so he could see the runes carved into it. "I helped create it," he said. "Or not completely. I had no role in the crafting of such weapons, but when Drake began to speak of creating something like this, he came to me to understand how to go about it."

"Remington collects rare items of magical properties," Ianthe explained. "He's the lead expert in any sort of magical relic, which is why I asked him to join us."

"You should have kept your mouth shut," Lady Eberhardt said.

Something darkened in Mr. Cross's eyes. "A set of relics to bind and control a demon? It seemed a prudent precaution, what with sorcerers over the years summoning them through from the Shadow Dimensions, with only a warded circle to contain them."

"How did they make the relics?" Cleo asked, for she'd always wondered. Her father, Lord Tremayne, had worked with Drake and his ex-wife, Morgana, to create the set.

"The Blade was forged from the iron of a fallen star," Mr. Cross replied. "The Chalice, as you can see is carved from ivory, and the Wand was cut from whale bone, and carved with runes. By themselves they are merely objects of the physical world, inscribed with powerful runes. The reason they're so dangerous, however, is because they were also formed within the dream plane—that realm that sits side-by-side with our world, and with the Shadow Dimensions. A demon can walk the dream-plane if it wills, though it cannot break through into our world. So the relics needed to be forged in both planes—physical and astral—in order to be able to kill it—"

"That's enough," Lady Eberhardt snapped. "There's no need to be spreading such information around. Once was enough."

"Where are the rest of the Relics Infernal?" Cross asked. "Where are the Wand and the Blade of Altarrh?"

"Morgana has the Blade," Bishop said. "We thought she'd destroyed it, however, she was using her illusion arts to make us believe the kitchen knife she held was the Blade."

"And the Wand was stolen by her over a year ago, unbeknownst to the Order," Ianthe said softly.

"I know where it is," Sebastian said.

The focus of the room shifted to him.

"Or I know who it was given to," he continued, looking coolly unperturbed. "Morgana needed a place to stay, and a means to find allies when she first arrived in London last year. There are few places in the city where no Order sorcerers dare trespass, and it is one of them. But she had to trade something of value in order for safe passage, and when she left she felt the Wand would be safe there, until she had use of it again."

"Where?" Ianthe asked curtly.

Sebastian rubbed his knuckles in his other hand. "There's a manor on the outskirts of the city. It belongs to a man named Malachi Gray."

Mr. Cross's gaze focused rather intently on Cleo's husband. "Gray has the Wand?"

"He did the last time I looked," Sebastian replied.

"Then he'll have it still." Cross frowned.

"My mother *might* have taken it back."

Cross shook his head. "Your mother has no idea who she was dealing with. Even she won't be able to take the Wand back by force, and Gray can see through any illusion she casts. You can bargain with Gray, but no sorcerer in this city can overthrow him. And if he took a liking to the Wand—or even owned some whim to keep it, just because your mother wanted it back—then there's nothing she could have offered him in trade."

Cleo shifted uneasily. "We need it. I saw the three Relics quite clearly. They're the only way to defeat the demon."

"Can he match the might of the Order?" Ianthe demanded.

"No." Cross looked contemplative. "But you don't need to bring the entire Order against him. That preempts a war with those of the Black Arts. Not every sorcerer in London cares for the Order."

"You know this Malachi Gray?" Cleo asked.

"We've met," Cross said curtly, "and if you think he's going to politely hand over something powerful, then you're quite mistaken. Not without an exchange of equal value."

"I wasn't planning to ask," Sebastian responded coolly.

Those hawkish eyes gleamed. "I do hope you weren't going to barrel in there and presume your strength gives you some sort of advantage against a powerful and dangerous foe? One who could possibly knot you in two? One who is very accomplished in the occult arts?"

"That's why I'm going too," Bishop said, crossing his arms over his chest.

"A seer," Cross tipped his head to Cleo, "and two fools who think what? That strength alone can conquer an unknown foe?" His voice dropped, a dangerously melodic quality entering it. "You know not what you're dealing with. Malachi is not even human. Not anymore. And I would be very, *very* wary to tread where he claims ownership. If Drake were here, then I think even he might refuse to make this assault, and your father is the greatest sorcerer I've ever had the pleasure of encountering."

"Just how dangerous is this Malachi Gray?" Ianthe murmured.

"Imagine facing me if I had no conscience, and all I cared for was the whim of toying with others. The demon you wish to bring down has as much empathy as Malachi does, and only twice the power."

"Could he face the demon?" Ianthe asked.

Cross's dark gaze shuttered. "It's not a matter of 'could he,' so much as, 'would he'? Could he survive? Maybe. But unless there was some interest in it for him, then your chances of finding an ally there are nonexistent."

Ianthe paced in front of the fire, her dark skirts swishing about her legs. "What would interest him?"

"Ianthe," Lucien warned, his hands in his pockets.

"You," Cross said bluntly, and Ianthe jerked to halt. "Your body, your heart, your soul." He held up a hand as Lucien stirred. "Simply because your bond with your husband—and your love for him—presents an impossible game to a man like Malachi. Could he win you? Could his allure defeat the strength of a soul-bond between two lovers? You wouldn't be half as interesting to him if your affections could be so easily swayed, but it's the game of it, you see. The temptation. If you want to trade him for the

Wand, or for his allegiance, then that is the sort of price he will ask for."

"No," Lucien said coldly, and his amber eyes locked on his wife. "He won't even get the chance to ask."

"I wouldn't even consider it, Luc. And neither of us can leave. There's been so much upheaval in the past month, what with hunting for a demon that's practically vanished. The Ascension Ball has been delayed too long. It is only days away and I have to prepare the house. The entire Order is going to descend upon us, and we need to present a united front. With Drake gone, there's been so much unrest, and my rule is so new." Ianthe pinched the bridge of her nose. "But we need all the information we can get, and if this Gray knows something...."

"I'll go," Bishop said. "Verity and I can hunt the Wand down. I'll take Sebastian with me."

"And me," Cleo added.

Ianthe nodded, as if in thanks.

"So we can't trade for it," Sebastian said softy, pushing away from the wall. "We can't steal it. And we can't hope he will use it as our ally. What does that leave us with?"

"No Wand," Ianthe growled under her breath.

"We don't have a choice. If we're to have any chance at saving our father, then we *need* the Wand," Bishop replied, pushing away from the wall. "I'm a Sicarii assassin, Verity's a thief, Sebastian's dangerous, and Cleo can predict the future. Together we—"

"Together you're all fools," Cross. "Children dabbling in things you barely understand."

"Remington." Ianthe looked up at him, her eyes full of some message only Cross seemed to understand. "We need the wand. We need Drake back. There's a demon inside him, and even if he weren't the father I never had, even if I didn't love him, then that fact alone encourages me to attempt this endeavor. What could a demon not do, with Drake's power? What *is* it doing?"

Cross considered Ianthe for a long moment. Something conflicted crossed his face, but he finally gave a curt nod. "Leaving Drake in the demon's possession is dangerous. And for friendship's sake, he deserves a chance to be rescued."

Ianthe breathed a sigh of relief. "Then how do we deal with this Malachi Gray?"

"You don't." Cross poured himself a cognac. "I'll deal with him. On one condition…."

"Anything," Ianthe promised, relief flooding her voice.

Cross looked at both Sebastian and Bishop. "I will get you this Wand, and I'll need the two of you at my back to do it, but the rules are simple: I'm in charge of this mission. Neither of you speak unless I permit it. You don't make a move unless I instruct you to, and you do not, under any circumstances, confront Malachi directly, or *offer him anything*. Do you understand?"

"Understood," Sebastian said, crossing his arms over his chest.

"We'll go tonight then."

CHAPTER SIX

"Will you walk into my parlor?" said the Spider to the Fly,
'Tis the prettiest little parlor that ever you did spy;
The way into my parlor is up a winding stair,
And I've a many curious thing to show when you are there."

—The Spider and the Fly, Mary Howitt, 1829

"DO YOU FEEL that?" Cleo whispered, as Sebastian helped her down from the carriage in front of the menacing iron fence that guarded Malachi Gray's estate. Patches of snow lined the driveway, but the rest of the place was clear.

"Feel what?"

A shiver ran over her skin, unlike anything else she'd ever felt before. Cleo looked down in surprise as her husband's faint touch upon her hand set off some sort of reaction within her.

He always set off that reaction.

But not to this intensity. The sweep of his thumb across her silk glove felt like it caressed something rather more intimate.

Their eyes met, then his gaze flickered lower, before he politely looked away. Her décolletage had been on the receiving end of some rather intense frowns ever since he'd helped her alight in the carriage. Her gown wasn't cut as low as Ianthe's evening gowns, nor did she fill her bodice out to that extent, but he seemed to have taken some fierce exception to the lowering of her necklines.

And so, she found herself wanting to flaunt it.

"It feels like... I've imbibed too much brandy," she whispered hoarsely, "and I can feel all that heat sweeping slowly through my veins."

A muscle flickered in his jaw. "There is a strange feeling in the air."

"Sweet mercy," she breathed, as that smoky touch seemed to settle heavily in the pit of her abdomen. Cleo clenched her gloved hand into a fist. She had the sudden shocking thought she wanted to grab her husband's cravat and yank his mouth down to hers. "What *is* that?"

"It's called allure," Remington announced, breaking the spell.

Suddenly she could breathe and think again, but a swift dart of her husband's eyes made the heat flare once more. Cleo held his gaze. *Liar.* He could certainly feel it.

"What sort of magic is this?" Bishop demanded with a frown. Or perhaps that was his normal expression, since he seemed to be perpetually glowering.

"Whatever it is," Verity said, with a laugh, "where can I get some more of it?"

"Malachi feeds on lust and violence," Remington said, leading them through the gates. He'd demanded they walk, preferring not to be trapped in the carriage if something attacked. The carriage driver cracked the reins behind them, heading for a place to rest the horses. "The closer we get to him, the stronger the allure will be. It's a subtle magic, designed to give him plenty of victims."

"Victims?" Verity repeated. "That sounds rather less alluring."

"Keep your heads," Remington warned, and among them all, he seemed to be the least affected.

He and Sebastian.

There was a party in progress, and it seemed as though someone had swept the snow from the lawn. The closer they came, the more it seemed as if they stepped into another world; flowers bloomed, here in the heart of winter.

Powerful magic, indeed.

Laughter roared in the night, and music swelled in the gardens behind the dark manor, though it was the sort of music that belonged in no respectable establishment. It seemed innocent enough—a string quartet—but there was something about the dangerous melody of the violin that sent a shiver down her skin. It whispered a song of lust and betrayal, aided by the soft huskiness of voices and the murmur of knowing laughter. The magic of Gray's allure wove between the notes, making her skin itch.

Lanterns gleamed through the trees as Remington led them up a gravel-lined driveway that circled to the back of the house. Cleo couldn't help looking about her in wonder. This garden was what Eden should have looked like. She'd expected naked statues, and raucous satyrs carved in the hedges, but there was nothing of the sort. Lush. That was the word. The greenery beckoned, with lanterns picking trails through the garden, and it seemed as though the closer they got to the house, the more they left winter behind them.

Dozens of red rosebuds reigned over them as they stepped beneath an arch, and she saw the entrance to a maze in the distance. "How on earth did they get them to bud right now?" she asked, brushing a drowsing rose. The air was still cold enough to make her nose numb.

"Magic, I presume," Sebastian murmured, his gaze locking on the rose. "I've always been able to make roses bloom."

"Yes, but it's a rather extravagant waste of magic for a party. This Malachi is an artist," she whispered, as Sebastian led her along a hedge-lined path that opened into the main garden beyond, and the beckoning party. "The music, the gardens…. It's all planned to seduce, but there's an elegance to it I hadn't expected."

Sebastian trailed his palm over a tightly furled white rose that belonged in *Alice in Wonderland*. "I'm inclined to agree."

"That would be a first."

The words broke from her lips before she could even consider them.

His gaze slid down to her, then back to the gardens, and she suddenly remembered how she'd found him that long ago day, tending to the roses in his mother's garden, while his mother plotted murder in the sitting room.

"Do you miss your garden?" she asked softly, for her previous words had been too sharp.

"Yes," he replied. "Bishop doesn't grant me the time to even consider his roses. He's too busy beating me to death with his magic staff."

"That sounds slightly titillating."

A faint breath of amusement broke from his lips. "He would kill you if he heard you say that."

"He might scowl at me a little harder," she admitted.

"Don't take it personally. He scowls at everyone."

"Except Verity."

"Oh, no, he scowls at Verity," Sebastian replied. "Particularly at Verity. She then proceeds to laugh in his face, or drags him off somewhere else, where—presumably—she teaches him to smile a little."

He stroked his finger along a rose petal as he spoke.

"You enjoy tending them," she realized.

"It's calming." He brushed another rose, a barely opened bud, and then broke it from the stem. Power whispered through him, and delicate pink petals began to bloom and open. A swift movement, and he tucked it behind her ear. "For you."

Cleo touched the soft petals, her breath catching. She looked up into his mercurial silver eyes. The stark black of his coat blended into the night, and he looked good. Too good.

I wish you'd make up your mind. There was no softness in that expression, but she could feel the rose behind her ear. Curse her if she could work out what it meant, though.

"Thank you," she whispered.

Fire spewed through the night, a man lowering a torch from his lips as he blew flame across the gathering. Sebastian turned toward it abruptly, his features tightening into a hawkish mask. The moment was gone.

People wearing garish masks of leering imps, painted satyrs and nymphs swirled across the marble dance floor. Despite the candelabras strewn across the lawn, it was difficult to see, almost as if some strange magic muted the garden.

The crowd clapped and cheered.

"It looks so beautiful," she breathed, doubt filling her. What on earth was Remington worried about?

"It's a mirage," Remington replied, as if he'd heard her. "You of all people should know there are shadows that lurk beneath."

Cleo blinked, centering her vision. A woman swayed toward her, wearing a vibrant red corset, pearls, stockings and little else. Her heart-shaped face seemed to bear a double image, almost as if there were something underneath the pretty doll-like expression, and then a leering face suddenly superimposed the woman's face, just for a second, and Cleo jumped back.

Remington was right. There was more going on than there seemed. Sucking in a sharp breath, she found herself clutching Sebastian's arm.

"What did you see?" he demanded softly, his hand resting against her hip. A light, protective touch, and one she didn't even think he was truly aware of, but it burned through her as though his hand rested on naked flesh.

"I don't know," Cleo said curtly, pushing away from him. "Something. Something not human." The ache between her thighs pulsed wickedly. She pressed a gloved hand to her temples, and tried to take a deep breath. What was wrong with her?

The woman in the corset slid her arms around Sebastian's neck and purred, "Hello, lover."

He swiftly disentangled her arms, looking sharply at Cleo as if for help, and she remembered what he'd said about women.

Morgana had made him entertain her allies. Or perhaps *made* was not the correct word. She'd put a sclavus collar on Sebastian when he was thirteen, which meant he'd had no choice in the matter. The collar forced him to the will of whoever wore the control ring, and Morgana had offered it at her whim to women who'd wanted him.

"Get your hands off him," Cleo said sharply, for the conflict was clear on his face. He would barely allow *her* to touch him, for heaven's sake.

The woman blinked at her in surprise, but then a pair of dancers swept between her and Sebastian. Cleo staggered back, and saw Sebastian reaching for her through the sudden press of dancers. At least he was no longer wearing the woman.

She shook her head at him. "I'm fine."

"Cleo, wait for me," Sebastian called.

Skirts twirled as Cleo found herself in the center of the dancers all of a sudden, as if they'd moved in some secret, choreographed sway in order to cut her off from the group. She was lost in a sea of wigs and silk, bodies pressing against her. A hand brushed her hip. Another stroked her arm. But when she spun around to see who had touched her, the dancers receded, much like the sea.

"Cleo!"

She turned back the way she'd come, as Sebastian tried to push his way onto the dance floor. He paused, crushed between two couples, and she saw frustration dance over his face.

"I'll meet you on the other side!" she called, pointing to the wide terrace overlooking the dance floor.

Something caught her eye. A masked face, watching her from across the crowd. Black feathers obscured the man's face, his crow-like mask capturing her attention before he vanished between people.

Cleo paused. She should return to Sebastian's side. But her divination instincts pulled at her.

Follow that man, they whispered.

But when she turned, there was nothing there.

"Isn't there?" came a wicked voice, deep inside her. *"Look again."*

Her powers were evolving. Ianthe seemed to think that without access to her Visions, her divination talents were trying to come through in other ways. Was this voice some sort of... intuition? It didn't come from without—her wards saw to that. So it had to be coming from within her. She was fairly certain she'd heard it whispering to her in the Labyrinth too.

Where had the stranger gone?

The dancers faded away as Cleo focused, and a single couple swam into view. The man was tall, his black velvet coat cut tightly around his narrow hips, and she caught flashes of his gaze through the mask, locked on her as he twirled the woman in his arms in devastating circles. She caught a flash of his smile, as if he were delighted to have caught her attention, and then he was gone again.

What on earth?

A shiver swept through her, blood rushing through her veins as the music began to die down. She found him again. The man lifted a hand to his crow mask, and slid it back off his face as he relinquished the woman he was dancing with, his gaze locked on Cleo's face.

Cleo swallowed.

Hard.

Sebastian was the most beautiful man she'd ever laid eyes upon, but there was something about this stranger that made her flush with heat. An intimate mocking in his green eyes, perhaps? A certain carnal slant to his full mouth? But beneath the handsome features lay a hidden undertone. Premonition surged through her. *Danger*, it all but screamed.

The kind of danger one desperately wanted to give in to.

This man was pure temptation, and from the look in his eyes when their gazes collided, he knew it.

Then the dancers twirled, and the man vanished and Cleo was left alone in the middle of the dance floor, feeling like she wanted to follow him down some dark, twisted rabbit hole.

Good grief. What sort of magic was this? For it had to be magic affecting her so badly. Her head was spinning, her body alight with the kind of anticipation only her husband had ever stirred in her before. She wanted to cast good intentions straight out the window, and do something shocking. *Lust, violence, hunger, need.* Remington had been underselling the danger significantly, and none of them had understood.

She needed to find the others.

Now.

Cleo turned and slammed into a hard body, all her good intentions evaporating from her mind. Hands caught her upper arms to brace her, and they were terrifyingly gentle. Every inch of her throbbed with lust. Cleo gripped his coat, trying to clear her head.

"Has he left you here all alone?" said a melodious voice.

Cleo sucked in a sharp breath. "Who?"

How had the stranger moved so fast?

"The man who watches you." That voice was molten honey, and it whispered through her like pure sin. Before she knew it, he'd captured her gloved hand and brought it to his lips. One finger stroked the inside of her wrist, even as his full, dangerous mouth whispered against the silk of her glove. "The man who hungers for you, but will not touch you." The dangerous stranger glanced up from beneath dark lashes. "The man you wish would touch you. You crave his touch so badly it calls to me." The stranger closed his eyes, a look of tortured pleasure crossing his face. "Sweet mercy, but the longing hurts so badly it's almost pleasure."

Cleo sucked in a sharp breath, and jerked her hand to her chest. The second he stopped touching her, she felt like she could think again, and her cheeks heated. "That man is my husband. And you are not he."

"No, I'm not." His expression turned dangerous. "For if I were your husband, you would have known my touch, and you would crave no other. And I would never allow such a rare bloom to wander so freely... where others might pluck it."

"Who are you?" she demanded, though she had a certain suspicion she knew.

Again she was the recipient of a hot-eyed look. "If you want my name, sweet dove, then you must win it."

"And how would I win it?"

His thumb stroked over the back of her gloved hand. "A kiss, perhaps."

Despite everything, the slow stroke of his thumb sent tremors through her. "Is your name worth so much?" she asked lightly, a little uncertain how to handle him.

Devilishly handsome strangers did not go around offering to seduce her. Or at least, they hadn't so far, in her limited experience.

"Shall you find out?" he teased.

"No kiss," Cleo insisted, though she didn't tug her hand away. "Besides, I think I do know your name, Mr.... Gray."

His eyes flashed pure heat, but his smile widened. "And now I am at a loss, for I don't know yours."

Cleo smiled a very dangerous smile. "What price would you pay for it?"

The sleepy, seductive mask fell away, replaced by a look of sudden interest. "Is your name worth so much?"

Her own words, thrown back at her. "The intrigue is in the mystery, Mr. Gray. I guess you shall have to find something worthy of my attention if you wish to find out."

"Not a kiss," he mused. "A dance then?"

Cleo's eyes narrowed, as she stared down at Malachi Gray's gently tugging fingers as he sought to draw her further into the crowd. Her heart yearned for Sebastian, as did her body, but she couldn't deny the treacherous little voice that whispered in the back of her mind: Sebastian had never asked her to dance.

Never flirted.

Never tried to kiss her, beyond that one disastrous time she'd tried to press her affections upon him.

She was a wife in name only.

A young woman who'd been locked away at her father's estate for far too long, her only introductions to other people being the strictly controlled meetings her father had forced upon her, where she was to supply Visions for a price.

He's dangerous..., Remington's voice whispered in her memories.

But they needed the Wand from him, and despite his intoxicating influence, she was certain she could handle him.

All she had to do was keep her head.

"I will grant you a dance. And if you're competent as a partner, then I might present you with my name when we finish."

"An excellent bargain." That thumb stroked across the fleshy pad of her palm. "Though I'm rather more inclined to win it."

Cleo smiled. She felt a little more clearheaded now. The press of his magic whispered against her skin, but she no longer invited it in.

Music swelled, as if at his silent command. Cleo hesitantly rested a hand on his shoulder, glancing up. "I'm told you host frequent parties, Mr. Gray."

"Please, call me Malachi."

"That wouldn't be proper."

His smiled flashed again. "What a terrible shame such impropriety would be. Imagine what my poor scandalized guests would think."

Another flare of fire belched into the air nearby, and a woman laughed raucously as a man swung her into the sky. "You have a point... Malachi."

To be in his arms was like floating on a cloud. The man danced divinely, and it felt as though she barely had to move, and he was twirling her. He kept the distance between them proper, but every touch of his gloved hands made her flush, and every heated look he sent her told a thousand naughty stories.

And yet... it felt wrong.

Almost like she'd had too much champagne, and her senses were dulled. Lust hung like a cloud in the air, like the sweet-smelling smoke of a hookah. She was drowning in the drugging kiss of it, and yet it felt vaguely distant.

It was nothing like the moment when her husband had unlaced her wedding gown for her. There'd been anticipation then, desire, nervousness, and a desperate sort of longing. This was merely skin deep.

Shallow. It could not penetrate her heart.

"I don't recall inviting you," he whispered, his breath caressing her bare neck as he turned her in his arms. "Or your friends."

Cleo twirled under his arm as he spun her, again and again, until she felt dizzy and breathless, and flushed with a heat that made her feel distinctly boneless. "Do you invite all of your guests personally?"

His smile seemed perfectly edged, as if it were merely a mask, and she realized he was watching her a little too closely. His game of seduction was precisely that. A game. And one he played with a certain sort of detachment.

"You're bored," she said, and wasn't certain if Premonition urged her to say it, or mere whim. "Bored of all the parties and the games. They satisfy some part of you, but they don't quite offer true fulfillment."

His green eyes sharpened. "What is true fulfillment?"

"Connection," she whispered. "One soul finding another in the dark, and realizing it's the other half of theirs."

"And have you found your other half?" he snapped, slowing just enough that another pair of dancers staggered into them.

A fierce glare cleared the space around them. The shiver of lust on her skin felt like it was evaporating.

"I'd hoped I had."

"But you're not certain." His face turned cruel. "No, he's not certain, or he would have had you by now. He'd be the one dancing here in your arms, drawn by my siren call. But he's not. And you're in *my* arms. He's a fool."

"I didn't mean to offend you."

Malachi slowed almost to a halt, his voice turning hard. "Who *are* you?"

"I think I quite enjoy keeping you in the dark," she said with a faint laugh. His attentions—as superficial as they seemed—were somewhat enjoyable, flattering. "You wouldn't be half as interested in me were you to know all of my secrets, would you? That's the game."

"And do you have many secrets?"

Cleo's voice dropped to a whisper. "Wouldn't you like to know?"

Flashes of other women in his arms, other men, cascaded through her mind every time she touched him. It was the closest she'd come to falling into a Vision since she'd lost the ability.

If she could just focus....

His mouth brushed against her cheek, and Cleo jolted. Her head was swimming again. "You could stay here with me," he whispered. "Leave your companions behind. Perhaps we could both find what we're looking for in each other?"

The smoky trail of his magic caressed her skin. Want surged through her. *Need*. But with it came the memory of Sebastian's hands upon her skin the night he'd helped unbutton her wedding gown. The gentle touch of his hands upon her back had stoked a fire this stranger's magic could not compare to. Malachi's magic was hungry and overwhelming, but it felt like a flame that would only burn too swiftly, leaving her unfulfilled. Sebastian's touch made her heart ache with a desire she couldn't even name, and she knew she would never forget that touch, never want another man, if only he'd give in to the temptation....

"It's tempting," she countered, and her smile softened a little. "But we'd be lying to each other. And to ourselves." Malachi turned her, and Cleo came up abruptly against that hard chest. Their eyes met. "Despite your magic, you're not the man I want. And I—I am not the woman *you* want."

"You don't know that."

"I do. I can feel it radiating off you, the same way I can feel your *allure* tempting me." Cleo reached up, pressing a hand to his cheek in an attempt to stir those flashes of Vision to life. They hammered through her, quicksilver darts of color, but nothing fully fleshed. Nothing like they'd once been.

A clock. A woman's laugh. The scent of lavender. The image of Malachi Gray standing alone in a hallway, his fist curling over a lady's glove as he looked down at it with an expression of such despair that her breath caught, and something began to suck her into the next image....

"No woman has ever captured my heart," he countered, but the words sounded very faraway.

"*Lie,*" Cleo countered hollowly.

The garden faded, the touch of his arms vanishing. Light began to glow in front of her. A candelabra swam out of the darkness as Malachi lifted a candle from its brass stem and used it to light another. Cleo blinked, and then he was circling a small room, lighting candle after candle.

"*You should never be left alone in the dark,*" he whispered, and Cleo began to make out the tomb-like structure he was circling.

A coffin made of glass, with something within it.

Someone.

A woman lay in serene repose, her blonde hair fanned across the pillow she rested upon. Malachi lit the last candle, his face implacable, but his eyes filled with a certain kind of desperation as he splayed one hand against the glass, reaching for his sleeping beauty, but never quite—

"What did you just say?" Malachi demanded, and his voice snapped her out of the memory—for that was what it was, she realized.

Then his face was in front of her, his skin paling even as she sucked in a sharp breath. What had she said?

"You should never be left alone in the dark...," Cleo repeated softly, her heart filled with sympathy. The Malachi Gray from her vision was not the one who stood before her now, his eyebrows narrowing tightly, and fury flaring in the green depths of his irises.

"Who are you?" he demanded in a hoarse voice. "What are you?"

"Are we bargaining again?" she asked lightly, but the spell was clearly broken, for his fingers locked around her wrist, and she realized they'd stopped dead in the center of the circle of dancers.

"Who sent you?" His grip tightened, and the pain swept from his eyes, replaced by a fury so intense it almost burned her. "Someone sent you, didn't they? Do you think this is a game you can win? You making vague comments that *mean nothing*, as if you know anything about me."

Sudden desire washed over her, swamping her in waves of pleasure. Cleo clung to his coat, her knees going weak and heat washing through her womb. She wanted to crush her mouth to his all of a sudden, to beg him for a kiss, just one kiss....

This was what Remington had warned her about.

Cleo dragged her hand to her mouth and bit into her knuckles, trying to break the lure of his magic. Sebastian. Sebastian.... But the thought of him only made her ache harder. "I know enough."

"I will break you," he whispered harshly. "You ignorant, foolish pawn. I will wreck you and make you beg me for more. Who *sent you*?"

Pain flared in her hand—her fingernails digging into the flesh of her palm. "Who is the g-girl in the glass c-coffin?"

The lust evaporated.

Cleo collapsed against his chest, gasping hard and shaking from the brink of pleasure.

His warm humor and faint smile vanished as if they'd never been. This time he looked at her as though he finally saw the real her, and not merely a toy to play with. "Leave," he warned, "before I lose all sense of myself and break you."

"I th-think," she managed to say, "that one of us is already broken."

A flash of rose-colored silk skirts swept past. Cleo. Sebastian's gaze locked on her as the ring of dancers cut him off again. It felt like a conspiracy, but the dancers all moved too perfectly, too in rhythm. They couldn't be keeping him from getting to her. Could they?

He saw her again, her golden hair shining in the candlelight like a beacon. And everything in him went still.

Cleo was dancing.

With a stranger who looked like he wanted to devour her.

And there was a smile on her lips, one Sebastian hadn't seen for a very long time. It hit him like a punch to the throat. She didn't smile for him anymore. Not like that. Oh, she might offer a faint curve of the lips, but this was a genuinely happy smile. The kind that wrapped fingers around his heart as if to claim it.

"What's going on?" Bishop demanded, grabbing him by the arm. "We lost you."

"Cleo was separated from me by these others." He prowled the edge of the dance floor. "Someone's dancing with her. Remington told us not to get separated."

"So I did," Remington announced, materializing with Verity at his side. He paused, every muscle in his body turning to stone as he peered onto the dance floor. "It appears your wife has found Malachi Gray. Or perhaps he's found her, more to the point."

"That's Gray?" He didn't know why he was so angry.

Remington looked disgusted. "It would have to be her."

"What do you mean by that?"

Bishop and Remington exchanged a long look. Remington sighed. "I thought Verity and Cleo would be protected by their soul-bonds. Verity clearly is, but I'm sure Malachi sensed your wife walking into this garden the second she stepped foot over the boundary."

"Verity and my soul-bond is complete and accepted," Bishop muttered.

And his and Cleo's was not.

"Cleo is young, she's innocent... the perfect temptation. If she can keep her head, then we might have a chance to distract Malachi," Remington mused, watching her dance.

Like hell. He wasn't going to wait here another damned second.

"Sebastian," Remington warned, grabbing his sleeve, "One thing you need to understand is that Malachi Gray is no longer human. He sold himself a long time ago, to a mistress who takes pleasure in ruining the souls of mortals. Being in his presence will make you feel certain things; lust, violence, hunger, need. All those dark little thoughts that whisper in your ear of a night, when nobody is watching. And you mustn't—whatever you do—give in to them. Do you understand?"

Sebastian twitched a brow. "Understood."

It wouldn't be a problem.

He'd spent years denying himself.

He wasn't about to succumb now.

Turning, he slammed through the first ring of dancers, pushing and shoving them out of his way as they flocked in front of him to slow him down.

If the bastard touched her again....

Power brewed within him, stark and dangerous like the roll of a thundercloud on the horizon. The dancers fled as a coating of frost began to settle over the grass, and Sebastian stepped through into the open space just as Gray swept Cleo's back against his chest, and caressed her throat.

Their gazes collided, but all his sorcery was for naught, as he could not risk assaulting the bastard, not with Cleo there.

"Let her go," Sebastian said, and his words echoed with a dangerous power.

Gray's eyes grew heavy and he did something that made Cleo gasp. "Perhaps I'll keep her. She's so ripe. So hungry. It makes me ache...."

Rage obliterated his reason, and he took a step forward, but something was holding him back. An iron shackle around his arm—or no, his brother's hand.

"Remember your lessons," Bishop hissed. "He's baiting you."

Sebastian forced the rage away, grinding his teeth together and reining in the sheer amount of power surging through him. The ground shook a little, and it scared him, for he hadn't been aware of how on edge he was.

The grass had turned into sharp little shards, tipped with ice.

"Or perhaps I'll keep her as a concession for trespassing." The bastard whispered in her ear, but his gaze was locked on Sebastian, as if he welcomed the rage, and the thrill of violence in the air. "There is a price for coming here, especially uninvited. And perhaps if you tell me who sent you I'll forfeit the payment. Perhaps. Why don't we retire to my parlor to discuss the issue?"

"A rather good idea," said a hard voice from behind them. "Why don't we?"

Remington's voice acted like a bucket of ice water thrown over Mr. Gray. He froze. Not in the way of a startled creature, but a certain stillness crept over his body in a way that made Sebastian want to tuck Cleo protectively against his side. There was a flash of surprise on Gray's face, followed swiftly by something else, something unidentifiable, before he settled that eerie gaze upon Remington as he gently pushed Sebastian and Bishop out of the way.

"Remy." The word was a soft-edged taunt. "You finally took up my invitation to visit."

"I'm not here to enjoy your pleasure gardens."

"No?" There was an edge in Gray's voice now, and all of them might as well be forgotten, for the two men locked stares in a way that indicated a past history Remington hadn't bloody well divulged when they were planning this visit.

"No." Remington shoved his hands in his pockets. "But we shall accept your offer to retire. There are things you and I need to discuss. In private. Take your hands off the girl. She's innocent, and if she's anyone's pawn, then she's mine."

"I'm fully aware she's innocent," Gray said, innuendo dripping off the words. His eyes locked on Sebastian's. "A dangerous thing, to let a young woman like this out in the world."

He stared back flatly. "A dangerous thing, to touch a man's wife."

"You look familiar," Gray said.

"I should."

But he didn't explain, and Gray's eyes slowly narrowed, curiously overcoming him.

"Very well. Come into my parlor." *Said the spider to the fly.* "Let us talk and become reacquainted."

And then he vanished into the crowd.

CHAPTER SEVEN

"WHAT THE HELL was that all about?" Sebastian whispered in Cleo's ear as he escorted her toward the manor house Malachi Gray had indicated.

"All what?" Cleo retorted under her breath.

"You know what I'm speaking about."

Cleo glanced up from beneath her lashes. Her body hadn't quite forgotten the sensual touch of Malachi, or the feelings his magic evoked in her. "No, I don't believe I do. Am I not to dance with other men? You could ask me yourself, you know. Am I not to talk to other men? It seems as though I—"

"Did you not hear what Remington said?" Sebastian's jaw clenched and he finally looked down at her, his silver eyes *glittering*. "The man is dangerous."

"He seemed quite charming to me. Playing word games, of course, but a great many of my father's allies did that."

"He was practically salivating over you," Sebastian snarled.

A little thrill went through her. She'd interpreted his displeasure as something else, but was he actually *jealous*?

Her first instinct was to reassure him, but the words caught in her throat. And Cleo realized she didn't want to reassure him. It might be petty, but *he* was the one who said this marriage needed to remain one of convenience. "He can salivate all he likes. I find men often do. It doesn't mean he's going to lay one pretty little finger upon me."

"You don't—"

"Oh, no, please," she interrupted, "continue with your lecture about how foolish I must be to dance with the man in a crowded place, when I knew you and the others were within calling distance—"

"Why didn't you call then?"

Cleo paused. There were a half dozen excuses she could have offered, all to do with the Wand, and their mission, and her intentions to take a reading of the man, but she'd never liked subterfuge, not even in her own thoughts. "Did you know, I've never had a man dance with me? Not beyond my dancing tutors, or perhaps my father dancing with me once or twice, when I was a little girl. I've never been kissed, or courted, or anything else."

"You wished to *dance* with him?"

I wanted to dance with you, but you won't even touch me. She steeled herself and tipped her chin up. "Yes."

She'd rarely seen Sebastian ruffled. He'd dealt with his mother with cold fury, and it had taken her hours of watching him to even realize his careful, controlled actions were intended to protect his inner thoughts and emotions from the world. But the muscle in his jaw flexed now, and he visibly swallowed before he glanced down at her. "I see."

No, you don't. Her lips pressed together firmly. "It was just a dance. Just one dance. And it's never going to happen again, so I don't particularly wish to speak about it anymore."

"As you wish."

"Let's focus on the Wand." At least they had a common mission in mind.

Sebastian offered her his arm, and the gesture was unusual enough she took it. His forearm flexed beneath her touch, but his gaze roved the area. She couldn't tell whether he was reading Remington's wariness, or whether he saw something else. But the three men might as well be lions prowling a dangerous new territory, prepared to fight at a moment's notice.

"I came here with my mother to hand over the wand," he murmured. "But it's different, seeing it now I can cut through illusions. This entire garden is full of a web of spell work. I can't quite see what it all hides, but there's something at work here. Something powerful."

"It's not just an illusion," Remington said curtly, as they climbed the steps to the manor. "It's an enticement. Allure. Or a lure, you could say. Malachi's no longer entirely human."

"So you keep saying," Sebastian muttered.

If a man like Remington Cross was nervous, then she was too. Premonition itched along her nerves like a trail of ants over her skin. "Something's going to happen. I'm just not entirely certain what."

She'd know if they were walking into danger, wouldn't she?

Sebastian gave her a sidelong glance. "Let me know if that itch gets stronger."

And if they couldn't speak? If she was somehow unable to warn him? "Perhaps tonight would be a good time to lower the shields on the bond? You would know the instant I would."

The forearm beneath her touch flexed, and he bent his head toward her. A long tense moment of hesitation stretched out, where she was certain he'd deny her, and then he nodded. "Agreed."

There was no warning. The bond was a distant, burning knot in the back of her mind one second, with her husband very firmly walled off behind it. The next... it was as if the bond suddenly slammed into place.

There were suddenly two of them in her head, tangled and meshed against each other. Thoughts whirled, some too fast to catch. But her sheer amazement radiated through the psychic link, returned with equal shock by him.

This was the first time he'd truly opened himself to her since the bond was formed.

She'd lost the sensation of it not long after she bonded him, and he discovered how to wall himself away, but it was only now that—compared to the loss of her Visions—she realized what else she had lost. It was like discovering an amputated limb had returned. A sense of wholeness.

Loneliness swept away.

Two hearts beat as one.

And she could feel him; his body, his mind, his thoughts…. An intimacy nothing else could compare to.

The world somehow faded around them. Oh, she was aware of it in some peripheral way, but it felt as though Sebastian was such a vibrant force of nature against her senses that the rest of the world simply mattered less.

Cleo managed to gain control of herself, realizing she was leaning against him heavily, her breast brushing against his arm.

"It's heady, isn't it?" Sebastian murmured. "I can feel your—"

"—every emotion," she whispered, trying not to delve too deeply.

It wasn't emotion he'd been about to comment upon. Cleo flushed, and looked up, falling into the depths of those silver eyes. He'd never once made any sort of innuendo, or attempt at seduction. Indeed, apart from that one kiss she'd pressed upon him the very first time they'd met, and the awkwardness of the night they'd shared a bed, there'd been little sign of his feelings for her, both emotional and physical.

And she wanted him to kiss her. So much so it was an almost physical ache deep inside her.

"Focus," Bishop warned. "We're almost there."

And somehow Sebastian drew back from her, just enough for them both to catch their breaths.

A dark-skinned woman dressed in a scarlet corset embroidered with what appeared to be tiny diamonds strode toward them, her skirts falling away from her knees and draping lower in back. She wore stockings the same color as her skin, with embroidered flowers upon them—or were they tattoos?—and a pair of heeled shoes that elongated her legs. Cleo almost choked.

"Don't look her in the eyes," Remington warned. "She's not entirely human either."

"What precisely does that mean?" Bishop muttered. "What exactly is this Malachi? And his servant?"

"Corrupted by the Shadow Dimensions," Remington replied.

"Corrupted?" the woman called in a melodious voice, as she paused in front of them. "Is that any way to greet an old friend?"

"Are we friends, Odette?" Remington drawled.

Odette was beautiful, her hair braided at the temples, with a halo of tight curls surrounding her face. She stalked a slow circle around Remington, inspecting him from head to toe. "Perhaps not." The smile on her face never died. "He's gone to refresh himself. He's been waiting for you to visit."

"He knew we were coming?" Bishop asked.

A quick flick of Remington's dark eyes. "He's been waiting for me for decades. Malachi likes to play at cat-and-mouse, and so far I've declined to entertain his notions."

"Tsk, tsk," Odette said, sliding her hands up under Remington's coat. "Poor Mal will be ever so disappointed to hear you disparage him so...."

Remington caught her wrists, just as her hands slid down his waistcoat en route to his belt. "He knows any friendship we once felt died centuries ago."

Centuries? Cleo blinked.

"What does he mean by that?" The words might have almost come from her husband's mouth, but she knew they didn't.

Just as he knew she'd heard them. *"I don't know,"* she said down the link. *"But he's been very careful about not going into too much detail about what these people are."*

"I noticed that too."

Odette gave another mocking little smile, and pushed away from Remington. "This way then. We don't conduct business out in the open, where the guests might hear."

"Guests?" Remington mused. "Is that what we're calling them these days?"

"Dinner seems a rather rude word."

Sebastian set his hand on Cleo's spine as he directed her into the parlor. Inside, the press of the allure wasn't quite as strong, but the exoticism of the place made her gaze wander. Intricate rugs lay all over the floor, and there were few chairs, merely large cushions scattered on the rugs. Sweet-smelling smoke lingered in the air. Some sort of glass device with a pipe extending from the end dwelled in the corner.

"A hookah," Sebastian said psychically.

Malachi awaited them, dragging his cravat from his throat and casting it aside. "A drink?"

"This isn't a social visit," Remington replied.

"Of course not." Malachi helped himself to the brandy, and then turned to face them. "So what is the purpose of this visit? It's not to reminisce about old times." His gaze settled on Cleo mockingly. "And it's not to bring me a gift for old times' sake. Hmm... is it possible you want something from me?"

"You have something we need," Bishop said darkly. "Something that doesn't belong to you."

"Everything on this property belongs to me," Malachi replied darkly.

"Not this," Bishop disagreed.

Verity touched his arm in silent warning.

"Oh, now I know what you want. Did your precious Order misplace something important?" Malachi sipped at his brandy, laughing under his breath. "Something a new friend gave me for safekeeping?"

"Morgana isn't your friend," Sebastian said. "You'd be a fool to think that."

"I'd be a fool to think anyone was my friend. So I don't." Malachi's eyes lingered on him. Recognition suddenly dawned. "Now I remember you. You were there when she offered me the Wand. Where's your collar, boy?"

"Long gone," Sebastian said coldly. "Along with my allegiances."

Malachi settled in one of the chairs, hooking his ankle up on his opposite knee. "Interesting," he mused. "I need the Wand."

"For what?" Remington cocked a brow. "Are you planning on conjuring a demon? I thought you'd learned your lesson."

"The Wand can command a Greater Demon from the Shadow Dimensions. So what do *you* need it for?"

"I don't," Remington replied. Their shadows loomed long against the walls, and there was a somewhat feral line to them, though both men played at repose. Remington gestured to their little party. "My friends do, however, and I'm inclined to help them."

Malachi cocked his head. "Does it have anything to do with the tremors moving through London at this moment?"

"The demon, you mean?" Remington remained nonchalant. "Let us not mince words."

"Did you bring a demon here?"

"I did not," Remington replied quietly. "One of us, at least, *has* learned their lesson."

This was going nowhere. Cleo stepped forward. "It doesn't matter who summoned the demon. The fact is, it's here now, and it's taken over the body of a powerful sorcerer. The demon intends to destroy London, and I have it on very good authority that we have less than two weeks before this destruction begins. Surely you can't want to see London suffer. There shall be no more parties, no more dancing... and whatever else it is that you do here. Even on the outskirts of London, you'll be affected."

Thick lashes obscured his eyes. Malachi considered his brandy. "And what if one is kin to demons?" He looked up emotionlessly, and his sudden smile held a certain sort of bitterness. "Perhaps I'll enjoy this new era."

"Please," Cleo whispered, going to her knees before him.

"Are you trying to appeal to my conscience, my dear? A wasted attempt, for I don't have one. Your good friend, Remington here, will tell you that."

She deliberately thought of the girl in the glass coffin, and the tender way Malachi kept the candles around her lit, so she wouldn't be in the dark. "I think you do. Though you might tread a dark path, not everything is lost."

Curiosity stirred in his gaze. "You never told me your name."

"Cleo Montcalm. Formerly Sinclair."

"Sinclair...."

"Lord Tremayne was my father."

Those emotionless eyes drew their own conclusions. "You're asking me to give up a very powerful object that was gifted to me, out of the goodness of my heart, which is decidedly not pure." He shook his head. "I don't know what to make of you. Good lord, you almost inspire a man to be better. But then one remembers what one is, and the idea of corrupting you is almost more tempting. Who would win? The innocent heart at my feet, or the devil before you?" He captured her chin with striking speed, bringing their faces closer together. His lashes fluttered over those pale cheeks, his expression languid. "I can see the temptation of the dark within you. You are not pure, not completely. There's a heart of darkness within you that hungers to be released...."

"Cleo," Bishop murmured, and she sensed him moving closer.

She reached up and cupped Malachi's face with her palm, seeing the young woman in her tomb again, the little room with all its candles... and something else.

"What happens when she wakes up?" Cleo whispered, low enough so the others couldn't hear. "What will she see when she looks at you? This man who plays his wicked games to amuse himself, or someone who has a good heart? What do you want her to see?"

Malachi cupped her palm against his cheek, but out of a sense of preservation, she thought, and not anything else. "She will see what she always saw: a wicked, wicked man."

"You could change that."

The sudden devastation in his expression struck her. Then it was gone and Malachi pushed to his feet, heading for the brandy again. He shot her a stark, angry look, but as she stood up, she knew she'd troubled him.

"I am not a generous man. I don't simply *give* anything away." He poured another brandy, eyeing them all dangerously. "I'll give up the Wand, but there is a price to be paid: one night in my and Odette's bed, with one member of your party. And that is not up for negotiation." He waved a languid finger. "Your choice, of course."

And his gaze settled eerily upon her.

Sebastian froze as the words echoed around the room.

"Any member?" Remington countered, sounding unsurprised.

"You know my predilections," Malachi replied smoothly, and it was all Sebastian could do not to plant his fist in the bastard's face.

As if hearing him, Malachi pushed away from the golden throne, sauntering down the dais toward him. "Perhaps this one?" His gaze shifted with predatory intensity toward Cleo. "Or perhaps—"

"If you complete that sentence," Sebastian said, moving with quiet, eerie grace toward him, "you'll regret it."

Silence fell.

"Don't," Cleo warned him, but he didn't dare look at her. The instant where she'd touched Malachi's face disturbed him, for he hadn't heard what she'd whispered to the man, but it had struck a chord.

Malachi circled him tightly, those predatory eyes seeming to see right through him. "Ah," he said softly, almost mockingly. "The lady has given you her heart—"

A flinch went through Cleo, and Sebastian stiffened.

"—but you have not given her yours," Malachi whispered. "What a tempting, tempting proposition." He turned abruptly, moving with a sinuous grace as he captured Cleo's hand. "Could I make her forget you?"

"How low the mighty have stooped," Remington pronounced.

"To the very depths," Malachi sneered, but he never took his gaze off Sebastian.

Sebastian hovered on the balls of his feet. Remington had warned them all not to threaten Gray. Power whispered through him. Emotion thrived, hot and rich and biting, until he wanted to lash out.

"He's trying to bait you," Cleo whispered, with some exacerbation. *"I almost had him. Don't ruin this."*

"If he bloody touches you again...."

"You will do nothing," she growled. *"Trust me."*

"I can almost taste your hunger." Malachi lifted Cleo's hand to his lips, and it took every ounce of will power for Sebastian not to smash him into the nearest wall. "A virgin. How utterly delightful."

Sebastian shifted on his feet, and those green eyes slid to him as if daring him to object.

Remington stiffened, as if prepared to leap forward, and even Bishop was shaking his head in a desperate, *don't do it.*

"Untouched," Malachi taunted. "A perfect rose about to bloom, but you've neglected her. And a neglected blossom is so, so easy to steal...."

Malachi pressed his mouth to the inside of Cleo's wrist in a mocking caress, and she gasped, before she suddenly *locked him out.*

What the hell? There was a wall between her emotions and his. Sebastian pressed against it, but her eyes glazed, her pretty lips parted, and she almost collapsed to her knees. *Trust me*, she'd said, but it was taking everything in him not to react. "What did you do to her?"

Tension simmered within him. Cleo was breathing hard, her body tight with tension, but he'd felt what went through her when Malachi touched her. *Pleasure. Need. Desperate longing....* And then she'd slammed shut the gates on her end of the bond, locking Sebastian out for the first time, and by all the demons in the Shadow Dimensions, he wanted to know what was going on in her head right now.

Was she attracted to the bastard?

Mother of night, did he even have the right to demand to know if she was?

Cleo drew her hand back against her chest as if burned, a flush of heat spilling through her cheeks. There was something in her eyes—sadness perhaps—as she caught and held Malachi's dangerous gaze. "I think perhaps you would know what it feels like to give your heart to someone, only to watch her turn to another."

Malachi looked down sharply. "I have no heart."

"That's what you'd like us all to think," Cleo whispered, "especially Remington. But I saw what *will* become of her."

She might as well have struck Malachi.

"One member of your party will share my bed," Malachi snarled, meeting Cleo's gaze with glittering eyes, "or I'll keep the fucking Wand and burn it."

"You will hand over the Wand directly, and allow the rest of us to leave without hindrance immediately, if we meet these conditions?" Remington asked.

Both Sebastian and Bishop gaped at him.

"Are you insane?" Sebastian snapped.

Bishop's face paled, but his eyes grew a little sleepy.

"You're not seriously considering it?" Sebastian demanded of his brother. Bishop would gut anyone who even looked at Verity sideways, and as for Bishop himself....

"We need the Wand," Bishop replied quietly.

Malachi turned on Remington with a predatory delight. "Safe passage and immediate transferal of the Relic, upon my word."

"And when the sun rises, whoever graces your bed is guaranteed the freedom to leave?" Remington continued.

Malachi flicked languid fingers. "If they wish to."

"So be it," Remington announced, stepping forward. "Give my friends the Wand, and I'll pay the price you demand."

For the second time that night, Malachi looked like he'd bitten into rotten fruit.

"I assume the lovely Odette will be joining us?" Remington said.

Odette stalked to his side, sliding a hand down his waistcoat. "I wouldn't miss it for the world."

"You bastard," Malachi said, without heat.

"Your rules," Remington challenged. "Fetch the Wand."

Malachi moved to a small cabinet, drawing a thin, dangerous knife from within his waistcoat and slicing his thumb with it. He pressed the welling blood to the cabinet, and a dozen layers of wards suddenly shimmered to life, before vanishing to their gaze.

Remington hadn't been wrong. There was no way any of them could have gotten through such warding. Not even Bishop.

Malachi withdrew an intricately carved box, and held it out. "Here it is."

Bishop took a step toward it, but Malachi shook his head. "No. The lady won the right to it." He held it out to Cleo. "Perhaps we shall see if your advice bears fruit."

She took the box solemnly. "Thank you."

"But before you leave.... a gift for the newlyweds." Malachi's mocking gaze captured Sebastian's, before he turned and took Cleo's face in his hands.

Swooping toward her, he kissed her swiftly. Cleo stiffened, before her body melted into his embrace, and then it was done, and Malachi released her.

Sebastian caught her by the arm as she almost fell to her knees, her eyes glazed, and her lips swollen and pink.

"Enjoy my gift," Malachi said, mocking him. "An unplucked bloom, just for you."

CHAPTER EIGHT

'Once one is touched by the Shadow Dimensions, they're never quite the same. The shadow lingers in the soul, until it slowly eats away at a person.'

—Lady Eberhardt

AT FIRST SHE hadn't quite understood what Malachi meant by "gift."

Cleo shivered in the cool night air as they waited by the gatehouse for Bishop and Verity to return with the carriage. Her body raged with unsuppressed desire she couldn't quite leash. Everything ached. From her nipples to the heat between her thighs, to the knot in her chest where the bond tied her to Sebastian... she was drowning in it. Drowning in Malachi's kiss. Her lips *burned*. "Do you think Remy is—"

"I would *really* rather not think about it," Sebastian murmured, his hands in his pockets, and his face cold and distant.

The woman, Odette, had been sliding her hands under Remy's waistcoat when they left, with Malachi watching them over the rim of his brandy with hungry eyes.

And she was *not* thinking of hungry eyes, or hands sliding under waistcoats, or... or Mother of night help her, any of those incendiary thoughts that only made the ache worsen.

"Gray's an incubus," she whispered, touching her branded lips.

As she drew her hand away, Sebastian shot her furious glare as if the kiss were *her* fault.

"I didn't ask him to do it," she protested. And the magic lancing through her was the sole cause of her restless desire. Wasn't it? "What on earth are Verity and Bishop doing? They went for the carriages almost twenty minutes ago." She rubbed her arms, trying to ease the ache beneath her skin. Sweet goddess, but she *needed* to be touched. "Do you think Bishop and Verity—"

"Yes," he practically snarled, and it was only then she realized how on edge *he* was, wound up tighter than a child's top.

Cleo stared at him. "It's just... it's been an awfully long time since they left to find the carriage, and Verity had that look in her eye...."

And the heavy magic in the air affected them all.

Perhaps even Sebastian.

"What did you say to him to make him change his mind?" he asked, staring into the darkness.

"It wasn't a complete vision." They still hadn't returned, and a part of her believed they never would. "I saw flashes of his past." When Malachi Gray had loved a woman enough to sacrifice everything for her, though he knew his feelings were unreturned. Cleo understood what it felt like to be the only one with her heart on her sleeve.

"He loved a woman once. I tried to appeal to his better nature."

"The man has none."

"Considering the Wand is now safely tucked in Bishop's pocket, I'd beg to differ," she replied coolly. Fever raged beneath her skin. It was getting worse. "Malachi was...." She trailed off, still feeling that invisible velvet glove stroking down her spine, Malachi's lips spilling pure heat through her body as he kissed her.

"Quite a kisser, by the look of it," Sebastian said.

Cleo tipped her chin up. "*Quite.*"

He *was* angry. Even though she couldn't feel it with the bond locked down, she could still see it in the tension of his jaw. Cleo wrapped her arms around herself and turned away. It all hurt. She felt knotted up inside and twisted.

Alone.

The lights of London spread out before them in the distance, and cool wind stirred through her skirts. This was almost rural here, exacerbating her sudden sense of isolation.

"I kissed you the first day we met but it wasn't... wasn't like this," she whispered. "You never responded that time. I've never been kissed. Not properly. Well, not until now."

And it ached that her first passionate kiss had been with someone else, and not Sebastian.

Sebastian froze, glancing down at her from beneath those dark lashes. For a long second she thought he wasn't going to reply, and humiliation branded her.

Quiet words: "I remember a second kiss."

So did she—the faintest brush of his lips against hers.... "When you thought you were dying. Just once. And you've never touched me again."

No matter how much skill Malachi Gray had, it didn't compare to that single moment. But how long could a simple kiss like that sustain her hopes and dreams? It had been *months*. She knew Sebastian had needed to focus on his training, but surely he could have written her back.

Surely he could have visited her, just once.

The ache intensified, as if the incubus's kiss sensed her unfulfilled desire. The spell wasn't just aimed at seeking pleasure, it seemed to hunt down every little scrap of need she'd ever felt, and to thrive on the edge of pain those memories wrought. Every twisted, bittersweet emotion she felt fed the flames.

Sebastian shifted. "It's not that I don't want to kiss you—"

"No? It certainly feels like it."

"It's not—"

"Then why will you not touch me?" she cried, nerves rubbed raw. It was starting to physically ache, just a little. "Two kisses we've shared, and neither of them lasted longer than five seconds."

Sebastian cursed under his breath, moving away from the hedge that lined Malachi's gardens. "Cleo," he warned, turning to glare at her. "Don't pursue this."

A horrible thought struck her. "Are you not attracted to me?"

His face tightened, and *oh, my goodness,* that was it.

Cleo's heart felt like lead. She turned away from him, her mind racing. He didn't want her. She'd thought once.... He'd touched her hair the night of their wedding with such longing. But what if she'd been wrong? What if—

A hand latched around her arm, and Sebastian spun her back to face him, even as a soft gasp of pain sounded in her throat. She could survive this. She could survive anything. If she could thrive beneath Lord Tremayne's roof—just wishing her father could love her when he very clearly did not—then she could live through this.

Even if her heart turned to ice in her chest.

"Don't think like that," Sebastian said sharply, both hands locking around her upper arms, and she realized her thoughts had somehow reached him through the bond. "I've never kissed you, not truly...," his voice fell, "because I don't know how."

"How...? What do you mean?" He'd serviced the women his mother pushed him toward. He was no innocent, no virgin, no— "Have you never kissed another woman?"

"Only you."

"That's impossible," she blurted.

"Perhaps we have more in common than we thought," Sebastian said, with a mocking, bitter little laugh. "Because the first time you kissed me, was the first time I'd ever been kissed."

Cleo stared at him with her mouth open. "You've never been kissed?"

Bloody hell, where were Bishop and Verity? Sebastian stared off through the fog that was beginning to settle in the lane, cursing inquisitive virgins under his breath.

"But how?" Cleo blurted. "I know... you're not...."

A virgin. He looked away again coldly. "What was required of me was never a kiss, though they begged me for it."

It was the one thing he'd been able to keep for himself.

He'd never been able to stop his body from reacting, especially at first when his mother plied him with certain drugs before sending him off to entertain her prospective allies. And once the numbness of it all washed over him and he'd stopped fighting, he'd swiftly learned to take control of the encounter.

It was easy to fuck.

To lock himself away, and let his body take over, and get the task over and done with. Sometimes he'd even come, though it made him feel dirtier than he already felt.

But he didn't know the gentler arts. Seduction, kisses, and gentle caresses were as unknown to him as another's love. A hollow fluttering compressed his ribs. Cleo was a complete innocent, one who dreamed of romantic aspirations. She wanted dances, and kisses, and a charming seduction. She wanted fairy tales, and when she looked into the future, she saw marriage, children, goddess-knew-what....

What do I see?

Nothing. It set off the panic inside him. All he'd ever wanted was freedom from the sclavus collar and from his mother. Freedom to make his own choices. And now he had it. There were dozens of choices each and every day in this new life, but the hardest to deal with was this.

Her.

If he kissed her here and now, then there would be expectations, and he didn't want to break her heart.

He'd vowed to help Bishop rescue their father, but he wasn't staying here forever. He craved escape from this entire world, and from the people who filled it.

And then what? said a dark, cynical part of him. *Do you think it would be easier to be alone in a new city, with no one who gives a damn about you?*

Baring his soul like this was torture. He never exposed himself. Never. But the look in Cleo's eyes when she'd thought he didn't want her.... Cleo stared up at him, her shoulders squared.

The wife he'd never wanted.

His wife in name only.

And it was all he could do not to shove her up against the wall of the nearest house and have his way with her. Sweet goddess, but a part of him wanted her so badly he ached.

"I'm sorry," she whispered, resting a hand lightly on his arm. "And thank you. For helping me to understand. I kept thinking...." She shook her head, but he read it in her eyes.

"That I didn't want you."

Cleo gave him a wavering smile. "It wouldn't be unexpected."

He closed his eyes. Her father had a great deal to answer for—but then, who was he to judge? "I think you underestimate your charms. You're a beautiful woman, with a pure heart—"

"Sometimes it's not so pure," she whispered, rubbing her hands along her arms as though she still ached.

And perhaps she did.

Sebastian's gaze dropped to her mouth. He'd hated seeing another man stake a claim there when he himself hadn't. *Hated* it.

If you take this step, then you cannot simply walk away from her.

"No?" he asked.

Those coffee-dark eyes lifted to his, and he knew a flush darkened her cheeks, for she was new at this too.

A whisper of need swept through him, his cock pressing fervently against the placket of his breeches. It felt surreal to want her, for his experience with sex had soured him of the need for it. But there was a sweet wholesomeness to his desire. Cleo's intentions were writ large upon her face, and her heart was open to him. There was nothing she could hide from him, and her need for him was simply that: she cared for him, and hence she craved him. Yes? Or no? Sebastian faltered in indecision, but it was her mouth that finally decided him. Those soft, luscious lips that another man had tasted....

And he couldn't bear it any longer. Gray had stolen something that was *his*, and the jealousy ate at him, stirred by the incubus's magic.

Sebastian captured her hand in his, locking their palms together, his fingers splayed through hers. "Cleo." A whisper, and a curse, for he didn't know how to deal with her. He never had.

She was a dream he'd never dared believe in.

"I've never had a man dance with me.... Never been kissed." He'd felt the ache inside her then, and it matched his own emptiness in some ways.

But it also scared him.

"I don't know what to do with you," he admitted roughly. "You want more than I think I can ever give you."

Her fingers clenched against his, a warming touch. "All I want is to know you care for me. Just a little bit. The rest we can figure out as we go."

It seemed too simple.

And far too complex.

And if he didn't act now, then perhaps he never would.

Sebastian cupped her cheek in one hand, his lungs arresting, and his heart beginning to quicken. Best to get this over with before he lost his nerve. "One kiss then."

And then he brushed his lips against hers, feeling her mouth soften to his touch. *Silk, soft as silk....*

His heart started beating a little faster. Sebastian brought his other hand up and captured her face in both hands. The drugging taste of her swept through him, stirred by an incubus's magic, but tempered by the pure flame of his own desire.

Cleo's lips parted, and he could feel the wetness of her mouth glide over his. His tongue whispered over her top lip, and she stilled, then the tip of her tongue danced against his.

Yes. There was no space between them as he swept her into his arms, pressing the heated steel of his cock against her belly. His mouth grew bold, and he sank his fingers through her silken hair, cupping the base of her skull so he could plunder her.

She stopped breathing. Started again. He had the feeling he ought to stop, before it went any further, because if he kept going, then it wouldn't end at this. Sebastian drew back, staring down into those black eyes from barely an inch away, their breaths mingling.

It was wrong. Terribly wrong, to start thinking of other illicit delights he could take, but his hand seemed to have a mind of its own. It wandered across the scallop of gold lace that decorated her décolletage, his thumb stroking the silk of her sleeve.

Cleo sucked in a breath.

And there were no words needed. Not right now.

For the "yes" was in her eyes. Eyes that made a man forget himself.

This time she kissed him, stretching up on her toes to blatantly capture his mouth. His hand moved, thumb tracing the curve of the exposed part of her breast. The sensation seared his brain. *Soft.* Softer than any silk could ever be. He had a sudden flash of what the rest of her skin would feel like beneath his hands, his mouth, the press of his body....

Cleo's fist curled in his cravat, as if she sensed his sudden urgency. He muscled her back against the wall of the gatehouse, their mouths parting for a brief moment as she gasped. Then his hand closed over her breast, and she pushed into it, her hips meeting his own, even as he sank his other hand through acres of silk skirts to grip the heat of her bottom.

"Cleo." He kissed her chin, her jaw, raking his teeth down her throat. The sharp edge of her clavicle met his hungry mouth, and he palmed the soft weight of her breast, focused on only one goal.

"Don't stop," she begged, and it was as though someone had lit a match and set it to oil. Need, fierce and furious, roared through her. A need to be fulfilled. He could feel it even through the muted shields he'd set on their bond.

Someone *had* lit that match, he thought, even as his mouth found the slope of her breast. Suddenly all he could see was the amused look in Gray's eyes when he noticed Sebastian glaring at him.

An incubus's kiss.

He drew back, capturing her face as he breathed hard, pressing their foreheads together. His lips tingled. His cock raged. He wanted nothing more than to lift those infuriating skirts and find the heat at the heart of her.

But he couldn't stop remembering Gray's smirk.

"Don't stop," Cleo whispered, her hands sliding under his coat and traversing the silk of his waistcoat.

A muscle jumped in his jaw. It would be easy to oblige. He *wanted* to. And that was amazing in itself, for he'd never, ever, wanted sex. "Verity and Bishop will be here with the carriage anytime soon."

Was that his voice? So low and raspy?

Cleo turned her face away, her fists clenching in his waistcoat.

"I'm sorry," he whispered. He shouldn't have started this. Not that he'd been able to deny either of them.

Fireworks exploded in the night, making him jump. "Merde."

A dozen dogs set up howling on nearby farmsteads, and then his arms were full of soft heat as Cleo practically wrapped herself around him. He'd quite forgotten where they were.

"Sorry," she whispered, looking up at the sky.

The red and gold flowers blooming in the sky above Malachi's manor painted their reflection across her skin, like one of Monet's watercolors. Something stirred in his chest at the sight of her face like this, all passion-flushed and softening into pleasure at the sight of the fireworks. Another racket of them went up with a boom, crackling into life in the velvet sky, but Sebastian couldn't tear his gaze from her face.

She could be the ruin of you. Your utter destruction.

For there was little in his life that he'd ever truly longed for.

His heart slowly kicked in his chest, and he tested the bond to make sure his shields were fully engaged, hoping she hadn't felt that thought.

But Cleo wasn't looking at him anymore. Her fingers curled around his upper arm, her head tilted sharply to the side, even as he lowered his face to hers once more. "Stop!"

Sebastian froze, feeling her fumble for him psychically. He slowly let her in.

"Can you feel that?" came her thought-whisper.

If he focused, there was a new itch afflicting her, this one curling dread through her.

"Feel what?" he tried to send back.

"My sense of premonition just started tingling down my arms and spine, and I don't think it means something good is coming this way."

Fog eddied around them in the night, thick tendrils of it seeming to creep out of the nearest lane. He scanned the quiet fields, stepping back and reaching for the knife Bishop had given him.

"It's too quiet here," Cleo murmured.

As if in answer, something scuttled over gravel, like claws.

"Quiet's good," Cleo squeaked, backing into him.

He stepped between her and whatever was hidden in the fog, hands held loosely at his sides as he opened himself to the pool of power deep within him.

By himself, he might have faced whatever was watching them, but not with Cleo here. Indecision gripped him. Stay and call for help? Or flee into the fog, and hope they came across Verity and Bishop?

Neither of them was truly trained in the art of sorcery.

His mother never wanted him to have control of the immense power he could wield, and Cleo's father considered it more important for her to dedicate her focus toward her tremendous gifts of divination.

Sebastian lifted his hand to the sky, summoning a mage globe of pure red with a word of power. He flung it into the sky, forcing pressure through the globe, the way Bishop had taught him.

The globe exploded, somewhat like the fireworks. In the quiet laneway it set the dogs off again, loud barking echoing through the neighborhood. A lantern blinked to life in a neighboring farmhouse and someone called out, "Shut up!"

SOULBOUND

"There's something behind us." Cleo spun, pressing her back to his. "I heard it in the dark."

Coppery eyes began to gleam in the shadows of the fog. All of Sebastian's blood ran cold. An imp. His mother had begun summoning them months ago, but they worked for the demon now.

"We need to get moving," he said, staring at the imp as it slowly materialized, creeping out of the fog on all fours, its tail slowly lashing behind it.

Where there was one, there were bound to be others.

Taking Cleo by the hand, he urged her in the direction Bishop and Verity had vanished in. Fog seemed to be rolling in across the fields now, gleaming pale beneath the moonlight. The only clear patch was the laneway they were in, and as they ran into the soft edges of the fog, it wisped away from them. Someone was clearly controlling it.

"Stop!" Cleo hauled suddenly on his grip. "We're not alone."

Summoning his power, he formed a ward that cascaded over them in a shimmering dome. It slammed into the dirt, and the fog within it evaporated as if summoned by sorcery. Nothing could get in or out, unless whatever was out there destroyed his ward. Some sorcerers could do that, Bishop had told him.

And there was definitely a sorcerer out there. Imps couldn't work magic.

"Safe for the moment," he whispered.

"But trapped," Cleo replied, her pulse pounding visibly in her throat. "Do you think Bishop will have seen your beacon? He won't think it merely another firework, will he?"

"Bishop's remarkably aware of his surroundings." Not surprising, considering the man was an assassin.

Cleo cleared her throat. "But if he's distracted...."

"I'll say this for the bastard... it would take a lot to distract him when we're in an unsafe area."

"Verity could do it," she pointed out.

He didn't let himself think of that. The situation vexed him. He'd needed to rely upon others before. But with Cleo here, he couldn't simply launch a full-scale telekinetic assault upon whatever was out there. Not and maintain a ward to protect her.

"Are any of your powers offensive?" he demanded.

She shook her head. "Not really. My natural inclination is telepathy. I know very little of the telekinetic arts."

The opposite of him.

"I can ward. And form a white mage globe, but there's not much impact in that."

Red globes were the color of war, or death; blue had significant impact; but white were almost harmless, and used mostly for light. He considered strategy. If he dropped the ward and stepped out of it to attack, he had to leave her to her own defensive capabilities.

"You're not invulnerable," Cleo blurted, as if she sensed his thoughts. "And we don't know what's out there. An imp or two hiding in the fog, but possibly something else. Be patient."

As if to underscore her words, something prowled the edges of the fog circling them. It couldn't get in, but they also couldn't move.

"Curious," he said, his gaze flickering to the manor, "that we're attacked by imps mere minutes after we leave the house of a man who pledged his allegiance to Morgana in exchange for the Relic."

"You think Malachi alerted her somehow?" Cleo half turned to him. "It's possible Morgana had someone—or thing—watching the manor. She wanted the Wand back eventually."

"Is there a reason you're defending him?"

"I'm not defending *him*." Her eyebrow arched. "Is there a reason the first thought that leaps into your mind is a conspiracy?"

Yes. *Jealousy.* "Life experience. If someone's able to stab you in the back, then they probably will."

"Well, I think—" Cleo hesitated. "Is your ward supposed to be doing that?"

He turned, finding a bizarre buzzing ring of red light at the base of his warded dome. As he watched, it began to fizz, evaporating upward.

"Something's breaking through," he said, trying to force more power into the ward. The power merely drained through, as though there was a leak in the ward somewhere. "Stand close to me!"

Another shadowy ripple stirred through the fog, as if an imp darted toward them, and then away. In the distance, a hollow boom sounded, and a patch of fog lit up in red. Fireworks? Or Bishop and his deadly mage globes?

Cleo pressed against him as the ward kept burning away from the bottom. A pair of claws flexed on the edges.

And Sebastian made a decision.

Grabbing Cleo, he dragged her into his arms, pressing her head to his chest to protect her. Letting go of the ward, he spat one of his power words, unleashing an enormous wave of force outward as the ward vanished. The fog evaporated, and something screamed in a high-pitched squeal as it went flying through the air. Timber groaned, and then a tree was tumbling down, its branches crushing through the gatehouse roof.

Sebastian stared at the damage. Served Malachi right.

"Behind you!" Cleo yelled.

He swung a hand, reverting to Expression to control his powers. Fear added a punch to his next blow, and he swept another imp out of the way with a flick of pure force. There was no finesse to Expression, merely destruction. He reined himself back in sharply.

"Warding!" Cleo yelled, and she glowed with faint light as a shimmering ward coalesced around them again.

The fog had swept away in the aftermath of his blow. A hooded figure moved out there. A human. Three imps circled them, but it was the man in the cloak who held his attention.

"What sort of coward hides in the fog?" Sebastian called.

The hood froze.

"He's not alone," Cleo pointed out.

There were two other figures out there. He could just make out a hulking form that towered over him, and a smaller figure, cloaked in a way that made him think woman. The three of them stood in a triangle shape around them.

"Take them," the first cloaked figure said.

Sorcery swirled, but it was the sort of thing he'd never encountered before. Cleo's ward began to evaporate the same way his had. The woman summoned a lash of pure electricity to life in her hands, and flicked it like a whip.

He couldn't take them all on at the same time, and he couldn't ward.

"Got the right!" Cleo called, casting a shield between the whip of lightning and the pair of them. She cried out as the lash struck her invisible shield, but it held.

A spinning ball of light came at him from the left.

Sebastian swung his arms up in a cross, forming an invisible shield. The impact of whatever the fellow threw at him staggered him back, where he tripped on Cleo.

They both went down. Sebastian rolled to his feet, catching a glimpse of a flurry of golden web heading his way. He shielded again, but whatever it was wrapped around his shield and obliterated it. The second it vanished, he saw an imp launching directly at his face.

"Get down!" someone bellowed, and a month of listening to that voice and obeying it made him slam Cleo onto the dirt.

A roar of fire shot overhead, the air turning hot and dry. Sebastian buried his face in Cleo's hair, trying to shield her with his body. The imp screamed as it was roasted, hitting the dirt and rolling wildly.

"Verity, get them out of here!" Bishop yelled, suddenly leaping over them with his cloak flapping behind him like wings.

A hand helped drag Sebastian to his feet, and Verity appeared, her face tight with worry, and her breath coming shortly as if she'd been running. "I've got you."

"Cleo, first," Sebastian insisted, pushing his wife into Verity's arms. "I'll stay here with Bishop."

It eased some of Verity's concern for her husband, but Cleo's dark eyes shot to his. "Don't get hurt."

Nobody had ever truly cared about him before, except as a weapon, or a tool to be used. "I promise." His voice came out dry, and he gave Cleo a curt nod.

Verity wrapped her arms around Cleo, and they both began to waver, then Verity punched out of there, translocating Cleo to safety. The bond between them vanished for a second, and then he felt her reform somewhere far to the south. Hopefully, Bishop's house, or Lady Rathbourne's.

"Remember how I told you to keep your power under tight rein, and hold everything back when we were dueling?" Bishop called. He flung a hand, his rings glittering with green light, and a ring of green flames raced to circle them.

"Yes."

"Ignore it," Bishop said. "You have carte blanche to annihilate anything that comes at us."

Finally. Sebastian began to channel power, sucking in the well of energy that filled the world around him. Every living thing thrived on energy, and he absorbed it, taking care not to pull from Bishop.

A red mage globe formed in Sebastian's hand, and he levitated it into the air, focusing on the first hooded figure. "*Ignitius!*" he bellowed, and the globe flew toward the stranger. It struck the man's shield, and obliterated it. The fellow landed flat on his back, his heels drumming on the ground.

The world lit up with red. Bishop was spinning at least a dozen red mage globes around his head.

"Show-off," Sebastian growled. He had more sheer power than Bishop, but none of the finesse. And mage globes were new to him. The best he could do was handle one at a time.

Bishop's globes darted toward the remaining two sorcerers. They hammered at hastily formed shields, exploding in washes of power. Imps flooded out of the shadows in response, racing across the ground toward them.

Fine. He didn't have his brother's finesse. That didn't mean he was defenseless, far from it. Sebastian sucked in energy from the imps, encasing some of them in ice. The second they froze, he flung another wave of force, and the frozen statues exploded into thousands of bloody shards. Black ichor sprayed across the ground.

It felt good to fight.

Something physical to burn off some of the tension Malachi Gray had left him with. Sebastian moved with oiled ease, echoing the moves Bishop had taught him, and locking down his focus until power words spilled off his tongue with ease.

He summoned globe after globe, all of them burning hotly red, until the world took on a bloodied tinge.

"Try not to burn yourself low," Bishop called, and Sebastian reined himself in.

A pair of imps took advantage of his sudden recalcitrance, stalking him from both angles. He formed the glowing quarter staff Bishop had made him practice with, twirling it around him. One launched at him, and he moved to the side, sending it flying with a well-timed heave. The other used the momentum to dash in and rake at him.

Claw marks sliced through his side of his ribs. The flare of pain made him flinch, and his countermove lacked punch. He got it off him. Somehow. Turned, the staff spinning in his hands, as the first one launched at him. Not thinking. Just reacting. Slamming it to the ground, and then withdrawing just enough to drive the end of his staff through its ribs. It screamed, pinned by his staff, and Sebastian forced a wave of energy through the length of the staff, detonating it inside the creature's rib cage.

Black ichor sprayed him like acid. He turned his face away, staggering on something in the grass.

Another imp came at him, and Sebastian rammed the end of the staff into its throat. Shadow flickered behind him, and he thrust back, keeping the newcomer off his flanks. They moved ridiculously fast. A month ago he wouldn't have had a chance. Sharp teeth bit into the end of the staff, and on the edge of his awareness, he saw red flashes illuminating the night as Bishop set to work.

BEC MᴄMASTER

"Eat this," he growled, as the imp shook the end of his staff. Another pulse of energy went through the staff, and he met its bronze eyes seconds before its head exploded.

"Retreat!" someone called.

And then the wave of imps vanished, shooting the pair of them cattish glances, and hissing at them as they melted back into the shadows.

Sebastian slumped over, letting his staff vanish. He rested his hands on his thighs, breathing hard. It was one thing to spar with Bishop, quite another to fight for his life.

It felt good.

Bishop's red mage globes flickered out, leaving him merely a shadowy figure. "I can't sense anything alive out there." He turned toward Sebastian. "You're bleeding."

"A scratch." He clamped his hand over his ribs and winced again.

"They have poisonous claws."

"Noted."

A hand reached toward him, and he drew back, before realizing Bishop only intended to touch his arm.

"I can heal you," Bishop said slowly, as if sensing his reluctance.

"Sorry. Habit." He'd nearly sent a punch of power in Bishop's direction. "Maybe later when we're home." Exhilaration thrilled through him, his muscles twitching as if they hadn't received the message that the fight was finished. "It's not safe here, and we need to get the Wand back to your house before they can send for reinforcements."

His vision was slowly adjusting to the moonlight. Bishop's eyes gleamed black, locked on his face. "Don't say I didn't offer."

"I won't." He strode toward the sorcerer he'd downed at the start of the fight, holding just enough power within him to deal with any threats in case the sorcerer suddenly sat up.

"He's dead," Bishop called, following him.

And as a sorcerer of the Grave Arts, Bishop would know. Sebastian released the energy he held. His legs and arms trembled from the rapid fluctuation of power he'd wielded. Bishop had warned him not to use his own energy reserves, but in the heat of the moment, he thought he might not have obeyed.

Or maybe the poison from those claw marks was working its way through him swiftly.

Bishop turned the body over. A pale face stared sightlessly at the sky. A man in his twenties by the look of it, his figure cut lean, pockmarks on his cheeks. A gold stud gleamed in his ear.

"Anyone you recognize?"

Bishop's lips thinned. "Not a face I know, no. He doesn't belong to the Order."

"There are plenty of sorcerers outside the Order."

Bishop revealed a black tattoo on the back of the corpse's left hand. A crow, by the look of it. Bishop sucked in a sharp breath. "This is a sign of the One-Eyed Crows."

"Isn't that a street gang from the Hex Society?"

"Some old friends of Verity's, yes."

CHAPTER NINE

"I'M NOT SURPRISED the One-Eyed Crows are involved. Daniel Guthrie wasn't very happy with me when I defected last month, and made him look like a fool in front of the entire Hex Society," Verity grumbled, brushing off Bishop's coat as she slid it from her husband's shoulders. "You've burned another one."

"Couldn't be helped," Bishop murmured.

Cleo watched the pair of them tend each other. There was something more important than words passing between them as Verity chided Bishop about sending her away. Verity kept clucking over the coat, but it was clear she was using it as a euphemism for her husband, and Bishop paused in his movements to tuck a strand of hair behind Verity's ear. A gentle moment from the assassin who rarely revealed his feelings.

And one that left Cleo feeling vastly left out.

Sebastian poured himself a brandy. Clearly favoring his right side, he ignored the byplay, though he rested one hand on the side table as if his legs weren't quite steady.

"Are you all right?" she murmured, crossing to his side.

"I'm fine. It's just a scratch," he murmured. "An imp took me by surprise."

"Of course it's just a scratch. That's why you look so pale."

"Are you all right?" he asked, his silky lashes shielding his eyes as he glanced down at her.

"Quite." She wasn't the one who'd been left to fight a pack of imps.

"No... remaining side effects?"

Her cheeks burned. "None."

Cleo's mouth still tingled from Sebastian's kiss, but he'd retreated into himself. He lifted the brandy to his lips, and then set it aside with a mutter. "I'm sorry, I'm not at all myself. If you'll excuse me," Sebastian murmured. "I think I need to go to bed."

"Should I find Cleo a bedchamber?" Verity called, and Sebastian barely glanced at her. He pressed a hand to his side as he vanished through the doorway.

"Well," Verity said, and looked toward her apologetically.

"I think I should sleep in my own bed tonight," Cleo told her quietly. As if there was any other possibility.

But Bishop was staring after his brother.

"What's wrong?" she asked him.

"I offered to heal him, but he wouldn't let me."

Cleo's heart jammed itself into her throat. "What do you mean? It *is* just a scratch?"

"Sometimes imps have poisonous claws, and I don't know how deep his wounds are. He wouldn't let me look at them." Bishop hesitated. "I'd go after him, but...."

But he doesn't entirely trust you. "I'll do it. Verity, could you see to making up a bedchamber for me?"

Cleo followed her husband into the hallway. He hadn't gone far, staring up the stairs as if they led all the way to heaven, and his legs already felt like lead. "Are you going to let me see to that wound?"

He blinked when he saw her, and her heart started to tick a little faster. Signs of fever made his eyes sink into his head. She pressed a hand to his forehead. Burning up.

"Let's get you upstairs," Cleo murmured, tucking herself under his arm and trying to tackle the stairs.

It wasn't easy.

"You don't have to do this," he murmured.

You stupid fool. Her heart twisted in her chest as she remembered their wedding night, when she'd finally realized he'd actually been shot. He hadn't told her then either, though he'd admitted his mother refused to heal him because he'd been responsible for foiling her plans.

Little wonder he didn't ask for help. What else had he suffered over the years because Morgana deemed his feelings unimportant?

Pain barely bothered him. He was clearly used to pain. But depending upon someone was his Achilles heel.

"I know," she whispered, finally managing to get him up the stairs. "But I want to help. I hate seeing you hurt."

He stared at her, then sighed and pushed open the door to his bedchamber. "You're not going to let up, are you?"

"Would you rather I didn't care?"

Those quicksilver eyes gave nothing away.

126

She closed the door behind her, helping him to sit on the bed. A quick glimpse beneath his coat revealed bloody stains. "Wait here while I fetch some water and a cloth."

When she'd returned, he'd managed to strip his coat off, and sweat dampened his hair. Fresh blood stained his shirt, as if he'd torn his wound open in trying to undress himself.

"Hold still," Cleo snapped, trying to lift Sebastian's shirt to see the damage.

"I'm fine," he snapped back. "It's just a scratch."

"Scratch or not, that's some mighty impressive bleeding," she countered, and then held up a hand when he moved to continue the argument. "You can continue talking if you wish, but know that no matter what you say, or how loud you are when you say it, the odds of me agreeing to leave you alone before I've had a look at that so-called scratch are rather minute."

Sebastian opened his mouth. Then shut it.

"A wise decision. Now remove your shirt."

Reaching over his shoulder with a wince, he hauled the shirt over his head, scrunched it into a bundle, and then threw it across the room. "Better?"

She'd tended his wounds once, and knew what his body looked like. But it was still a slap in the face, especially after the visit to Malachi's. A sleek sheathing of muscle covered his ribs, and his abdominals flexed as he sank back onto the bed. He'd been lean before, but not quite like this. The month of working with Bishop had honed his body into a finely wrought weapon.

"Lie down," she insisted, bringing her small bowl of water closer to her, and eyeing the ragged edges of the claw marks that sliced across his abdomen. One of them came perilously close to his belt. Another half an inch deeper, and the imp would have torn through gut muscle. Cleo swallowed, "You're lucky, by the look of this."

He lay flat, one hand cupped beneath his head. Cleo gently wiped his wounds clean, the sound of water dripping into the bowl as she rung out her cloth the only noise.

"You promised you wouldn't get hurt," she said softly.

Wringing the water into the bowl, she tried to ignore the red hue it now bore.

"I was trying not to," Sebastian replied, those silver eyes turning distant. "Two of them came at me at once, and one of them got lucky."

"I felt it," she whispered. "Through the bond. I nearly made Verity go back and fetch you, but then I sensed you were all right."

He looked down, silky lashes fanned across his cheeks. The second Verity had whisked her away, he'd shut down the bond again, as if he simply couldn't allow himself to be so vulnerable for so long.

Cleo captured his fingertips, unable to help herself.

"Are you ready?" She gathered her power. She'd healed him once before, and despite her lack of education, healing was one of the arts she had a natural inclination for. "This might sting a little."

Sebastian sucked in a sharp breath, and his fingers tightened in hers. Cleo burned the poison from his body, closing her eyes as she worked through the complex healing weaves.

It was only minutes later, when she opened her eyes, that she found him watching her.

"It's done." And she was run ragged, exhausted by the day's events.

"Thank you," Sebastian whispered.

She should leave now. But something caught her tongue. It hadn't felt right to question him earlier, and she'd been too overwrought with emotion to think, but there was something she needed to know.

"I have a question for you," Cleo whispered. "I didn't wish to bring it up before everyone else, and there hasn't been a chance to ask it since."

He looked at her, perhaps sensing danger. "Yes?"

"I caught a glimpse of one of the demon's allies in my scrying. She's someone from your past I think. I suspect she has the ability to scry too." Cleo gave a brittle laugh. "She's probably serving the demon in the same capacity I'm helping everyone here. Do you... do you know of anyone?"

Nothing in his expression changed, but an arctic chill somehow seemed to emanate from him. He knew what she was asking. "Not off the top of my mind, no."

"Could you think about it? I think it's important to discover her identity."

His lashes obscured his eyes. "I'll try."

There was no further reason to remain. Any warmth that had existed between them in the previous moment had vanished. Cleo swallowed, and gathered her bowl. "Thank you."

"Well, don't you look like you lost a fight with a pack of rabid cats," Lady Eberhardt announced as Sebastian made his way to the dining room the following morning.

There was no sign of anyone else, and Cleo hadn't roused from the bedchamber beside him. She'd been exhausted last night, closing his bedchamber door quietly, and leaving him alone with his thoughts.

A part of him had wanted her to stay.

"Any reason you're plaguing the household this early in the morning?" Sebastian examined the sideboard with a hunger he didn't usually feel. The healing had taken something out of him.

"Careful." Lady Eberhardt snorted, lifting her teacup to her mouth. "I might take offense at some of your sass."

Despite himself, he almost smiled. The old bat had proved an endless source of frustration in the past month, but she treated him precisely as she treated anyone else. The first time she'd swatted Bishop over the ears for being impertinent had been the first time he'd almost relaxed beneath this roof.

"Where's Bishop?" she demanded.

"Probably in bed," he replied, and began loading up his plate with coddled eggs. "Why don't you go haul him out?"

"Because Verity deserves some time with her husband, the poor gel."

He gave her a look. "Verity's no lamb."

A snort. "She is to me."

Verity's clear inability to do any wrong in Lady E's eyes made Bishop roll his and often. Sebastian shook his head. What did it take to get on the right side of Lady E?

"Take a seat," Lady E told him, as if he hadn't been about to do precisely that. "I have something for you."

"A present, just for me?" Something told him he wasn't going to enjoy it. Lady E was of the opinion that people should be given what they needed, not what they wanted.

Lady E gave him a sweet look over the rim of her teacup. "Well, we could sit here and discuss the reason your wife isn't keeping you in *her* bed, like Verity is with Adrian, but something tells me you'd prefer to have a tooth pulled."

He gave her a sour look. "That's none of your business."

"Oh, boy." Lady E reached out and patted his cheek almost tenderly. "Haven't you realized yet? Everything that happens in my sphere *is* my business." She set her teacup down. "Adrian tells me you ran into an incubus."

"Could we not discuss this?"

"Well, it's been a good thirty years since I came across one. They're quite rare." Her expression grew distant and fond. "Damned good in bed, though one doesn't appreciate being used as fodder."

He almost gagged on his mouthful of eggs.

Lady E's dark eyes locked on him. "I heard... he might have given your lovely wife a kiss."

Sebastian grabbed his plate and stood, pushing back his chair. Done. He was done with this. "I swear to God—"

An iron hand locked around his wrist. "Oh, sit, and I'll leave you and your wife alone."

Anything was better than this. Anything.

"Here," she said, reaching for the chair beside her and pulling out a slim package bound in brown paper. "I've been searching for this for the past week, and finally found it last night."

He tore the package open, revealing a slim brown leather book. "Is it going to bite?"

"Perhaps." Her voice turned serious. "I want you to read it."

He turned the book over, and then untied the string holding it closed. "What is it?"

"Your mother's journal. I made her write it many years ago when she first came to the Order, and I was named as her master."

Sebastian froze, his thumb sliding from the middle of the book. He set it aside firmly. "I don't need it."

And he was done with breakfast, done with Lady Eberhardt... done with this whole cursed house. Wiping his mouth, he avoided her grasping hand, and escaped his chair.

"Why not? Know your enemy and all...."

"I know my mother," he said coldly, "perhaps better than any of you do. I don't need her bloody diary to understand her strengths, or weaknesses, or what she plans to do—"

"I'm not asking you to understand her strengths and weaknesses. Take it," Lady Eberhardt said, pushing the diary toward him. "And promise me you'll read it. Within the week."

Frustration itched beneath his skin. He didn't want to do this. Plunging himself into his mother's youthful mind would be like drenching himself with poison, and besides, there was little point. "Why?"

"That's an answer I hope you can tell me."

He glared at her. There were few things in life that had so utterly foiled him. Lady E was one of them. Not only did she not fear him, but she seemed to treat him like... like she treated his brother, Bishop. *I could make her fear me....* But no. Sebastian looked down at the diary. That was arrogance speaking. Not himself.

"Perhaps the more interesting question is, why are you so against reading Morgana's diary? There's nothing to be frightened of, Sebastian. Just odd musings and the ramblings of a young woman with a vindictive outlook on life. What can her diary do to you?"

Sebastian turned away toward the window, feeling restless. "She put me in a fucking collar that made me little more than her slave. I was thirteen."

"She could have loved you and nurtured your talents," Lady E continued, "but she feared you instead. Her fear is the reason you suffered, and you need to understand that. Bishop claims we don't have the time to help you overcome all your... issues of trust... but I think it's important. Especially when it is certain you will face your mother again, and she knows how to manipulate your emotions."

Sebastian stared through the window, rocked by the knowledge. It hurt. But more than that, it sounded like the truth. "She wasn't... wasn't always cruel," he finally admitted, in a careful voice. "Perhaps that's the hardest thing to deal with. Sometimes I remember when I was a small child, and she bought me a new book, or kissed my cheek. She did that once. I mean, she was never a perfect mother, but she knew I liked chocolates, and books, and sometimes she would smile at me...."

"Few people truly are rotten through and through." Lady Eberhardt sighed. "Your mother does come close, but that is my own prejudices showing." Her lips thinned. "And *if* I were being truly honest with myself I could *perhaps* admit I bear some blame for the path she took. I was arrogant and heavy-handed as her master, and I never did trust her. All I ever did was counsel your father against her."

"That doesn't sound like a mistake."

Lady E smiled bitterly. "Perhaps it doesn't. But what if all your mother ever needed was for someone to love her? To accept her? A female mentor who could teach her a better way? She never truly trusted men, but perhaps a woman could have reached her. I failed in that. And I never truly realized until I held that journal in my hands. Sorcery is about understanding yourself intimately. One cannot wield immense power with blatant disregard to their own desires or weaknesses. All it ever does is end in someone dying."

He stared at the journal as though it were a mistake.

"Nobody likes to see truth in the mirror," she muttered. "But if you want to become a sorcerer, then you need to understand what drives you. Read the journal, Sebastian. It might enlighten you in ways you never expected."

"Why are you telling me this?"

Lady E's gnarled hands curled around her staff. "Like I said, Morgana made the wrong choices for the wrong reasons." Heaving herself to her feet, she strode toward him.

"And you think I'm about to make the same wrong choices," he realized.

"I understand you have suffered. I do understand that. But what I see is a young man who walls himself away, keeping everyone at arm's length. In a way you have more in common with Adrian than you realize." Reaching up, she patted his cheek, and for a moment the feel of her warm, cupped hand on his skin almost took his feet out from under him. How long since anyone besides Cleo had offered simple human comfort?

How long since he had trusted it?

"We all have our crosses to bear. Even Adrian. Even me." Those black eyes stared deeply into his soul. "You're not alone, and you're not the first to feel the weight of your past. But you're also no longer a child. The choices you make now could hurt people. They could hurt you. If I'm being honest, I could be staring at your mother right now, as much as you hate the notion."

He slowly, carefully, curled his hand over hers. He trusted Lady E, he realized, or at least he trusted her as far as he could ever trust anyone. "That could be the worst thing you've ever said to me."

"If that's the worst thing I've ever said to you, then you have little to complain about." One eyebrow arched.

"Or perhaps it's a horrible notion because you know there is some truth behind it."

Patting his cheek, she stepped back and picked up the journal for him. "Read it. It might prove enlightening, even if you find it distasteful. To understand yourself, you need to understand your mother and what swayed her from her path."

"I'll consider it," he replied, as she handed him the book.

"And you need to stop avoiding your wife."

This time his cheeks burned with heat. "That's really none of your business."

Another snort, as she turned for the door. "I didn't think you were a coward, but time will tell."

Curse her. He had to get out of here. "Tell Bishop I'll be back by lunchtime. I'm going for a walk."

"To clear your head?"

"Something like that."

Gulls squawked overhead, pinwheeling between the masts of numerous ships as Sebastian wandered along the docks. He'd come here often enough when he could slip away from Morgana's house, though the collar he'd worn then limited how far he could go. The scent of the river left much to be desired, but it was the one place in London where he felt like he could relax.

Sebastian's gaze slowly came into focus, and he realized what he was staring at. The ticketing office's sign showed a ship, cast in bronze. It wasn't the first time he'd considered it.

It was, however, the first time he'd stepped inside.

The bell over the door tinkled. The small agent looked up sharply from where he was writing in a book. "May I help you?"

"Perhaps."

Half an hour later, he stepped out of the ticket office, tucking his purchase into his waistcoat pocket.

Liverpool to Manhattan.

He didn't know what had driven the purchase—he'd given Bishop an oath after all, to help destroy the demon—but this aimless jaunt in the city had ended here. The moment he saw the steerage ticket office, he'd known what he was looking for.

Escape.

A steerage ticket to Manhattan was all he could afford, but it offered him something he'd never had before. He could almost see a new city unfolding before him, filled with opportunities, and a new life.... Far away from the mess here, and the haunting reminder that his mother was still out there, no doubt plotting revenge against him for all he'd cost her. Lady E might think all he needed to do was embrace his past, and learn to control his emotions, but that restless itch was back.

He didn't belong here.

And last night... last night only reminded him of everything he couldn't have. It would be better this way.

He stopped in his tracks at the sight of a young woman sitting on a barrel, kicking her heels and sending her green skirts fluttering. "Verity."

"Fancy seeing you here," she said, biting on the apple she held and lifting her gaze to the sign on the shop.

"Indeed," he replied. "Were you following me? Did my brother put you up to this?"

Verity ignored him, as she was wont to do, but then he expected that living with his brother's glowering moods gave her some sort of immunity to anything he could throw at her. "Bishop wants to pay a visit to the One-Eyed Crows after lunch, so he sent me to find you. He thinks they might know the whereabouts of your father—"

"The demon."

"Technically. So, yes, he put me up to this, but no, I wasn't following you. I tracked you."

"Tracked me?"

She rolled her eyes. "All I need is a possession from somebody to be able to find them. It's a gift."

"From when you were a thief?"

"Touché, big brother." She grinned. "Mind you, utterly redeemed now."

He couldn't find it in him to remain angry with her. Verity's charm was often insufferable, but he liked her. Particularly when she was standing toe-to-toe with Bishop.

He also had her to thank for saving his life, when his assassin brother had thought he'd be better off dead. Instead, she'd made Bishop reconsider, and offer to teach him to control his dangerous powers.

"I don't think you'll ever be redeemed," Sebastian said dryly. He pulled his pocket watch out and looked at the time. He had two, but only this one worked, and the other... well, it wasn't as though he'd have thought himself sentimental, but it was the first gift his mother ever gave him. He really ought to destroy it. "We're going to be late."

Verity seemed in no mood to hurry. She kicked her heels slowly, staring at the ticketing office. "It's a long way to the Americas."

His gut twisted into knots. "Verity—"

"Of course, I suppose it seems easier to run away," she added. "No demon to contend with. No sign of your mother, or her murderous cronies. No more torturous lessons with Bishop. And not to mention your wife...."

"I'm not running away. And this has nothing to do with the demon, or my mother, or my wife."

"Does Cleo know you're leaving?"

"No."

"You would leave her in a bit of a quandary."

"If I left now, I could offer her an annulment. This marriage was only ever one in name. She would have the chance to remarry, and to create a family of her own."

"And if you don't leave now?" Verity asked quietly.

Then it would be too late. The taste of Cleo's mouth had haunted him all night. "If I don't leave, I doubt I'll be able to offer her an annulment." Not on the grounds of nonconsummation anyway.

"Last night bothered you," she murmured, tucking her hand through his arm as if he'd offered, and settling into a stroll. "I could see it on your face when Gray kissed her."

"I don't have the right to feel that way."

"Some could say you have all the right."

"I can't give her what she needs," he countered.

"Have you ever asked her what she needs?"

To be loved. He rubbed at his mouth. "Verity...."

"All I ever wanted was a family, and a home, and perhaps a husband who cared for me," Verity said. "I never believed it would be possible. I was the best thief in the Dials. But I had nothing—no family, really—beyond the girl I was raised with. Who could have loved me—a girl who lied, and stole, and knew little more than how to watch her back? I owed the Crows money for the roof over my head, and the food they put on my table. And no matter how much I stole, I could never pay back that debt. There was always something to add to it." She looked up. "I know what it feels like to be trapped, Sebastian. And then your brother walked into my life, and told me I was owed more. I deserved to be loved, and treated with respect. I deserved the right to learn my magic. I deserved my freedom. And he took me away and offered me his heart, and suddenly I have everything I ever wanted." She took a deep breath. "But the transition was hard. It took me a long time to realize I could trust him, and my first instinct is always to watch my back. He's patient enough with me, but he doesn't understand you, or what you're going through."

She looked at him, her green eyes shining. *She did,* he realized.

"Give yourself time," she murmured. "You have a family here, if you could only open your eyes to it. And I've seen you with your wife. Your first instinct is always to protect her, did you realize?"

"How do I protect her from me?" He breathed the words. "She had a Vision—"

"I know." Verity patted his hand. "London's doom."

"Me," he said hoarsely. "She sees me in the middle of a hexagram, and the skies tear open above me, and I bring death and destruction to London. It's not the demon you should be worried about."

"She sees you, and she sees destruction, and it's somehow linked. It doesn't mean you're the cause of it."

"Is that what Bishop thinks too?" He'd seen the look on his brother's face whenever Cleo mentioned her particular Vision.

Verity hesitated. "One thing at a time. Let's deal with the tangible. The demon. Your mother. The enemies we can see. Cleo sees a lot of things, but she's only just learning to dream-walk. Now she's claiming this black queen is the true threat. Maybe you're not the one who causes the destruction? Maybe you're the key to stopping it? We don't truly know what is going to happen."

He looked away. "Can we take that chance? If I'm not here, then perhaps the Vision doesn't come true."

"If you're not here, what happens to all of us if it does come true? What happens to Cleo?" Verity asked quietly.

His mouth twisted. "I haven't even decided if I'm going yet. It was just a whim."

"But you have a ticket...."

"I.... Yes."

"And an annulment doesn't happen overnight."

"*Verity*," he said, more of a warning than anything else.

"When do you leave?"

"Ten days. If I choose to go." He could feel power welling within him, sending a chill through the air around them. Expression. He was letting his emotions overpower him, and drive his sorcery. Exactly what Bishop warned him against, and was trying to teach him not to do.

With limited success.

Verity bit into her apple, chewing thoughtfully, as if she couldn't feel the air chilling. "I suppose that's a decision you'll have to make," she said, and then tossed the apple core in the gutter. A hungry rat slipped out of a pile of crates and darted toward it, whisking the core away.

Verity held her hands out to him. "Coming?"

He looked down. Verity's gift of translocation was a little unnerving. He didn't know how it worked—by all rights it shouldn't have—but Bishop had muttered something along the lines of "she doesn't know enough about the rules of sorcery to be able to comprehend the illogic of what she can do." As long as Verity believed in her magic, then she'd be able to pop in and out of midair, no matter where.

"Aren't we catching a hack?" he asked cautiously. "And what do you mean by 'that's a decision I'll have to make?' You're not going to tell my brother?"

"Do you want me to?"

Hell, no. "He'll think I'm reneging on the bargain we made."

"Yes, he'll be disappointed. I know this month hasn't been an easy one for either of you." She nodded slowly. "But it's your secret, Sebastian. Your choice. I hope you change your mind before your ship leaves."

"He'll probably be relieved," he muttered under his breath.

Verity smiled sadly. "I wish you could both trust each other. Sometimes I see so many similarities between the two of you that it makes my heart ache to see you both stubbornly butting heads, purely because neither of you will yield. He's not your enemy, Sebastian."

Similarities? She had to be joking. "Bishop wanted me dead."

"You're right," she said, holding out her hands. "He was afraid of your power, and how uncontrolled it was. The same way you once wanted your father dead, because you thought he'd abandoned you. But he changed his mind, as it seems you have too."

His father *had* abandoned him. And then he'd turned around and sacrificed his body to the demon in place of Sebastian's. A muscle in his jaw ticked, and he stared down at Verity's gloved hands. "How on earth can you look so optimistically on the world, when you know what it's like? You're a fool."

"Maybe. But if I don't have hope the world will turn out to be a better place, then what is the point in going on?"

The words struck him, right to the heart. And he put his hands in hers before he could consider just what exactly it meant.

He hadn't made a decision yet.

He had ten days to make it.

"Do you have something to tell me?" Bishop murmured, as he followed his wife inside the carriage that would take them to Seven Dials.

Verity blinked at him, her green eyes guileless. "Do I?"

He tested the soul-bond between them, coming up against the small hard shield that blocked him from a certain section of her thoughts. The shield hadn't been there before he sent her to find Sebastian.

She'd never locked him out before.

"You're hiding something, and it has to do with Sebastian." And he didn't like it one bit. "What did he do? What did he say?"

"Why don't you ask him?"

Bishop flexed his fingers inside his leather gloves. She had to be jesting. She, better than anyone, knew how poorly the past month had gone. He could teach Sebastian how to attack with sorcery. He could teach him how to defend himself. But he couldn't reach him. "Because he won't tell me."

"If you push the issue, then I daresay I will reveal it. My loyalties lie with you, after all," Verity said, then pursed her lips. "But I would prefer not to. Your brother needs to know he can trust someone."

Words Agatha had been drilling into him for weeks now. He knew she was right.

"He doesn't trust me," he said.

"No."

Bishop looked at her. Then away. "Then I won't ask. And I won't push." He reached for her hand, stroking her fingers. "I trust your judgment."

Verity let out a long sigh as she crossed the carriage and slid onto his lap. "I hate keeping secrets from you."

Bishop pressed his face against her neck, squeezing her tight. Verity brought so much lightness to his life. He couldn't remember what it had been like before she tried to steal the Chalice from him.

"I just hope I'm right in keeping it," she whispered.

CHAPTER TEN

THE DEMON COULD sense the thinning of worlds. It kept its eyes closed, channeling enormous amounts of raw power into its great spell works, feeling every little rune and charm it had cast in the past two weeks wake up as it tested the pattern.

Perfect. This body had so much potential, so much power. All was nearly ready. All it needed was—

A door slammed shut, breaking its concentration.

"They have the Wand," said a strident female voice. "That piece of filth betrayed me. And you."

Morgana.

The demon opened its eyes, the golden patterns across the lawn winking out of existence as he withdrew his power. He looked toward the back door of the manor he was currently residing at, and saw her striding across the back lawn, her red skirts swishing about her legs.

"I know they have the Wand," it said.

Morgana drew up shortly, as if surprised by its lack of emotion. "That makes two of the Relics Infernal, Great Lord." She lowered her eyes as if suddenly realizing how much she dared when she confronted him. "They could destroy you if they get their hands on all three of them."

"That is why the remaining Relic is safely in your hands." He turned and gestured toward the two women kneeling nearby.

Both women rose, shivering slightly. He noted the small signs of weakness.

It's not weakness, Drake whispered inside him. *You've had them kneeling in the snow for three hours.*

The demon sometimes forgot about human foibles. What it did not forget was how often Drake seemed to be speaking to it these days, and it crushed the former Prime down deep.

He's stronger than I thought.

Morgana wrapped her cloak around her. "Well, what are we going to do about it?"

Nothing. I am going to do nothing. "Drake's hold on this body is remarkable for a vessel," he said. "I dare not risk a direct confrontation with his sons. I swore I would not harm them when he allowed me to take this body. I will not engage them until I need to."

"You can't just allow such a challenge to go unmarked." Bitterness flashed in her green eyes.

He repressed the urge to simply slit her throat here and now. *She still has some use.* "I am not ready for a confrontation." It gestured to the lawn. "I still have days of preparation ahead of me."

And the Relics are unimportant. For now.

"You don't have to confront them," Morgana said, peering across the lawns, though she didn't understand what he was trying to do. "I could do it. *Let* me do it for you, great lord."

He stared at her. "Kneel."

Confusion flickered across her face, and then she went to her knees before him. The demon captured her chin, tilting it up. Seeing it in this body caused her some pain. This body had memories for her. An ex-husband she'd never quite forgiven. Or forgotten.

"I will allow you to make a strike in return," it said. "I need time. I need them distracted. If they focus on the remaining Relic, then they are not focused upon what I do here. How do you intend to do it?"

Her mind raced behind her green eyes. "They'll all be gathering for the Ascension Ball. They'll never expect an attack there. Only a madman would attack an assembly of nearly four hundred sorcerers."

"Perfect."

Morgana smiled.

"I have only one rule: You shall do no harm to your son's wife."

"Cleo Sinclair?" she said incredulously.

"I want her alive. And well." It looked toward one of the other women. "Lady Beaumont."

Lady Beaumont stepped forward, her dark curls shining in the afternoon sunlight. "Your faithful servant, Great Lord."

"Work with Morgana. Create a distraction. Make it bloody." He turned toward the remaining woman, eyeing her up and down. "And you will share my bed. I need to replenish my strength."

The woman's dark eyes flickered toward the others, and she sucked in a sharp horrified breath. "Yes, Great Lord."

After two days of fruitless hunting through Seven Dials, Sebastian and Bishop were forced to concede defeat. There was no sign of the demon in the Dials. Nobody knew anything about the Relics, and the One-Eyed Crows claimed the men who'd attacked them at Malachi Gray's were outcasts from their hex gang.

The day of the Ascension Ball arrived, bringing with it Ianthe's first act of command as Prime of the Order, and they were all forced to set aside the hunt for a moment.

Though Sebastian questioned the necessity of the occasion—*a ball, right now?*—he'd been assured by Lady Eberhardt that such an act was more necessary than he could ever guess. The Order had been shaken by Drake's resignation, and the demon's assault at the Rite of Ascension. It needed to see its new Prime and be assured of her strength, and the cohesion of her allies.

And they needed the Order behind them.

Sebastian watched from the base of the staircase to the ballroom at the Earl of Rathbourne's manor as guest upon guest arrived. Ianthe and Lucien greeted them all politely, with Lady Eberhardt scowling mercilessly at anyone who was less than effusive in their greetings.

Eleanor Ross—his father's lover—leaned on a cane in the corner. Sebastian tried not to catch her eye. The left side of her body was still stricken, and his fingers flexed as if remembering the moment he'd flung a wave of force at his mother, and she deflected it.

Directly into Eleanor.

She'd be able to stand straight if it weren't for him. And he'd overheard Bishop murmuring that Eleanor still couldn't use her magic.

He'd cost her everything.

Including Drake.

Dozens of guests were arriving, and the crunch of wheels on the gravel of the driveway heralded more. Sebastian helped himself to a glass of champagne as one of the waiters went past. He'd never been to a ball like this. All the ones Morgana made him attend descended into orgies, and he'd been the centerpiece in most of the auctions. The memories made him sweat a little bit, and he felt somewhat on edge.

One of the musicians began to tune his instrument. The jagged saw of the violin thrummed through him. He gulped a mouthful of champagne. These people would recognize him as the instigator of the melee at the night of the Ascension, despite the fact the demon had worn his skin and he'd been merely a passenger. There was no hiding here, though Lady E had dared him to look them in the eye and arch a cool brow.

"You're your father's son," she had said, straightening his collar, and patting it tenderly as though for a second she thought she stood in front of his father, many years ago. *"Don't ever forget that."*

He wouldn't. But he also couldn't forget that these people knew him as his mother's son as well.

The music broke into a quiet little riff. Sebastian glanced at his pocket watch. Cleo should be down at any moment. She'd been locked away all day with Verity and Eleanor Ross, and he'd only caught the odd snatch of her thoughts—enough to realize she was terribly excited about such goings-on.

He'd barely seen her in the past two days. Cleo had spent that time reading some sort of book she'd called *Sidestep Through Time*. The sudden anticipation in his chest surprised him, though perhaps it shouldn't have.

He'd kissed her.

And not just sweetly. He could still feel the ghostly imprint of her mouth upon his, and at night, when he had nothing else to distract his mind, he'd let himself imagine what might have happened if they hadn't been interrupted by the imp attacks.

Almost as if the thought of her brought her to call, the bond swelled, and he blinked back to reality, realizing his wife was approaching.

Turning toward the stairs, he looked up, just as a swish of silk skirts whispered over the carpets up there. A crown of blonde hair caught his attention. Cleo paused at the top of the stairs, and his breath caught in his lungs.

She was—

Jesus.

She wore a ball gown of the palest pink, more of a blush of color than a full wash, and it emphasized the creaminess of her skin. It was beaded with what looked like pure starlight, gilded by the warmth of the light from the wall sconces. The skirts bunched around her waist in swags of wispy fabric before falling to the floor, and tiny little cap sleeves sat just off her shoulders, though the bodice was not virginal. No. Heat stirred in his groin as his gaze traced the slopes of her breasts. He'd never seen her wear such a daring neckline, and some part of him wanted to take his coat and cover her up, to shield her from every other man there in a protective burst of instinct he'd not felt before.

She's not yours.

You can't have her.

But some part of him laughed at himself, as though it saw straight through the lies.

This was no longer the virginal miss who'd first caught his eye.

Nor was she openly enticing, the way most of the female sorcerers in the ballroom were. No, she stood apart.

Shy. Breathless. Somehow untouchable, and yet yearning to be touched. Cleo gazed down over the ballroom, her eyes covered by a delicate gold mask. He saw the moment she noticed him staring at her, and the sense of connection slammed through him.

The soul-bond roared to life through his veins.

"Cat caught your tongue, *brother*?" Bishop appeared out of nowhere, bringing him back into the present. There was a knowing look in Bishop's eyes as Sebastian sucked in a sharp breath and looked away from her.

"Don't you have somewhere to be?"

Bishop straightened his gloves. "If you won't have her, then some lucky man will. Look at them. They're all watching her with appreciation."

Bishop might as well have been bloody prophetic, for there were heads turning all across the ballroom. Appreciation was one word for it.

And she'd be free to take up any offers she received if they got an annulment. A knot tightened in his gut. He wanted her to be happy. He did. But there was something ugly inside him too, something primeval that wanted to beat its fists on his chest and claim her for his own.

The thought of another man touching her almost undid him.

"Well, she's mine for tonight," he said coldly. "So they can all go hang." Sebastian drained his champagne glass, setting it on a passing tray as he strode away from Bishop.

Catching her skirts up in her hands, Cleo began the descent, her eyes hesitantly meeting his through the eyeholes of the mask. This was her night, the ball she'd always dreamed of. He couldn't destroy the moment for her.

And maybe it would be something he could remember when—if—he left England.

Playing the part, he captured her hand as she took the last step, lifting it to his lips. "You look beautiful."

She smiled shyly. "So do you."

His smile slipped. Women had called him beautiful as they'd forced him into their beds.

The heat in Cleo's eyes as she eyed him appreciatively made him feel uncertain. Lust mixed together with the horrible sensation of other women's hands pawing at him. He wanted this to be her night, and he wanted to be the man she thought him, but it was too late. He'd thought of the past, and his mouth tasted sour.

"Are you all right?" she asked with a frown.

He lowered her hand from his lips, holding on to it tightly. He wanted to hold on to the purity of her. Not think of the other. "I'm fine. Are you going to save me a dance?"

"Do you want to dance with me?"

He needed something more than flirtation to take his mind off things. Stroking her cheek, he bent his head and swiftly kissed her on the mouth. "Yes."

As far as kisses went, it hearkened straight back to their first awkward attempt, when she'd caught him by surprise. He hadn't reacted then, and he'd surprised her now.

Cleo blinked. "What was that for?"

Merciful mother of night, but he was making a hash of this. "I'm sorry."

"Don't be sorry." Her hand pressed to his chest. "Never be sorry for kissing me."

"Even if it is as terrible as that?" Simply holding her hand was relaxing him, though the back of his neck still felt clammy.

She touched her lips. "Terrible is not the word I was looking for. Perhaps we simply need more practice?"

There was the distraction he needed. He looked down and finally saw her—truly saw her—pulling out of the spell that had bound him for several seconds. "Are you offering to practice kissing with me?"

A heretofore-unknown flirtatious side emerged from her. "Only if you promise to lure me somewhere dark and mysterious."

Sebastian stroked the back of her hand. "I could potentially do that." There were dozens of places around Rathbourne Manor that were secluded.

But once there, would he be able to contain himself to mere kisses? *I want to do many, many things to you beyond kissing.* Heat stirred through his skin. What would it be like to hold a woman in his arms who meant something to him?

What would it be like to kiss her naked skin? To take his time exploring all the secret dips and valleys that made up Cleo's body?

It would be perfect.

"I will hold you to that promise," she said, with the smile that left him breathless.

The smile that captured his heart and squeezed it.

Sebastian took a minute step toward her, half tempted to steal her away now, lust coursing through his veins. He couldn't always promise that it would feel as pure as it did now, and he wanted to capture the moment. To bottle it. He almost suspected he could do this in truth—be her husband—if he could only continue to feel this way, pure and clean.

"Don't look at me like that," she said breathlessly. "Don't you dare. I want my dance first."

His gloved hand brushed against her skirts, and he captured a fold of it between thumb and forefinger, the movement so subtle only she would know. His voice lowered, "We don't have to dance in the ballroom."

Cleo rapped him on the arm with her fan, glancing over his shoulder as if to see if anyone watched. This was allowed. She was his wife, and he could damned well touch her when he wanted in the eyes of the world, but he felt the illicit thrill sweep through him too.

"The waltz?" she whispered. "Just once. In the ballroom."

Over the top of her head, he caught a glimpse of a woman in a feathered black swan mask eyeing him with appreciation.

The sight froze him.

Utterly.

Full red lips curved as the swan realized he'd seen her, and then the woman in black turned and sauntered into the hallway, casting one more glance behind her as if in invitation.

"Are you all right?" Cleo asked, resting her hand on his arm. "You've gone awfully pale. Don't tell me I've frightened you away from dancing forever? I promise I won't step on your toes."

He reined his emotions in sharply, and gave her a thin smile. "Sorry. I thought I saw someone I knew. Would you care for some champagne?"

He didn't fool her. Cleo's lips pressed together. But then she nodded. "That would be wonderful. Are you sure you're—"

"I'll fetch it for you," he said curtly, striding away, an icy sweat springing up along his spine.

It had to be a mistake. The lighting in here was dim, after all, and it had been over ten years since he'd seen her last. Champagne. He turned, trying to think where he'd seen the servants last. Sweeps of color swam around him as he found himself in the middle of a waltz; every woman in here looked like some floral bloom, and the press of swagged skirts brushed against his trousers, making him shake. They couldn't know, but right now he didn't think he could stand to be touched, even if it were the innocuous brush of a skirt. The crush of perfume became almost overpowering, and he wiped his numb mouth.

Too many people. Too much scent. Sebastian shoved his way between a woman in red and her dancing partner, escaping through one of the doors—

The swan waited for him at the end of the hallway, lowering the mask she held to her face.

There was no mistake.

It was Julia Camden.

Sebastian shoved blindly through a doorway in the wall, heading for the terrace. He had to get out of there, before he drenched the entire ballroom in ice.

Sebastian burst out into the gardens, sucking in a lungful of cold air. He was shaking, practically vibrating with energy and fury. He held his hands out and stared at them, trying all of Bishop's methods to control himself; his breathing, clearing his mind, trying to focus on something, anything else...

Skirts swished.

Sebastian gathered himself, turning to face his worst nightmare. The black swan eased the glass doors shut behind her, leaning back against them for a moment, as if to capture the look of his face.

"All that youthful promise," Lady Beaumont whispered, twirling a lock of her brown hair around her finger. "Haven't you more than fulfilled it?"

"What are you doing here?" Lady Beaumont had allied herself with Morgana in the past. The only reason for her to be here right now was for mischief's sake.

"Greeting my new Prime," she said, with a pout. "Who was far more welcoming than you."

"We're not friends."

"We were... once." She took a step toward him, her words dropping to a purr. "We could be friends again, Sebastian."

He caught her hand as she reached for him. "If you touch me, I'll make you regret it."

Lady Beaumont gasped, but he could see the words thrilled her, more than they should have. "You weren't nearly so forceful the last time we met."

"I was seventeen," he said bluntly. "What did you expect?"

Her free hand stroked his waistcoat, and he could feel that touch on his skin, see her laughing down at him from his memories, as she kissed her way down his chained body. "The boy has grown up," Lady Beaumont said in a smoky voice that made him want to vomit, even as her hands delved beneath his waistcoat. "What I wouldn't give to renew our acquaintance. You liked it the last time I—"

Sebastian shoved her away, the world around him vanishing. He could barely see for the sheer, blinding rage that obliterated his thoughts. All he could smell was her perfume—the sickening, overpowering scent of orange blossom, a scent that had stayed with him all these years. Lady Beaumont hadn't been the first to use him, but she'd been the first to wring any sort of reaction from his helpless body.

"Don't touch me," he warned again, and this time his breath misted in the air in front of him.

Tendrils of ice began to crawl up the windowpanes, almost as if Jack Frost painted delicate stars upon them. The air was so cold it bit the back of his throat, making his chest heave, and Lady Beaumont shook the ice from her skirts.

He'd done this.

Sebastian swallowed hard, trembling with power he couldn't even recall gathering. It took everything he had to disperse it, letting the trembling ground subside.

Lady Beaumont eyed him with hungry eyes. "You want to hurt me."

"I want you to leave."

"I'd let you, you know?" She pressed a hand to her throat. "Think of all the things I'd let you do to me—"

"I'm married."

"So I'd heard. Tremayne's brat. The blind girl. She wouldn't have to know."

Killing her wouldn't solve a damned thing. But he had to remind himself of that. How could he touch Cleo after having the feel of this woman on his skin? "You disgust me. You always have."

"That's not the entire truth, is it now?" Lady Beaumont's skirts whispered over the tiles, and he could *feel* those skirts slithering over his bare thighs again, her nails raking down his chest.

Sebastian turned his face away, breathing hard. "What do you *want?*" he repeated, a little more coldly. "I assume there's a reason for this?"

"I could be your friend, Sebastian. And from what I hear, you could use a friend right about now."

Her words caught his attention. He shot her a dark glance. He'd thought her an old friend of his mother's, and knew Lady Beaumont wasn't brave enough to play her games too far in the open. But what if she was still allied with his mother?

What if there was a *reason* she was here?

He moved swiftly, slamming her back against the walls of the house. Lady Beaumont gasped, then laughed her husky laugh, biting her lip as she looked up at him.

"No games," he told her. "Did my mother send you?"

"I haven't seen your mother in an age," she taunted, though her eyes glittered. "It would be rather foolish of me to make an appearance here if anyone were to know I had ties to Morgana, wouldn't it?" She *tsked* under her breath. "And your mother is known to stab her acquaintances in the back."

Sebastian's hand settled over her throat. She'd liked that once, and her eyes told him she liked it now.

"A little harder," she breathed.

He let his voice drop to a whisper. "If you know anything, you would be wise to mention it before you try my patience. There are people inside whom I care about. I wouldn't like to see anything happen to them. Indeed, if something *were* to happen to them and I thought you knew anything about it—"

He let his power spill through his fingers, controlling the sorcerous weaves with ease. Ice was his natural inclination, and the first element he'd ever controlled. Lady Beaumont choked as he froze the inside of her throat, her eyes popping wide in disbelief.

Sharp nails raked his hand, and she clutched at it, her chest heaving. Sebastian held the weft of power for another three seconds, before letting it vanish.

He turned away from her as she slumped, a hacking cough tearing through her slim frame. The thin glove he wore couldn't seem to check the touch of her skin. He stripped it off, casting it aside, but he still felt dirty.

"Do you have anything to tell me?" he asked, turning around to survey her.

There was blood on her lips. She'd bitten her tongue, and she smiled at him with bloodied teeth. "I hope your mother *is* working against you. Perhaps I'll even look her up, and see if she'll offer me your leash for the night, once she brings you to heel again. Or maybe a month." Lady Beaumont licked her lips. "Breaking you would be almost enough incentive for a girl like me to do something foolish...."

He took a menacing step toward her.

"Ah, Sebastian, there you are," called a firm voice.

He came back to himself, staring down at her, every muscle in his body locked tight. Her mocking laughter grated across his nerves as he tilted his head to watch Lucien saunter along the terrace.

His half brother looked relaxed, with hands in pockets, and a loose step, but his amber eyes locked on the pair of them. "Lady Beaumont, what a surprise to see you out here."

"Oh, please," she said coyly, dropping one shoulder. "Call me Julia."

"We missed you inside during the receiving line," Lucien said, still smiling that faint, graceful smile, though his eyes sharpened in a predatory manner. "You must go congratulate my wife on her Ascension. Before she thinks you've slighted her."

She'd lied about meeting the Prime. Sebastian turned toward her swiftly.

Lady Beaumont's smile froze. "Of course. I... must have missed her in the crush."

"Ianthe has quite a temper," Lucien said fondly. "Perhaps you should go now, before it has time to brew."

"An excellent suggestion, my lord." She glanced coquettishly at Sebastian. "It was lovely to see you again. I've missed you, darling. Until we meet again...."

"We won't."

Lady Beaumont merely smiled, as if to tell him he was deluding himself, and then she slid her greedy little hand over Lucien's sleeve.

Over. It was over. Sebastian turned away as Lucien hastened her inside, with firm instructions for the footman to deliver her to the Prime.

He strode down the stairs, into the garden. He couldn't go back in there.

Stalking through the gardens mindlessly, he found a small clearing where the moonlight streamed down upon him. It was nothing like Malachi Gray's estate, but he touched one of the pruned rosebushes, stroking the bare branches. Channeling his power into the plant, he forced a flower to form, its lush petals tightly budded and pale. Another lash of sorcery, and those petals opened like the twirl of a lady's skirt, color staining them and darkening as he let his magic surge.

A red rose.

Plucking it from the bush, he pressed it to his nose, thinking of Cleo. The tight band around his chest eased somewhat, as the sweet perfume filled him.

It took him a long time to realize he wasn't alone. Lucien had returned with two glasses of champagne, his shoes slowly crunching on the gravel path.

"Shouldn't you be inside?" he asked flatly, lowering the rose.

Lucien handed one of his champagne flutes to Sebastian. "Here."

Everything he'd been holding inside him burst out, sending chills all across his skin. He gripped the champagne flute, turning and staring blindly into the garden. A thorn pricked his finger, and it was almost the only thing holding him together. "I think I should take a carriage back to Bishop's."

"You have rooms here for the night," Lucien said.

"I don't think I would be very good company." He turned away.

A hand settled on his shoulder. Bile soured his mouth—that Lucien should see him like this—but he didn't force him to remove his hand.

"I take it your acquaintance with Lady Beaumont is not a happy one."

She raped me. Sebastian ran a hand over his mouth instead, swallowing down the bile. *Worse than that, she got a reaction from me.* "No."

"Do you want me to evict her from the manor?"

The offer shocked him a little. He barely knew this brother. All his attention had been focused upon Bishop, and Lucien... Lucien had more cause to hate him than even Bishop did. "Won't it cause a commotion?"

"Probably." Lucien shrugged.

"But isn't tonight meant to allay the Order's concerns? Won't it fracture Ianthe's support base if they see us casting one of them out?"

"Haven't you heard? I'm the mad, bad Earl of Rathbourne, fresh out of Bedlam. They'll expect that sort of thing from me." Lucien's amber eyes locked on his. "And the Order's not as unstable as all that. Ianthe's worried, for she wants everything to be perfect. Yes, it will cause gossip, but I can quell it. Or threaten to set Lady E on any rabble-rousers."

"Thank you." He barely breathed the words. The bubbles in the champagne fizzed down his dry throat. "I wouldn't take your eyes off Lady Beaumont though. She dabbles in the Black Arts, and she's enjoyed my mother's games in the past."

"I won't." Lucien hesitated. "I don't know everything that's happened to you, but I'm an Empath. Your emotions when you saw Lady Beaumont... they sliced right through me. I would have said you were screaming on the inside."

Sebastian cringed internally.

"She was my mother's ally," he said hoarsely, looking across the gardens. "She did nothing more than any other young lad might have dreamed of."

"But you didn't."

"I never had a choice in the matter," he said softly, oh so softly. "They used to have auctions...." He couldn't say any more, but there was one question that was bothering him. "Why are you doing this? I helped kidnap your daughter."

Lucien remained silent. Then a hand clapped on his shoulder and squeezed. "Did I ever tell you about my father?"

"Which one?" he asked. For Lucien was secretly Drake's illegitimate child.

"Lord Rathbourne," Lucien replied. "The earl despised me for most of my life, and it wasn't until recently—a year or so ago—that I finally realized why. Rathbourne claimed he needed my help to perform a great working. He'd neglected me for so many years it never crossed my mind to question him. Or maybe it did, and a part of me didn't care. I wanted to please him.

"And he brought forth this... this sort of metallic link he claimed could increase my powers, and help us to link. There were runes in each link of the metal, and it gave me an odd sensation when I touched it." Lucien released a sharp breath. "A sclavus collar is illegal. It's forbidden to have anything to do with one. We don't speak of them anymore. We tear pages from books that show you how to make one. And it wasn't until I put it around my throat that I even knew what it was."

Sebastian's head jerked toward the other man. "You wore a collar?"

"Out of all of us here, perhaps I alone know what it feels like to be bound to another's bidding." Lucien looked up at the night sky. "The sensation as your will is turned against you.... There's nothing you can do. Nothing you can say. Your body's no longer your own, nor your mind. And it hurts to fight it, fuck it hurts. It felt like every nerve in my body was on fire. There comes a point where you don't think you can survive, and you give in." He glanced down at his feet. "And afterwards you wonder: did I fight hard enough? Did I surrender too early? Did I have anything left to give?"

Sebastian's mouth felt dry.

"You want to know why I can forgive you for your role in Louisa's kidnapping?" Lucien's voice firmed. "It's because I know there's nothing you could have done to have stopped it."

And they weren't merely speaking of Louisa anymore.

Nor were they speaking of Lucien's forgiveness.

Something was wrong.

Cleo smiled at everybody who greeted her, but she couldn't help craning her neck to try and find Sebastian. The bond between them was fiercely shielded on his end, but she felt as though something had happened to him. Her skin was itchy—not quite Premonition—but more an innate sense of Sebastian's emotions.

Excusing herself, she went to find him, brushing through a pair of dancing sorcerers, and slamming directly into another woman's shoulder.

"Oh, I'm so sorry," she said, as the pair of them staggered apart. "I didn't see you there."

Premonition lit through her like wildfire.

The other woman—wearing black silk from head to toe, with a ruff of black swan feathers around her neckline—sneered a little at her. "Quite all right, considering the circumstances."

"Circumstances?"

"Your husband's in the garden," the woman whispered, leaning close to her. "But I'd give him a few more minutes to regain his composure at least."

With a knowing smirk, the woman withdrew a small compact mirror from her reticule and began to powder her nose.

Cleo blinked at her. Sebastian... in the garden. "Are you trying to hint that you and my husband were having a rendezvous out there?" she asked incredulously.

The woman snapped her compact shut, and gave her a world-weary smile. "Oh, my poor sweet child. Don't take it personally. Men have such appetites—"

"I don't take it personally," Cleo interrupted. "I find the idea ludicrous."

"*Ludicrous?*"

"You would have to know my husband," Cleo explained politely. "He's not the sort to take a lover, or even to flirt with other woman."

"I *do* know your husband." The woman brushed past her, as if to go, but paused at the last moment. "Intimately. Perhaps you should thank me. Everything he knows, he learned from me."

And then she was gone, leaving Cleo gaping behind her.

A sliver of unease went through her. He didn't want to touch *her*, but he'd been with... with this woman?

And then it all suddenly made a perfect sort of sense.

"It was never about making love, Cleo. All they ever wanted from me was fucking."

His mother had sold him to others for the night, and he'd hinted that there'd been nothing he could do about it. The heat drained out of her face. "That bitch," she whispered. For she'd bet her entire life the woman had been one of Morgana's friends, and Sebastian's tormentors.

And now he was out there in the gardens alone, and that uneasy feeling she'd been having for the past half hour suddenly made sense. Despite the way he'd locked her out of his mind, his emotions had been leaking through his shields. *That* was what made her skin itch.

Whatever the strange woman might claim, Sebastian wasn't recovering from an interlude. He was violently angry, and.... She felt a mix of a half dozen other emotions; guilt, rage, some horrible, twisting emotion that made her stomach want to roil.

She had to find him.

Cleo pushed through the doors, standing on the terrace and staring out into the night. Lantern-light warmed the garden, but there were a dozen pockets of darkness. Closing her eyes, she felt for him.

There.

And not alone, either.

Scurrying down onto the gravel path, she headed for the fountain where Sebastian and Lord Rathbourne were deep in conversation.

"Ah." Rathbourne spotted her first, a sure sign her husband was emotionally compromised. "I think your lovely wife has come to call, and I'm sure you'd prefer her company to mine."

Sebastian looked over his shoulder, and she was struck by the sharp lines of his face. In the pale moonlight, his eyes looked like black holes. Empty of even a single emotion, though she could feel them through the bond.

Muted now. Not quite as furious. Not quite as murderous. Whatever he'd been speaking about with Rathbourne, it had calmed him a little.

Rathbourne excused himself, giving her a faint nod, and she saw the warning in his eyes as he moved past her, heading back to the ball to give the pair of them a little privacy. *Proceed with caution*, his eyes said.

Cleo waited until he was out of earshot, and then moved closer, the wind stirring her skirts.

"I'm sorry," Sebastian said, in a hollow voice. "I find I'm not very good company tonight. You should go back to the ball. It's your first one. I wouldn't want you to miss it."

Cleo rested a hand lightly on his sleeve, and he stilled. "I couldn't go back," she said. "I wouldn't enjoy a moment of it, knowing you were out here, and that she'd hurt you."

"*She?*" He looked dangerous tonight, the moonlight reflecting silver in his eyes.

But she'd never been frightened. This was *her* Sebastian. Despite everything, he'd never scared her, and though he might not love her, he'd protected her against her father and his mother. He'd *sacrificed* himself for her, when his mother kidnapped her.

"I had a moment with a certain woman," Cleo admitted. "Looked like she'd massacred a black swan for tonight's event. She tried to tell me the pair of you had a passionate interlude out here."

Rage blanked his expression. He took an unconscious step toward the house, but Cleo lifted her hand and pressed her fingertips to his cheek. "She hurt you," she whispered. "Somehow. I could feel it through the bond."

"Cleo." He stepped away from her touch, flinching a little. He didn't like to be touched sometimes, and now was clearly one of them. "What did Lady Beaumont say to you? You do know I'd never—"

"I know," she replied dryly, trying to ignore the little rejection. It wasn't personal. He was upset; overwrought over something the woman had said or done. "It seemed a desperate, grasping ploy. I assumed you'd humiliated her, and she wanted to gain back her confidence by trying to trick me into thinking my husband was having an affair. I felt a little sorry for her, to be honest."

"You shouldn't," he said bleakly.

"I know, but...." Cleo toyed with her gloved fingers. "What sort of person lies about such a thing? I have to assume she's a terribly sad woman, with nothing in her life—"

"She's not. She's the sort of woman who'd lie to amuse herself, or to crush your dreams, or simply because she thought it might be some form of retaliation against me. She's a cruel bitch who deserves everything she gets. And the very fact you can feel even the slightest shred of sympathy for her only highlights your good qualities."

"You knew her."

"I don't want to talk about it."

And there was just enough hint of pleading in his voice to make her bite her tongue. Sympathy vanished. If Lady Beaumont had been one of the women who forced him into her bed with the sclavus collar.... Sebastian was right. Some people didn't deserve sympathy.

And it made sense why he didn't want her to touch him right now. She tucked her hands inside the crooks of her elbows. "If you ever do, then you know I will listen.

But for now... why don't we take some time away from the ball?"

"Are you certain you're not going to miss it?"

"There'll be other balls."

"I'm sorry."

"It's not your fault. And it's not the same without you. You seem to think all I care for is the ball, but I wanted to share it with you. This way," Cleo whispered, holding her hand out to him. This time he let her take it, and she led him toward the shadowy gardens, relief flooding through her. Maybe she could make him forget what had happened, just for a moment. "I know you'd never been here at Lord Rathbourne's manor, until the other day. I want to show you something. I think you'll like it."

Julia Camden, Lady Beaumont, circled the ballroom once more, gathering a glass of champagne and pausing by one of the French doors. A pair of figures rippled through the gardens outside; one stark and imposing, carved of shadows, and the other an insipid girl in a ball gown that overwhelmed her insignificant figure.

Julia smiled and brushed her earring, bringing the glittering bracelet she wore up to her mouth, and the spell that lingered there. "They're in the gardens. I doubt he'll return to the ballroom anytime soon, especially now he knows I'm here. I'd suggest you move quickly."

She glided along the wall of French doors, heading for the entrance. She had no intention of greeting that bitch who called herself Prime. It was time to take her leave. Setting the empty glass on a side table, Julia glanced once more at the ballroom: all the glittering lights, the laughter, the gloating smiles of the Prime and her two companions as they greeted some pompous lord or other....

The Prime's smile would soon fade.

Julia sent the footman for her cloak, her gaze alighting on a small glass globe she'd deposited behind a picture frame earlier in the night. There were over a dozen scattered through the house, tiny glowing strands of spell craft glimmering in the light every now and then within them. Lady Rathbourne's static wards shimmered over the manor like a cloak of spider silk, but there were ways to pierce them.

"Give me five minutes to get clear," she whispered once more to her bracelet, smiling at the footman as she tucked an errant curl behind her ear. "Then I'll fire the spell and bring the wards down."

Julia swung her cloak over her shoulder, and gathering her skirts, she strode down the front steps of the house, heading for her carriage. She couldn't wait until Morgana brought her son to heel, because then Julia would get the chance to remind him of everything they'd once shared.

She almost shivered in anticipation.

CHAPTER ELEVEN

THE NIGHT AIR smelled of jasmine and roses.

Cleo led him to a walled garden, tucked near the end of the house. Near enough to still see the lights from the ballroom, and hear the sweet notes of the string quartet, but just far enough away that he felt like he could catch his breath again. Regain his equilibrium.

"I used to come here," she admitted, "whenever I needed to think."

He brushed his fingers against the long-dead bud of a rose. Somebody had neglected to snip the old growth away. The bushes were wild and overgrown, clearly lacking any sort of restraining hand, but he liked the way it felt like they protected the walls, as if to guard this little garden against the outside world. "It's beautiful."

"It reminded me of you." Her voice sounded wistful. "I kept thinking how much you'd enjoy it here. I imagined what it would be like if we rescued Drake, and your mother and the demon were vanquished, and all of us had a chance to catch our breaths. I know you barely know your father, but I thought... it would be nice to get to know him."

She was speaking of a future in which they were married in truth. Playing happy families, and spending time with his brothers and their wives.

"After the last month," he said, instead, "I was hoping to have some time away from the others once this is all done." If it was done. *If* they all survived.

Cleo glanced up from beneath her lashes. "Others? Or Bishop?"

He sighed, and scuffed the back of his hair. "It's been an intense month."

"He wants to teach you."

"He wants to use me to get his—*our*—father back." Sebastian circled the garden, suddenly impatient. "I know you want a family, Cleo, but I don't want you to expect too much. Lord and Lady Rathbourne haven't forgiven me, not entirely, though they're polite enough, and I'm sure Verity and Bishop will be relieved to have their house to themselves again."

She seated herself patiently on the stone bench. "I'm not quite certain which one of us you're trying to convince."

He looked at her sharply.

"It seems your shield isn't quite as impermeable as you'd like to believe," she pointed out, and he tested it immediately. Cleo smiled a little sadly, as if she'd expected it. "Your emotions have been trickling through tonight, though I think I'm more in tune with than you are."

Sebastian stared at her. "What do you mean?"

"If you expect the worst, then you can't ever be disappointed, can you?"

His nostrils flared. *Devil take her.* "I'm not the one lost in dreams that will never happen," he said sharply. "You don't know the world. You've been sheltered and locked away, and say what you will about your father, but he kept you protected, Cleo. You might have seen horrible things in your Visions, but you've never *lived* them."

What else had she sensed through their bond? What would she say if she knew about his ticket to Manhattan? He looked away. *Tell her.*

But he didn't.

It.... It wasn't the right time.

And he wasn't entirely certain if he'd made that decision. The ticket represented a possibility.

A choice, when he'd had so few of them.

Cleo took an uneasy breath. "Is it wrong to want to live in hope? Is it wrong to trust, and believe that things can be better? That there is a home here for me? For us?"

"Us?" he said hoarsely.

And their eyes met.

"I'm sorry," he whispered. More than she could ever know. He squeezed his eyes shut. *I can't give you what you want. I know that.* "We come from two different worlds."

She turned away, her face stricken for a moment. And he felt like the lowest bastard who ever walked the earth.

The cool air made her shiver. Sebastian dragged his coat off, and slid it around her shoulders, his hands resting there.

Cleo looked up in surprise.

"It seems I'm not the only one who's having trouble keeping their emotions to themselves," he murmured. "I never wanted to hurt you."

"I brought you here because I thought you'd like the roses." Her eyes suddenly glimmered, and she blinked a visible tear away. "I just wanted to make you happy."

He drew her into his arms, his hand cradling the base of her skull. "You do."

And it was a shock to realize the words were true. He drew back and gazed down into her face. "It *is* beautiful. And thank you. For bringing me here, and for... trying." His mouth twisted. "I ruin everything."

"I should have known better. She hurt you, and you weren't in the right mood—"

"That's not an excuse."

"Yes, but—"

"No." He turned toward her, and breathed out slowly. "It's no excuse. I don't know how to manage you. I don't know how to *be* a husband. And I don't want to hurt you, but it feels like every time we're in the same room, I inevitably do."

"At least you're willing to be in the same room with me now."

"It wasn't you I was hiding from."

"Now who's the liar?"

Sebastian stepped closer, capturing the lapels of the coat she had over her shoulders. His knuckles brushed together, and he tugged her a little closer, until her skirts pressed against his trousers. "When you speak of dreams it's hard for me, because I've never dared dream. And I can see it. What you speak of." His voice grew heavy with longing that even he heard. "It's like a snow globe, filled with a beautiful scene I can't quite touch, and it fills me with fear, for what if I drop the globe? What if I smash the dream?" His thumb skated over her cheek, as he searched her gaze, hoping she understood what he was trying to say.

"You won't drop the globe." Cleo brushed her cheek against his hand. "I trust you... more than you trust yourself."

He breathed out a laugh. "I ruined your night."

"Lady Beaumont ruined my night," she said, a little fiercely. "And I have a very great desire to have words with her over that."

"Don't," he warned. "She's not the type of woman who'd stop at mere words."

"When I used that particular statement, it wasn't exactly what I meant."

Cleo had always been a warrior when it came to him. "When did you become so fierce?"

"When I realized I had something to fight for. Why don't we start the night over again?" she suggested.

"How do we do that?"

Cleo looked up at the stars. "You tell me I look beautiful. Indeed, you're quite welcome to tell me such a thing every day if you feel like it."

"You look beautiful," he said, looking down at her upturned face. His voice softened. "You look like everything I've ever dreamed about."

"And you—" She paused for a moment, as if sorting through her words. "—seem a rather intriguing gentleman."

"You came for the ball," he said.

"It's my first. My father never allowed me to attend the balls. But... I always dreamed about them." A soft smile graced her lips, her eyes staring into the distance as if she saw something he didn't. "I used to imagine I was some sort of princess, and a handsome prince would sweep me off my feet and insist on taking all of my dances."

"And is the night living up to your expectations?"

"No princes. No dancing. But it's been quite lovely, and I guess I must grow up someday and shed such dreams."

Silence fell between them.

The night was still, the gardens awash in lantern-light and mage globes.

He didn't quite know what came over him, but Sebastian cleared his throat, as strains of a waltz began to creep from the ballroom. "May I have this dance?"

Those beautiful brown eyes widened, but it was her hesitation that made the muscles in his gut clench. Cleo was brave and bold, but he'd been pushing her away for too long. Done too well at keeping the distance between them, and now he could see the wariness written all over her face.

"No expectations, Cleo," he whispered, holding out his hand. "No promises. I just want to dance with you. Just once. Why not celebrate the Ascension together? Fulfill at least one of your dreams?"

He could do this, at least.

"All right," she whispered, and shrugged out of his coat. The silk of her gloves slid over his hands, and she stepped toward him. "Just once."

Some distant part of him knew this was a mistake. Especially if he intended to grant her an annulment. Sebastian drew her into his grasp, his thighs pressed against her skirts. Cleo didn't quite fit against him—she was half a foot shorter than he—but somehow it worked.

It felt so right.

And he knew in that moment a part of him longed for something more between them.

More than sex. More than longing. Forever, perhaps, if he could dare believe it.

Music whispered against their skin. Sebastian swept her in a slow circle, taking the lead firmly. Cleo's steps were hesitant, as if she wasn't entirely certain what she was doing, but she gave herself into his hands, and somehow it was as if they'd been dancing together for years. Her trust in him echoed his in her. He'd never felt this way before.

How long since he'd looked at someone and known they would never betray him? How many years had passed since that first crippling betrayal from his mother turned his world to a landscape of enemies?

Being free of the sclavus collar had felt like he could breathe for the first time in years, but it wasn't until this moment he realized he hadn't truly been living. He'd merely been putting one wary step in front of the other, trying to work out this new world he'd been thrust into, and keeping the one anchor point he had at arm's length.

Until now.

The heat of her body drew him like a moth to flame as he swirled her in a graceful pirouette. Cleo shot him a delighted smile, her entire face lighting up as they came back together, a breathless laugh escaping her lips.

Not for her a lifetime of wariness. She embraced each moment as if it might be her last, or as if she'd never been burned, when he knew she had. Her bravery made his throat feel dry. In so many ways, she was stronger than he, for she too bore the brunt of years of neglect, and yet *she* was the one flourishing, when he was barely holding his head above the floodwaters.

And somehow, simply having her in his arms felt like the world opened up before him. An endless proposition of hope, if he only dared take it.

Each step felt effortless, as if he'd been born to do this. Or perhaps, been born for her arms.

What was he doing?

Creating dreams....

But were they her dreams? Or his?

"You dance very well," Cleo whispered, as if she didn't want to break the spell between them.

Her words were like a dash of icy water to his face. His grip on her tightened. "Morgana insisted I learn. My body was always a weapon for her to use, to entice her allies with."

Sympathy flooded through him along the bond they shared. He closed his eyes, feeling the press of her in his arms.

"I'm sorry," she whispered.

Perhaps it was time to let go of the past?

"I'm not," he admitted, slowly opening his eyes. Cleo's heart-shaped face sprang into being; the center of his world. "For then I wouldn't be here. With you. I wouldn't be able to do this—"

He sent her whirling beneath his arm. Once. Twice. A breathless dervish that swam back into his arms, her skirts wrapping around her legs. A gasp of shocked delight escaped her, lantern light gleaming on the gilded curls that tumbled down her back.

Sebastian smiled. "Nor this."

And he bent her back over his arm, her body wilting like a lily, and his lips devastatingly close to the smooth skin rising from her bodice.

Cleo laughed, trying to return to her upright position, but something in him couldn't step back. Her hands slid up his collar, and then their faces were but an inch apart, and he tugged her tightly against his chest as he slowly drew her upright.

The thrill of her heartbeat seemed to pound in time with his. The music in the distance softened. Or perhaps he was no longer focusing on it, lost in the allure of her rosy lips.

He hadn't dared kiss her since that night at Malachi Gray's.

And the urge to do so was suddenly ferocious.

Cleo's laughter died, her breath catching as if she felt it too.

And Sebastian eddied to a gentle halt, both arms around her waist. The waltz played on in the distance, but he was breathless with wanting her, and intoxicated by the scent of the roses she'd found for him.

"Was your first dance to your liking?" He needed to know.

"It was better than I ever expected."

He lowered his face toward hers, his hands sliding up her sides to cup her face between them. Cleo sucked in a sharp breath, staying still. His thumbs stroked the sides of her face.

The music ground to a halt. Sebastian could barely breathe. "Cleo...."

Perhaps his problem wasn't trying to stay away from her, or resisting the feelings she incited within him.

He no longer felt dirty. Cleo had cleansed the taint from his skin, and maybe, just maybe, he could do this. He captured her cheek, lifting her chin even as he lowered his mouth to hers. Their lips brushed, her hand coming to rest, hesitantly, on his chest.

The first time he'd kissed her, he'd almost been overwhelmed by the sensation of it. He'd not had a chance to savor it. But now.... His tongue pressed against her lips, parting them. One hand slid to her waist. Cleo's breath caught, and he could taste the sweet, champagne taste of her tongue as she lightly caressed his own.

It wasn't the same as the night at Malachi Gray's. Neither of them were affected by magic. And this wasn't a first kiss, hesitant and unsure.

This was raw hunger. Sheer need. A gentle exploration of Cleo and the art of kissing. He wanted to make it good for her, but the second their tongues touched it no longer mattered.

He forgot where he was. He forgot everything but the feel of his wife beneath his hands, her arms sliding around his neck as her body wilted against him. Suddenly it wasn't enough. Heat stirred in his cock. He captured a handful of her bustle, dragging her against him, and plunged his tongue inside her mouth. It felt as though the two of them became one, and everything around them receded until he was lost in the touch and taste of her. Cleo. Cleo, the girl who'd saved his life. The girl who'd shown him what trust was, and invited him into another world. One that both terrified him and enticed him. He could almost see himself pressing her down onto the sheets in his cold bed, dragging the silk of her night-robe open....

The crush of her breasts against his chest dragged his mind to darker, hungrier places, imagining his lips on her bare flesh.... To tongue her nipples like this, teasing her, igniting her....

Mercy.

Sebastian's hand fisted in her skirts, though he didn't drag them up. He wanted to. Sweet mother of night, how he wanted to. His fist clenched.

But he needed to break this spell, and he needed to break it now. Before he crossed the point of no return. He broke from her mouth, breathing hard. "You make me forget myself."

You make me forget everything.

Cleo looked up with passion-drugged eyes. Her soft smile sent an arrow of need straight through him, but he was captured by the poignant thought that he never wanted to forget what this particular smile looked like. "Not entirely a terrible thing."

It brought a laugh to his lips. "Someone's pleased with themselves."

"Considering how often you've held me at bay, it's nice to know you find me difficult to resist at times too." She bit her lip, those dark lashes shuttering over her eyes.

Sebastian slid a finger under her chin, insisting on looking at her. "Impossible to resist," he told her hoarsely.

If she only knew....

But there was no time to tell her, for that was when the screaming began.

CHAPTER TWELVE

'There are many types of hell spawn one can drag from the Shadow Dimensions, but imps are the worst. A vile plague, and difficult to kill... though not impossible.'

—Lady Eberhardt

SEBASTIAN BROKE AWAY from her.

Cleo drew a ragged breath, her head turning unerringly toward the manor, her body a mixture of cooling desire and sudden conflicting fear. Every muscle in Sebastian's body was hard, a look of predatory intensity upon his face.

"What was that?" she whispered.

Light flared; red light. Glass exploded out through the French doors that lined the terrace, and then the screaming started again.

Attack. They were under attack.

"Stay here," Sebastian said, but Cleo caught his wrist as he turned toward the manor.

"Are you daft?" she demanded. "You don't know what's happening!" Neither of them did. "We're both barely trained."

Indecision flickered over his face. "This is my mother's work. I'll stake my life upon it."

Only Morgana would dare attack the majority of the Order at Ianthe's Ascension Ball. Perhaps as payback for their theft of the wand.

And that was enough to break any restraining hold she might have held upon him. Sebastian despised his mother more than anything.

Cleo grabbed fistfuls of her skirts and scurried after him. "Then I'm coming with you."

"You're safer out here—"

"Oh yes, so much safer," she drawled, "considering we don't know what is happening, where the attack is coming from, and just who precisely is crawling through these gardens. Or what."

Sebastian paused and glared down at her.

"We're safer together," she pointed out. "We're a bonded pair. My powers run to divination, but you could use my strength...." Cleo winced. It wasn't as though he needed more power. "I just.... I'm not leaving you. I'm not letting you walk in there alone. And that's final."

She hadn't liked it the other night at all, being sent off with Verity.

The clench of his jaw dared to refute her, but he gave a sudden brief nod. "Keep beside me at all times. I'll protect you."

"I do know how to ward," she retorted, scurrying after him once again.

"Aye." Sebastian pressed his back to the stone of the terrace, his voice dropping to a whisper. "But do you know how to kill?"

It made her flinch.

"*I* do," he said, in that same, deadly soft voice. "And if my mother is behind this, then neither of us can afford to hesitate."

Cleo swallowed. "Understood."

An errant streak of pure power blew out all the windows above them. Sebastian flung his arm over her head, pressing her into the stonework, even as Cleo crafted a ward around them.

"To me!" someone cried. "To me!"

"Over here!" yelled another voice, and this time she recognized Lucien.

"We have to help them," Cleo gasped.

Grabbing her by the hand, Sebastian hauled her through the greenery, her skirts snagging on the pruned rosebushes. The ballroom was a mess of shadow and flickering red light. Mage globes, clearly, and the red color meant that someone wasn't mucking about. Red was the color of war; of death.

"Stand firm!" Ianthe called, and Cleo caught a glimpse of the Prime gathering dozens of sorcerers to her side.

They stood back to back, but there were pockets of them scattered all through the ballroom, which was overrun with imps. The hell spawn must have been dragged straight out of the Shadow Dimensions, and the sheer number of them....

"My gods," Cleo whispered. "Who could conjure so many imps?"

"The demon," Sebastian replied grimly, flinging his hands wide.

A lash of power sent half a dozen imps tumbling across the polished timber floors.

One leered at them and leapt from the balcony above them, its claws flared wide. Cleo formed a ward about them and it hit with a splat, sliding down the amorphous bubble.

"Drop the ward," Sebastian bellowed, and she did, just as he sent another sheer wave of force slamming through a pack of imps.

Black blood stained their bronze skins. One hissed at them, its long tail lashing back and forth like a cat's. Together she and Sebastian moved through the room, alternating between attacking and shielding. Cleo was breathless by the time she reached a small pocket of frightened apprentices, but Sebastian only seemed buoyed by the fight.

His eyes gleamed a merciless silver, and sparks spat from his rings as he wielded his sorcery like a brute scalpel. Imps were nearly impossible to kill, but he was succeeding. Ripping them apart like rag dolls with sheer force, his head turning to and fro as if he sought something.

Morgana. A shiver ran through Cleo. Seeing him like this was a brutal punch of truth. He'd told her a thousand times he was dangerous; she'd never truly believed it. Not *her* Sebastian. Her quiet, genteel husband, who took such care of his precious roses, and hid his raw pain behind a cool, emotionless mask.

She might not be able to see new Visions, but her old ones haunted her. Especially the one she called London's doom: an enormous shadow of rippling darkness that took over London, sweeping away every light that lit the city, and leaving nothing but ruins.

She'd thought it was the demon, once upon a time.

Now, watching her husband, she wasn't entirely certain.

But: *The key to defeating the darkness lies with Sebastian.*

She had to maintain hope.

"This way," Cleo whispered, gathering a pair of young girls who hadn't even earned their first apprentice ring. She didn't take her eyes off him, however. "Sebastian, we need to join the others."

Those silver eyes glittered. "Go," he said. "I'll join you in a moment—"

"No." Cleo stood her ground. "There are other sorcerers here who need help. *Your* help. Morgana can wait."

Grabbing the first young woman's hand, she pushed them ahead of her, warding the three of them. "Through the door! Into the gardens!"

The young girls screamed as every window along the sidewall smashed into little shards, one by one.

"Run!"

A static buzzing echoed in Cleo's ears. Her face went numb, then hot with sudden heat. She didn't understand what was happening until a wave of force smashed through her half-tended ward and sent both her and Sebastian sprawling.

"Cleo!" Something grabbed hold of her, and then she was slammed against a warm body, the pair of them tumbling head over heels.

It finally ended, and Cleo sucked in a sharp breath, looking up from where she was shielded by Sebastian's arms. Everything hurt. She was lying atop him, and half his coat was melted, stinking of burned wool.

Ears ringing, Cleo looked up.

"Hello, my sweet, sweet son," said a hooded figure who stepped out of her crowd of imps, reaching up to draw her hood back.

Morgana's black hair was heavily streaked with white, and the last Cleo had seen of her, the woman had been crippled, but now her stride was firm. The demon must have healed her.

Sebastian staggered to his feet, dragging Cleo with him. He'd been a vicious whirlwind of sorcery, obliterating large swathes of imps with a wave of his hand. But the second he saw his mother, his powers seemed to wane, turning into chaotic golden threads around him.

Emotion was his weakness.

It always would be. And when it came to his mother, the storm within him was too volatile to control.

Shoving Cleo behind him, he held both hands splayed, plunging the room into a frigid environment as he sucked in enormous amounts of energy. *No!* Cleo breathed through a raw throat, her heated breath steaming in the suddenly icy air. *Sebastian*. She tried to say it, to warn him, but her voice wasn't working. Catching hold of an enormous Chinese vase, she tried to stay upright against the sudden draining whirlpool.

"You," he spat, and lashed out, lightning sparking from his fingertips.

Morgana merely smiled, and waved it away. "Your father sends his regards."

"You mean the demon in his body," Sebastian snarled, and enveloped his mother with a wave of pure darkness.

A storm of force lashed back in return, and Sebastian went down on one knee, his wards blown behind him as Morgana stepped forward, her red skirts whisking around her legs.

"*Get up*," Cleo whispered, crouched behind her vase.

"Tsk, tsk," Morgana said, circling him slowly. Light flickered off the seven rings she wore on her fingers; a sign of just how far she'd progressed through the Order ranks in the past. "Someone's forgetting all the lessons he's clearly been taught. Did you think you could defeat *me*?"

Sebastian flung another wave of pure force at her, which Morgana parted with ease. The wind rippled past her, sending her skirts and hair flying, but she responded with something that made him cry out and fall backwards, scratching at his arms, his face, his eyes—

"What's wrong, dearest?" Morgana mocked. "Can't you focus on your weaves? Is it *difficult* to concentrate right now? It's so tempting to fall back on Expression, to forget everything you've clearly tried to learn. Come on, Sebastian, show me *your wards*."

Sebastian screamed as his mother made a claw with her fingers, his body arching obscenely on the floor.

A wave of bile rose in Cleo's throat. *Come on. Get up!*

But he wasn't getting up, and Morgana was tying him in knots, all his skill evaporating in the wake of his emotionally compromised power.

Morgana drew her hand back, giving him an instant of relief, before she threw a vicious blue mage globe at him. Sebastian rolled to the side, narrowly avoiding it, his face tinted blue and his eyes black as the globe exploded, pitting the marble where he'd been.

Cleo's thigh muscles bunched. She couldn't simply stand there and watch. No matter how drained she felt.

But she couldn't defeat a powerful sorceress like this.

Unless...

Farshaw's book sprang to mind. *Some say those disciples of the Light discipline of sorcery are the weakest, with their gifts tending toward Elemental magic, Healing, and Divination. But one forgets the most dangerous weapon of all: a skilled practitioner of the divination arts can see the future. And if that practitioner learns how to future-walk—to see ten seconds, twenty... or even a minute in advance—while still maintaining their grip in the current timeline, then they are well nigh invincible.*

Cleo wasn't trained, but she knew how to open her Third Eye, and she knew how to see the future. Not in

Visions anymore, but in odd flashes, in Premonition. Could she both see *and* react?

"All that power," Morgana whispered. "Wasted. It should have been mine."

And she drew her hand back for another strike. A red globe formed, Cleo's heart clenching in her chest in horror.

"No!" Cleo yelled, sliding to a halt between her fallen husband and his vicious mother. She wrenched back some of the power he'd stolen from her, fairly thrumming with it. "I won't let you hurt him."

"You're beginning to become something of a nuisance, girl." Morgana's eyes glittered as she flicked the battle globe directly toward Cleo.

Cleo flung her arms up, crossing them at the wrists, and her ward sprang into being; a shiny, flickering bubble that enveloped her and Sebastian. She'd been working on her wards with Ianthe in the past month, and Morgana's mage globe shattered against it, violent red sparks showering across the marble floor. The force made her stagger back a step.

Then she was staring at her adversary across the blistered ruins of the ballroom, her ward amorphous and flexible around her—but still intact.

Morgana's mouth fell open.

"Sebastian's not the only one who's been learning new tricks," Cleo warned. And whereas he might be purely offensive in his magic, she'd revealed a heretofore-unknown ability to defend herself.

Open yourself to probability, Quentin Farshaw's book had said.

Open your Third Eye.

Cleo bloomed like a flower, power flowing through the tenuous soul-bond between her and Sebastian, only this time it flowed toward her. The world suddenly changed, flat lines flowing from almost every surface as if she could see through distance. Golden threads glimmered over everything. An aura of soft white energy surrounded every human in the room.

She pushed *forward*. Five seconds forward perhaps.

As if in a trance, she saw Morgana unleash a shining net of golden strands that Cleo knew would destroy her if they hit.

Part the weaves, instinct told her.

And then she was back in the moment as Morgana drew her hand back to send her deathly net directly toward Cleo—

—who held both hands together, slicing apart the core of Morgana's magic network, in some method she'd never used before.

On either side of her, imps fell screaming, tangled in the remains of the treacherous web.

And Morgana's eyes widened.

The next assault appeared in her trancelike state, and Cleo countered it before it had even begun. It was so easy, so brutal, to stay several seconds ahead of her opponent, a sharp ache beginning to form behind her right eye like the insistent stab of an ice pick slowly being driven into her brain as she neutralized every single one of Morgana's assaults.

She couldn't keep it up forever. Seeing through time was a heavy burden in itself, let alone manipulating spells as well.

But neither could Morgana, and Sebastian was slowly getting to his feet behind Cleo.

"You little snake!" Morgana hissed, her hands falling at her sides as she breathed hard. But she looked perplexed. "You're an apprentice!"

"I warned you once," Cleo whispered, feeling something hot slide down over her lip, saltiness flooding her mouth, "that I could see the future—"

"He took your Visions from you!"

Her own father. Cleo blinked, the world going a little blurry. "As Drake said, nobody can take another's magical gift from them. Not without sundering their ties to sorcery completely. My gift is still there. I just have to find a way... a way to unblock it...."

"*Cleo?*" She could hear the words distantly. Feel someone shaking her.

See the imps starting to flee.

Fury danced in Morgana's eyes, but Cleo blinked and then there were two images before her; Morgana slowly backing away, even as her reflection started to flee.

"Cleo!" It was Sebastian, looking down at her with frightened eyes.

She was on her back on the floor. She couldn't remember falling.

"It's all right," she whispered, or thought she did. The world was starting to blur. She could see a hundred images of him, reflecting into the future. That ice pick was working its way into her brain.

"You little fool, what did you do?"

She thought she was going to vomit.

Then Ianthe was there, sweeping a cool hand over Cleo's brow. "Close your Third Eye. Now, Cleo!"

A thousand Ianthes.

A thousand Sebastians.

"I don't think... I can...."

Then a surge of coolness washed through her as Ianthe brought peaceful, blessed darkness to Cleo's fractured world.

CHAPTER THIRTEEN

"WHAT'S WRONG WITH her?" Sebastian demanded, placing his unconscious wife on her bed in Rathbourne Manor. "She's not waking." Panic swept through him. "She hurt herself."

Hurt herself to save you.

Gods, would he ever stop bringing destruction down upon those he cared for?

Ianthe twitched the curtains shut. "I've sent for help. There's not a great deal I can do at this moment." Her cool face momentarily looked younger, the mantle of power slipping just enough to let him see her indecision. "Divination isn't one of my gifts."

Lucien eased a hand over Cleo's brow. "Yes, but it's one of mine." He winced. "She's overtaxed herself, I think. Severely. I can sense the strain around her aura and her mental faculties. Eleanor? You have divination gifts too."

Sebastian had been ignoring her until now—he still couldn't look her in the eye—but Eleanor Ross sat on the edge of the bed and took Cleo's hand in hers. "She's still projecting something."

"Will she recover?" Sebastian demanded, pacing by the bed.

Lucien looked up flatly. "I don't know."

"What she did is extraordinary," Eleanor breathed. "I've only ever seen one other person display even the slightest gift like this. She was future-walking, and it's a dangerous gift, to See one timeline, and react in another. She's clearly untrained too, which is why she couldn't draw back."

"This happened because of me," he said hoarsely.

The three of them looked at him sharply.

Merde. Sebastian's nails dug into his palms. "I wasn't strong enough to face my mother. I thought I was. I thought I could destroy her." And in trying to do so, he'd forgotten everything he'd been taught in the past month. The second he'd seen Morgana, his careful attempts to harness his will and work his sorcery through ritual and sigils evaporated, and were obliterated by the rash power of Expression.

All he'd dreamed about in the last month was facing Morgana and making her pay for everything she'd done—to him and to others. He'd spent long restless hours staring at the canopy of his bed, planning exactly how to defeat her.

And the second he saw her, it all went wrong.

"Can you heal her?" he croaked, sliding his hand over Cleo's pale fingers.

"There's nothing to heal," Ianthe said sadly. "Nothing but rest, and hope—"

"There is one person we might be able to turn to," Eleanor murmured, meeting the Prime's eyes.

"Who?" Sebastian demanded.

"Madrigal Brown," Ianthe replied grimly.

"I don't know her." And while he'd do anything to save Cleo, the expressions on both their faces concerned him. "Neither of you like this idea. Why?"

"This information doesn't leave this room," Lucien murmured.

Sebastian gave him a dangerous look from beneath his lashes. "Who would I even mention it to?"

"Good point." Lucien sighed. "Madrigal's the head of the Sicarii. While you might not know her, she knows who you are. She was the woman who stood against Ianthe the night of Ascension in order to try and gain the seat of Prime. The moment you walked into the gathering with a demon inside you, she saw something in her future that made her resign. Ianthe won by default, which means you cost her the chance to be Prime. She's no friend of yours."

An assassin. And not just any assassin, but the head of the Order's Sicarii. "Does she know Bishop?"

"Yes."

He looked down at Cleo, pale and still upon the bed. His heart twisted in his chest. "What will it cost me?"

"Probably nothing," Lucien admitted, but there was a hesitancy to his voice.

Sebastian looked up. "What will it cost you?"

It was Ianthe who answered. "Goddess knows. A favor. My soul. I'll pay the price, however. Cleo is dear to me."

He didn't know what to say. "Thank you."

Ianthe's cool gaze settled upon him. She slowly nodded. "I'll assume you'll stay here with her?"

"Of course."

"We'd best see to the ballroom. Cleo's not the only one who took an injury," Lucien murmured.

Ianthe looked grim. "I hate owing that bitch a favor." She swept toward the door. "Let me go send Jeremy to beg Madrigal for help. Then I have to make sure everyone else is all right downstairs."

The door closed behind them, and Sebastian paced by the bed. He could feel Eleanor's steady gaze upon him.

"It's not your fault," she said.

"I shouldn't have confronted her—"

"I'm not talking about your wife."

Sebastian turned toward her helplessly. Eleanor slowly levered herself to her feet, limping toward him with her cane in hand.

"Your mother was going to cut out my heart," she said. "If you hadn't defied her, I would be dead."

"I cost you your magic." And Morgana had only captured her, because Eleanor had tried to save him from his mother's collar.

"It's still there inside me," Eleanor said simply. "I have a long path of healing in front of me, but I will be a sorcerer again. And I have a chance to try, because of you. You should stop blaming yourself for the actions of others."

Eleanor leaned up on her toes, lurching unsteadily against him as she lost her balance, and pressed a kiss to his cheek. "You remind me of your father, very much so. He always bore the weight of the world on his shoulders too." Lowering herself to the floor, she patted his arm sadly. "He loved you, even though he never knew you."

"Until it was too late," Sebastian whispered.

Eleanor merely smiled. "It's never too late. I still have hope I will see him again. The demon has him for now, but we'll get him back. I know we will."

He only wished he had half her confidence.

Three hours later, Madrigal Brown swept inside Cleo's chambers like a woman going to an afternoon soiree, rather than one who'd been roused from her bed at dawn.

Sebastian looked up from his seat at Cleo's side, his hands curled over the carved arms of the chair, though he'd been warned not to make any sudden moves.

The assassin looked no more dangerous than a Pomeranian. A fox stole was draped around her throat, and as she entered the bedchambers, she began to unpin her broad-brimmed green hat.

She had to be sixty if she was a day, and the chip of marble in her Order ring indicated she belonged to the Light Arts, which were usually wholesome and beneficial. Divination gifts often pushed one into the Light Arts. However, Madrigal's gift of Foresight made her a formidable opponent, Ianthe had warned, and she'd been the other contender to take Ianthe's position as Prime until he'd entered the fray, his body a vessel for the demon.

Madrigal examined him as she tugged off her lace gloves. "The last time I saw you, your eyes were pure black."

"The last time I saw you," he countered, as he'd been aware of what happened when the demon used him as a vessel, even if he couldn't *stop* it, "you turned white as snow, and surrendered your claim upon the mantle of Prime."

Madrigal's lips thinned, and she palmed her gloves, a considering light in her eyes. "You cost me a great deal that day."

"You could have confronted me," he replied. "The way Ianthe did."

"The problem with Foresight, however, is that one can see their death coming. I wasn't ready to greet it. Now"—Madrigal turned to the bed, running a mercurial eye over Cleo's prone body—"what have we here?"

Sebastian rested his hip on the edge of the bed, and curled Cleo's pale hand in his as he told Madrigal what had happened.

"The girl was countering all Morgana's weaves?" Madrigal reached out and pressed a thin, paper-skinned hand to Cleo's forehead. "Oh, the little fool. She's overreached. Someone has learned the basics of how to future-walk without taking the time to crawl."

"Can you help her?"

Madrigal brushed a soft curl off Cleo's forehead. "And why should I?"

Their eyes met. This was the side of human nature he knew well. "To avoid having me as an enemy," he suggested coldly, before letting his gaze rest on Cleo's heart-shaped face. He couldn't feel the lively flicker of her energy against the shield he maintained against her. He'd even dropped the shield several times, trying to reach for her down the bond they shared, but there was... nothing there. A hint of her, perhaps, the bond still in place, but... distant.

"There are very few things in this world I hold dear," he whispered. "My wife is the one person who I would kill for. Die for. She's the only reason I'm here, working with Lord Rathbourne and Bishop to save my father."

"Bishop?" Madrigal murmured.

"My brother." He looked up. "And one of your Sicarii, I believe."

Seconds ticked out. Madrigal peered through him, almost as if she were seeing something else. He'd seen that look on Cleo's face often enough to know she probably was. Slowly her vision came back into focus, locking on his face. "I'll help her."

"Thank you."

Madrigal's lips pursed. "Do you know how many seconds ahead your wife was projecting?"

"I wouldn't have a clue. It's not something she's done before. I didn't even know she could do it."

"Here." Madrigal reached for him, and Sebastian froze. The last time another woman—aside from his wife—had touched him, he'd suffered a flashback. It hadn't ended well. A surge of nausea washed through him, and he captured her wrist, the leather of his gloves protecting him from touching her skin.

"Don't." Even to his ears, it sounded deadly.

Madrigal flinched back, her eyes widening as if she saw something she didn't like. Skirts swishing, she circled the bed, keeping it between her and him. "Your wife needs energy, and as fond as I am of holding a favor over the Prime's head, she's not having any of mine."

"What do I do?"

"Take her hand." Madrigal cocked her head. "Are you bonded?"

He nodded.

"Then reach for her through the bond...."

Madrigal talked him through the transfer, until Cleo's color had settled and she shifted slightly on the bed.

"She's still lost in the currents, I think," Madrigal murmured. "We have to reach her before it's too late, and drag her back. Overreach like this could destroy some of her gifts."

"How do we get her back?"

"You," Madrigal said. "*You* get her back. You use your bond to reach her, and convince her to return. I'll talk you through it. I can't reach her without you."

"What do I do?" He could sense her gaze upon him. "What is it?"

"There is a great darkness within you." Madrigal curled her hand protectively against her chest. "It's going to destroy you one day."

"Maybe."

Madrigal reached for Cleo once again. "She's the only thing holding your darkness at bay. So I will help her, not you. For all our sakes. For London."

"To find the black queen you need to go back to your past," Quentin Farshaw had told her.

Cleo floated in a world of nothing. She'd spent her nights walking her dreams, trying to remember, but she hadn't found the point in time that he referred to. Yet something felt different now. The second she'd begun to future-walk, something opened up within her, like a long dormant gift had been hiding—or waiting perhaps for the right moment to show itself.

She knew now, how to find what she was looking for.

"Find me the black queen," she whispered, and began sifting back through her past, seeing it flash by in endless years of blindness, until suddenly there was color again.

Black queen, black queen, black queen. She locked on the thought, using it to track her hidden nemesis. Something pulled her back deep into the past, slamming her into a single moment.

Cleo opened her eyes.

She stood like a wraith in the hallway of her father's mansion, many years in the past. Holly decorated the mantle in the sitting room, and the scent of pine needles filled the air. Christmas. He'd never celebrated it. Cleo frowned.

Or had he once?

"Show me the black queen," she whispered, and the tug drew her along the hallway.

The drone of her father's voice began to echo through her mansion. Cleo walked along the marble floors she knew so well, her bare feet flinching at the cold. Winter, judging from the snow on the windowpanes. And December if she were to use the holly as a clue.

But at what point of time?

"*Hecarah di asmosis. Solaris ni tenduin.* Come forth, my lord. Come forth," her father called.

Cleo winced. The language he used hurt her ears. What was he doing?

Light beckoned along the hallway, behind a half-closed door. There was no sign of the servants, though Lord Tremayne sometimes gave them the night off when he was performing his darker works.

Trepidation filled her as she reached for the door. *Black queen, black queen, black queen....* Her heart pounded in time to the words. Seeing this would change everything. She just knew it.

She pushed open the door, finding herself in a cellar that had been fitted out with her father's ritual altar. A hexagram was painted on the floor in blood, and a woman knelt in the center of it in her nightgown, another bloody hexagram painted on her forehead. Her long silvery-blonde hair cascaded down her back, her brows dark in her heart-shaped face.

She could have been Cleo's twin.

Mother. Cleo clapped a hand to her mouth. Her mother had died when she was two, which meant this had to be over twenty years ago. She couldn't remember her mother, and she'd never seen a picture of her, thanks to the blindfold.

She looks like me....

Lord Tremayne circled the altar with a knife in one hand, and a grimoire in the other. He kept droning the words in that hideous language, until something began to appear above the hexagram.

Silence chilled the room. Tremayne's eyes lit up when he saw the shimmer in the air. "Come forth!"

A heart of darkness began to form above him, turning into a malevolent black cloud, and the bloody rune in the middle of Tremayne's head suddenly glowed.

The black cloud swirled over Lord Tremayne's head, and he opened his arms wide, looking up and staring into the heart of the cloud. "One night I grant thee," he boomed. "Use me, my lord. Let me beget the child that was prophesized."

The black mist began to swirl, then plunged down, entering her father's mouth and ears. He roared in pain, his body jerking, and then the mist was gone, and he froze.

Cleo's mother opened her eyes. "My lord?"

Tremayne grasped the silver cup on the altar with both hands, lifting it to his lips and gulping it down. Blood dripped down the sides of his cheeks, and droplets of it dripped off his chin and spattered on his white shirt.

"Tremayne? Did it work?" her mother whispered.

He slowly lowered the cup, and his eyes were pure black. Whatever this was, it was no longer her father.

"Give me my child," her mother whispered, tugging at the drawstring of her nightgown. "Give me the child he cannot."

Tremayne went to her, capturing her chin and lifting it harshly. "You little fool. Do you have any idea what you have wrought?"

"You have one night," her mother cried. "Use it, or begone."

He tore her mother's nightgown clean down the center, shoving her onto her back. Her mother cried out, fisting a hand in Tremayne's shirt as she drew him down over her....

Cleo whirled away from the room, slamming the door behind her as her mother cried out again. Her ears were ringing. What did this mean? What had her father summoned into himself?

A demon, said the little voice of intuition inside her.

Her mother....

The black queen?

No. No. She'd died. She'd died when Cleo was two, in a carriage accident. Her father had always said....

Her father was known to lie.

"Cleo?" a woman whispered. "Are you there? Can you hear me?"

She twisted and turned. Something was pinning her down. Hands upon her wrists. Her heart started racing. The vision vanished and she found herself in the dream plane again, the skies as dark as midnight. Not a blank canvas, but one filled with possibility that could take her anywhere she wanted to go.

"You're safe," the woman added. "Your husband is here. He's holding you down so you don't thrash. Can you hear me?"

She stared up at a night sky with a thousand stars. One of them flickered a little brighter. Not stars, but souls, she realized, as she drew nearer. The bigger one flamed into a beacon. *Sebastian.*

"I can hear you," she whispered.

"I've got her." A cool palm rested on her forehead. "Come back, Cleo. Come back before you burn yourself out."

Tears leaked wetly from her eyes. She'd finally found the black queen. And it hurt. It hurt so much.

Why did she leave me?

"Hush," Sebastian murmured, drawing her into his arms. "I'll never leave you. I promise."

Cleo blinked back into the real world, and found her wet face pressed against his shoulder. Her ruined ball gown was crushed up between them, and his coat was smoke-stained and scarred from the battle downstairs. How much time had passed? They'd won, hadn't they? She pressed her hand to his chest, feeling the steady thud of his heart.

"We won," Sebastian whispered, as if he were sensing her thoughts. "Morgana and her coterie of sorcerers fled. Only thirteen sorcerers died, and the rest are being treated by the Order's healers. Ianthe's taking charge."

None of it mattered.

She saw again the demon enter her father, and shivered. *Give me the child he cannot....*

What did it mean? A demon... sired me. There was a horrible, horrible feeling inside her. She'd seen something about this in Farshaw's book, she was certain of it.

She cried for a long time, feeling the stroke of his hand down her spine as he rocked her. And then she finally gave in to exhaustion, her forehead slumping against his shoulder, where she could feel the beat of his heart through her palm.

Everything hurt.

Cleo blinked slowly, the intense stab of the afternoon light making her wince. She could barely see.

"I'll draw the curtains," a woman murmured, and then the blaze of light vanished, leaving her able to breathe again.

Cleo tried to sit up, her throat dry and her head thumping.

"Here," a man murmured, his arm sliding behind her, as he pressed a glass of water to her lips.

Sebastian. Cleo nearly choked on the water. "What are you doing here?"

Watching the other woman like a hawk, it seemed. He eased the glass away from her, his body shockingly warm. "You've been sleeping for nearly three days," he said tightly. "I've been trying to call you back to me, through the bond."

A bond that was intricately stronger, she noted, brushing against it... and flinching. "*Ouch.*"

"Yes, 'ouch,'" said the older woman who pushed away from the windows, her silver hair swept up into an elegant chignon. "You foolish child. Where on earth did you learn to future-walk? Have you *any* idea of how dangerous it was to blindly go forth, without learning even the basics?"

"Yes, I knew how dangerous it was!" Cleo retorted. "I didn't have a choice. I'm no match for Morgana, and none of my powers are offensive ones—at least, not yet. I was trying to protect my husband."

That earned her a steady look. Oho, Sebastian didn't like that, did he? Cleo glared back at him. "Which I wouldn't have had to do, if he'd been thinking rationally, rather than trying to murder his mother the first chance he got." She flung back the blankets, realized she was wearing a thin cotton nightgown, and tugged them back over herself again, blushing fiercely.

Sebastian leaned back in his armchair, his arms crossed over his chest, as if to dare her to cast her blankets aside again. No doubt as payback for her comment about his mother.

Oh, yes, my dear. Do grant me a glimpse of those shapely calves....

Cleo looked between the two of them, touching her temples lightly. Was that her thought? Or was she actually hearing his? It felt like their auras brushed against each other, now he'd lowered the shields he'd kept up against her. "Who are you?"

"Madrigal Brown," the woman said, leaning on her cane like a silver-haired hawk. "Sorcerer of the Seventh Level, Foreseer, and Mistress of the Sicarii."

Sicarii? The heat washed out of Cleo's face. The assassins protected the Order and the Prime—at all costs.

And it suddenly terrified her that they might see Sebastian as a threat.

"Madrigal's the only other Foreseer in the Empire," Sebastian murmured, his hand coming to rest over hers.

Almost... protectively.

"She's not going to hurt you," he pointed out. "She and I have reached an agreement. She's going to help teach you how to control your powers."

Yes, but what about him? He'd let a demon use his body, after all.

And you have some part of the demon within you. She went cold and locked down her end of the bond.

Sebastian looked at her sharply.

"I have been told you've not truly been taught your sorcery. You've never truly served an apprenticeship, though technically you wear three rings. I am offering to grant you a true apprenticeship, where I will teach you everything I know."

Cleo looked between them. A true apprenticeship? Her father had taught her... enough. But what if there was more? "What would I have to do?" There was too much ahead of them... "I can't. Not now."

But she wanted to. She wanted very desperately to learn everything this woman knew.

"I know what's coming," Madrigal said stiffly. "I caught some edge of your Visions, and I've seen my own. Something dark settles over London. And if you survive it, then come and find me."

This was a deal she could accept. Cleo nodded.

"Firstly," Madrigal said, with an arched brow, "I want to know how you learned to future-walk."

"I'll tell you... on one condition," Cleo said, not forgetting who this woman was.

Again that eyebrow.

"You swear on your power never to raise a hand against Sebastian," she told the other woman fiercely. "No matter what you think is best for the Order."

"She's not going to hurt me—"

Cleo hushed him with a fierce glare. "You don't know that. She's Sicarii, Sebastian."

"*She* is standing right here," Madrigal said dryly. "And *she* will promise not to make a move against your husband, unless he makes one against me."

It would have to do. "Swear it," Cleo suggested.

"I swear by the Light of my powers not to attack your husband without provocation," Madrigal replied softly, and Cleo felt the power of the oath settle over the room like a heavy blanket.

Everything was hushed. Sorcery dimmed the candlelight, and even the fire in the hearth flickered.

Then it was gone, the weight suddenly lifted.

"There was a book," Cleo muttered, gesturing to her dressing robe. "Could you fetch that for me?"

Sebastian returned with her robe, and helped tie it on.

Madrigal's eyes glittered. "Which book?'"

"I can show you," Cleo promised, slipping from under her blankets. Her knees shook as she stood, her stomach tight and dry. Hollow. "But first... I need to refresh myself, and eat something."

CHAPTER FOURTEEN

"QUENTIN FARSHAW'S *Sidestep through Time*," Madrigal breathed, turning the book over in her hands. "The full copy.... Sweet goddess, it looks like a hand-written version of it. It must be the original!"

Cleo rested by the fireplace in the sitting room, with an audience this time. Ianthe and Lucien had gathered to see how she was feeling, and although he'd vanished long enough to bring her soup, Sebastian was tethered to her side as though he'd rather be no place else.

It shocked her a little.

Yes, there'd been that kiss. Several kisses now. And a dance. But his sheer attentiveness since the ball led her to believe there was something else going on within him.

He'd barely left her side.

She didn't know what to think. Or how to feel about it.

It was one thing to get her hopes up, quite another to see them dashed. And she'd been brave once, before she lost her world: her father, tyrant though he was; her home; her Visions... everything, in reality. Could she risk her heart, only to lose it again?

Sebastian shot her a quizzical look, almost as though he'd caught the edge of her thoughts, and Cleo flushed.

"The book is important?" Ianthe mused.

Madrigal finally seemed to realize where she was. "Important? It's been missing for centuries, and was named the greatest living treatise on the divination arts." She tuned on Cleo. "How did you get a copy of this?"

"You wouldn't believe me if you tried," she said.

And Madrigal did try to get the truth from her, giving up in pure frustration an hour later, when all Cleo could tell her was that Quentin Farshaw had put it in her hands personally.

"Enough," Sebastian finally said, a dark look upon his brow. "Cleo needs her rest, and I cannot see how this is serving any purpose. You were brought here to help my wife, and you have done so. Her Third Eye is closed. What she needs now is rest."

"I will be back," Madrigal said, peering down her nose at Cleo.

"To train Mrs. Montcalm," Ianthe said coolly, linking her arm through the assassin's.

"Yes," Madrigal murmured. "To train her in the art of future-walking."

Sentenced to a day of bed rest, Cleo succumbed with frustrated grace. If she couldn't get out of bed, then at least she could put the time to good use.

Dragging out *Sidestep Through Time*, and thanking every god she still had a copy, considering the avaricious gleam in

Madrigal's eyes, she set to reading it. She'd managed to snatch a glimpse at a few chapters the other day, but this was the first chance she'd gotten to truly delve inside it.

Instantly she knew she held a book unlike any other. Most sorcerers could rise to the seventh level of the Order of the Dawn Star if they spent many, many years practicing their art, and various Primes and Triad Councilors—the three wise sorcerers who ruled in conjunction with the Prime—had reached perhaps the eighth or ninth level. But Quentin Farshaw had been the *only* sorcerer to ever reach the tenth level.

The tests for the tenth level required one to manipulate time, or to communicate directly with the divine. To prove his task had succeeded, Farshaw had been required to take an object he was only made aware of during the testing period, and return it to some point in the past, with a letter instructing the sorcerer who found it to appear at the precise time and location of the final test with it.

Nobody had expected him to succeed.

Even to this day, some said he hadn't. But she'd seen him vanish into thin air with her own eyes. Farshaw either owned the same skill as Verity—in itself a rare gift—and was hosting some elaborate scheme, or he was telling the truth.

"More soup?" Sebastian asked at some stage of the afternoon, and Cleo forced herself to smile and waved him away.

He knew she was hiding something from him, and she hadn't dared allow her shields to drop between them.

She'd glimpsed something earlier about demons and time. And with the recent revelation about her father, she needed to know more about it.

She reached a chapter on demons, or the Shadow Horde, or whatever one liked to call them. Premonition became a soft whisper. This was why Farshaw had given her the book. She was certain of it.

Divination is a particular gift, and a truth universally recognized within the Order is that one cannot be taught anything more of the divination arts than vague scrying, which is rarely successful. Think reading tea leaves, tarot cards, and gazing into crystal balls. Objects of focus that allow the sorcerer to perhaps catch a glimpse of future events, if they are well-trained.

But the true divination arts are not these vague predicting agents. Foresight is a powerful gift—or curse—depending upon how one looks at it. Backsight can see right through the annals of history. Psychometry, dream-walking, and future-walking all set the sorcerer of the divination arts aside, and it is a rare sorcerer who can sidestep into a different plane or dimension, or project astrally.

I have spent years cataloguing those with the true gifts. They have nothing in common that I can see. Male, female, child, crone, British, Indian, European, African.... What brings rise to this gift?

Two years ago, I began to study a sudden rash of "miracle children" in Cornwall. Scattered between the ages of thirteen to seventeen, over a dozen children in several villages began to predict things. We have seen such groupings occur in many places and times, however, this was the first time I've heard of them before they were turned to the flames and named witches. I managed to interview the children, and none of them knew where their gifts came from. At first I turned my attention to a nearby leyline, and a ring of standing stones close by. Was pure power leaching up through the earth and affecting such vulnerable minds? I had no conclusive evidence, and it remains but a theory. There is, however, only one common element I can link to these "miracle children," something far more sinister that turns my stomach, but sets my prediction senses reeling.

Eighteen years before, a group of untrained so-called witches raised a creature in the midst of the standing stones. Barely anyone would speak of the occurrence, but there were hints of the truth, told in vague suppositions. It was a devil, they whispered, and it lured many nearby into sin. It fueled itself on blood, and ruined many an innocent woman before it was finally hunted down and destroyed, though I wonder, if it was demonic, whether it did not merely flee instead.

And the question I must ask myself, is if any of these unions with this "devil" bore fruit.

Is the answer in the blood? Is there something unnatural about those who own the divination gifts? It is said that demons first taught us the gifts of sorcery, many, many years in the past, opening our minds to the possibilities of the world. What if they gave a certain group among us other gifts?

I have spent many nights pondering this question, even tracing news of any disturbances within my own village. There was nothing in the gossip in my home town, but I note that seven seers arose at the same time I did. We range in age, but at most five years separates us.

Why does time seem to part around me, when others cannot even see the individual threads? I think the demon is in me.

Cleo swiftly looked up, to see if Sebastian was watching her. Her heart threatened to stop in her chest, she swore it did, and a breathless, slightly horrified feeling ran through her.

For if she was reading this correctly, then she bore some part of the Shadow Dimension within her own veins, and that alone had given her the great gifts she could work with.

CHAPTER FIFTEEN

'I don't even know why I keep writing in this bloody thing. But if they won't listen to the words that spill from my lips, then perhaps they will read these. I hope *you read this, Agatha. I hope you understand you have ruined everything. I hope Drake reads this, and knows he has committed an innocent woman to die. For I have been guilty of many things, but this one time I am innocent of the charges against me. I did not kill Drake's nephew. I had no need to, for I am with my own child, finally. And my baby would have been heir. I knew how Drake doted on little Richard. It would have been foolish indeed to strike against him, but nobody will believe me... Nobody. You would think I would have learned this lesson, would you not? I trusted Drake. I trusted him, and when I needed him, he was not there. No, he too, points a guilty finger toward me. The only thing I have left is this child—this precious child within me—who has stayed my execution until I deliver him. But I swear to every god out there; Drake will never know this child. I will kill it before I birth it into its father's world.'*

—Morgana's journal on the day of her judgment

SEBASTIAN MOVED THROUGH the twilight quiet of Rathbourne Manor, uneasy with himself. Cleo was resting, and he should have been doing the same, considering his exhaustion. He'd barely been able to sleep in three days.

What if he'd lost her? He felt ill just thinking about it. It was one thing to consider an annulment, and a new life away from her. In his dreams she'd always gone on and remarried, finally forging the happy family she desired so much. It gave him some sense of peace to consider he could make her happy by removing himself from her life. All he'd ever wanted was to make her happy.

But to lose her to death....

The thought froze him every single time it passed through his mind. He saw his mother again, and his wife standing between them, her wards blazing.... A part of him died in that moment. There was nothing Morgana could do to him now or in the future that could ever compete with that single, heart-wracking moment when he'd thought Morgana would destroy Cleo.

But she hadn't.

No relief there. He'd seen the expression on Morgana's face as she realized Cleo was more than her match.

If you can't defeat an enemy, then you take them out of the equation no matter what you must do....

Cleo had just found herself at the top of his mother's destroy-at-all-costs list. He knew Morgana too well to think otherwise.

Mother of night, he had to protect her. No matter what the cost was, no matter what he had to do. The second he returned to Bishop's house he was going to take that fucking ticket to Manhattan and rip it into little pieces.

But first.... He'd been a reluctant partner in this entire scheme to overthrow the demon and save his father. Guilt was a strong motivator, but sometimes he'd wondered if it wouldn't be better—easier—to simply vanish into the world.

Now he had a new reason to throw himself behind this cause.

Tracking down his brother wasn't easy, particularly with Ianthe buried in paperwork at her desk. The last thing he wanted to do was stir that dragon. As much as the Prime had been cordial, he wasn't fool enough to think she'd forgiven him.

The soft murmur of his brother's voice drew him upstairs, to where Louisa had her bedchambers and nursery. There was another girl up here somewhere— Ianthe's apprentice, Thea, if he remembered correctly—but the level was quiet, except for the patient sound of Lucien's voice. Three bears and three bowls of porridge, and yet it sounded like there was nothing Lucien would rather be doing. Bloody hell. It felt like Sebastian had suddenly awoken in another world. This was so different to anything he'd ever experienced.

Or was it?

She read to me once. When I was a little boy....

Hatred surged, and anger, and goddess-knew-what-else. This was all Lady E's fault for putting the diary in his hands. It was easier to deal with the collar and the abuse when he didn't have to remember Morgana being a mother at all. *Why?* Why had she suddenly changed? She'd never been perfect. Indeed, she was hateful some of the time, and absent the rest. But every now and then she'd brushed his hair off his forehead as if she gave a damn, and sometimes she'd smiled at him, or been proud of him for his lessons. Those were the moments that made his heart ache, for he'd been so hungry for them as a little boy.

Why had she hated him too?

What had he done to turn her against him so suddenly on his thirteenth birthday? She'd been so proud when his powers first came in, and she'd marveled at the strength of them.

"You're everything I've ever hoped for, Sebastian."

But as time went on, he'd seen wariness compete with pride in her eyes.

Sebastian rested a shoulder against the cracked door to Louisa's bedchamber, watching as Lucien drew the covers up over his child's chest, and leaned down to press a kiss to her forehead. No wariness there. Only tenderness and love and a father's protective spirit.

Sebastian couldn't look away. Something in the moment seemed incredibly alluring. Maybe it was the trusting expression on the girl's face as her eyelashes fluttered closed. Or maybe it was the way Lucien looked down at her as if he'd just been given the world.

And a new image arose: a little girl with moonbeam-pale curls, blinking sleepily as *he* was the one who put her to bed.

A child.

One with her mother's dark eyes, and her stubborn mouth. Sebastian froze uncomfortably, for this was not a dream he'd ever had before, and he was surprised at how much he suddenly wanted it.

Nothing.... Nothing had ever frightened him more.

Lucien put his finger to his lips as he stood up, moving silently through the room. Sebastian stepped back into the hallway, waiting for his brother to close the door. His heart beat a little raggedly. He could still see that little girl, but hell, he wasn't even anywhere near ready to accept the idea.

"How is she?" Lucien asked.

"Sleeping," he replied, for Lucien had been in several times during the day to check upon Cleo. Whatever anyone thought of him, they loved his wife. "She wants to delve back into her *Sidestep Through Time* book, as she thinks there's something important within it she needs to know, but I made her put it aside. She needs rest."

"A premonition?"

"I don't know." *She was hiding something from him.* "It gives me an itchy feeling. A knowing."

"Cleo's intuitive senses are the best I've ever encountered," Lucien admitted. "She's probably picking up on something, and you're probably feeling the echoes of it."

"She can read the book tomorrow," he replied, still troubled. "I don't want her to overtax herself."

"If I can give you a little bit of advice in regards to handling your wife... don't give her any ultimatums. Try and make her think that resting is her idea."

"Oh, don't worry. I'm learning that lesson."

Lucien shared his dry amusement. "If it's any consolation, it's worse when your wife is mistress of over four hundred sorcerers. Especially when you were the one who suggested she take the role."

Sebastian's smile died. "Your wife hates me."

Thunder grumbled in the distance, as if to agree.

"She doesn't hate you. But this is not a conversation to be having here, outside Louisa's room. This way," Lucien murmured, heading toward the orangery at the end of the house.

There was little choice but to follow. It wasn't as though he had anything particular to say to the man, but it wasn't as though he had anything better to do either, and there was an odd yearning in him tonight. The urge to talk to someone, though damned if he knew why.

Or what about.

These people were getting to him. He barely knew them, but there was something about belonging here that made him feel itchy.

A ridiculous notion, for he'd never belong. Ianthe had all the reason in the world to hate him. He'd helped kidnap her daughter, and his mother had used the opportunity to blackmail her into stealing the Blade of Altarrh from Drake.

They ought to hate him.

Collar notwithstanding.

Lightning flickered on the horizon as Lucien led him inside the orangery. The windows faced the city, with beautiful views over the Rathbourne gardens. No sign of those views now, with a rainy darkness descended over the house, but the view within was glorious enough. Someone had clearly spent a great deal of time cultivating the orangery of late. The leaves of over a dozen fruit trees beckoned lushly.

Summoning a white mage globe, Lucien left it sitting on a shelf, and shut the door. The ease with which he tied off the sorcerous weaves made Sebastian vaguely envious.

"Ianthe doesn't hate you," Lucien murmured, sinking into one of the overstuffed armchairs in the corner, and gesturing to the other.

Sebastian shook his head to the seat. Too restless for that. "If she could poison my tea, I'm fairly certain she'd consider it."

"With a strong emetic, perhaps. Her feelings are conflicted. Every time she looks at you she sees your mother, and she sees her daughter in the hands of your mother. But Louisa says you protected her." Lucien clasped his hands over his middle, eyeing him with those enigmatic eyes. "Lou's quite fond of you. Apparently you're terrible at tea parties though, which gives Ianthe pause. The idea of you sitting down to a child's tea party is a difficult one to swallow."

Heat stirred in his cheeks. "It was one afternoon. Morgana wasn't at the house, and Louisa was upset."

"Nobody quite knows what to make of you."

"Likewise." He circled the room. "You're potting lemons." It seemed such a strange thing, to connect with Lucien on this level. The stillness of the room brought him peace. He felt like he could breathe here, the way he couldn't elsewhere.

"Drake thought it might help me to meditate and heal my aura." Lucien shrugged, pushing to his feet as if to follow. "This close to winter, it's not as though I can go and walk around barefoot on the lawns."

"Bishop said your powers have..."

"Waned?" Lucien arched a brow. "My psychic senses scarred? I believe that's the description you're looking for."

He shifted awkwardly.

Lucien turned toward his potting station, running a hand over the marble slab. "I told you Lord Rathbourne put a sclavus collar upon me. I didn't tell you why. He demanded I raise a demon—the demon we're currently facing—and use it to destroy the Prime.

"It's the only reason I'm still alive. When I summoned Lascher—the demon—and sent it to attack Drake, it wasn't by intention. I had no choice. Drake was forced to lock me in Bedlam afterward, as the entire affair scarred my aura and my abilities to channel power, but it meant I wasn't executed."

Hell. He hadn't known that. Sebastian toyed with the timber handle on a trowel. "You still feel strong to me." He thought about it. "I'd almost say your raw sorcerous strength is greater than Bishop's."

"The amount of power I can probably wield is immense, yes, and no doubt similar to what I used to be able to hold. But my ability to channel that much power is greatly affected."

"It bothers you to be so scarred?"

"Yes, it bothers me, though not as much as it did once. I have a wife and child now. A home. To have lost a significant portion of my strength seems a small trade in hindsight." But he looked discomforted. "It bothers me most at night, when I consider what's coming. How can I protect my wife, my child, when I am only just relearning how to use my sorcery?"

Sebastian leaned against the potting counter. How could he protect Cleo when he could barely control his burgeoning powers? All along he'd been focused on overthrowing his mother, but the second he saw Cleo collapse, everything changed.

This was no longer about revenge.

It was no longer about guilt.

They would have to confront the demon at some stage. It had sworn an oath to Drake not to harm any of them, *unless* they made a move against it, but they couldn't leave it out there, running amok in London. It felt like no matter which way he looked, he was heading for an inexorable collision with a creature that could destroy them all. Bishop had been heading toward this collision with single-minded focus for the past month, but it was the first time he'd begun to think in tune with his brother.

The only way to protect Cleo was to face the demon.

A creature that had the power to destroy them all.

"Can we defeat it?" he asked softly.

Lucien frowned. "With the Relics, perhaps. It will take the three of us, however...."

"And you're scarred," he whispered, "and I'm untrained, and Bishop... well, Bishop can probably manage. I haven't seen anything he can't do yet."

Their eyes met.

We'll fail, he thought bleakly.

But he was done with running away from his future. Perhaps it was time to deal with the past.

And with his wife.

Cleo stirred as her bed dipped. Alarm roused, but then she came awake just enough to realize who the intruder was.

Sebastian slid beneath the covers in the dark, his weight heavy in the bed. "I didn't mean to wake you."

Her heart beat quickly. "What are you doing in here?"

He'd never ventured into her bedchambers, and the only time they'd ever shared a bed—their wedding night—he'd finally fled to the sanctity of the trundle in his dressing room.

Sebastian sighed, as he rolled onto his side to face her. "I couldn't sleep."

She didn't have to worry whether he was wearing anything beneath the blankets. He wouldn't be unclothed. He never was.

Cleo lay back down, though how on earth he thought she was going to sleep like this, she didn't know. Her nightgown felt like a thin shield against him. Naked or not, she felt like she was. "Are you going to... sleep here?"

What a stupid question. She pressed her hands to her face. He'd been at her side all day, reclining in the armchair beside her bed every time she woke. Last night bothered him. She knew that. But it was one thing to find him at her side, another to lie beside him, with her breath coming shortly, and her body horribly aware of him.

"Do you mind?"

"No," she whispered.

Silence stretched out, and she didn't know whether that was worse.

He wouldn't want her to touch him.

He'd made that quite clear on their wedding night. Especially if he was asleep and he didn't know who she was....

"All right," she said hoarsely, rolling away from him. She could do this. "I'll see you in the morning then."

Sebastian shifted, and she stared at the far wall, trying desperately not to wonder what he was doing.

"May I hold you?"

For a second she almost didn't realize what he'd said. Cleo froze. "O-of course."

The mattress shifted, and then a warm, callused hand reached out and found her arm. She flinched. Not in shock or horror, but in anticipation.

Sebastian nestled in behind her, a fold in the blankets keeping their bodies apart, his breath stirring her hair.

Darkness, ever her ally, kept him from seeing the pink stain on her cheeks. They lay stiffly together, her head snug against the pillow, and his body politely aligned against hers. Slowly, his palm closed over her side, resting there. All she could hear was the sound of her heartbeat in her ears, and the soft rush of his breath past his lips.

What had happened to provoke such a response from him? He'd been cool and unreadable most of the day, his shields irrevocably in place, and she'd been distracted enough not to notice anything amiss. The book consumed her attention.

But now she found herself wondering....

Slowly she relaxed and closed her eyes, surrendering to the moment. She'd spent so many nights dreaming of what it would feel like to lie in his arms.

"Is your head still aching?" he murmured.

"No." Some part of her hated to break the silence. It seemed like a single word could destroy this fragile truce, and she wasn't prepared to let him go.

Love me. Please love me.

But she didn't dare say the words aloud, and she kept her own shields in place so he wouldn't hear her thoughts.

"I have been thinking," he murmured, his breath caressing the back of her neck, "about what you asked me the other day."

"Asked you?"

"About someone from my past."

She turned her head to glance at him.

"I vaguely recall seeing Julia Camden reading tea leaves once," he said, his lips pressing thinly together. "And it seems more than a coincidence to see her at the Ascension ball barely an hour before Morgana attacked. They were allies once, and though she claimed she hadn't seen my mother since...."

Julia Camden reading tea leaves. Cleo's heart beat swiftly. Was Julia Camden her black queen? "Any trained sorcerer can read tea leaves," she said, more to herself than anyone. "It doesn't make her a seer."

Was it enough proof? She almost wanted to believe it.

"It's just a thought. Is there any reason you wanted to know?"

Cleo slammed the gates shut on those particular thoughts, and knew he'd felt it. "No reason. Just trying to deduce who might be working for the demon."

His hand settled on her arm, and he stroked his fingers down it.

"Can you promise me something?" he murmured.

Anything. "Of course."

"If we meet my mother again, you're not to get involved," he said, and hesitated as if he wanted to add more.

"I can't promise that." Sebastian stirred, but she rolled back into his embrace, her spine meeting his chest as she glanced over her shoulder at him. "I *won't* promise that, because I don't know if I could keep such a promise if your life was on the line."

She couldn't see his face in the dark, only the sharp outline of his nose, and the slope of his brow.

"What's wrong?" she asked.

The shadowy shape of his face dipped toward hers, but only to rest near her shoulder. For a second.... She quenched her sudden hope, toying with the sheets.

"I keep thinking Morgana can't hurt me anymore," he admitted. "But the truth is... she can." His hand curled tightly over her hip, as if he sought to reassure himself. "She knows you're my weakness, Cleo. And seeing you there, the only thing standing between her and me.... And I couldn't move in time, I couldn't do anything.... That moment was the longest moment of my life. I thought she was going to kill you, and then all of a sudden you warded."

Cleo relaxed into the blankets. "You were worried about me."

"Of course I was," he suddenly growled. "Do you think I don't care about you?"

She had no answer to that. "I know you care. You would never have traded yourself in my place when your mother kidnapped me, if you hadn't."

"But...?"

But.

"You've been distant," she whispered quietly. "You never wrote me back, you never visited, and you were never 'at home' when I called."

Frustration echoed in his throat in a sound that was purely primeval. "I couldn't handle the thought of you. Not on top of... of Drake's sacrifice." He shuddered. "I had my freedom, finally. But at such a cost. I didn't know what to do. I didn't deserve freedom. Not like that." His voice broke. "I didn't deserve you."

Oh.

She stroked her fingers down his arm gently, her mind reeling. "You fool. You deserve more than you can ever know. Your father sacrificed himself because he *loves* you." She bit down on the words that wanted to come next, trying to rearrange them carefully. He wasn't ready for them. And nor was she ready to speak them. "And you're more than deserving of my affections. I thought you didn't want them."

"I'm sorry," he whispered, stroking his hand down her side so faintly she barely felt the ripple of her nightgown. "I'm trying."

Silence fell, but this one was full of a thousand unspoken words. Her heart swelled, and she felt the first soft stirrings of hope, along with a flush of heat behind her eyes. All she'd ever wanted was for Sebastian to try to love her.

His questing hand became firmer, stirring her nightgown now. Cleo sucked in a sharp breath, her fist clenching with need. She didn't dare touch him, especially in the wake of such momentous words.

But their first true kiss sprang to mind, the heat of his body pressing against hers. This was a purer longing, untainted by the incubus's touch, and somehow far more painful. Sweet torture.

For she didn't know if he would take another step down this fated path.

"I want you," Sebastian murmured into the stillness of the night. "I want you so badly I ache, but to take this step scares the hell out of me." His voice became very small. "I've never made love to a woman. I don't know if I'd even know how to begin."

Her heart broke a little. She hadn't known. "I wish you'd told me."

A shudder went through that hard body. "I've never been very good with words."

She thought she understood. It wasn't his words that failed him, but the emotions behind them. Sebastian had never known love, nor kindness, nor true friendship. She'd been mired in doubt, thinking of her own inadequacies, thinking them the *reason* for his distance.

And she'd been horribly wrong.

Cleo held her breath. Did she dare? "Then show me."

Lips grazed the back of her neck. Little goose pimples erupted all over her body. Cleo gasped, holding a fistful of the sheet for dear life. She couldn't see a thing. Her world narrowed down to the rasp of his stubble against her nape, and those soft lips, so tender, barely brushing against her skin....

The wet tip of his tongue traced the hardened nubbin of her spine. *Oh, mercy. Mother of night.* Cleo sucked in a sharp gasp.

And then his fingers stirred, tracing small circles on her shoulder. "Sometimes I cannot bear to be touched, but it's growing easier with every kiss. Easier to forget, easier to remind myself I'm with you, and not trapped beneath someone else. If we could take it slowly...."

What was he trying to say?

"Would you let me?" he whispered. "Let me try to make love to you?"

She nodded desperately.

"I would have to be in control." That hand stroked down over the lawn of her nightgown, as if he soaked in the sensation of the fine fabric. "Don't move."

Cleo's nipples pebbled. The ache between her thighs grew hotter, wetter. But she didn't dare move.

And maybe in not daring, it became somewhat more indecent indeed. Denial became a fierce ache, until she could barely breathe for the need to reach her hand between her thighs.

How far would he take this?

Sebastian was barely touching her, his fingertips skating lazily over her hip and up the side of her ribs. Her breasts felt heavy and full, desperately aching for his touch, but she was not in control here. He was.

"I dream of you sometimes," he murmured, brushing the backs of his knuckles over the side of her breast. "I think of the taste of your mouth." He caught her chin, tilting it back toward his for a kiss. "And how sweet the sounds you made...."

Their lips brushed against each other's. Sebastian lazily traced her tongue with his, a slow seduction that grew deeper, and deeper.... Heat stirred deep in her belly as the kiss turned hungrier. All her attention was focused on the teasing circle of his thumb as it grew closer and closer to her nipple.

Cleo shuddered as his hot mouth moved down the column of her throat, his hand finding the fullness of her breast and palming it firmly. She couldn't help noting the practiced way he manipulated her. He knew her body better than she ever could. And it would have bothered her a little, if it weren't for the soft noises he made, and the rasp of his teeth against her shoulder.

She wanted to touch him too.

To drive him half wild with lust, the way he was doing to her.

"What is it?" he murmured.

She lifted her shoulder off the bed, dragging his arm beneath her, and curling her fingers through his. "May I touch you too?"

"Later," he breathed. "It's not the touching that bothers me, so much as the being touched. I would need a lantern there, so I could see your face."

Those fingers brushed down her hip, leaving her gasping in great ragged breaths. She turned her face into the pillow as he began to stroke upward, skimming her nightgown out of the way, until she could feel his callused fingertips tracing those small, teasing circles up her thigh.

"Part your thighs," he breathed, hot breath caressing her ear, and his body pressed tightly behind hers.

Heat burned in her cheeks, but there was no place for embarrassment here. Cleo complied. "What are you doing?"

Grabbing a fistful of her nightgown, he dragged it slowly up, leaving her bare beneath the sheets. His hips gave a small thrust, and she felt something hard press against her bottom. His erection, no doubt.

"What do you think I'm doing?" he whispered.

His fingertips circled her bare hip, leaving her twitchy and restless, but she sensed the question they asked: Yes? Or no?

"I think you're trying to torture me," she whispered back, capturing his hand. Their fingers twined together, and then he was kissing her neck again, breathing in the scent of her hair as if it anchored him.

His hand slid beneath hers, curling over her thigh, and nudging them apart a little. Cleo died a thousand little deaths as she let him guide her hand lower.

Fingers dipped between her thighs, stroking idly through the soft curls there. Cleo's eyes widened, and Sebastian captured her gasp in his other hand, his breath stirring the curls behind her ear again. "Shhh," he whispered, almost as if he enjoyed forcing her to be silent and still while he mastered her body.

Shhh? She cried out as his questing fingertips found her wet and swollen. Sensation speared through her as he located the precise spot where she needed to be touched. A jerk went through her. *Oh, God.*

He toyed with her lightly, and suddenly she could barely breathe. There was heat beneath her skin, dark and delicious. And a rush of feeling stirred through her, almost like the sensation of her predictions, only within her, not on top of her skin.

The darkness within her stretched and awoke. She didn't want to be a young woman anymore, uncertain of her welcome and shy beneath his touch. She wanted to own him. Heart and soul.

"You're so wet," he murmured. "So fucking wet."

Two fingers stretched her, as he buried them up to the first knuckle. Despite her inexperience, her body parted easily, slick and moist to the touch. Cleo writhed. "More. Please."

The sharp bite of teeth bit into the sensitive skin between her shoulder and her neck. "But you're not in control here, my love."

His fingers slipped from her body as if to remind her of this fact, and he circled that sensitive spot again, leaving her crying out into his palm. Cleo's entire body shivered.

"That's it," he breathed, bringing her right to the edge. "I can feel it rushing through you. Are you ready?"

For what?

His thumb speared flat over that sensitive little nubbin of flesh between her thighs, his teeth sinking into her shoulder. Cleo cried out as everything within her turned molten.

"Come," he whispered down the bond. *"Now."*

And she screamed into the cup of his hand.

He'd never experienced anything like this in his life. It went beyond the earthy thrust and pull of flesh. Sinking into Cleo's arms felt like coming home, to a place he'd never known. It was powerful. Defining. Soul-shaking.

Each kiss felt momentous. To kiss her like this was strangely freeing. His choice. His desire, unfettered and furious. For all his vast experience with a woman's body, he was ridiculously naïve when it came to this sweeter seduction. Kissing Cleo was the simplest, purest task he'd ever committed himself to, and nothing could tarnish it. Not even the blunt demand of his cock, heavy and aching against her hip.

He wanted to take her.

Sweet goddess, how he ached.

But fear lived in his heart too. Fear that he'd break, and forget where he was, or whom he was with. Fear he couldn't live up to her expectations. Fear that this untarnished moment would somehow be consumed by more blatant desires.

It was perfect. Utterly perfect. Like an arrow straight to the heart. Sebastian drew back from her mouth with a gasp, shaking slightly. The evidence of his arousal jutted between them, bolstering his nightshirt like a mast on a ship.

Cleo's night-dark gaze slid between them, and he sensed her sudden nervousness. "Do you wish me to—"

"No."

Cleo cupped his face with her palms, and he could just make out her eyes in the dark. He could sense her mind stroking his through the bond, an unusual feeling, almost as if she were trying to tell him she knew. That it didn't matter.

"We'll take it slow," she whispered, as her palm slid over his nape, dragging him toward her.

He sank into her trembling embrace, closing his eyes as she gently stroked her palms over the back of his nightshirt. Burying his face against her throat, he tried to think of other things to still his pulsing desire.

"I've been in many beds," he whispered. "But the only one I've ever truly wanted to be in is yours."

And he closed his eyes and pressed a kiss to her cheek, one so sweet it ached.

CHAPTER SIXTEEN

THE NEXT DAY Sebastian went hunting with Bishop, trying to track down the demon, Julia Camden, or even Morgana. His expression had been cool and locked down over breakfast, but as Cleo reached for the jam, their eyes met, and he smiled the faintest smile. Suddenly she was blushing.

He'd been there in her bed this morning, gently stroking her arm. She didn't know if he'd gotten any sleep—to fall asleep beside her and not know her seemed to be his greatest fear, and she knew something horrible had happened in his past—but he'd stayed the night and her heart felt strangely light this morning.

Until she turned to the book again.

Madrigal Brown arrived for a sparring session in Lady Rathbourne's salon. Cleo wasn't ready to even attempt to future-walk again, as her mind still ached, but she watched as Madrigal showed her how it was done, and went through the theory of the process. No matter the walk of life, every sorcerer she'd ever known loved to speak on the theory of sorcerous gifts, and assassin or not, Madrigal was no different. It was clearly the first time the woman had ever come across anyone with a skill set even remotely similar to her own, and though she'd been wary at first, as Madrigal opened up, there was a hunger there to connect that she hadn't expected to find.

If Farshaw's theory was correct, then Madrigal had to have a demon's blood somewhere within her veins too.

She didn't ask. *She couldn't.* But it was all she could think about.

Did the gift pass down through child after child? Was that why some sorcerers were strong in the divination arts, but others were barely amateurs? How many generations could the gift sustain itself?

And if she was considering strength as a particular pinpoint of how far in the past the demon had mated with a female in her bloodline, then she shouldn't be looking too far. A shiver of dread ran through her at the thought. Her mother had died when she was very young, and she couldn't even recall her, but Cleo knew she was *the* strongest seer in the Empire.

Her father—sweet heavens, was he even truly her father?—had seen that she was named Cassandra of the Order at the age of twelve, when her Foresight truly bloomed. It was an honor at the time, and it made him so happy he even threw a party for her, but the memory felt warped now.

She had to know the truth.

And she needed to know if this was why the demon had singled her out and begun to invade her dreams.

Did it know her in some intimate sense? Was there a connection there between them? Was that why she was the white queen?

And if she was the white queen, then who was the black queen? *Two sides to a coin....* What if the black queen bore demon blood in her veins too?

Her mother? There had to be a reason her quest for the black queen drew her back to that particular point in time.

But then of course, there was Julia Camden.

Who had no ties to *her* past.

It gave her a headache, and she finally set the book aside, but the questions didn't vanish, and deep in her heart she knew why.

Cleo rapped hesitantly on the door.

"Come in," Lady Eberhardt barked.

She slipped inside Lady E's parlor and closed the door. Lady E looked up from where she was meticulously placing her tarot cards. The old woman sighed and gathered her tarot cards into a pile. "Well, your arrival makes my petty divinations obsolete."

"A month or so ago, perhaps." Cleo smiled wanly.

"Nonsense." The snort that accompanied the word made Cleo's lips twitch. Lady E owned the ability to communicate entire sentences in a single lip curl or *tsk*. "The second you stop believing that rubbish is the second your mind disavows its stranglehold on your gifts. Belief in oneself is *the* most important aspect a sorcerer can learn."

"Perhaps it *is* belief that holds me back. I prophesized I would lose the ability of Foresight the day I saw the world again through my own eyes, and so far that has held true." She took a seat across from Lady E. "But if I believe my Visions are true, then how do I disbelieve the very first Vision I ever had?"

Lady E made a harrumphing sound, but she had no articulate answer to that. She scooped the pack of tarot cards into her hands, and held one card up, the back of it directed toward Cleo. "What card is it?"

Cleo hesitated. Reached out and held her hand up to the card. "Six of Pentacles."

"And this one?" Another card.

"The Empress." Cleo sighed. "I've been doing this since I was three."

Lady E put her cards down and leaned forward. "You, young lady, are an utter fool. I hear you've been future-walking and dream-walking. Gifts you didn't own before your blindfold was removed. Perhaps the blindfold wasn't safeguarding your Foresight abilities? Perhaps it was holding you back from exploring your other gifts?"

Cleo looked down into her lap.

"I've been speaking to Madrigal Brown. Did you know, you're already future-walking better than she can? Her outer limit is a minute in advance at her absolute best. She tells me she thinks you were predicting almost half a minute in advance in your first *attempt* at it. You're still the Order's Cassandra, Cleo. Nobody can take that away from you."

Tears pricked at her eyes. "I know. I just.... A part of me feels like it failed my father. All he ever prized in me were my gifts of Foresight. And he was the one who tore my blindfold from my eyes. He *wanted* to destroy my gifts. He hated me so much in the end, because I betrayed him."

She pressed her face into her hands. Lady E shifted to the cushion beside her, patting her shoulder. "Your father deserved his fate. He didn't respect the gift that he had, right beneath his nose."

A barrage of tears suddenly overwhelmed her. She'd known her father never loved her. It was all she'd ever longed for, and she'd tried—so hard—to make him proud of her. Cleo furiously dried her eyes. He didn't deserve her tears.

"Something else is bothering you," Lady E said, watching her hawkishly. "Spit it out. Reticence never suits anybody."

"Is there any chance we can send for tea?" She wasn't stalling, but she needed a moment to gather herself.

Lady E arched a brow, then sent down to the kitchen for tea. Considering the woman's penchant for nosiness, Cleo was almost surprised she waited until the tea actually came up before she turned that demanding look upon Cleo.

"I want your oath that what I am about to tell you doesn't go any further," Cleo said. "A blood oath."

Arching a very pointed brow, Lady E cut her finger, dripping blood into a spare teacup. "I solemnly swear on my power, and my blood, that I will not reveal the contents of this discussion to anyone... until you grant me leave to do so."

Her sorcery flared, and Lady E gasped as the oath bit through her.

"I saw something in my dreams the night of the Ascension Ball," Cleo admitted. "You knew my father. Did you know my mother?"

Lady E poured them both tea. "Lila Sinclair. Aye, I knew her. I warned her not to marry Tremayne, as he was dabbling in occult areas he shouldn't have, but she wouldn't listen to a single word I said. I told her she'd come to a bad end."

"She had the gift of Divination," Cleo murmured, fingering the small silver charm on her necklace in the shape of a moon. Her mother's charm. She hadn't worn this necklace in years, but today it seemed... fitting. "Not like me. Her gifts were quieter, and limited to reading tea leaves, and scrying." *And mine are either gift or curse, depending upon how you look at it....*

"Aye. It's the reason your father married her. His powers were purely telekinetic, and he was quite powerful within his ranks, but he wanted to breed telepathic gifts into his bloodline. He hoped to produce a child with equal strengths in both disciplines."

"It doesn't always work like that." Sometimes two sorcerers produced a child with no penchant for sorcery at all, and at other times a child with no sorcery in the family lines suddenly learned how to manipulate the world, through sheer willpower—or desperation.

"No it doesn't, though it sometimes helps. Most sorcerers are one or the other, though they can be taught the other discipline to a certain degree, if they're dedicated enough. It's very, very rare to find a child who is equally telekinetic or telepathic."

"And I am almost purely telepathic." Cleo sipped her tea. Her mouth felt dry.

"Aye, well, your father went funny in the head after he, Drake, and Morgana quarreled five years earlier. He was furious when Drake became Prime of the Order. He always believed he was the better of the two, and I think Tremayne decided this was a means to prove it." Lady E helped herself to the butter cake. "But you're not asking about him, are you. Why do you want to know about your mother?"

"My father said she died in a carriage accident." Cleo met Lady E's eyes. "I begin to suspect it's not true."

"Are you sure you wish to know?" Lady E asked bluntly, and Cleo's heart plummeted in her chest. There *was* more to this story.

"I think I need to." Trepidation stirred. She hadn't spoken of the black queen to anyone. "Please."

"You were a little girl, barely off her short strings," Lady E murmured, "when Lila found herself with child again. Your birth wasn't a kind one, and the pregnancy drained her. It took her almost a year to regain her strength, and she was warned not to try again. Not anytime soon.

"But she didn't listen, or perhaps there was someone else whispering other suggestions in her ear, someone with more influence than Lila's contemporaries."

"My father," Cleo said leadenly, for it was the sort of thing he would have done.

"He wanted a dynasty, and it was far too early to tell whether you had inherited both gifts from your parents' bloodlines. I think he believed that the more children they had, the greater the chances were. So she fell with child again. And the second pregnancy was much the same as the first. I've never seen a mother so drained of vitality like that…. The healers could barely keep her alive, and they couldn't find a single physical reason for her to be fading so fast."

There could have been a very good reason for that. Cleo saw that moment again as her father let *something else* inside him, before he reached for her mother. Her teacup rattled on its saucer, and she looked down before Lady E saw it in her eyes.

Lady E sighed. "Lila died in the birthing chambers, and the baby was stillborn. It wasn't…. Tremayne locked himself away for days. I think he regretted encouraging her to try again so early. He did care for her, despite everything. I will grant him that. And in the end I think he felt he'd killed her and the child, which left him only with you."

A child. He'd always said it was a carriage accident. "Did you see my mother's body?"

Lady E paused with her teacup to her lips. "Yes, I saw her laid out in the parlor, while we all paid her our respects." She put the teacup down. Suspicion narrowed her dark eyes. "I've played along, my gel, but enough of this fiddle-faddle. I won't believe you've suddenly got a hankering for the family history without good reason. Spit it out."

How much could she trust Lady E? Cleo pressed her fingers to her temples. It didn't make any sense. Her mother died...

...and the baby was stillborn.

Or so it was claimed.

Heat drained from her face. "Did you see the child's body?"

"Of course not. It was a closed coffin." Lady E folded her arms over her chest and presented a menacing brow. "That's a rather unpleasant question. And a very curious one. As far as I know, the child was in that coffin. But you think otherwise."

Cleo pushed to her feet in a swish of skirts. "I haven't told anyone this... but the demon's been visiting me in my dreams ever since Morgana stole the Blade of Altarrh."

"*What?*" No one could enunciate a word quite like Lady E.

"It lures me into the dream plane, I think...." The second the words tripped over her lips, the floodgates opened. Lady E stared at her, face paling slowly as Cleo told her everything; the chess board, the game, the pawns.

"I'm the white queen," she whispered, "but there's a black queen on the board too, and... I get the impression the black queen is going to set this entire mess off. She's the ace up the demon's sleeve, and she's somehow tied to me and Sebastian. I was told to look in my past for the answers—"

"Told by who?"

Cleo's shoulders slumped. "You wouldn't believe me if I told you."

"Try me, my gel." Lady E's voice cracked like a whip lash.

"I saw a man who claimed to be Quentin Farshaw in Balthazar's Labyrinth. He said he was part of some collective that watched over England's safety. He gave me the book, and he told me the black queen can be found somewhere in my past, and she has divination gifts."

Lady E merely waved a dismissive hand. "Meddling bloody Travelers."

"You know of them?" she said incredulously.

"I'm a Triad Councilor," Lady E said haughtily. "There's not very much that goes on within the Order that I'm not aware of." Thoughts swirled in her dark eyes and she looked at Cleo with a very disconcerting look. "Hmm."

"What?"

"You think you have a sister out there somewhere?" Lady E asked. "You think she might be the black queen."

Cleo's shoulders slumped. "It's the only answer I can come up with. In my dream, there was only one woman in that room and she is confirmed dead, by you. But was the child that was conceived *me*? Or was it a sibling? If I'm looking for the black queen, then it makes sense. A child with the same gifts I have. A child...." She looked down into her lap. A *sister*.

"Have you told anyone else about this?"

"No," she said, meeting the old woman's eyes. "And I don't intend to. Not until.... Not until I know more about it."

"Good," Lady E said, pouring them both another cup of tea. "I would keep what you have learned very close to your chest. And keep scrying. Sometimes Visions aren't quite what they seem."

Later that night, after another fruitless day of searching, Sebastian sat in the window seat, reading by the light of a small mage globe that burned above him. It was the journal, the one he wouldn't let Cleo look at. Frost gleamed on the window, though she didn't think he was aware of the cause of it.

But she was.

She was.

"We missed you at dinner," Cleo murmured, leaning her shoulder against the doorjamb as she returned from scrubbing her teeth. "How does your reading go?"

He closed the book with a gentleness that belied his expression. She'd learned to recognize the gentleness as a mask. When he was emotionally conflicted, he became quieter, and yet colder. His movements became very, very careful, as if he'd burst out once upon a time and hurt someone or something, and knew better now what he was capable of.

"As expected. Morgana blames everyone but herself. I can't see what Lady E hopes for me to learn."

Then why are you so absorbed in it?

She didn't say it though. Instead her eyes took a small tour of the room.

A bottle of brandy on the vanity. A sticky-rimmed glass on the floor beside his seat. And her husband, moving with such precise, gliding movements as if he were locked down so firmly that merely moving required a conscious level of control others didn't bother with.

She knew not to touch him when he was like this. This was the man who'd faced his mother with icy rages, the man who locked his heart away and guarded it with cruel words and dangerous smiles.

Perhaps the journal meant nothing to him, as he claimed, but she didn't think so. It was cutting him to pieces, and the only method he had of surviving was to fall back into old habits.

Cleo took a deep breath. *Let me in. Please let me in.* She wanted to hold him so badly, even as she knew he wouldn't accept such a thing. Not tonight. *I hate to see you hurting.*

"I don't think she would have insisted upon it unless she thought there was some value within it."

He snorted. "Lady E probably finds it amusing."

"To torture you?" Cleo arched a brow. "Well, you're in a mood tonight."

He looked up, and sighed. "Sorry. It gets to me. What could I possibly learn about my mother I don't already know? I pity her in some ways, yes. She was beaten and raped by her uncle for years. But...."

She saw the conflict in his eyes. If Morgana had suffered so, then why had she not protected him from the same horror? Had she hated her son enough that she didn't care? How could a woman who'd been through such a thing then turn that same abuse upon her own child?

"She wasn't worthy of you," Cleo said. "The fault lies in her, not you."

He moved restlessly, circling the room. "My mother saw me as a weapon she'd designed to unseat my father. All she ever wanted from me was to use me. To kill her enemies, to fuck her friends, to threaten those she despised with my strength.

"And Bishop wants to use me to get my father back. It's a different kind of leash, but all he cares for is my sorcery too."

"That's not true," she said, stepping forward. "He's your brother."

"She was my mother." He'd found the brandy again, and the room was very, very cold. "And you. What do you want from me?"

"Nothing," she whispered.

If it were a test, she would have failed. His entire expression shut down, those silver eyes glinting in the moonlight as he sipped at his brandy. "That's not entirely true, is it, Cleo?"

Cold. He moved with predatory intent toward her, and she sucked in a sharp breath. There was something languid to the movement now. Something predatory.

"You want my body—"

"Only if you wish to give it," she protested, taking a step back. "Last night was special." Wasn't it?

"You want my heart."

She had nothing to say to that. She captured his cheek in her hand, and perhaps it was that which confused him. She meant to comfort him, but his eyes turned to molten silver, and he swooped down and took her mouth in a searing kiss.

Cleo kissed him back desperately, aching with his pain, and frightened of this mood of his.

As far as kisses went, it was sublime. Perfect. Designed to arouse her, but also designed to give nothing back. A kiss like this could consume, but it left one hungry, denied the substance she craved so much. Each stroke of his hands set her on fire, for he knew what a woman wanted from him.

Hands moved with ruthless intent toward her robe, and he tore it open with a sharp tug, breaking the kiss.

And that was when she realized she could not heal him with a kiss, or a gentle touch.

This was not love. This was sex, and Sebastian was playing the role that had been predetermined for him by all those other women.

The glitter of his eyes cut her with sharp knives. "You want this," he whispered, tracing those tormenting kisses down her throat. "And this."

Hands on her breasts, his thumb circling her aching nipple....

Stop. She placed a hand, very firmly, upon his chest. "No."

"I can give you my body." His thumb stroked the side of her breast, and it ached both within and without, for a part of her yearned for his touch. Even as she knew he wasn't there. Not tonight.

This was Sebastian at his cruelest. Sebastian with his mask firmly in place. A hollow, gilded man.

"I said no." Cleo sucked in ragged breath, and pushed him away from her. "This isn't a transaction. This is... a gift. I would give my heart to you, my body, and ask for nothing in return." She looked up. "Though yes, I desire it."

The shock on his face turned to uncertainty, and then a brief flicker of horror went through his eyes. He looked down at her as she tried to control her ragged breathing, and she knew what he saw. Her robe agape. and her hair tumbling in a messy braid over her shoulder, her lips kiss-stung and swollen.

"You want me," he said, as if to try and understand, and a little piece of her heart broke because she knew he was trapped in the past right now, seeing sex and lust as a bargaining chip, as a game of control and hate.

"Not like that." Cleo tucked her robe back together. "And not this particular incarnation of you. I want the man who makes a rose bloom for me, and asks for his first kiss. I want the man who danced with me because he knew it

was my first ball, and... because I'd always dreamed of it."
She took a trembling breath. "I want the man who looks at
me and sees me. *Me*. Not other women, not other times. I
know what you have been through. I sympathize. And I
will always be there for you if you wish to talk about it. But
if you think I will let you use me like that even as you're
pushing me away, then I suggest you think again."

She tied the knots on her robe. "I don't want anything
from you that you're not prepared to give to me. All I want,
all I've ever wanted, is to see you happy. And... and if you
cannot be happy with me," she whispered, her mouth
tasting like ash, "then I would grant you an annulment. The
marriage remains unconsummated."

"But what of you?"

Cleo sat on the edge of the bed, trying not to think of
all she'd lost. "I shall make do. It will hurt, I would expect."
Voice firming, she looked up. "I care for you. You know I
do, and I cannot hide my feelings. But my happiness does
not depend upon you. With or without you, I will make my
own way in this life, though I would like it very much if you
were by my side." He looked so lost, and her heart ached.
"I would like that very much."

"I'm sorry." He went to his knees before her, and
there was *her* Sebastian again. "I don't understand you
sometimes, or what you want from me."

"Yes, you do." She stroked his black hair back from
his face, caressing the roughened stubble of his jaw. "It's
yourself you do not understand. I love you."

His face twisted. "I don't know what that means."

Cleo sank to her knees too, still caressing his face. "It
means I wish only the best for you. Love is not a chain,
Sebastian. It's not something I seek to tie you with, or to
trap you with. Love means I would protect you, and that it
hurts to see your pain, and I know you don't understand

any of it... I don't ask for it in return. I don't. But I must love myself too. Enough to expect more than what... what happened here tonight."

He looked down, capturing her hands against his cheeks, and shaking violently. "My head is a mess tonight. I shouldn't have allowed you in here."

"I knew," she whispered. "Do you want to talk about it?"

He sank back against the wall, dragging one knee up to his chest. "No."

"Do you want to be alone?" she whispered, dragging her knees up to her chest too.

The "yes" was in his eyes, the thought of what his instincts probably told him. But the word that came from his lips in a single breath was, "No."

A hand slid toward hers, resting over it with lax attention. A question lingered in that touch. She silently replied, turning her palm toward his and locking their fingers together. A single touch that meant more than any others that had happened within this room tonight.

"My mother used to ask me to brush her hair," he said softly.

Cleo's head turned sharply. "Pardon?"

He was staring toward the window again. "She had this brush. Her mother's brush. And sometimes she'd let me brush her hair."

The words made no sense, but then she saw his gaze alighting on the journal. *Oh.*

"Sometimes my father would send for me for dinner," she whispered quietly. "He never had any time for me during the day, or unless he wanted to see how my lessons were going. And when I grew older all he wanted from me were my Visions." She could see the lavish spread of the dinner table. "But sometimes we had dinner together.

Perhaps they're the hardest moments to recall, for he neglected me, severely, and yet no matter how much I tell myself it wasn't my fault—that I was worthy of more, and he was a bad father—it's those moments that break me sometimes."

A thumb stroked across her palm. "The first time my powers came in was a sunny day in Provence," he admitted, and the stroke of his thumb turned a little desperate. "I liked Provence. There was a serving girl who was kind to me, and that was a rare thing. And Madame Cook always set aside an extra pastry for me."

"What happened?" she asked, for the first act of sorcery was nearly always Expression. An emotional outburst, and usually destructive.

"One of my mother's lovers was in the house, and they were quarrelling." Sebastian looked down at their entwined hands. "He barreled out of the house in a rush, calling for his carriage and his hounds, and when he alighted, he took the whip and sent the horses racing out of there at a gallop. The serving maid—Sybil, her name was Sybil—had been collecting eggs. She was walking through the gates to the courtyard when he drove straight into her."

Sebastian released a slow breath. "He didn't even care. He was worried about the horses, and shouting that the stupid girl should never have been in the road. My ears sounded hollow, and the world around me felt so distant. And he didn't care, even as Sybil lay there in the dirt." Tears shone in his eyes. "I killed him as my mother watched. I... I crushed him somehow, slowly, as he screamed. And when I looked at my mother's face, I saw her smile somehow fade. She'd been waiting for my powers to come in, but when they did, she didn't like what she saw.

"I'd been bred and trained to be a weapon to use against my father, but I think Morgana finally realized I was everything she'd ever dreamed of. Ridiculously strong. The perfect heir to two powerful bloodlines. *Dangerous*." His silky lashes swept down as he looked at their clasped hands.

Cleo squeezed his hand.

"She was never the same after that day," he whispered. "And on my next birthday, she collared me. I'd... forgotten about brushing her hair, about the books she sometimes bought me, for it seems so long ago now."

"The journal's bringing everything up," she said softly.

"She lost a first child before I was even born," he whispered, his gaze dropping to his lap. "A daughter. I never knew that. It's all through her journal. What she dreamt the child would look like, the little dresses she would buy for her, a trip to Paris for the pair of them when the girl was older...."

"She was threatened by me," he continued in a hoarse voice. "Because I was not a daughter. Her uncle.... The things he did to her as a child.... It broke her somehow, I think. And when she married my father, she could not see past her uncle. Whenever she'd speak of Drake, it was always with vitriol. *'He betrayed me.'* With another woman. With the divorce, when she was accused of murdering his nephew and only heir." Sebastian buried his face in his hands. "And I was my father in every way in her eyes. *'You're his mirror image,'* she used to say, but it was not in pride. But she loved this daughter. She loved the idea of her in a way she could never love me."

Cleo brought their clasped hands to her lips, pressing a kiss to the back of his hand. *This* was the heart of his turmoil, and her heart broke for him.

"I was a threat," he rasped, and this time his eyes gleamed from emotion, not the moonlight. "But once upon a time, she was occasionally kind and... I'd forgotten that."

Cleo gently tugged him into her arms, and he rested his head on her shoulder. "I think the worst thing about hateful parents are those small moments of kindness. For they give you a glimpse of hope. They make you crave it, and you can never understand why they withhold it so frequently." Cleo stroked his hair. "Your mother didn't deserve you."

He was silent for a long moment. "Your father didn't deserve *you*."

Cleo sucked in a sharp breath, for it hit a little too close to home. For what if Lord Tremayne wasn't truly her father?

CHAPTER SEVENTEEN

SEBASTIAN SAT UP from deep sleep with a gasp, rubbing at his throat. The collar was gone, but he could still feel the ghostly caress of it from his dreams, as if it were branded in his memories. He could feel Julia Camden's touch as she worked his body like a puppeteer.

He couldn't stay here. *Mother night.*

Scraping a hand over his mouth, he shoved the blankets aside and found his feet. A restless energy swept through him, one that demanded movement, and then he slipped his trousers and robe on, and escaped his bedchamber.

The hallway was cooler, his bare feet slapping on the timber floors.

He turned to glance at Cleo's room. He'd insisted that she stay in her own room tonight, knowing the diary would stir his nightmares. He couldn't go to her now either. Not with the stain of his past upon him.

Sebastian made his way downstairs, a silent ghost in the dark. Easier to breathe here. Easier to get some perspective. Curse Lady E for asking him to read that bloody journal. It stirred old wounds, dragging him back into a past he'd rather leave behind. And for what? What fucking purpose? Was he supposed to remember all the times he'd tried to please his mother? The gifts—her little reward system.

The fact that once upon a time he would have done anything—*anything*—for one kind word from her.

His chest felt like a gaping hole, his ribs splayed wide and bloody. He couldn't fucking *breathe*.

Pressing a hand against the wall, he rested his forehead on the cool plaster. He needed silence and cold. Something to ground him and remind him he was in the here and now, and not trapped in that nightmare.

A sharp *crack* made his eyes jerk open, and he lifted his head.

Turning, he caught a glimpse of a slash of warm candlelight lighting the hallway floor toward the back of the house.

A shadow rippled through the light, moving with predatory intensity, and he froze, instantly recognizing its owner.

Bishop.

Who should have been tucked up in bed with a warm handful of his beloved wife.

The last thing Sebastian wanted was to be caught out here. To have to explain his actions. He tensed to go, listening intently, but his brother never stepped through the door.

And curiosity began to lash through him.

From what he'd seen of his brother's marriage, Bishop and Verity were happily bonded. But his brother was clearly haunting the other edge of midnight for a reason, and as much as he wanted to snort at the notion, he doubted it was because Bishop had nightmares too.

It was foolish. Resentment rose in his chest as he moved silently down the hall, but he simply couldn't help himself.

The door was open, just enough to see through. The back end of his brother was bent over something—a table perhaps—and it all suddenly made sense when he realized Bishop held a billiard cue in his hand. He saw the stick move sharply, and then heard the crack of a pair of balls. Bishop stepped back into view, scowling at the table, and Sebastian froze.

"Are you coming in?" Bishop called softly, in that scarred-velvet voice. "Or going to stand out there pretending you can sneak up on an assassin who can hear the beat of your heart calling to him."

Caught.

Bishop tilted his head, those dark eyes meeting and holding Sebastian's gaze through the slender opening. Sebastian breathed out through his nose, and then slowly pushed the door open.

He didn't want to be here. Didn't want to have to talk to this man. "That's incredibly creepy, you know."

Bishop chalked his cue, and gave a faint shrug. "I'm a practitioner of the Grave Arts. Brandy?"

Sebastian sauntered around the table, rolling one of the balls under his palm. "I thought abstaining from anything that was supposed to weaken my resolve was the key to mastering myself?"

Bishop poured himself a brandy, then held the bottle up as if to ask again.

Sebastian nodded.

Liquid splashed into the glass, the warm amber glinting in the firelight. Bishop set the bottle aside, then turned with a tumbler in each hand. "Can't sleep?"

Sebastian looked away as he took the tumbler. "I'm not the one with a wife upstairs and a warm bed waiting for me, while I'm trying to beat myself at billiards."

"Right." Bishop snorted. "If we want to play that card, then I could counter with the fact you have a wife. And a warm bed waiting for you, if I'm not mistaken."

That was part of the problem.

"Fancy a game of billiards?" Bishop asked.

"What? No lessons?" Sebastian arched a brow, and gestured to the cue stick. "No throwing mage globes at each other, or having my teeth handed to me while you show me just how proficient you are with that thing?"

"Not in the house. Verity would have a fit if we broke anything."

"Verity wouldn't give a damn. She was raised in the streets of Seven Dials. I daresay she's seen her fair share of broken furniture."

Bishop ran his hand along the billiards table. "She's quite partial to this."

Sebastian paused. *Did he just...?* He glanced down at the table and swiftly removed his hand from its surface. It wouldn't be the first time Bishop had seduced his wife in an area other than his bedroom—or perhaps it was the other way around. He was never quite sure.

"And this is the first time Ver's ever had a home," Bishop pointed out. "I'm not about to let you destroy that for her."

Sebastian slunk around the table, uneasy still. He liked Verity. Probably more than he should, considering how few people he could truly trust, but there was something about the look in her eyes at times. Shadows haunted her, and despite her quick wit and smile, she had the look of a survivor.

She'd also kept his secret, if Bishop's rare good mood was anything to go by.

"You just want to beat me at something else," Sebastian said slowly. He should make his excuses. Leave. But what was the point? He was only going to stare at the ceiling for half the night.

"That's what brothers do, don't they?"

Their eyes met.

He'd been Montcalm, and Sebastian, and "apprentice," but he'd never been called brother. Not by this man. Not without sneer or sarcasm. "I wouldn't know."

Bishop screwed up his face as if he'd bitten into rotten fruit. "Neither would I. You're not the only one trying to find your feet in this scenario." Bishop looked frustrated. "I can't reach you. Not as a tutor. You don't trust me. We're getting nowhere. The ladies told me to play nice."

As suspected. Sebastian stared at this brother of his, hands in his pockets. "I appreciate the truth. Subterfuge doesn't sit well with me."

"In the interest of truth then, I'll also admit that beating you at billiards *does* entertain me. Just a little."

"You might lose."

"Care to wager on it?"

Despite himself, he was drawn. This was one area where they stood on even footing. "What do you want? My soul?"

Bishop flashed him a dangerous smile. "I think you've already traded that. It didn't go well, from what I've seen."

Sebastian's eyes narrowed. "Are you actually joking about the demon? Verity's right. You do have a terrible sense of humor."

"In? Or out?"

"In. If you lose, then you have to wear a pink waistcoat." He smiled as Bishop blinked in surprise. "For a week."

"Going straight for the throat, I see." Bishop considered him. "If I win, then you have to offer to clip Agatha's toenails."

He almost choked.

"Best of three," Bishop said, with an evil smile.

"I'm not going to lose." Not now, with so much at stake.

Bishop racked up the three balls, setting them with precision into a triangle. "Your break."

"Too kind."

Bishop flashed white teeth at him in what was probably the first true smile he'd ever shared. "I wanted you to get one good innings in before I demolish you."

"You do realize you've never seen me play? There wasn't a lot to do for a boy in the countryside in Le Havre." And if *big brother* thought he was being a sport in offering the first cut to Sebastian, then he wasn't going to return the favor. It was about bloody time he was finally better at something than Bishop.

"Le Havre? That's where you grew up?" Bishop stepped back from the table, and tugged his cheroot case out of his pocket.

"Calais for a while, then Geneva for a few years, and on to Vienna. Morgana sent me to the Consular Academy—a boarding school there—while she vanished for a few years, presumably leading the Order's assassins on a merry chase. Ghent, Munich, Le Havre, then on to Paris." Paris, where his mother's friends first laid eyes upon him. The name of the place flinched through him, and predictably, he missed his first shot, sending the balls scattering, but not pocketing a single one.

Sebastian looked up, but Bishop seemed preoccupied with lighting his cheroot. It wasn't as if he could have known the effect asking about Sebastian's past might have had on him.

He split the pair of balls in the corner, sending them flying around the table as Bishop poured them another brandy. One hit the pocket, and Sebastian showed his teeth in an equivalent smile as Bishop passed him his drink. "I'm out of practice."

"And two shots in."

He considered the play of the table, sighting along the cue. There was no way he could manage this in fewer than three shots. He sank the second ball, and then moved intently to set up the third.

"The Order had an execution warrant out for your mother," Bishop said, leaning against the fireplace. "But it's almost like she vanished once she left England. They had Sicarii assassins hunting her for years, and even they couldn't find her. Nobody even knew you existed."

"Morgana's a master of the Art of Illusions," he breathed, lining up the final ball. "From my very first memory, I wore a watch covered in runes that cast an illusion every time someone looked at my face. I was never allowed to take it off. I'm certain she had her own version."

He hammered the final ball into the end pocket. "Four shots. Your turn."

Bishop looked interested as he took the cue. "A watch to wield the illusion? That's an incredible amount of fine detail to set up in the spell work. Illusions work best when they're being managed directly."

"Whatever else she might be, my mother's an excellent sorceress," he said begrudgingly as he racked up the balls for Bishop. It was part of the reason they were having so much trouble finding her.

"How would you even...? You'd have to keep powering it. No, maybe a rune to channel your own power, but then you said you were young when she gave it to you, not fully fleshed into your powers yet, so...." Bishop looked like he was trying to solve some complex mathematical equation.

And enjoying the idea of it.

Sebastian fetched the balls from the pockets. "I had to wind it each morning to power the spell for that day. There was a rune in the side of it to gather energy into the device, and when you wound it, the spell was triggered until it ran out of power. If I forgot to wind it in the morning...." His stomach knotted at the memory.

"If you forgot...?"

"Then she put me in a travelling trunk and locked me in," Sebastian replied, and made sure the balls sat in a straight line. No point in handing Bishop the victory.

There was silence.

He looked up.

"A trunk?" Bishop asked incredulously. "How old were you?"

It wasn't the worst thing he'd ever endured, though it had given him a fear of the dark for a long time. "Perhaps five or six."

"For how long? Did she feed you? Did she...." Bishop seemed as though he didn't know what to say.

"The worst was a day or two," Sebastian replied coldly. "It didn't take me long to remember to wind the watch. She said it was to teach me responsibility."

Bishop scowled, and paced around the table. He considered the placement of the balls, but looked through them as if he saw something else. "Damnation."

"What?"

"Agatha's right, as bloody usual," Bishop muttered, sending the balls careening around the table. None of them landed, a sure sign he'd upset the other man. "You don't respond to punishment. You've been punished too often."

He laughed under his breath. "Not a single thing you've done to me this past month is what I'd call punishment."

Bishop paced around the table, but his lips were pressed firmly together. Flashes of his dark eyes kept sweeping over Sebastian, but he finally focused on the billiards table. He potted two balls off his next shot, muttering under his breath, before he chalked his cue and considered the play. "Then what do you respond to?"

Nothing. But that wasn't entirely correct. "Rage. Fear. Anger.... Violence." He thought for a little bit. "Being chained up."

Being chained down, and whipped, and raped.

"All emotions, or a physical threat that inspires emotion," Bishop said. "And you can't use that forever. Expression is too dangerous, you need to learn to—"

"—master your will," he echoed, as if he hadn't heard it a thousand times before.

Bishop missed his next shot.

"It appears this round will be a tie, at best," Sebastian mused.

"There's also guilt," Bishop said, taking his time to set up for the fourth shot.

Guilt. He felt leaden. "That doesn't inspire me."

"The only reason you're here attempting to rescue our father is because you feel guilty," Bishop pointed out. "It took me a while to realize you even cared."

Sebastian headed for the brandy. This was not the sort of conversation one wanted to have whilst sober. *Fuck.* "I *don't* care for him. He's a stranger, and all he's ever meant to

256

me was a windmill to tilt at. My mother's dreamed of Drake's downfall for years. I just.... I just want to know why he did it."

It plagued him at night. He drained his drink, poured another. "I mean, why would he sacrifice himself to the demon in my place? He had to know he might never escape its clutches. He had to know how horrible it would feel. It's been using him as a vessel for over a month, and I could barely handle a single day with it inside me."

Sometimes when he woke, he could still feel that vile thing inside him. His soul had been locked away deep within his own mind, passenger in a body he could no longer control, but he'd seen what it was doing. He'd felt it pressing in upon him, until it was a wonder he could stand to be in a dark room at all these days.

"And you never think about how he feels, with it inside him?" Bishop murmured. "You've been there. You *know*."

"Of course I bloody do." He drained another snifter of brandy, feeling the urge to pace.

Bishop turned back to the table. "Guilt," he pronounced.

It wasn't that fucking simple.

"I barely know the man." His voice rose. "He got my mother with child, then divorced her when he realized she'd poisoned his nephew. The only part he's played in my life has been a name my mother's cursed for years—the reason we're even here in this country to begin with. He was a target. Nothing more. What do you expect from me?"

"Drake thought you were dead. Your mother sent him a bloody rag and told him that was all that remained of the child she carried. He believed it. He mourned you for years."

"Then he didn't know my mother. Morgana doesn't cast aside a potential weapon, no matter how angry she is." Sebastian's lips thinned. Something had been plaguing him. "What happens if we can't get him back? I asked Lady Eberhardt but she said I should ask you."

Bishop's face blanked of all emotion, and he examined the billiards table with ruthless intensity. "That's not an option. We will get him back."

He sighted down the cue, but he didn't fool Sebastian. Not this time.

Especially not when his next shot went wide, and he turned to the chalk as if it alone could save him.

"Everyone keeps saying Drake's the greatest sorcerer of this generation. And the demon within him isn't going to be so kind as to relinquish its hold." Sebastian could remember the feel of its claws raking through his mind, and swiftly swallowed the rest of his brandy with a shudder. "Not after it went to so much trouble to trap him into being its vessel. We have the Wand, and the Chalice, but not the Blade. Not the real one. And even if we do get our hands on it, can we vanquish a First Tier demon?"

"We will do whatever we must."

"What happens," Sebastian repeated softly, "if we fail?"

Bishop finally stopped chalking the cue, his voice turning to ice. "Then I have to kill him. I'm the only one who can."

CHAPTER EIGHTEEN

'Any seer has the ability to scry; to seek another's whereabouts. But there are ways to Veil against scrying, if one knows how. And ways to break through that Veil.'

—Quentin Farshaw, *'Sidestep Through Time'*

THE NEXT MORNING, Cleo reached for the map of London and her scrying crystal. She was still under orders not to engage her divination arts, but she *needed* to know.

Taking a small knife, she cut her finger and dipped the crystal in her blood, before turning to the map. And then she hesitated.

What if there *was* a child out there who shared her blood? There was a hollow feeling in her chest. She almost didn't want to know.

A sister?

Imagine the hallways of her childhood then, filled with laughter instead of silence. Imagine being able to curl up in bed together, knowing their father cared little for them, but at least they had each other.

If the child survived, then why had her father sent her away? To be raised as this... this black queen?

"Blood reaches blood," she whispered, opening herself to her power. "Show me the blood."

Setting the crystal swinging over the map, she closed her eyes and felt for any answering tug. Sweat dripped from her upper lip as the minutes ticked by. Cleo finally opened her eyes.

Not in London.

She rifled through Bishop's desk, coming up with a map of the British Empire. A droplet of blood slid from her nose, but she dashed it away and turned back to the crystal. She *needed* to know.

But there was no sign of anyone sharing her blood in London. No one in the entire Empire. Cleo finally let the crystal spin to a halt.

Nothing.

It made no sense.

Unless the child truly hadn't survived childbirth.

"Do you remember the runes your mother used for your illusion watch?" Bishop asked, as Sebastian sat down for breakfast the next day.

"I can do better." He reached inside his waistcoat pocket and produced the bloody thing, sliding it across the table toward Bishop.

"What is *that*?" Lady E demanded, peering at it over the top of her teacup. "It makes me feel wretchedly queasy."

Bishop examined it. "Morgana etched the watch with illusion runes. When Sebastian wound it, the watch changed his appearance in the eyes of all who saw him."

"It's been broken for years," he said, seeing where this was going. Surely Bishop wasn't that desperate?

Last night reared up in his mind. The camaraderie they'd shared for a few brief minutes had evaporated when Bishop pronounced Drake's fate if they failed.

It made Sebastian uncomfortable. The only thing they shared was blood, but his brother loved Drake. It was clear in every plane of his face when the man's name was brought up. Killing him would destroy something inside Bishop, and while he might have wished all manner of curses upon the bastard, that... that was a line he didn't think he wanted Bishop to cross.

Bishop snatched the watch up in his palm. "Then it's a good thing I have a certain knack for restoring spell-crafted mechanisms—or creating them."

"You're going to fix it." Lady E's eyes narrowed. "And you think to use it against Morgana and the demon?"

"Why not?" Bishop suggested. "Perhaps we can use it to spy, or get close to them before they know it."

She turned and settled that beady gaze upon Sebastian. "Did your mother ever not recognize you when you wore the watch?"

"No."

"Is your mother the greatest Mistress of Illusions the Order has ever seen?"

He almost enjoyed ganging up on Bishop. It chased away the last of his moody thoughts. "As far as I know. She made me believe I'd destroyed the Blade of Altarrh, when all I bloody melted into slag was a kitchen knife."

"Adrian," Lady E raised her voice, "do you have any gifts of Illusion at all?"

Bishop laced his arms together over his chest and scowled at her. "I'm an assassin, Agatha. The answer is yes, though I'm not Morgana. And I wasn't planning on sending

Sebastian in wearing a disguise. I was planning on sending myself in."

Bishop suddenly flinched, as if something invisible swatted him across the ear.

"Utter codswallop," Lady E muttered, slurping her tea. "While you might fool Morgana, there's a possibility you propose to waltz beneath a demon's nose. A demon can see through *time*, you fool, let alone any cloaking spells you intend to use. Then there is the matter of your father, and *he* would never fail to recognize you, no matter what face you wore—"

Sebastian tuned out, sensing the sudden strengthening on the soul-bond. He turned his head toward the door, drawn unerringly toward the focus point of his sudden awareness.

The ladies appeared, Verity linked arm in arm with Cleo. The second she walked in the room, his heart started to skip. A dark green gown caressed her slender curves, and the bodice was cut far lower than anything he'd ever seen on her before. The jacket was black velvet, with ribbons of green silk and black lace adorning it. He sensed Lady Rathbourne's hand all over it.

Sebastian looked away. He almost missed the virginal lace Cleo's father had draped her in, if only for the sake of his sanity. Green suited her pale skin, and his fingers itched to begin unhooking those little brass buttons down the front of her jacket. Touching her that night hadn't been enough. His long-dormant desire was stirring, and it had a particular destination in mind.

Verity blinked when she saw her husband. "What the devil are you wearing?"

Distraction, thank goodness.

Bishop scratched at his jaw. "Sebastian thought my attire needed brightening up."

262

"That's hideous," she continued, looking amused as she lifted the tureen lid on the kippers. "Where on earth did you find it?"

"Sebastian loaned it to me."

"Oh, no," Sebastian broke in. "Don't pretend that came out of *my* wardrobe."

"Is that my old dress? Is that what you wanted it for this morning?" Cleo frowned. There'd been shadows under her eyes earlier, but she seemed to have rallied. "You said it was an emergency."

He relaxed back in his chair. "It was. I'm hardly about to let him get away with losing a bet. It's a worthy cause, if only to see Bishop wear it for a week. I cut the skirt, and Agatha helped me hand-stitch it to the front of his waistcoat. It took almost two hours."

Cleo smiled her secret smile—the one that made his insides stir—and took her seat. "In that case, I'll consider it a worthwhile loss." She poured herself some tea, and appraised the man. "You look positively smashing in pink, Bishop."

Verity chortled.

"Thank you, my dear," Bishop drawled.

"So what are we up to?" Cleo mused. "I'm well rested and if I stay in the house one more day, I think I shall scream."

Verity touched the watch. "What is this?"

Bishop swiftly explained.

"I have a plan to steal the Blade back," Bishop said. "The only problem is we still cannot find Morgana. Lucien's tried scrying since the ball. Lady E tried. And Verity attempted to lock onto her location using her particular talent for finding anything she sets her mind to. Ianthe's had all her contacts out searching. She even set the rest of the Sicarii to hunting last night. And Verity and I have been all through Seven Dials, and Balthazar's Labyrinth. None of her usual allies know where she is."

Cleo's dark eyes locked on Bishop. "Are you trying to tell me you asked *Lucien* and *Lady E* to scry for Morgana's whereabouts and you didn't think of me?"

"I thought of you," Bishop said, resting one arm across his neighboring chair, revealing his delightfully pink waistcoat. "But you've been under the weather since the ball, and I was under strict instructions not to bother you."

Sebastian didn't quite look at his brother.

"Give me the watch," Cleo growled.

Bishop crossed his arms and looked quite pointedly at Sebastian. "Is she allowed to use her scrying gifts?"

"I am sitting right here," Cleo said sharply. "Oh, for heaven's sakes." She reached across the table and snatched up the watch, shooting him a particularly challenging look.

"Madrigal said you'd overstretched yourself," Sebastian pointed out. "I didn't want you to harm yourself. And I thought you couldn't scry her either?"

"Something's shielding her from Sight," Cleo said grimly. "We've all tried. But that was before I laid hands upon Farshaw's book."

"Something?" Bishop murmured.

"Fine," Cleo replied. "The demon. Lascher. I could sense it watching over me the last time I tried to scry. I can feel Morgana out there, but Lascher obscures her whereabouts with some sort of shadow I can't penetrate."

The last thing he wanted was the demon's gaze lingering upon his wife. "Cleo."

"I need to do this," she told him, and he heard the catch in her voice. "I'm the greatest seer of this generation. I have an item Morgana once touched in my hand, unlike last time. And Farshaw spoke of how to break through a Veil. I can do this. I can *find* her. I have to find her."

He stared at her determined face. This was more than merely an attempt at scrying out their enemy. She'd lost so much, but most of all she'd lost her belief in herself.

"If anyone can do this, it's you," he said, circling the table and sitting beside her. "Hold my hand. If you need me—my power, anything—then it's yours. Just don't push yourself too far. Madrigal spoke of knowing your limits."

Cleo took a deep breath, her shoulders relaxing as he squeezed her hand. "I won't push too far."

She closed her eyes. Started muttering under her breath. Long moments stretched out as he stared at her moving lips. She shook her head. "The Veil's still there. The watch isn't enough."

Shoulders slumped, all around the table. He'd actually thought she could do it.

Cleo's eyes suddenly popped open. "I'm an idiot."

"You are?"

"Here, give me your hand," she said, reaching for him. "Bishop, do you have a knife?"

Bishop produced one—of presumably many—from within his coat. "Always."

She took the knife and met Sebastian's eyes. "Blood calls to blood. You have a direct link to your mother. Do you trust me?"

He nodded, holding out his hand.

Cleo took a deep breath, and sliced a small line across his finger. Blood welled, and she smeared it across her hands, before taking both of his palms in hers. "You might see some strange things, considering how we're bonded. Whatever you do, stay calm. And close your eyes."

He obeyed her, seeing nothing but darkness.

Cleo started murmuring her ritual words under her breath again. Suddenly he was floating high above London among fluffy gray clouds, even as he sat in a chair in

Bishop's dining room. London seemed so far away, church steeples spearing up toward him, and a thousand miles of cobbled streets lying in wait, should he fall. He would have panicked, if not for the hand in his.

"Relax. We cannot fall. We're not truly here."

It felt real enough. Sebastian discovered a hitherto unknown fear of heights. He looked stoically at her bloodied hand in his, realizing he was clinging to it.

Cleo floated beside him, wearing a gown of pure white, with her silvery hair cascading down her back. He could barely make out her face. Some sort of diamond of pure light gleamed in the middle of her forehead. She looked like an angel.

Dark eyes flashed toward his, and she smiled. *"That's very sweet, Sebastian. But I'm no angel. This is merely my astral form. What you're seeing is my Third Eye."*

"Can you find her?"

Cleo turned her attention toward London. *"This is where it will get strange."*

Merde. He'd almost reached the levels of strange he could handle.

A throb of heat began to beat between their linked hands. The world around them pulsed in response.

"Blood follows blood," Cleo whispered. *"Find me Morgana Montcalm. Find me blood of blood."*

They swooped down, and he was fairly certain he screamed. Streets flashed past him. A cemetery ringed in an iron fence. Oxford Street, bare of any pedestrians. Covent Gardens theatres. Kensington.... Each image pulsed past him, until his heart was racing.

Then there was a hazy gray barrier in front of them, almost like a wall of pure fog.

Sebastian found himself standing upon a cobbled street, with Cleo's hand in his. Sweat dripped down his spine. Solid ground. Bloody hell.

"Here's the Veil," she said, her brown eyes fueled with pure determination. "I could never get through it in the past. But now I know how."

She began whispering again, strange words he almost, almost understood. Reaching forward with her free hand, she began to trace runes in the air, channeling power into them. They glowed with golden light, vanishing one after the other.

And then a thin golden strand of pure light latched around him, driving from his naval through the Veil.

"There it is," Cleo whispered. *"Where is it taking you?"*

Something tugged at him. Then he was flying forward, hungry faces swimming through the fog to meet him, their mouths opening toward him—

They punched through the Veil, the golden line hauling him faster and faster. He could hear himself screaming, gasping, trying not to react.

And then they landed in the middle of a garden.

A house stood before them. A beautiful house, glimmering all over with a cascade of wards. He was on his knees, the golden strand at his naval tugging him toward the house.

"There it is." Cleo took a step toward it, slowly letting go of his hand.

Sebastian opened his eyes, finding himself on his knees on the carpet inside Bishop's dining room. *Mother of night.* There was a hand on his shoulder. Bishop. An empty tureen in front of him, just in case he wanted to cast up his accounts.

"A pleasant journey by the look of it." Bishop looked amused.

"Fuck," he said, scraping a hand over his sweating face and shaking. The world had stopped moving around him. He wanted to kiss the floor.

Cleo remained sitting in her chair, her eyes closed. "I've got her now. Morgana's in a house... a beautiful house. The West End somewhere, I suspect." Cleo's head cocked to the side, almost as if she were listening. "I can't see inside the house. It's warded quite heavily. I'm only just getting through. Not enough to give me any details."

Her eyes blinked open, staring into nothing. "Get me a map."

Bishop hastily produced one, scraping the tea setting out of the way.

Cleo took a deep breath, and hovered her hand over the map of London, shutting her eyes once more. She moved her hands slowly across the map, pausing over Knightsbridge.

The rest of them leaned forward. A sliver of tension went through him. After last night, Sebastian felt a little conflicted about confronting his mother. She deserved to die, but... it all felt a little raw.

"There," Cleo whispered, her eyes flicking open and her bloodied finger stabbing into the map. "She's right there."

"Hammerton Lane," Bishop mused, launching into action. "Let's go."

Lascher looked up from its working, halting the flood of power as he sensed a distant tickle at the back of his mind. Bloodied lines crisscrossed the lawn, and seven bodies lay discarded, their throats and wrists slit in sacrifice.

It turned his head toward London, and opened himself up to his Sight. For a second it saw the girl standing in front of Morgana's townhouse in her astral form. She glowed like a perfect beacon. The White Queen in all her glory.

She was learning. She'd pierced its Veil, and found the decoy.

The demon smiled. *Run little rats.*

And then it turned back to its work.

Nothing could stop it now. Plans were proceeding perfectly. And she still hadn't found its black queen.

"Slight problem," Verity said, popping out of thin air.

Sebastian would never get used to that. "What sort of problem?"

Ianthe, Lucien, and Agatha were leading a scouting party to find out if the demon was with Morgana. He hoped the problem wasn't coming from them.

"The house is warded. Bishop can't get inside. He tried to cross the threshold and it nearly knocked him out." Verity's face paled. "The illusion works. Even I wouldn't recognize him, but we can't get the Blade."

"Can he get through the wards?" Cleo asked. "He said he could slip through Drake's."

"He's studied Drake's wards for years," Verity replied. "With time he could get through Morgana's, but we don't have time. The demon's not inside the house, but it might return at any moment."

There was one solution. Sebastian scraped a hand over his mouth. "I might be able to get inside."

Both women blinked at him, but it was Cleo who shook her head. "No," she said, her dark eyes softening.

"You can't face Morgana. You know you're not ready for that."

"If they're the same wards she's been using for years, then I can get through them," he argued. "It's tied to aura, or blood, which means it might still recognize mine. And there's one problem with harnessing your will, and using ritual to power spell craft; it's very difficult to change the ritual, or the runes, or the charms you use after so many years of using the same ones. She might not have been able to change the wards."

"You can't go alone," Cleo argued.

"Yet nobody else can get in," he pointed out.

"What about me? Our auras are linked. There's a chance that if you can get inside, then I can too. It might work."

Like hell. "If I go in alone, then she has no one to use against me. Bringing you is like gift-wrapping my weakness."

"That's very touching." Cleo crossed her arms. "I can ward better than you can. I also have this rather convenient innate detection guide. If something's about to go wrong, then I'll know it."

Her Premonition.

"Besides, perhaps I can lead us straight to the Blade. I've held it before in my hands. I know what it feels like, and my gift of psychometry might help me find it. You don't even know where she might be keeping it."

True. His nostrils flared. "Cleo, she might kill you."

He couldn't quite say the words—that Morgana knew exactly what his wife meant to him, and if she thought she could cripple him by killing Cleo... she wouldn't hesitate.

Cleo arched a brow. "She might kill *you*. She did threaten revenge. Link with me. We're stronger together."

"I work better alone," he snapped.

She actually rolled her eyes at him. "*Tick, tock,* Sebastian. You're not going to win this argument. If you want to sneak inside before the demon returns—if it *is* staying with her—then I suggest you save your breath."

He shut his mouth. She was— He could just about— He turned to Verity, but she was frowning, staring into the distance as if she listened to some private conversation. And chances were, she wouldn't take his side anyway.

It would be a cold day in hell before Ver agreed that a lady's place was waiting at home for her husband.

"Fine," he said curtly.

"Bishop doesn't like it," Verity said, blinking back into the here and now. "He doesn't think you're ready."

Sebastian arched a brow. "Bishop doesn't have to like it. It's time he cut the apron strings. Tell him he can either let me try, or we might have to fall back on Plan B. I need that watch. If Morgana recognizes me, she'll attack instantly."

"He's coming."

"What's Plan B?" Cleo asked, helping him shrug out of his jacket.

"Drake has to die."

Cleo froze, her fingers on his lapels.

He met Verity's eyes, and saw the distress in them. Verity slowly nodded, and clearly passed the message along. "Fine. You have this one chance. *Don't* fail."

CHAPTER NINETEEN

THE WARD SHIVERED over his skin as Sebastian slipped the window on the second floor up, and slowly edged over the sill. The ward quivered a little bit, plucking at him as if it didn't quite recognize him, and so he cut his finger and pressed the bloody pad of it to the wall.

His aura might be slightly different, thanks to Cleo, but it definitely recognized his blood. The prickling sensation vanished. First success.

The house was quiet, and he couldn't sense any sign of alarm. Morgana could have altered the wards, but these particular ones were ingrained in her memory. Changing the template would have required a lot of time, effort, and meditation.

Cleo took a deep breath, perched upon the branch they'd both climbed. It was becoming easier to see her, thanks to familiarity, but the cloak she wore was embroidered and spelled with runes, courtesy of Bishop. Not quite an Invisibility Cloak, but one that kept telling him to *look away, look away*, and he was developing a slight ache behind his right eye by forcing himself to see past it.

She reached out, testing the wards... and her hand passed through open air. They both released a faint breath.

Morgana's wards recognized her as an extension of him. Just as their heartbeats had aligned with the formation of the soul-bond, so had their auras.

He reached out to help Cleo inside, heart beating a little quicker. Her skirts slithered over the sill, and she fell against his chest, his arms wrapping around her.

They both froze.

Silence. He pressed a finger to her lips, and then opened his link to her. Instantly it felt like a weight eased from his shoulders, heat and life spilling through him, and cocooning him in the psychic scent of her.

This was what it felt like to be whole these days. Sometimes, in the dark of night, he wondered what if would feel like if he were to accept the bond completely. Right now, he could sense more of her than she of him, thanks to her initiation of the ritual. They were linked, but he was in control of how far it went.

What would it feel like to share thoughts with her as freely as Bishop and Verity clearly did? Or Ianthe and Lucien?

But she didn't know about the ticket to Manhattan, and he couldn't bear for her to dredge the depths of his nightmares or memories. Some things were never meant to be shared, especially those.

"Can you feel anything?" he asked.

Cleo closed her eyes and reached out to press her palm against the wall. The Divination Arts were completely foreign to him.

Her head tilted to the side, as if she were listening to something. Then her eyes shot open. *"Got it. It's faint, but it's definitely inside the house. Lower, I think."*

"You focus on the Blade. I'll keep an eye out for guards."

Cleo nodded, and he glided ahead of her, careful of his footsteps.

"There's no one on this floor," she whispered, in his mind. *"But there are at least three people in the house. Downstairs, of course, which happens to be where the Blade is."*

Sebastian untied the small bag at his hip, and plucked out one of the glass orbs Bishop had given him, planting it behind a statue as they slipped along the hallway. As much as he hated to admit it, the man was pure genius when it came to spell craft. Bishop was better suited to being a scientist, or an engineer, but he somehow managed to put those instincts to use to make himself a better assassin.

She grabbed for his arm, just as alarm screamed through her. *"Someone's coming."*

Sebastian shoved her behind a curtain, into a small window alcove and followed her in, hand resting on her ribs. This was the hardest bit. The second he embraced his power, any sorcerer nearby would feel the prickling sensation of it.

Cleo sucked in a slow breath, her breasts crushed against his chest, and despite the urgency of the situation, he couldn't stop his gaze from shifting lower. From this height–this position—he had a prime view directly down her bodice. Black lace teased him, tantalizing more than hiding her assets from view, and those creamy swells thrust up as if to tempt him.

He felt her gaze on his face and glanced up, beneath his lashes, realizing he'd been caught looking.

"Later." Even her mental whisper sounded husky.

Later. Jesus. His cock swelled at the thought, a muscle ticking in his jaw. Now was definitely not the time. Or the place.

But there was no telling his cock that.

Footsteps stalked past, a man muttering under his breath. "...ain't here to be at your ladyship's beck-and-fuckin'-call."

Those stern boots hammered up the stairs, and Sebastian breathed out. *"Anyone else setting off your Premonition?"*

Cleo shook her head slowly.

Easing aside the curtains, he backed out into the parlor, setting another of the glass orbs beneath a stuffed parrot's tail where it wouldn't be seen. Five left in the bag. He planted them in the rooms they passed through as they followed Cleo's hesitant tugs toward the Blade.

"Down." Cleo sent the thought to him as they covered the entire bottom floor. *"I feel like it should be right here, but it's not. The Blade must be below us."*

He sighed. *"Of course it is. She'll have set up her altar in the cellar. No doubt it's warded too."*

They hurried through the servants' hallway, and Sebastian pushed into the next room—

—right into another man.

The fellow's eyes widened, his moustache quivering as he opened his mouth, and Sebastian slammed him back into the wall, clapping a hand over the bastard's mouth. A knee drove into his thigh, narrowly missing his groin, and he staggered back, taking the stranger with him.

A blistering fist hammered into his head. He caught a flash of Cleo's startled eyes, as she hovered helplessly. *No sorcery! No sorcery!* He didn't know whether it got through to her, for his back hit the kitchen bench, and pain sliced through him.

A month's worth of hard training suddenly opened up in his mind. He blocked the next blow, getting his feet under him, just as power bloomed within his attacker.

He was dangerously open to any metaphysical attacks. And so was Cleo.

Grabbing a fistful of the man's hair, Sebastian wrenched with both hands, snapping the man's neck.

The hard weight landed on him, driving him back against the bench again as they both slumped. His heart was pounding. He held them both there, listening, gradually hearing the sharp rasp of Cleo's startled breath over his ravaged heartbeat. She'd clapped both hands over her mouth, and slowly lowered them, swallowing hard.

"Are you all right?"

He nodded, and there was a second where his gaze dipped to the body in his arms, and he realized he'd just killed a man—

Not his first time. Probably not his last, but she looked shocked.

"Cleo." He let the man's body down, hauling him toward the pantry by his boots. *"There's no time for panic. Can you feel the Blade?"*

Color seemed to be flooding back into her cheeks. *"Definitely below us."*

"Richard?" a man called from above. "Was that you?"

Silence lingered in the house. Cleo shot him a look.

Jesus. They must have heard the scuffle, as quick as it was. She held her hands out to him as if to say, *what are we going to do?*

He cleared his throat and called gruffly, "Aye. Just tripped on somewhat."

"We're going to have to move quickly," he sent. *"Find the cellar."*

Cleo swirled her *look away* cloak off her shoulders and handed it to him. *"Cover him."*

Then she scurried toward the pantry, as he lowered the fellow to the floor and swung the cloak over him. Instantly he was encouraged to see past the lump on the floor. It would have to do.

"This way!"

He followed her past the pantry, to a rickety staircase.

There was a faint tingle as he reached for the door at the bottom. This ward was stronger and more aggressive than the one protecting the house.

He hadn't come all this way only to be deterred now. Footsteps creaked somewhere above them, but they were far lighter than the other two. A little flurry of nerves stirred in his gut. He hadn't seen his mother in the house yet, but the signs of her were everywhere. Perhaps they were in luck. Perhaps she wasn't at home.

His fist clenched. A part of him hoped she was.

Cleo rested a hand in the middle of his spine, as if she sensed his tension. *"My Premonition is itching again."*

They either needed to break the ward on the cellar and search for the Blade, or try and escape.

This wasn't the time for a confrontation. He had Cleo at his side, and the fate of Drake rested upon his ability to steal the Blade out from under Morgana's nose. Escape wasn't an option.

"The second I break this ward, she'll know," he told her. *"Time for Bishop's distraction. Are you ready?"*

"To thwart one of your mother's schemes?" Cleo's thumb stirred against his spine, though her breath still came shortly. *"I'm all in."*

Sebastian swelled with power, and triggered the globes he'd left all through the house.

The second they were inside the cellar, he called a mage globe of pure white to life so they could see.

The tingle of the broken ward skittered over his skin, and he could hear cries of surprise from above. A woman's voice came to him, just distant enough that he couldn't make out the words, but the sound sheared through him like a knife. Morgana.

Focus on the Blade.

"Find it," he snapped. Bishop's distraction wouldn't last long. The smoke pouring through the house, and the small detonations would cause confusion, and make it difficult to see, but Morgana was no fool.

There was a low altar in the corner of the room, and a hexagram engraved in the floor in silver. Cleo moved perilously close to it, and he hauled her up short. "Don't step on that."

Red velvet gleamed in the corner, covering a globe of some description. A scrying device, probably. Sage hung in dried clumps from the walls, and he caught a glint of silver on the bench along the side wall, but it was only his mother's athame, a ritual blade used to draw blood to power her spell work.

Power brewed in the house. It felt like a gathering storm.

"Cleo!"

"Here!" she cried desperately, placing her hand flat on one of the flagstones on the floor. "It's drawing me to this stone."

"Stand back." No time for finesse or stealth. Not anymore.

Sebastian triggered a small spell, and the flagstone exploded in a little hail of stone that he contained within a ward. Kneeling down, he fumbled in the hole, hauling out a larger slab of stone that was all that remained. There was something beneath it. More velvet. Something long and sharp. "Got it."

No denying it was the Blade. He'd touched it once before, and felt the malevolent, oily stain of its aura, for lack of a better word. The Blade was stained with blood, involved in numerous sacrifices over the years, and those deaths haunted it.

"Let's go." He grabbed her by the arm, and hauled her toward the staircase.

They slammed into an invisible ward at the top, and he swore under his breath. Of course. "I thought it was too easy." Getting inside the cellar was the easy part. Getting out, another matter entirely.

Cleo pressed against that invisible wall. "Damn it. Sebastian, my skin's on fire, my Premonition setting off all sorts of alarm bells." Her pale face flashed toward him. "She's coming."

Morgana.

The world dropped away from him, that familiar icy chill sliding through his veins. He had years and years of pent-up violence stored within him. *Revenge*, whispered the darkest part of him, hungering for it. No longer weak. No longer powerless. Bishop had granted him the chance to finally, finally match up against his mother and see which one of them emerged the victor.

He severed the link between he and Cleo, not wanting her to be a part of this.

"Stay behind me," he said, handing her the Blade. "I'll cover you. You need to get the Blade to Bishop, no matter what happens next."

CHAPTER TWENTY

HE WENT COLD. That was the only way to explain it.

"How are we going to get out?" Cleo whispered, resting a hand on his arm, and holding the Blade in her other.

"Stand back," he said, flexing his hands.

Static wards like this could be broken with an enormous influx of power; a hammer-blow of immense proportions. Cleo glanced at the roof above them. "Bastian, be careful."

"I know what I'm doing." For once he sounded confident. "Bishop's had me cracking wards for the past month. This is something I can do."

Power swelled through him as he sucked it up through his feet. She could almost feel him vibrating with energy, and the surge of it she felt through the link buoyed her.

"*Shusharah*," he cried, bringing all his power to bear upon the invisible ward.

The backlash was immense. Sebastian flung up a ward to protect them, driving her into the wall and covering her with his body. Dirt shivered from a crack in the ceiling as the entire house shook.

The second it died down, he took her hand. "Move!"

They bolted out of the cellar, through the kitchen, and straight into chaos. Black smoke clung thickly in the air, and Cleo bumped into Sebastian as he stopped abruptly. Neither of them could see a damned thing.

"Didn't think of that," Sebastian muttered, groping for her hand in the dark.

She coughed as the thick smoke filled her lungs, and his hand came to rest between her shoulder blades, pushing her low where the air was clearer.

"We just need to find a window or a door."

"Not a door," he called. "It's her first rule. If we were ever under attack, then she locked down the house wards. The second we open a door she'll know where we are."

Cleo couldn't stop coughing. *"I'm fairly sure... she's going to know anyway."*

Wind stirred through the air, sending the black smoke roiling. Sebastian stumbled through a doorway, and they found themselves in the main entrance, where the air was considerably clearer.

A swish of red skirts appeared on the main staircase, the last remnants of Bishop's smoke globes thinning to mere threads in the air as Morgana stirred wind through the house.

It was a shock to suddenly see her, face-to-face, and Cleo squeezed Sebastian's hand.

Morgana froze on the stairs, the rings on her fingers glittering where she rested her hand on the bannister as she and Sebastian finally faced each other again.

"Hello, Mother," he said, in a voice practically dripping with ice.

A hammer strike of Vision suddenly slammed through Cleo's head. *Blood. Everywhere. An explosion of red light; a mage globe.* Then she was blinking past it, trying to suck in the air to breathe. Bang. Bang. Bang. Little Vision vignettes struck her, one after the other. *Morgana screaming. Sebastian's hands closed over her throat, his eyes black with pure rage. The walls trembling. Parts of the ceiling ripping away as he lost himself to his power.*

Expression. Always dangerous. Always uncontrollable. This was why it was considered illegal, and all practitioners either forced to learn to harness their will and control their powers, or be executed.

She came back to the world huddled against the nearest wall. There was an icepick in her brain. She could barely breathe. Premonition screamed through her, leaving her virtually crippled.

It was the first time the full force of her Visions had stirred since her father took her blindfold. Instead of relief, she wanted to vomit.

"Fancy seeing you in here, Sebastian," Morgana drawled, advancing down the staircase, her skirts trailing sinuously over each step. Green eyes flickered toward Cleo. "And your precious little wife. I have a bone to pick with her."

Morgana's smile could only be considered menacing.

He stepped between them, blocking Cleo's view. Frost crackled up the walls, but he was still in control of himself. For now.

"Sebastian," Cleo rasped. "*No.*"

They needed to get out of there, before her Vision came true.

"We have the Blade," he said. "And you're not going to manipulate me today."

"Aren't I?"

The carpets crunched with little particles of ice as Sebastian took another step toward his mother. "No."

"Look at you," Morgana drawled, pausing on the stairs. "Almost reined in. It's quite impressive."

"Perhaps it's time we finally had that little discussion I've been promising all these years," he threatened.

"I can hardly wait." Morgana lashed out, power lancing like a dart toward him—

Cleo screamed, but a bubble of iridescent power shimmered around him, and his mother's attack skittered harmlessly aside, sheering through the wall.

Sebastian advanced upon her, hands clenched at his sides. For the first time, something else flickered in Morgana's eyes. Fear.

"You've been learning," Morgana chided, clucking under her tongue. "Who was fool enough to teach you how to ward?"

"My brother."

Morgana retreated up the stairs, one step at a time.

"You might recall him," Sebastian's voice sounded dark as midnight as he took the first step. "He's the assassin, remember?"

Cleo staggered to her feet, holding on to the wall. *"Don't do this."*

"Get the Blade out of here," he told her.

"Not without you."

"And what is your assassin brother going to do when all of this is over?" Morgana chided. "Do you think he's not going to look at you and see a threat? An educated one?"

The arrow struck its mark. Cleo sensed his confidence falter through the bond. "Do you think you have a place with your father *if* he ever gets that creature out of himself? One big happy family... is that what you see? You'd like that, wouldn't you? You always wanted a brother or sister."

His fists clenched. "You know nothing about what I wanted."

"No?" Morgana reached the top of the stairs, and glanced behind her, as if to search for someone to help her. "What about Lord Rathbourne? Do you think he looks at you and sees anything more than the man who helped kidnap his daughter? And his wife, what does *she* think of you?"

Cleo frowned. Something about the woman's manner struck her as odd. Morgana had never fled before. "Sebastian, don't listen to her. She's trying to poison your thoughts."

He tilted his head as if he were half listening to her, but she could feel him locking himself down inside, so even she couldn't reach him. "I know."

Morgana locked eyes with Cleo and smiled. "Ah, the sweet young bride. Always your champion, my dear boy. How long do you think she's going to look at you with those loving eyes? How long before her hope starts to fade?"

"That's enough," he said.

"Have you fucked her yet?"

The walls began to shake.

"If not, then I'm sure the demon could take care of her virginity for you. It's got an insatiable appetite these days."

"I'm sure you would know that," he spat. "It's the only way my father would ever touch you again."

For the first time, something real flickered in Morgana's eyes.

"No," Cleo whispered to him, *"You're not your mother. Don't stoop to her level."*

His fists clenched, lightning flickering across his wards. "Do you remember when you said you would destroy everything I ever loved?"

A shard of glass from the chandelier dropped from the ceiling, shattering on the marble below. Morgana didn't look at it, but she faced him at the top of the balcony, her calculating eyes gauging the damage she'd done. "I remember. I remember everything. Did you know Julia Camden is working for me? The bitch is practically frothing at the mouth to get her hands upon you again."

A red mage globe formed in his palm. He threw it toward his mother, but Morgana flicked it aside and it exploded as it hit the wall, sending chunks of plaster flying.

Another formed. And then Morgana brought her own to life. Seven red globes circled her head as she twisted her wrist, and she smirked at her son. "Let's do this then. Show me what you've learned."

"Sebastian!" She tried to reach him, but the link between them was locked down tight now, and only he had the power to open it.

Hand fisted around the Blade, Cleo scurried up the stairs after him. Another hammer-strike of Vision sent her swaying into the wall—a white painted hexagram splashed over timber floorboards, a timber hall runner dragged over it.

A trap.

Then the image was superimposed over the sight of Sebastian finally reaching the top of the staircase. Morgana backed away slowly, lashing out at him with crackling blows, trying to find any weakness in his wards.

Sebastian brushed away each attack almost contemptuously, advancing with sure and steady strides, and Cleo suddenly realized Morgana was not bringing all her power to bear upon him. Just enough to distract him as she took stealthy steps back. Panic flickered over the woman's heart-shaped face, but her eyes gleamed hot and steady.

"Is that all you've got?" he asked in that dangerously soft voice.

Premonition dug into Cleo's skin like knives as he started to take another step, and she could almost see her prediction colliding with real time, the spelled star hovering beneath his unsuspecting foot—

Cleo gathered her own power and reached out, hauling him back sharply. He staggered as she used telepathy against him, ripping at his coat. It was never her forte, and she barely managed to stop him in time, but he didn't take that final, fatal step.

"Under the rug," she gasped, as he looked back at her. "It's a trap."

Cold green eyes cut her way, Morgana's lips thinning. "You're starting to get on my nerves, dear daughter-in-law."

Cleo dragged herself to her feet, and cried out in surprise when one of the mage globes suddenly hurtled toward her.

Cleo crossed her wrists at the last moment, a ward coalescing around her. Red heat exploded over the ward, the impact driving her to the floor.

Sebastian's heart leaped into his throat, his hand outstretched toward her.

But the heat died down, and Cleo looked up at him, wary, but untouched. "I'll shield myself."

He turned back to his mother, rage turning into crystalline clarity. There was nothing Morgana could ever do to him to break him. But this... this crossed every line he owned.

The walls of the house started shaking again, and wind whipped through the house as he summoned it into a vortex. Glass smashed somewhere else as the pressure in the house mounted, and the windstorm increased. Pottery smashed, Morgana's skirts blowing back behind her, and her arm flung up in front of her face to protect herself.

"You won't touch her again," he said, in a deadly soft voice, utterly devoid of feeling.

The center of his own deadly whirlwind, he took the attack to his mother.

Mage globes hammered her, one after the other. A new one formed above his hand just as the previous one battered his mother's wards, and he could feel his strength fine-tuning itself. Morgana went to her knees, holding her wrists crossed, strain twisting her face.

Yes. He stepped around the hall runner with its deadly trap and advanced. A heat spot formed in his mother's shield. His next mage globe struck it in the dead center and Morgana's wards exploded.

She hit the floor, sliding back on the polished marble several feet. Blood dripped from her nose, and a sense of exhilaration choked him.

All of Bishop's lessons seemed to coalesce in his head. He formed a manacle of pure energy and flung it toward her wrist. The glowing manacle snapped shut, locking her hand to the floor.

"You want to know why I could never be your mother?" Morgana spat. "Because I was warned this would happen. Your wife's not the only seer out there. I was always going to die because of you." A sob broke loose. "You're a monster. A monster I held to my breast."

The words picked him apart, and Sebastian paused, only to have her throw a tangled golden web of spell work at him.

It wrapped around his body, cutting into his skin like snaking wires. He screamed and went to his knees. Fire in his blood, wrapping around his bones... then his mother was upon him, lifting a knife and trying to drive it into his chest—

Bishop's training made him react in time. He slammed a palm to her shoulder, shifting her deadly trajectory. Sharp pain slashed across his shoulder, as he used her momentum to drive her murderous hand toward the floor. The knife clattered free from her outstretched hand, and Morgana scrambled to get it, the glowing manacle sucking her toward the marble again.

It buzzed suddenly, the current in it evaporating.

One hand wrapped around her throat and the other scrambled for the knife. There was blood all down his arm. Everywhere. She'd genuinely tried to kill him. It broke him. *If you'd only fucking loved me, I would have been yours....*

A seer had done this. Turned his mother against him as a boy. Years of abuse hammered through him: the collar locking around his throat; the first time Morgana used the control ring to drive him to his knees with the pain; the last time she'd locked him in a box as a little boy; women touching him, pawing at him....

He lifted the knife. She'd been more torturer than mother, but.... But....

"Do it," Morgana hissed at him, her nails digging into his wrist. "Go ahead and fulfill your destiny."

Cleo. His heart broke again, and he held the knife in the air above her, suddenly realizing what this all looked like.

Morgana started laughing. "She'll never look at you the same way."

"Sebastian, no!" Cleo reached out for him, her hair whipping behind her in the whirlwind.

He looked up at her, the knife in his hand. His mother sprawled beneath him, still spewing her vile poison.

"This doesn't end until she does." His voice broke. "You don't understand, she'll never stop! She'll keep coming, she'll try to ruin me every second she still draws breath, and she'll... she'll destroy everything that I... that I care for. I can stop her. I can stop her."

"If you do this, you become her," Cleo said softly.

And it finally struck him, why Lady E wanted him to read his mother's diary so bloody badly.

Everything Morgana had ever done to him had been because she'd trapped herself in her own vile circle.

...I just wanted somebody who loved me...

...My uncle raped me...

...Your father betrayed me...

...It was the only time in my life I haven't been responsible for what I was accused of...

And he saw her for the first time. Not as the woman who was evil, but someone who, at various stages in her life had made a dark choice. Someone who'd turned down the wrong fork in the road.

In that moment he had the power over his mother, and he actually saw her cowering beneath him.

Emotion was his weakness. Lady E knew that. Morgana knew that. She'd said she could manipulate him better than anyone else on this earth, because she knew him, and he was her son in so many ways.

Truth. Truth so piercing that he'd always known, deep inside, that she wasn't lying. *"You're your father's son,"* Morgana had always told him.

But there was another part of him that existed. A darker half that aligned more with his mother's side than with his father's.

Because, at heart, he *was* who his mother had been, before she'd made those choices.

Abused. Tormented. Powerless. Bitter. The only thing that separated them was the fact she had finally killed her tormentor, and never again trusted another soul. Not his father. Not Lady Eberhardt.

Not even him.

It struck him then, how things could have been so different for her if she'd been able to move past her torment.

"Sebastian?"

The knife lowered, his grip on Morgana's throat softening as he beheld her. The winds slowed.

There'd been a cage around him the last month, despite the mirage of freedom. Something that held him back from the people who cared for him, and now he finally understood it.

Him.

He was the key to his own freedom.

And this moment here, was the catalyst for it.

The whirlwind stopped. The air stopped pressing in upon them, frigid with ice. Furniture dropped out of the air, and Morgana flinched as Sebastian slowly lowered the knife.

Killing her would be too easy. He wanted to. He wanted her dead so badly his fist actually shook.

But the second he did that, he became her.

And as she crawled back across the floor, her legs dragging behind her, he finally shattered his mother's hold over him.

"Sebastian," Cleo whispered, her hand held out before her, as if she sought to placate a wild animal.

He took in the room. A mess of fury. He took in his mother, her eyes narrowing in that familiar hiss of rage. "You'll ruin her. You know you will. She'll never love you."

And he pitied her.

But nothing else.

Power bloomed within him. All his telekinetic lessons sprang to mind. It was ridiculously easy to reach out and pluck the table upright. To set the room below to rights. He used a cushion of force to pin his mother to the ground where she couldn't move.

Sebastian gained his feet, staring at his hands. He felt like he could do anything.

Glass smashed as someone in black hurtled through the window, and then Bishop rolled to his feet, shimmering knives of pure etheric force forming in his hands as he took in the scene. Verity punched into midair, fists raised as if to block a blow that never came.

Bishop blinked in surprise to find the room already locked down. "Heard someone screaming, and then the house wards went down."

"It wasn't us," Sebastian replied, still holding his mother pinned to the floor with telekinesis. Sweat slicked his temples. The effort it took to keep her in place without crushing her was immense.

"I can handle this," Bishop said, seeming to note the strain. A pair of shimmering golden manacles suddenly appeared in his hands. "Let me in?"

He dropped the pressure wards, and Morgana threw something at him. Bishop slapped it away almost contemptuously, and knelt down to slap one of the manacles around her wrist.

"No!" she cried, fighting him.

"Morgana, I have a warrant for your arrest and execution," Bishop said, "for the murder of Drake's nephew, Richard de Wynter, twenty-seven years ago. You will face the Prime of the Order, and the Triad Council for your crimes, including the use of a sclavus collar on your son, the murders of many others, theft, blackmail, and the summoning of a demon to this plane. If you make any sudden moves, it is within my powers to eliminate you, do you understand?"

"Sebastian!" his mother hissed, reaching toward him. "You treacherous little cur. Do you think they'll stand by you when this all comes to fruition? Do you think you can ever be part of them?" Her green eyes locked on Cleo. "You'll ruin her. You know you'll ruin her."

"That's enough." The heat drained from his face.

"You're my son," she spat. "You'll never be free of me! I'm in your bones, in your soul, in your—"

Bishop muttered under his breath and she suddenly gaped, her mouth freezing around an invisible gag.

"That's better," Bishop said. He looked up. "Are you all right?"

You'll ruin her. You know you'll ruin her. He held out his hand, only to find it was shaking.

Cleo took hold of it, squeezing it gently. "I think it's time to go home."

And he had nothing left within him to argue.

Morgana had scraped him raw.

CHAPTER TWENTY-ONE

"ARE YOU PLANNING on this being a regular occurrence?" Cleo asked as she helped Sebastian out of his bloody shirt. "I don't know that my nerves can handle it."

His ears were still ringing. He could barely remember the carriage ride home. The last he'd seen of his mother, Bishop had been dragging Morgana to the cellars, where he planned upon questioning her about the demon's whereabouts. Nobody thought Sebastian needed to be there for the questioning, and neither did he.

"Sit," Cleo said, pushing gently upon his shoulders.

He sank onto the chair by the fireplace, exhausted right to his bones. Slumping his head into his hands, he let her dictate his movements as she clucked over his arm. He barely felt it. The wound to his heart was far deeper. Nothing had changed. His mother had taken a damned good shot at killing him.

He was a weapon to her, nothing more. And now he'd become a threat. He couldn't even understand why he'd... hoped... for anything different.

Water rippled as Cleo squeezed out a clean rag, and checked the wound to his shoulder. "Not too deep. I think I can heal it. Are you ready?"

He nodded, and felt her hands suddenly heat. Then energy swirled through him, and there was no more pain.

Sebastian caught her hand, looking up. "Thank you."

He didn't know how to ask for what he wanted, but she knew. He saw it in her eyes as she slid onto his lap and wrapped her arms around him.

"I—"

"No." She pressed her fingers to his lips. "Just let me hold you."

He couldn't recall anyone ever simply holding him before Cleo, and the sudden hunger to be in her arms was overwhelming.

This tenderness was something he was unaccustomed to. Holding her hand last night for hours had felt like more of a connection than anything he'd ever felt before. Desperate to hold her closer, he drew her into his arms, pressing his face against her throat. A shiver ran through him.

"Let it out," she whispered, but he couldn't. He couldn't.

Soft hands slid up and down his arms. "It hit me hard the night of the Ascension," she admitted. "When my father died. I knew it was going to happen. I'd Seen it." She made a little strangled sound in her throat. "I'd tried to turn him from his path. But it was inevitable in the end, for he didn't want to stray from it. Not if he had a chance at confronting Drake and killing him. His hatred for your father ran too deep for him to listen to me."

Cleo slid her hands into his hair, letting the black strands run between her fingers. He looked up, focusing on her soft mouth.

"It still hurt," she whispered. "Even though he earned his own death. Even though he was barely a father to me. No. He was a horrible father. There. I've said it."

"The Order will execute her," he said softly. "She deserves it."

"I know she's horrible. I know she's evil. But it's all right to grieve her loss, or the loss of what she could have been. What you hoped she could have been. She was still your mother. A terrible mother, but... I understand."

Sebastian shuddered, turning his face into her palm. "She tried to kill me."

Cleo's expression softened, and her eyes shimmered with the tears he could not shed. She leaned down and pressed a soft kiss to his mouth, her thumbs stroking his cheeks.

He set his hands on her wrists. Not now. He couldn't.... He wanted the comfort she offered, but after the other night, he didn't dare touch her like that when his head was such a mess. She deserved better than for him to use her body to make himself feel better.

"Maybe later, Cleo." He sat back, and raked his hands through his hair. "I want to burn her fucking journal."

"I'll fetch it for you." She moved to the pile of books Sebastian had set on his bedside table.

He stared leadenly at the wall, feeling empty within.

And it was only when it was too late that he realized what he'd tucked inside the journal, to keep it safe from prying eyes.

At first she didn't quite realize what she held in her hand. Her mind moved slower than her eyes could perceive. A ticket... Liverpool to Manhattan... Mr. Sebastian Montcalm. A steerage ticket made out in her husband's name. *But why would he...?*

A soft inhalation of breath sounded behind her, and Cleo looked up just as Sebastian turned sharply in his chair.

His gaze dropped to her hand.

To the ticket.

And the second she saw the expression on his face, it all suddenly made a great deal of sense.

"You're leaving." The date was printed right there—a week. No, less than that. The room spun around her. She felt like she couldn't gather her thoughts.

"Cleo—"

And suddenly time snapped back into place, an odd clarity pervading her thoughts even as her heart curled into a small, tight knot in her chest, oddly painful. "No," she whispered. "I think I understand. You never wanted this. You never wanted any of this. All you've ever been focused upon is the destruction of your mother, and—"

"I wanted freedom," he snapped. "You don't know what it's like... to spend the past fifteen years bound to Morgana's will by that fucking collar. All I've ever dreamed of is escape. And... I didn't know.... I hadn't made up my mind yet, but—"

"Hadn't *made up your mind?*" She shook the ticket at him, the heat of her anger suddenly scalding. All she'd ever demanded from him was the truth. It was her own damned fault she felt something more, but she couldn't begrudge him that. But he'd *lied* to her. He'd let her believe there was something more growing between them. "This looks like it's quite made up to me. You *bought* a ticket. Were you even going to tell me? Or your brothers? Or would I have just woken up one day to find a letter on the bed? Did you plan to help us with your father, or have you simply washed your hands of him—"

"It's not like that."

"Then tell me what it's like!"

A rap at the door interrupted. Cleo swallowed down the hot words she'd been about to spill. She couldn't deal with this. Not right now. Not on top of everything else. And she was dangerously close to tears. The last thing she wanted right now was to betray how upset she felt.

"I won't hold you to this bond," she whispered, setting the ticket in his hand as she strode past. "And if you wished to get an annulment, then I would not protest. Perhaps... perhaps this was all a mistake."

And then she fled, before her emotions could get the better of her.

Sebastian stared after her, the ticket clenched in his hand. He knew his wife, he knew she wanted to say more, and yet she'd closed herself off to him in a way she'd never done before. She'd even locked down the bond from her side, muting her emotions—but not before he'd felt the sharp slash of pain that rippled through her.

Jesus. She hadn't let him explain.

And he didn't know if he *could* explain, for he didn't even know precisely what he wanted to do.

The ticket mocked him. The lure of escaping all this mess still attracted him. He could feel the pull of it even now, even in the face of Cleo's distress; a fresh start away from his mother's machinations; away from the guilt of Drake's sacrifice, and the frustrating lessons Bishop was pushing him headlong into; away from responsibility, the concept of family, commitment, and a world he didn't understand. One he'd never known, one where other people expected things from him—no, demanded them.

A world where Cleo existed, trying at every moment to connect with him, when she was the one thing that utterly destroyed him.

A world where he feared her disappointment, feared the loss of her affection, of never being able to measure up to the image of him that she'd somehow concocted—a hero who could save her, a good man, one who rescued kidnapped children and protected his wife of convenience. A husband who could offer her love, when he didn't even know *how*.

But he wasn't that man.

He'd killed people, mostly at Morgana's will, but sometimes... sometimes of his own volition. He'd fucked women he cared nothing for, learning how to lock himself away from his body while it performed. He'd walked away from innocents, knowing any interaction of his would only earn them worse punishment from his mother's schemes. He'd deafened his ears to screams and cries for mercy. He'd locked himself away, locked his heart away, and turned himself into something that lived and existed, and didn't own hope or dream of anything more, because sometimes the most brutal thing his mother could do to him was allow him a chance to hope, only to tear it away.

It was the only way he knew how to survive.

Until suddenly he was free of his mother's command, and a whole world had unfolded before him. Choices. The ability to make his own decisions, to imagine possibilities. A future he'd never had before. Escape.

And yet he'd found himself in a new set of chains. A wife. Brothers. Sisters-in-law. A father he'd never known, but had hated. A father who'd sacrificed his own life so Sebastian could know this freedom. Family. *Family*.

It was too much. It had *been* too much.

Sebastian stared at the ticket. Morgana had been captured. He had no reason to stay. But he knew events here weren't finished.

No reason, except a wife who was trying not to cry, right at this moment. *"If you wish an annulment...."*

He didn't know what he wanted to do with his future, but he knew the answer to that one question at least. No annulment. Cleo evoked a thousand different emotions within him, including ones he couldn't even name, and yet walking away from her, never seeing her again.... That knot in his gut was back, but the longer he waited....

"Is something amiss?" Bishop asked, staring through the open door. "I came to see how you were."

How you were....

"Shouldn't you be questioning Morgana?" he asked.

Bishop blinked. "I was just on my way down there."

A sharp knot began to untwist within his chest. Morgana was important. The demon was important. And Bishop was obsessed with rescuing his father.

It struck him then, what the man was trying to say. He'd come here first.

He... cared?

Another thought struck him. Bishop hadn't been happy to let Sebastian break into his mother's house. *Watch your back,* he'd said at the time, and Sebastian had thought it meant, *don't fail.*

But Bishop was still wearing the pink waistcoat— though he'd taken it off for the mission—and he was here, instead of trying to wring questions from the one person who might know how to find the demon.

Merde, he was looking at this all wrong.

"You are definitely not all right," Bishop said, his dark brows drawing together. "Do you want to go spar? Or hit something? It always makes me feel better."

Sebastian stared at the ticket. He'd made a ruin of this. These people cared for him. It felt... surreal. His feet were moving, faster than his thoughts. "Not now. I have to find Cleo."

Sebastian went after her, tracking her through the house. The library. Of course. It was where she always sought refuge, hiding in that bloody book she'd become absorbed in.

He stepped through the doors, taking a punch to the heart when he saw her dashing away her tears, and resolutely opening the book to the page she'd marked. Duty gave her something to focus on, a means to sidestep the press of her emotions, and he didn't know why he hadn't seen how thin she was stretching herself. He'd been so busy trying to sort through his own turmoil that he'd barely given thought to hers.

"Cleo."

"You don't have to explain," she said, clearly trying to be brave. "I won't hold you to this—"

"If you'd give me a chance to speak," he said sharply, through gritted teeth, "then you'd know I *want* you to hold me to this marriage."

Dark eyes flashed to his.

Bottling his turmoil, he stepped through and closed the doors, locking them behind him. Then he turned and looked at her hungrily. Despite her reddened eyes and splotchy skin, she'd never looked more beautiful.

His decision had been made, perhaps long ago, before he even knew it himself.

"I never wanted to marry you," he said. "You were simply one more thing my mother forced me to do for her.

Imagine my shock when I couldn't resist trying to see what sort of woman my mother was binding me to, and found you. You with your endless hope, and helpless charm. You with your belief the world was a happier place if only one strived for it. A woman who betrayed her father in order to help rescue me from a collar that bound me to my mother's will. A woman who fought for me every step of the way, pushing me to do what was right. A woman who argued there was something better within me, when I couldn't see it myself." His voice softened. "And now you're giving up? Now you won't even give me a chance to explain, when it's my turn to fight for you?"

Her chin tipped up, her lower lip quivering. "There's only so much of my heart I can give you without destroying myself."

"Well, that's too bad," he said, starting toward her. "Because I want it all."

Wariness filled her gaze. Cleo found her feet, pressing her bottom to the desk as he advanced. "It's not yours to give or take."

"No?" Lifting the ticket, he tore it into little pieces, dropping it on the carpet as he made his way toward her. Her eyes widened in shock, and he took a step to the side as she shifted to escape. "I think I already own it."

He'd known for a long time how she felt about him. Cleo had bonded him, so there was no way for her to hide the truth from him. And he'd learned to shield far quicker than she ever had.

She darted one way, and he caught her in his arms, dragging her against his chest. Cleo's arms were trapped between them, and she squeezed her eyes tightly shut. "*Please*. Please don't do this. Not unless you mean it. I don't think I can handle it if you were to toy with my affections right now."

"I'm sorry," he whispered. "So sorry I haven't been able to give you what you wanted until this moment. When I woke in chains after Drake sacrificed himself for me, I knew I was free of my mother for the first time in my life. Free of her sclavus collar. Free of everything that weighed me down. I've never known freedom before. I've always hungered for it, but I never considered what I would do if I ever actually gained it." He paused, sliding the mass of her hair in his hands and beginning to tug the pins restraining it free. "I wanted to leave England, and to leave this mess behind me. I thought perhaps I could strike out for the Americas. No Morgana. No demon. No…."

"*Me*," she whispered. "Our bond is just another chain around you. I'm so sorry, Sebastian—"

"If you hadn't bound me," he pointed out, "then I wouldn't be here to even wonder about my life. I was dying. You bound me to save my life."

"At the cost of your freedom," she whispered, still looking horrified.

He brushed her blonde curls over her right shoulder. "That's not what I'm saying at all."

Cleo looked up at him. From this angle the green gown she wore hung just haphazardly enough he could see the smooth slope of her breasts and the lace edge of her corset. His cock pulsed, and Sebastian forced himself to swallow. Capturing her face in his hands, he drew back from her.

"I bought the ticket one day when Lady E was pushing me too far. It was a spur of the moment whim. I don't even know if I was ever going to set foot on that ship, but it gave me… room to breathe when I didn't think I could cope with everything." He pressed his cheek to hers, breathing in the scent of her soap. "I wanted a new life away from all this mess. But I was dreaming of the wrong sort of life. The second you fainted at the Ascension Ball I knew I could never go through with it. There you were in my arms, helpless and in danger. I didn't know what was happening to you and *it broke me.*"

He shuddered. "Cleo, you consume me in ways I've never known before. And you terrify me, for you ask me to be something I've never had to be. You want a husband, and you want a family, and those are things I've never wanted, until now.

"I don't know what love is," he whispered hoarsely. "You say you want my heart, but you don't know the truth. You have *my soul.* You've had it from the moment I first saw you, standing there feeding your ducks without a care in the world. You saved me. Time and time again, and I've never wanted anything in my life the way I want you." He clutched her close, breathing her in, trying to absorb the essence of goodness within her.

A soft cry came from her throat, and she slid a hand up between them, pressing her palm to her chest. "Sebastian."

"I choose *you*, Cleo," he whispered, hovering over her. "I choose us."

And then their mouths were meeting, his hands softening in her hair as he cupped her face and fused their lips together. He let his shields fall, becoming fully, irrevocably hers. The soul-bond roared to life within him like a flame given fresh air after being starved for so long.

He bound himself to her, knowing he could never hide from her again. Knowing there would be no annulment, no separation, nothing but a future, which they could forge together.

Their breathing harshened, becoming thick, ragged pants. He couldn't get enough of her. She was under his skin now, within his heart, their bond fusing them into one being, and the only way he could feel more complete would be to physically fill her.

Reaching beneath her, Sebastian captured her bottom and set her on the desk. Leaning toward her, he set both hands on the desk beside her hips, effectively trapping her. Their breath mingled, their gazes locking together. He couldn't look away from her if he tried.

"I want to be your husband in truth." Capturing her knuckles, he brushed his mouth to the back of them. "If you will have me."

Heat stirred pinkness through her cheeks. "You fool. I've been yours from the start."

And then she grabbed a fistful of his shirt and tipped her mouth to his, her body wilting in his arms.

His. Finally his. Sebastian's tongue drove into her mouth, his body screaming for sweet release.

He'd worried he might ruin this, earlier in their marriage, when all he knew of sex was pain and prostitution. But it was impossible to even think of Cleo the same way he'd thought of sex—of those other women his mother had forced him to service.

This felt new. Wondrous. A drugging sort of feeling that could consume a man, and make him whole again.

Sebastian drew back, gasping for breath, and their eyes met. Then his hand was sliding down the soft green silk of her skirts and capturing a handful of it, dragging it up. The brush of his fingers against her thigh made her suck in a sharp breath, and he could see every emotion she felt in her eyes; shock, pleasure, wonder, curiosity.

"Last chance, my love," he whispered, stroking his thumb up her inner thigh and feeling that delicious tension shiver through her.

"For you? Or for me?"

He captured her soft mouth in a kiss, sweet and gentle. "I made my choice, Cleo. Yes. The answer is yes."

She had no idea how very much he wanted to make love to her.

Or perhaps she did, for the walls between their bond were softening, and he was starting to catch a glimpse of her thoughts.

Oh, God yes. "Have we finished talking about it?" she breathed, and then that old flicker of mischief lit her brown eyes. "I swear I'm going to die of curiosity."

His fingers found her, brushing against the warm cotton of her drawers. Sebastian kissed her jaw, nipping at her throat as he worked his fingers through the slit in her drawers, and found the lush, wet heart of her. The blunt tip of his finger stroked its way down her seam, earning a shocked gasp.

"Sebastian!" Cleo captured his wrist, but she didn't push him away.

"Is that answer enough?"

He stroked her slowly, parting her wet folds, and staring into her eyes as if he could capture the moment.

She writhed, sinking her teeth into that fleshy lower lip. A certain sort of shyness came over her. It had been different the other night, in the dark, when she didn't have to look at him. He felt it too.

"Cleo." He stroked the soft little nubbin of flesh between her thighs and she moaned and rolled her hips, "Don't hide away from me. Look at me."

Their eyes met.

Her beautiful, beautiful brown eyes wide with wonder and desire.

"Have you never touched yourself before?" His lips skated across her throat, nuzzling at her ear.

"No," she gasped. "I just cannot believe.... Oh, oh, that feels.... *Ohhh*."

And he knew how it felt, for she was writhing now, her thighs pinned wide around his narrow hips.

He had the sudden, distinct urge to kiss her between her parted thighs, to plunge his tongue inside her, to shock her well and truly. And he was smiling to himself at the thought, surprised at how very innocent she was, she with her Visions, who claimed she knew exactly what went on between a man and a woman in bed.

Easing a finger inside her, he bit her throat as he worked his way within her. He wanted her wet and aching. He wanted this to be perfect. She clutched at his shoulders, holding on for dear life, her hair brushing against the mahogany surface of the desk. "Oh God, oh God, oh God."

Sebastian tugged at the buttons on the back of her dress, his lips working their way down her throat. He flicked his tongue against her skin, earning a small moan. "Lie back."

"On Bishop's desk?" She sounded scandalized.

"I'm fairly certain it's not as innocent as it looks."

Cleo clapped a hand over her eyes, her cheeks scarlet. "I cannot believe.... Oh, my goodness!"

"I've wanted to do this for a very long time," he whispered, nuzzling his face against her gown. It slipped from her shoulder, the lace of her corset clinging to the rosy tip of her nipple. Sebastian tugged it down, licking the gentle slope of her breast, his tongue darting over that pert nipple.

"Sebastian!"

He slid a second finger slowly inside her, an assault on two different territories as his heated mouth captured her nipple and he suckled.

Cleo clutched his shoulders, her eyes going very wide, and her mouth parting in ecstasy. The clench of her body around his fingers told him how close to the edge she was, and he speared his thumb over her clitoris, earning a helpless thrust from her hips, and a muffled scream she captured with her hand.

Yes! Please…. Oh, please. She was open entirely to him now, any separation between the two of them vanishing in the maelstrom of her pleasure. The room faded. The world vanished. All he could feel was Cleo, her pleasure and her thoughts overwhelming him in the moment as lightning swept along her veins.

Capturing her mouth, he swallowed her cries, working her through the orgasm. It was a miracle he didn't spill himself, crushing his erection against her thigh, and gritting his teeth at the pressure.

And then it was over, and both of them could breathe again, their tangled thoughts separating just enough for him to come back to himself.

Cleo's fists curled in his collar, and she pressed her forehead to his shoulder, aftershocks milking his fingers. Embarrassment blazed through her as he curled the tips of his fingers slightly, finding the slightly softer pad of pure sensation within her. She trembled again, lashes stirring against her cheeks, and one hand capturing his wrist as if to say it was too much.

"I love hearing you scream," he whispered, kissing the sensitive skin below her ear, then nuzzling the fleshy pad of her earlobe. He withdrew his fingers slowly, then lifted them to his lips and suckled her wetness from them.

A helpless laugh shook her shoulders. "You love twisting me in knots."

"That too." Sebastian dragged her drawers slowly down her thighs, giving her a hot, silky-lashed look. He went to his knees before her, sliding his hands behind the back of her thighs and dragging her to the edge of the desk.

Cleo's breath caught. She swallowed. "What are you about now?"

"Can't you tell?" He slid his thumbs up the inside of her thighs, pushing them wider, deliberately picturing himself lapping at her flesh.

She saw it through the bond, and pressed her cool hands to her hot cheeks. "My goodness," she blurted, and it was such a lovely, very Cleo moment that he laughed.

"Lie back," he teased, "and let me ruin you."

"You've already ruined me."

He buried his face in the tuft of blonde curls between her thighs, breathing her in. Cleo cried out as his tongue lapped at her, fingers sinking into his hair, and her hips thrust up, up, desperate for more. He circled her clitoris teasingly, suckling it into his mouth when she was close to the edge, wringing every scream from her that he could.

It was different to seek her pleasure. He knew how a woman's body worked—he'd been taught where to touch, where to stroke—and he'd always kept himself disconnected from the action. It was a means to an end.

But the feeling inside his chest right now was too large for his ribs. Cleo threw her head back and screamed in pleasure, and something proud reared within him. Something utterly masculine and possessive.

He was her first.

And in so many ways, she was his.

"You do realize what comes next?" he murmured, standing and looking down at his lovely, soft and disheveled wife as they both gasped.

"Next?" she murmured sleepily.

Sebastian deliberately thought of sinking his way inside her, picturing the soft cry of surprise on her face as he took her virginity. A hand curled in his collar. Her eyes softened beneath the dark fan of her lashes, and she bit her lower lip again.

"Yes," she whispered, a little saucily. "*Please.*"

Tugging at the flaps on his breeches, he let his cock spill free, stroking the firm length of it with a shudder. He wanted inside her. Now.

"Can I see you?" she whispered, sliding her hands up over his shoulders, but there were limits to what he could handle, and he shook his head, nibbling on one of her questing fingers.

"One day, maybe." When the past no longer haunted him. "Are you ready?"

"Yes," she blurted.

Sebastian pressed forward. Heated flesh parted, Cleo's nails digging into his back as he slowly worked his way inside her. He'd never taken such care before, but he didn't wish to hurt her more than necessary. He could feel the slight sting through their bond, feel the burning intrusion, and Sebastian rested there, waiting for her body to grow used to him.

He could barely hold himself back.

God, it felt so good. Home. Finally home.

And then his mouth met hers, and he was thrusting, slowly at first, still trying to make it good for her. He needed to be in control, but it was slipping through his fingers. His cock had a mind of its own, and he thrust hard, earning a soft cry from her lips.

"Yes," she breathed, biting his lower lip. "Like that."

Harder.

He had permission, and now there was no point in fighting for control over his body.

It felt glorious to pin her wrists to the desk, to fuck his way into her. Their eyes met again, hers wide in shock, and then he was kissing her again, their tongues tangling together with delicious intent.

Cleo. It had always been Cleo, from the moment he met her.

Of all the plots his mother had orchestrated, binding him to Lord Tremayne's daughter in a marriage of convenience had turned out to be the greatest gift Morgana had ever given him.

To think of how he'd dreaded that day, not knowing what Cleo would be like, and picturing a miniature Lord Tremayne in his mind, a woman with thick, beetled brows and a defined nose.

She'd been nothing like her father. Blindfolded, curious, sunny-natured, and prone to prattling. Sebastian's hands slid up her sides, as he let her feel how much that moment in time had changed his life.

Their thoughts tangled together, the bond swelling between them. He knew what was coming. A soul-bond was like a marriage, and needed to be consummated for the connection to form completely.

Heat soared through his cock, and he ground his teeth together, trying to prolong the rush of pleasure. The soul-bond began to tingle. It was all coming together. Sebastian cried out as he came, burying his face in her throat as he pumped his seed within her.

There was a new sensation within his mind. No longer two joined together, but one.

Hers forever.

Until death did them part....

He collapsed atop her, both of them slick with sweat and panting. He wanted to spend an eternity in this moment, clasped between her thighs, his seed spilling between them.

"That sounds lovely," Cleo whispered with a laugh, "but I think you'd start to crush me after a while."

He couldn't speak—heart pounding so hard it felt like it was lodged in his throat—and the words he wanted to say wouldn't form. Instead, he captured her mouth, hard and intense, pouring everything he felt into that kiss.

Much simpler than finding the words.

He couldn't get enough of her.

Taking her back to his bedchamber like some Viking lord with his plunder, he stripped them both bare and rolled her onto her back, capturing Cleo's mouth as his hips slid between her thighs. He'd worried once that he might hurt her in his sleep if she moved and he didn't know who she was, but that concern was long gone. With the bond between them there was no mistaking who was in bed with him, and the bond wrapped around him like a silk glove. A cocooning presence. A warm body pressed against his. Never alone. Ever again.

Everything coalesced into one single thought: this was worth fighting for.

Sebastian took his time with her this time, gentle and torturously slow. Both of them bore bruises from the encounter in the library, and yet his shuddering, scarred heart felt like it had finally healed. Losing himself in their bond, he thrust and rocked within her, hooking her knee up between them so it was crushed to her chest, and his cock rode over that exquisite little region within her until she cried out.

Not done. Not yet. But he stilled within her, rubbing his palms up her thighs and lean flanks. This had become less about his pleasure, and more about hers.

Soft hands stroked up his back, a finger caressing the hard knobs of his spine. He drew back, unable to look away from her beloved face. He'd never been able to bear her touch before, but he suddenly found he wanted her hands all over him.

He pressed inside her, moving in one smooth glide as Cleo gasped. And he watched her throw her head back beneath him, firelight gilding the smooth column of her throat as he lowered his face to press his lips there.

She was worth fighting for. Worth dying for.

And Sebastian lost himself in the promise of their future as he buried his need within her slender body.

She was finally a wife.

Cleo lay curled in Sebastian's arms, as her husband slept, his breath stirring her nape. Her body ached in several places, but she was fairly certain she wanted to do this again. Many times.

Her cheeks ached, but her smile slowly faded as the grim reality of the situation crept in. They'd captured Morgana, and now they had all three relics. She and Sebastian couldn't hide in here forever.

And then of course....

She stared up at the ceiling, nerves twisting within her. Curse Farshaw's book.

Sebastian stirred, drawing her into his arms with a sleepy murmur. "Care to tell me what's bothering you?"

"Bothering me?"

He traced a finger between her breasts. "There's a darkness in your heart. A shadow. I don't know what it means, but I know you're scared about something."

Enjoyment flooded from her like a shroud someone tore from her skin. She sat up, raking her hair back from her face. It wasn't as though she could hide things from him anymore, but if she didn't think about it too strongly, then he wouldn't know.

But was that fair?

He'd given her all his secrets. They were in this together, no matter how nervous her latest suspicion made her. She couldn't stop thinking about her flash into the past and what she'd seen there.

...the demon is in me.

She was almost absolutely certain she knew where her divination gifts had come from, but there were other implications she'd only recently begun to dwell on.

Her mother was dead. No matter how much she tried, she couldn't find any trace of her blood out there when she scried. There was only one other possible candidate in that scene who could have been the nemesis she'd been preparing to meet.

"Cleo." He watched her making her decision, his silver eyes patient, but narrowing. "Who is the black queen?"

CHAPTER
TWENTY-TWO

CLEO SAT UP abruptly, the soft languidness of the prior moment washing off her as if it had never happened. "How did you know that name?"

Sebastian rolled onto his back, slinging his arm above his head. "I sensed it through the bond. You were thinking about it as we lay there."

Cleo threw the sheets back, slipping from the bed, a nervous exhilaration suddenly running through her veins. "I n-need something to drink."

Finding her robe, she slipped it on, feeling far too naked all of a sudden. There was a flagon of wine on the sideboard. Two glasses. A celebration for two that she'd prepared earlier, and needed now.

The rustling of sheets behind her told her he'd shifted to watch her. Cleo gulped her first mouthful of wine, clinging to the sideboard. What was she going to tell him?

"The truth, preferably," he murmured.

And she realized the bond between them was wide open. Cleo slid her shield neatly back into place and turned to look at him, her heart seizing in her chest.

He was beautiful. Intelligent. Everything she'd ever wanted. And he was finally in her bed, their marriage consummated. It should have been a dream come true, and yet the first cold tendrils of fear slid through her.

"I told you about my prophecy," she whispered. "London's doom."

"Me," he murmured.

Cleo's throat locked tight. "You were always there. The dark clouds swirled around you, seeming to overwhelm you, and you screamed a cry of such loss and fell to your knees and the entire sky ripped open, destroying London. And the only thing that seems to offer any hope is a flurry of white lights, beating back the tide of darkness." She paused. "I thought it was you. I thought you were the creator of such destruction, the wielder of the portal. I thought every light represented a person who might be able to hold you back. Me. Drake. Bishop. Lady E... all of them. But I misread the Vision."

That brought his gaze to hers, a sudden predatory intensity highlighting the hard lines of his face.

"It's not you," she whispered, setting the wine aside and pacing to the windows, staring sightlessly through the glass. "The night we bonded—just before your mother kidnapped me—I awoke in a dream. It was the first time I've dream-walked, and I don't think it was of my own volition. The demon was there, sitting across a chessboard from me. It told me to make a move, that I was the white queen, the one who directs the play. The one who could see the future. And so I made a move. I set Bishop into play, and the demon moved his own rook—Verity. The night Drake sacrificed himself to the demon, I received a second dream. My father was dead, which meant I'd taken one of the demon's major players. Verity was now wearing a white sash, and I'd won her over to my side, but… the demon had taken Drake. The game ended in a stalemate."

"We're all chess pieces?"

"To the demon, yes," she replied.

"And what color am I?"

"You were black," she whispered, "but now you have a white sash, and you're my king."

The tension in his shoulders dissolved as he began to think. "Can you recognize the other pieces the demon is wielding?"

"Yes."

Sebastian sat up, the sheet concealing his lap. "Then there's a way to discover who's working for the demon. You might recognize them."

There was a horrible feeling deep inside her; the thought that she could let him distract himself from the original question. "Sebastian," she whispered, and he seemed to realize there was something more she hadn't told him.

His mercurial gaze sharpened. "That's why you asked me about my past. About Julia Camden. Who is the black queen?"

She didn't want to answer. Doing so unleashed her fears into a world she'd just begun to claim as her own. It would turn him against her, perhaps bring about everything she'd seen.

And yet she needed someone else to know. She needed him to be there for her, to hopefully help her fight her terrible prophecy. "At first I assumed it was Morgana. But when it became clear it wasn't… I needed to go back into the past to find her. I began to suspect it was my mother, but in questioning Lady E about my mother's death, I learned it couldn't be. My mother died in childbirth. There was a sister, and for a moment I thought perhaps she'd lived. Perhaps my father spirited her away for some reason..." She wrapped her arms around her waist. "But I have been scrying, and scrying, and I can't find even a trace of her existence. And Lady E said something to me that day, about reading the Vision correctly. If I... if I assume the reason I can't find a trace of a blood relative out there is because there is none, that leaves me only one other possibility. One that makes sense in so many ways."

Especially the demon's interest in her, and Quentin Farshaw's insistence she was going to have to make a choice very shortly, toward the Light, or the Dark.

"Which is?"

"I think the black queen is also me."

"How can you be both white and black queens?"

It made no sense. But Cleo seemed to wilt under his regard, her misery and fear plain to see. She sank onto the windowsill, her arms wrapped around her, and her eyes shining within unshed tears.

"I've been reading about Quentin Farshaw," she replied.

"The first true seer."

"The only sorcerer who's ever ascended to the tenth level," she corrected.

"You thought you saw a man pretending to be him in Balthazar's Labyrinth."

"I think that truly *was* Quentin Farshaw. He dabbled in demonology and he was obsessed with seeing through time. He thought there was a connection between being able to

See the past or the future—and the ability to slip into the time stream physically."

"He also died in the middle of one of his experiments," he pointed out.

"Did he?" Cleo's voice was a monotone. "There was no body. No blood. No viscera. Nothing human left in his laboratory once they broke the doors down. So did he die? Or did he finally achieve what he'd been trying to do all along?"

Sebastian flung the covers back, dragging his trousers up his legs and buttoning them. Her line of thought was troubling. "You think he finally learned how to walk through time."

"I think he's out there somewhere," she admitted. "In some different time. I think he gave me the book deliberately, because he could sense what was coming and he wanted me to stop it."

"Then why doesn't he stop it?"

"I don't know." She threw her arms wide. "I could only fathom what it would be like to even try and change the future. It's difficult enough to see it, and to make minute changes. Every step you take down a different path opens up a different future. Visions constantly change. But to slip through time, into a period not your own, and shift even a single thing could potentially…. I don't even know what it could do. Perhaps we can stop the demon because we're in the here and now, so he gave us the clues to do so."

"It could have been one of the demon's allies, trying to distract you. To walk through time…. That's impossible, Cleo."

"So is translocation," she pointed out.

Verity, with her unpredictable gifts.

"You're confusing me. What does Quentin Farshaw have to do with you being the black queen?"

She picked up the book, flipping through it swiftly before reading: "A notion that has constantly plagued me has been a curiosity about why I see the future and the past with such clarity, when other sorcerers can barely glimpse it. Where do these dreams come from? Why does time seem to part around me, when others cannot even see the individual threads? I think the demon is in me."

A light fluttering began to swim through his gut. "What does that even mean? He was possessed?"

"No." Cleo took a deep breath. "Sebastian, what's the one creature with the ability to time-walk? The one creature who can see through time, and manipulate it?"

A demon.

"Every act of sorcery can be learned, even if one is never very good at it. Consider myself with telekinesis, for example. But not.... Divination is a gift that cannot be taught. One either has it, or one does not."

"What are you saying?"

She cradled the book to her chest. "What if the gift of Sight is not a gift, but something in one's bloodlines? I've been... researching. The first time a demon was called through from the Shadow Dimensions was in 1497, according to our records. The very first recorded seer showed up some twenty years later. And what do demons do when they get here? They possess a body, but they require the energy derived from sex and blood in order to survive. What if there are children born of such couplings? Children with their parents' bloodlines, but a hint of the demon inside them too? Maybe it leaves a mark, a stain on the soul? Maybe—"

"You think there's some part of a demon in you? Cleo." He crossed to her side, kneeling at her feet, and rubbing his palms up her silk-covered legs. "You're the very opposite of a demon. There's a light inside you even I can see. That I've always seen. You wouldn't even begin to know what true darkness was."

A tear slid down her cheek. "The night of the Ascension Ball you and Madrigal pulled me from a dream about the past. My father was fascinated with demons too. After he, Drake, and Morgana created the Relics Infernal, and they betrayed him, he turned to darker arts. I saw my father the night I was conceived. He was at his altar, and he summoned something into him, before he went to my mother."

Sebastian froze.

She could barely continue, the fall of her hair covering her face. "I'm human, Sebastian, but there's something of the demon inside me too. Something from the Shadow Dimensions. And I think it's starting to wake.

"A stain, Sebastian," she whispered. "Something dark that whispers to me at odd moments. I can feel her, even now. I'm the white queen, but I think the black queen is inside me too. I think I am… both. And I don't think you'd like her very much."

He stared up at her, hating the doubt he heard in her voice.

"Quentin Farshaw said I had to make a choice between the Light and the Dark," Cleo continued. "I don't know what he means. Do I have to choose to be the white queen? Or the black queen?"

"Farshaw said quite a lot," he muttered. And she hadn't told him any of it. "Come here."

Sebastian dragged her into his lap, where she finally succumbed to her tears. The bond between them was shielded, and maybe this was why. Maybe she'd begun hiding her thoughts and emotions from him the moment she realized something was amiss within her.

The very way she clung to him told him something else though. She hadn't wanted to tell him. Doubt, perhaps, that he would deny her. Or cast her aside. Sweet mother of darkness. A growl of fury vibrated in his throat, and he crushed her close to him.

"What did you think I was going to do?" he whispered, capturing her tear-stained face and tilting it up to press a kiss to her lips.

"You were leaving," she said in a ragged voice.

"You didn't know that. Not until you found the ticket. You've known all this time, or suspected there was something dark inside you."

"Well, you weren't *there* for me. You wouldn't reply to my letters." She pressed her face into her hands and sobbed. "You didn't want to see me. You've *never* wanted this marriage."

"You're right," he whispered, cupping her face and tilting it to his. "I never wanted this marriage. I didn't know what to do with you, or how to be a husband. But I want this. I want you. Let me be your husband, Cleo. Be my wife in truth. No matter what we face."

And then he kissed her, knowing that this time she needed him to fight for *her*.

CHAPTER
TWENTY-THREE

The Shadow Dimensions are gray, lifeless planes where creatures of the Void exist. They constantly hunger for life, and yet it is denied them, so of course when they are summoned through into this world they crave the light and life and wonder they see. They wish to absorb it, to drink it down, to glut themselves on sex and blood and energy—and to destroy the Summoner who called them. For when summoned, they wear a leash. And it chafes....

—Lord Gilderoy in *Of Demons and Imps*

"GOING HUNTING?" SEBASTIAN asked, as he poured himself a cup of tea the next morning.

Bishop paused in the act of sliding his black leather gloves on. "Verity's going to use a lock of Drake's hair to try and track him again. We had no luck the other day, but he's got to be somewhere out there. I'm going with her."

Cleo crunched into her piece of toast. "Best of luck."

"There's no chance *you* could find the demon?" Bishop asked her.

"I've tried. There is no Veil shielding it. It's simply not there." Cleo glanced down, and Sebastian knew she lied.

He said nothing. There were reasons she might not dare confront the demon, especially considering her recent revelation.

Verity leaned down to kiss her on the cheek, and murmured something in her ear that made Cleo blush.

"What are your plans?" Bishop asked, trying to pretend both ladies weren't discussing something not meant for polite ears.

Cleo set her toast down. "We—"

"Intend to continue reading Farshaw's book," Sebastian cut in, lifting the cup to his mouth and meeting his brother's eyes. "Cleo thinks there's something inside it she needs to know, for when we face the demon."

Bishop shrugged into his coat, and Verity helped brushed him off. "Good. I don't want any surprises when we finally track this demon down. It's going to be a hell of a campaign to face it even with the Relics Infernal, let alone anyone else it can drag out of the woodwork."

Verity grimaced. "It *has* to have gone to ground in either Balthazar's Labyrinth or Seven Dials. They're the only two sorcerous communities in London that don't belong to the Order, and it needs allies with power. It knows we're coming for it."

"Happy hunting," Sebastian said.

"Good luck," Bishop responded curtly, and then he and Verity slipped from the room.

Why did you lie to him?" Cleo kept her eyes on her plate.

"Because Bishop sometimes believes the best way to make a problem go away is with a very sharp knife."

"You don't trust him."

"I don't trust anybody," he replied. *"Present company excluded."*

She chased a spoonful of coddled eggs across her plate. *"He wouldn't hurt me. He's not like that. He's... kind. Sometimes."*

"He's not going to ever have reason to consider it." Sebastian frowned. It was one thing to face his brother in a sparring match. If Bishop ever discovered Cleo's secret, then Sebastian knew he couldn't stop his brother if he decided to bring her before the Prime. Not one-on-one.

They'd never truly gone head-to-head. Every encounter had been a lesson, Bishop restraining himself. And every encounter, his brother defeated him, regardless of his overwhelming strength.

It made him wary enough to keep this a secret.

"But what if it helps to counter the demon?" Cleo bit her lip. "Do you think we ought to mention—"

Verity punched into the room. Cleo's knees hit the table in surprise, and Sebastian's cup rattled on its saucer.

"Bloody hell," he swore, trying to mop up the tea he'd spilled before it dripped into his lap.

"Sorry." Verity stole an apple from the bowl in the middle of the table, looking utterly unrepentant. "I almost forgot it wasn't safe to simply translocate into a room where the two of you were sitting. Not now anyway." She grinned saucily. "Who knows what I could have walked into?"

Now? Sebastian stared at her. "Verity!"

"Don't be a prude." She rolled her eyes. "It's lovely to see the two of you getting along."

Getting along wasn't quite the way he'd describe it.

"Just... don't do anything I wouldn't do." Verity winked at them, and then vanished into thin air.

He made a choking noise in his throat.

"Well, I did suggest we not desecrate the desk in the library," Cleo said, as if it were entirely his fault.

"Did you say something to her?"

"I didn't have to." Cleo shook her head. "Verity's been, ah, giving me tips on how to seduce you for weeks. She knew."

Tips? He stared at her. It wasn't as though it should surprise him, as Verity was quite free with her affections whenever she thought she and Bishop were alone. "I don't think I want to know."

Cleo cleared her throat. "I might be able to change your mind on that later."

He definitely didn't want to know. Not now. Not with an entire day ahead of them, and the need to focus.

He glanced at the door, draining the last mouthful of tea from his cup. "Ready?" Then he added, *"That's why we need to keep these conversations private. Don't breathe a word of what you told me last night. Not to anyone. Especially not Verity."*

He thought she looked a little sad. "What's wrong?"

Cleo shook her head and pushed away from the table. *"Nothing. I just.... I hate lying to my friends."*

So did he, but when it came to keeping Cleo safe, he'd do anything.

"Where are we really going?" Cleo asked breathlessly as she hurried down the back stairs of Bishop's small townhouse onto the street. They'd waited almost fifteen minutes to make sure Bishop and Verity weren't likely to return, before slipping out the back door when cook's back was turned.

"I've been thinking about what Morgana said the other day when we stole the Blade of Altarrh back from her."

"I think it best to ignore almost everything that leaves that woman's mouth," Cleo muttered. "She's the most horrible woman I've ever met."

"You're the one who didn't want me to kill her."

"For your sake, not hers," she pointed out.

Sebastian strode ahead of her, lifting a hand to hail a hansom cab. A pair of glossy black geldings trotted toward them, and he helped her up into the carriage, leaning out to give an address to the driver. As he closed the door, he settled on the seat next to her. "She said Lady Beaumont *was* working for her."

Cleo's chin jerked up in surprise. "Julia Camden?"

His gaze slid to the window as the hack started moving, the *clip-clop* of horses' hooves ringing on the cobbles. "Yes. Considering Morgana doesn't seem to have much to say to Bishop, I thought Lady Beaumont might be more inclined to speak."

"And you didn't tell Bishop?"

"I can handle Julia. And if she is working for the demon, then she might know the true identity of the black queen. I just want to make sure she knows nothing before I turn her over to Bishop," he said, his gaze meeting hers.

Cleo wished he didn't sound quite so cold. "Are you certain you're up to that?"

"I have you by my side."

"Little help I may be when it comes to confronting dangerous enemies."

"No, you're here as my conscience." Sebastian's hand settled on her knee, and he let go of a small breath. "And you're more of a help than you might think. You did singlehandedly bring my mother to her knees."

"And Madrigal Brown warned me I wasn't to future-walk anytime soon."

"When have *you* ever listened to reason?" he teased.

"I listen to reason all the time," she scoffed, but she folded her hands in her lap. She could feel his gaze upon her face, and knew he'd picked up on her small deception.

Cleo sighed. "All these new abilities I'm discovering....
What if.... What if they were from the demon that sired
me?" Her voice dropped to a whisper. "Perhaps I shouldn't
use them."

"The demon that used your father's body as a vessel
when *he* sired you."

"Semantics," she said, arching a brow at him.
"Tremayne's seed, the demon's stain."

Sebastian turned a cool brow upon her. "You said you
thought all your Divination gifts were inherited from the
demon and you've been using them all of your life without
any dubious side effects. I doubt there's anything to worry
about with your new gifts."

Gifts? "You're not the one dreaming about playing
chess with a demon," she muttered, trying to ignore the
chill in her chest at the thought. She'd always thought her
Foresight a gift, but what if it was something far more
sinister?

His hand squeezed her knee. "We'll get the answers. I
promise. There's no point worrying about it in the
meantime."

Cleo slid her fingers into his hand. It was easy for him
to say. He wasn't tainted by a demon's blood.

"I've spent most of my life being told I was a
monster," Sebastian said, squeezing her hand. "If there's
anyone who knows how you feel right now, it's probably
me."

Her heart broke a little. He'd spent years with no one
at his side to assuage his fears. She could do this for a week
or two.

"Be brave," he said, bringing her hand to his lips to
press a soft kiss there.

"I'll be your conscience," Cleo whispered, "if you'll be
my courage."

"Deal."

Lady Beaumont lived in Knightsbridge, not far from Bishop's home. Cleo rested her head against Sebastian's shoulder as they travelled in silence, trying not to think grim thoughts. She could stay there forever, she thought, with his arm around her and the soft thud of his heartbeat echoing near her ear, but all too soon they were pulling up, and the hack driver called out, "Whoa there, lads."

And how long was forever, anyway?

They disembarked from the carriage, and Cleo stared up at the mansion while Sebastian paid the driver. Breath steamed hot from the horses' nostrils as they nickered, and Cleo wrapped her arms around herself until she grew used to the morning's chill. Choking clouds of soot stained the murky morning, and someone had left the gaslights burning faintly in this section of town, an extravagance she didn't expect to see elsewhere, except perhaps Mayfair.

Lady Beaumont certainly held a posh appointment. Sharp little spears of wrought iron circled the property, and one could barely see past the lush foliage and the hedge of sharply pruned conifers. The house loomed out of the greenery, its shutters peering back like beady little eyes.

Behind her, reins slapped on the horses' rumps, and then the hack was moving off with the heavy jingle of tack and the rush of its wheels on the cobbles. Sebastian appeared in the corner of her eye, staring coldly up at the mansion as if he saw more than just a house.

"I'm never certain what inspires people to mount those horrid structures on their roofs," she murmured.

He followed her line of sight. "Gargoyles?"

"They're considerably eerie."

The coldness in his mind dissolved, and the faintest of smiles etched his lush mouth. "Every sorcerer has to have at least one. Isn't it written in the Order's handbook?"

"There's a handbook?" She bantered with him as they strolled along the street arm in arm, pretending there was naught amiss.

"How do you intend to go about this?" she murmured, pausing by the end of the fence. "A frontal assault? Or are we going to break in and tie Lady Beaumont to a chair?"

"Breaking in and scaring the devil out of her is tempting, but she'll have wards in place." Taking the *look away* cloak out of the small bag he carried, he shook it out and swung it over her shoulders. "Julia hinted she'd like to continue our acquaintance at the ball."

"Acquaintance? Is that what they're calling it these days?"

His mouth twisted a little, and she felt the sharp stab of unease slide through him. It was so different now with the bond unshielded. All those minute quirks of his expression suddenly made sense.

"Fine, she wants to fuck me," he said, a little coldly.

It wasn't a coldness meant to warn her off, she realized, but a means to protect himself. Whenever his emotions were severely compromised, he shut down, until only ice remained.

"When hell freezes over. You're mine," she said. "And if she lays one finger on you, then I will give her hell, regardless of whether Madrigal thinks I ought to future-walk or not."

His expression remained cool, but something unknotted within him. "She's not going to touch me. I just need her to open the door."

"I'll stay here then," she said.

Cleo waited just inside the gate in Lady Beaumont's gardens as her husband knocked on the door. Minutes ticked past. What was taking so long? Peering around a ruthlessly pruned satyr, she caught Sebastian's eye.

"A servant should have answered by now," he sent. *"I can't feel any wards in place. Are you coming?"*

Cleo slipped onto the porch, holding her breath. *"What now?"*

He turned the doorknob, and the door opened. Both of them looked at each other as the dark hallway beyond beckoned.

"There should be static wards on the doors," Cleo told him. No sorcerer kept a house without wards. There were too many closely guarded secrets of sorcery, and precious grimoires and relics lying about.... *"I don't like this."*

"Maybe she didn't ward the house?"

"A woman allied to your mother leaves her back door open, so to speak?" Cleo arched a brow.

His eyes turned dangerous. *"Be careful. And watch my back."*

There could be numerous reasons to have no wards, but one sat forefront of her mind. *"It could be a trap."*

Power flooded through him, making his aura emanate around him. *"I'm in a mood to spring it."*

The grandfather clock in the hallway ticked ominously. Nothing else stirred. Cleo crept through the house on Sebastian's heels, barely daring to breathe. The kitchens were far too clean, and a fine layer of dust settled over everything.

"It feels like nobody's been here for a few days." Cleo ran a finger along a mantle in the parlor. No self-respecting parlor maid would turn a blind eye to this.

Above them, someone's weight shifted. They both froze, looking up.

"Upstairs."

Sebastian moved with starling alacrity, the hem of his coat flaring as he made for the door. He took the stairs almost silently, and Cleo ghosted along behind him. Wearing a blindfold for most of her life had made her hearing startlingly acute, and she was used to moving quietly to avoid her father's notice whenever he was in one of his rages.

No sign of movement in any of the rooms, and they carefully opened each door. The wait ate at her nerves. *"Maybe the floor was settling?"*

"No, there's someone here." Sebastian eased the next door open, as Cleo kept a watch in the hallway. Sudden horror leapt along their bond, and she turned to see what had struck him so, only for him to wrap an arm around her waist and force her back, out of the room.

"Don't look."

Too late. A bed flashed into view, red streaks painted across the pillows and sheets, and a woman's pale leg hanging from the edge of the mattress carelessly. Dark bruising mottled the woman's skin, hinting at death.

Sebastian shut the door in a hurry.

"What.... Who was it?" Her mouth tasted sour, and terror set a stranglehold on her throat. That poor woman.... Cleo's mind refused to make sense of the shapes she'd seen, and the angle of the bloody gashes in the woman's side, and she was grateful for it.

"Lady Beaumont, I think." Despite the gloom, his face seemed drained of color. It was one thing to wish a woman

dead, quite another to see it done so horrifically. *"That's why there weren't any bloody wards. The second she died, her wards evaporated. We're getting out of here. Now."*

A creak sounded along the hallway. And Premonition, that willful, unruly bitch, began to skate along the fine hairs of her arms.

Cleo's fist curled in his coat.

"What is it?" The midnight taste of his mind brushed against her own.

"Someone's inside the house."

Another floorboard groaned, as if something momentous tested its strength. In the gloom at the end of the hallway, a pair of glowing red embers suddenly lit up.

"Merde." Sebastian shoved her behind him.

"What the hell is *that*?" she gasped.

"A gargoyle," he said, taking a careful step backward. "Don't move too suddenly. My mother had a house guardian once. It's been primed to take down any intruders, and if we run it will pounce."

"Who the hell ensorcels a gargoyle?" Of *all* things!

"Some sorcerers use stone constructs in place of watchdogs."

She knew the theory behind magic constructs. The Jewish called them golem, though she'd read that a golem was created when a power word was etched upon a scroll and placed within the golem's clay casing. Constructs were resurrected by a single spoken power word, and a sorcerer could create one of the soulless, mindless automatons out of anything: stone, wood, paper, shadows....

"If Lady Beaumont died, then all her spell work should have died with her," Cleo said, "unless she embedded the spell in a rune."

"I can't see one. Someone else must have created this construct," he said.

The gargoyle's head turned to face them suddenly, and Cleo took a startled step back.

Those red eyes locked on her. Oh, mercy. She froze, but it was too late. The construct saw the small movement. *"Sebastian?"*

He stepped between them, funneling energy out of the air. "When I tell you to run, then run."

The gargoyle launched forward on all fours, it's heavy wings tucked tight against its body. Sebastian detonated one of the pre-prepared charges in his rings, and a wave of force unleashed. It smashed the construct back into—and through—a wall.

"Run!"

No need to say it twice. Cleo grabbed her skirts and raced along the hallway with Sebastian at her heels. A thunderous crash sounded behind them, sending her heart rabbiting in her chest.

"If we can get outside the house, there's a good chance it won't follow!" Sebastian yelled.

The front door had never seemed so far away. Growling sounds echoed behind them, hot on their heels. They'd never make it.

"Yes, we will," Sebastian snapped.

Sebastian warded, and the gargoyle flew into the shimmering dome surrounding him. The impact drove him off his feet, and he landed on the hall runner, sliding several yards along the floor. Cleo hesitated, turning toward the creature as it regained its feet. Sebastian's ward protected him, but the fall had disorientated him enough to leave him unsteady as he rolled onto his side.

If he dropped his ward....

She glanced around, and snatched an urn off a nearby pedestal, hurling it toward the creature. Priceless antique porcelain shattered on the gargoyle's wings. "Over here, you ugly lump of stone!"

Red eyes locked upon her, and the sleek muscle in its haunches gathered itself.

Cleo sprinted toward the stairs. Snatching at the railing, she hauled herself around the corner where the staircase met the upper hallway, chancing a glance behind her. Scrabbling claws peeled small scrolls of timber off the floorboards as it tried to bank, and the gargoyle slammed into a wall, tearing the delicate Chinese wallpaper and knocking a picture frame to the floor.

Its eyes flared red with vicious need. Cleo's heart stopped, terror choking her. She fled down the stairs, her boots catching on the last step and sending her sprawling onto the marble floors in the foyer, the sting to her palms and knees jolting her. She rolled onto her back, summoning her power and flinging up a hasty ward.

A man stepped into the foyer, avoiding the patches of hazy sunlight that lit the floor. He flexed a hand, and sorcery filled the air, tainting it with a coppery taste.

"*Hezhrazahd.*" A single horrific word of command, and the gargoyle exploded into a million small shards, raining dust everywhere.

Cleo lowered the arm she'd hastily flung in front of her face. The word seemed to pulse in her ears, as if it ate its way inside her.

Wiping his hands and a cutthroat razor upon what appeared to be an old shirt, Drake de Wynter looked down at her, his lips thinning and his eyes no longer the pale gray they'd once been, but a demon's merciless obsidian depths.

"I truly wish the pair of you hadn't walked in here," it said.

CHAPTER
TWENTY-FOUR

THE SIGHT OF the man who'd sired him punched through Sebastian's chest, shocking the breath from his lungs.

The duke might have been his mirror image if he were thirty years younger. The duke's shoulders and chest were broader than Sebastian's, his build solid and filled with a quiet menacing strength. The faint cleft of both their chins matched, and he recognized his mouth in his father's face, though the shape of his eyes was more like Morgana's.

They'd only met in the flesh once, and several times upon an astral plane Drake had dragged him to when he was trapped in a cell in his mother's house. Drake had been trying to rescue him then, begging him to hold on and not unleash the almighty powers brewing within him like a thunderstorm.

But there was no sign of his father anymore.

Sebastian rose to a crouch, and then froze when the demon stared at him. Any sudden movement.... He glanced at Cleo. She was far too close to it. He'd never reach her in time.

The demon cast the bloody rag aside, its eyes unblinking as it took in the debris from the ruined gargoyle. "That took me over an hour to create."

Cleo scooted backward on the floor, her back meeting the wall. *"What do we do?"*

"Keep it talking." He didn't take his eyes off the demon.

"How did you find me?" Its lips quirked. "I've made arrangements to befuddle young Verity Bishop's talents, and no scrying device can track me on this plane." Its head turned sinuously toward Cleo. "And I've accounted for you."

Pure bad luck. Sebastian slowly placed his foot on the stair below him. "We wanted to question Lady Beaumont."

"If you move suddenly, I *will* gut her," the demon said, turning back to him.

He froze, putting his hands in the air.

"*Tsk, tsk*, Sebastian." His father's voice, but it sounded wrong coming from that throat. "You've found yourself another weakness."

"She's not a weakness."

"A pressure point then." It smiled, a thumb running along the edge of the razor. "All you have to do is know the right place to press."

"You look better than you did in Noah Guthrie's body." He eased down another step. Another.

"This body is stronger than Guthrie." The demon seemed pleased. "No matter how much your father screams at me inside."

Merde. He'd housed this creature within his own body once. A desperate, unthinking ploy when he'd lost all hope, and the only escape he could see was to work with it. Barely a single day with it inside him, feeding upon him, knowing his every thought.... Hearing its thoughts, or the ones it allowed him to hear. Sebastian swallowed hard. He'd blocked that day from his memory, but seeing it now brought everything back to the surface.

Including a hint of what it wanted.

The demon hauled Cleo to her feet, his hand manacling her upper arm tight enough to make her cry out.

"If you hurt her," he warned, finally reaching the foyer floor. "You won't get out of here alive. I promise you that."

"You wouldn't dare."

"I think you're the one who wouldn't dare," he said softly, advancing one step at a time.

Interest flickered in the demon's eyes. "You and I worked together once, to trap your father into his bargain. I have no wish to kill you, unless you get in my way."

I was desperate to escape my mother. I never meant to cause any of this.... "I don't think you *can* kill me."

Definitely interest. Cleo cried out as its grip on her arm tightened. "How so?"

"You made a bargain with my father when he traded his life for mine," Sebastian said. "You can't harm any of us, or he'll be able to take control of his body again. Demons can't lie."

Its nostrils flared. "True. Unless you attack first and I am forced to defend myself."

"Then I won't."

Dragging Cleo back against its chest, it put the razor to her throat. "Are you certain of that, Sebastian?"

His heart stopped, and the whirlpool of emotion threatened to suck him under. *Cleo.* There was no magic in the world that could stop the demon from hurting her if it willed it. He'd never felt so powerless. "Let her go."

"You shouldn't make threats you can't keep."

"She's included in the bargain," he replied. "Drake said you couldn't harm any of us *or* our wives."

"Ah, Drake. That constant thorn in my foot...." The demon smiled. "I didn't lie. He can try to take his body back if I hurt you. I never said I wouldn't fight him for it."

The razor slid lower, slicing through the thin lace at Cleo's décolletage. She sucked in a shallow breath, and he felt her trying not to look down.

"And there are things I can do to your wife that have nothing to do with hurting her."

"Don't react," Cleo babbled in his mind. *"It wants you to react."*

There were hands pawing at him, leaving his skin feeling oily, stained, dirty.... "No." Sebastian shook his head, unable to bear it as the razor parted the silk covering her breast. Only her corset remained, thin protection against the world. Cleo trembled, and he felt it within. "If you fucking touch her...."

Not her. He could bear the pain, but he never wanted her to know what the world was truly like.

"How are you going to stop me?" The demon laughed.

He couldn't attack it, not with Cleo in its arms.

He couldn't defeat it with his sorcery, for demons were creatures of pure magic....

Only one card left to play. Sebastian stared into the demon's eyes, trying to find any trace of the man he barely knew. "If you're in there, then you need to fight it now. I *need* you."

And he threw himself forward, capturing the demon's wrist and slamming the pair of them into the wall. Tendons strained in Drake's arm, and Sebastian forced the razor away from Cleo.

A hand locked around his throat, squeezing with inhuman force, but it wasn't the first time he'd been breathless. He remembered a belt around his throat, choking him as Lady Beaumont kissed her way down his torso. He slammed the bastard's hand back into the wall, trying to force him to drop the razor. Couldn't breathe. His face tightened, blood pounding in his ears. All he had to do was hold on just a little longer.

"Sebastian, let him go!"

He danced back, just as Cleo hurled something at the demon. A mage globe of white, barely a threat, and yet it was enough to distract the demon. The demon brushed it aside contemptuously, and white light splashed up the walls as it exploded.

Then it was slashing with economic grace, and Sebastian had to duck and weave, slamming a fist into its ribs as he went…. A punch strong enough to fell a mortal man, but the demon barely flinched. Did it not feel the blow?

Pain was an old friend as the razor kissed his cheek, splattering blood across the walls….

Sebastian clapped a hand to his cheek, yanking Cleo out of its grasp, and summoning all his power to bear. Energy thrummed through his veins, but the demon paused, hunching over, choking a little….

"What's it doing?" Cleo cried.

The demon's face rippled, and it snarled at him. The darkness drained out of its eyes, replaced by pure silver.

It went to its knees, one hand splayed over the marble floor tiles and its entire body shaking until… a man knelt there, slumping as if he'd fought a mighty battle.

"Run," Drake rasped at him. "I can't… hold it for long."

His father. Sebastian's heart leaped into his throat, guilt searing his nerves.

"Drake!" Cleo gasped as she staggered free, sliding to her knees beside the duke and trying to help him up.

Color mottled Drake's face as if he were still choking. "Not much time." He pushed her away from him, and looked toward Sebastian. "Eleanor?"

He couldn't take another step forward. His father. His *father.* They'd spoken only a handful of times, but this man had set him on a path toward freedom, toward Cleo. And he couldn't even answer him.

"She's fine," Cleo said, squeezing Drake's hand. "Ianthe's had her healers in to see to her, and she's almost as good as new."

"You don't have... much time." Saliva dripped from Drake's mouth. He hunched in upon himself. "It's setting everything... into motion."

"When?" Cleo demanded.

"Tomorrow." Drake shuddered. "It needs the full... moon."

"What for? What is it planning?"

Drake looked up. "It wants to tear a hole in the Veil between worlds. It wants to bring forth... its brethren."

Demons. Imps. All the monsters and beasts within the Shadow Dimensions. This was how London would be destroyed, and all Cleo's Visions had him at the center of it. The cause of it.

"How do we use the Relics against it?" Sebastian demanded.

Drake's teeth gritted together, and his entire face screwed up in strain. Gasping, he ground out, "Use the Blade.... Only Cleo can wield it. Sink it.... Sink it into my heart."

"No." There had to be another way.

"*Only* Cleo," Drake stressed, gasping again. A wild ripple of movement slithered inside his cheek, and the veins on his temples stood out. "Agatha knows what to do with the rest of it."

"Stay with us!" Sebastian called, suddenly feeling like he could move again. *Please.* There was so much he wanted to say.

"It's too... late."

Drake shuddered on his hands and knees, sucking in breath. Those things were moving beneath his skin now in angry waves. Drake screamed, his knuckles straining white. "*Run!*"

The sound of his scream cut off so abruptly, Sebastian froze. Drake's body began to still, and slowly he looked up, bringing his breathing under control.

It wasn't his father. Not anymore. Even though the demon tried to hide it, Sebastian could see the frustration and rage turning those silver eyes to liquid obsidian.

It laughed, but there was no humor in the sound. "He's stronger than I thought." And it pushed to its feet, locking murderous eyes upon the pair of them. "And I am done playing by his rules."

Flinging a hand toward Cleo, it hooked its fingers and yanked its hand close to its chest. Cleo soared across the room, clutching her throat and choking as she sank into a pile of ruffled skirts at its feet.

"*No!*"

Sebastian darted forward, but the demon hauled her to her feet, and yanked her back against its chest.

"Oh, I wouldn't," it warned in a dark voice, its hand sliding up her throat and forcing her chin high. Silver glinted as it flicked its wrist and set the edge of the razor to the pulsing beat of her carotid artery.

A single red bead of blood formed, and Cleo sucked in a wild breath, her spine arching to alleviate the press of the razor. Her wild eyes met his.

"Pressure points, Sebastian. Don't forget that."

His hand lowered, and he didn't dare reach for his sorcery. Pressure points. He knew a little about pressure points. His mother had taught him the price of having them all his life. "What do you want?" he demanded flatly.

The demon laughed. "Now you're starting to play the true game." Its laughter shut off abruptly, as if it had never been. "You've been very busy, haven't you? You have my pawn. You have my Relics. I want them all back."

"Your pawn?"

"Morgana."

It had wanted to kill his mother last month. Sebastian's mind raced. Cleo had said something about chess pieces.

"Don't," she whispered, clinging to the demon's sleeve. *"Don't give them to him."*

The demon caressed her throat with the razor, dragging the tip of it down to rest in the hollow of her collarbone. It slowly looked up. "You have twenty-four hours to deliver what I want, or I'll do to your lovely wife what I did to Lady Beaumont. I'd suggest you take a good long look at Lady Beaumont before you make your decision."

It was no decision. "Where am I to deliver them to?" he asked hoarsely.

"I'll send a message." It dragged Cleo back toward the door, opening it with a twist of telekinesis. "All three Relics, don't forget. If you double-cross me, she's worse than dead."

"Alone?"

It smiled. "No. Bring whomever you want. I'm hungry."

Sebastian stole one last pleading glance toward her. He'd never felt so helpless in all his life. *"I'll come for you."*

"Don't. Please don't." A tear slid down her cheek. *"I don't want to see you hurt. Use the Relics against it."*

"I'll come for you," he repeated. He would do whatever the demon demanded. Even cut his own throat to save her life. *"You are my everything, and I will not risk you."*

Pressure points. He'd once thought love was a weakness, swiftly learning his mother would only ever use such a thing against him. A puppy. A childhood friend. A servant who was kind to him. He'd stopped letting the world in, stopped allowing himself to have such weaknesses.

Until now.

"Don't follow me," the demon suggested, holding the razor to Cleo's throat as it stepped back through the door. "And I won't harm her."

The carriage rattled as it made a sharp turn, a horse neighing loudly as the driver cracked the whip.

Cleo sat stiffly on the seat, not daring to take her eyes off the creature sitting opposite her. The sight of her husband's father only twisted the knife in her chest. He looked so much like Sebastian.

Sebastian. Oh, mercy. Heat swam behind her eyes. He wouldn't listen to her. He wouldn't destroy this monster. She knew it. He'd hand over everything it wanted, just to save her life.

If it hurt him....

"We meet again, Cassandra," the demon mused, resting its chin on its hand as it leaned against the carriage door and watched her. "You look well."

Look well? The bloody thing had held a knife to her throat. "Do you think this a game?" she rasped, gripping her skirts in fear.

Its lips twitched. "Of course it's a game. I'm trying to teach you a lesson. Who do you think is winning?"

Cleo stared at it. There was no sign of the menace it had exuded in Lady Beaumont's house. Indeed the expression it wore was similar to that of a long ago tutor, only... slightly more unblinking.

It leaned forward, resting its elbows on its knees. "You disappoint me. I thought you were ready to be instructed, but in some ways, you're still wearing your blindfold." It reached out and brushed its gloved fingertips down her face before she could flinch away. "Look deeper, Cassandra. Look beyond everything beneath your nose. Think about everything that's happened in the past twenty or so years."

There had to be a reason it picked that timeline. She swallowed hard. "Was it you?" An image of her father formed in her mind, drawing something into his body the night her mother conceived. "Or some other demon?"

"What do you think?"

Her mind began to race. She felt ill. The puzzle pieces fit together. "What do you want with me?" Not to play chess. No. There had to be something more.

"Now she begins to ask the important questions. Your father wanted a child of unimaginable gifts."

Children like Quentin Farshaw and the Travelers, and all those "miracle children" out there.

"He began to dabble with other planes and dimensions in his youth. He was obsessed with power, with knowledge. He hungered for the world, and he used his friend, Drake de Wynter, and the woman they both lusted after, Morgana, to create three relics that could control me. Me." It laughed. "But he did not know what he called into this world when he brought me forth. All others who have come before me were Lesser Demons, seeding their ilk in this world." It spread its arms wide. "And I am a prince of the Shadow Dimensions."

"Prince or not, that doesn't tell me why *I'm* so important."

"Did you know, I was going to go to all the trouble of having you kidnapped this afternoon, only for you to wander straight into my clutches."

"If you speak of destiny, or fate," she warned harshly, "I shall throw myself from this carriage."

"Destiny and fate are mere words." It snorted. "There is only intention. My intention. My game. You all waltz to my tune."

"Why did you want to kidnap me?" A shudder of unease filled her. It had always been a little too interested in her. "I doubt it was simply familial duty."

"Did you not want a father to love you?"

The blow struck her deep. "You're not my father."

"There are parts of me within you. I know you've felt them stirring."

She looked away.

"I wanted to take you off the game board momentarily," it said, as if bothered by her lack of reciprocation. "You had the Blade, you had the Wand and the Chalice... and you're the only one who can use them, apart from this body." It gestured to itself. "Drake is powerful enough, and skilled enough in astral projection to cross planes. But you walk them."

"That's why you went after Drake," she whispered, her nerves starting to light up. "It wasn't revenge for having raised you twenty-eight years ago. He's the only one who could defeat you." The implications staggered her. Drake had told her she was the only one who could use the Blade against him, but what did that mean? She'd thought he'd meant for her to kill him... but what if there was something more to all of this?

She needed to find out what it was.

And to do that she needed to know the truth, despite her disgust. "You were never going to kill me in there, were you? You wanted Sebastian to think you were going to do it...." It had everything in the palms of its hands, manipulating events until they lined up for it. Cleo tried to focus. She'd always wondered.... "Was it your idea to send Morgana in to try and destroy the Ascension Ball?"

"Yes."

"You had to know Morgana and whatever sorcerers you dragged out of the bowels of London's depths had no chance against a gathering of nearly four hundred sorcerers."

"Yes," it whispered, looking amused. "Keep going, White Queen. You're almost there."

None of its actions in the last month made any sense. Her brow furrowed. "Morgana was a decoy. The Blade and Wand were decoys."

"I have spent many days walking these parks you humans have created. And I have discovered something. What happens if you poke an anthill?"

They all stir and rush about, tilting at windmills.

"Morgana enjoyed the assault. She thinks only of revenge, for hers is a small mind."

All along they'd misconstrued its intentions. "Drake, Morgana, and my father raised you twenty-some years ago, and bound you to the Relics Infernal and their will. But you don't truly care about that."

"I never said *I* wanted revenge, though a part of me would enjoy it." Its lips twisted. "I can't lie, after all, for words are power."

A breath shivered through her. "Then what do you intend?"

"You're the one who's seen it."

London's doom. A sky filled with black clouds. Sebastian. Destruction. Screams.... And a thin slit of light peeling apart in the sky. Drake had said it himself. "You're going to bring more demons through. You're going to open a gate between dimensions."

"I'm going to tear a hole between dimensions," it told her. "This world has so much to offer, and my vassals hunger."

No. No. This was worse than anything she'd ever predicted. And she suddenly realized it wouldn't be telling her any of this if it thought she'd ever have a chance to thwart it.

She reached for the bond, to try and alert Sebastian, but the demon's cage kept her locked within herself. Panic sucked sharply at her. "I won't let you do that."

"How are you going to stop me?"

She reached for the door handle and threw herself at the door, but he flicked a finger and she slammed back into the seat, pressure forcing her to desist.

"Don't hurt yourself," it said. "I just put my queen into play."

The black queen. "I'll never help you."

"Won't you?"

Cleo's heart felt like it stopped in her chest. Was this.... She could barely breathe. Something rippled within her as if it heard its name.

A taint.

Something the demon had seeded within her body at the moment of conception.

"Yes," it whispered, as if reading her mind. "You are my queen too. White queen and black queen. I wonder which will win? It's a risk, I know, but the idea intrigues me."

Something sinuous glided beneath the skin on her arm. Cleo gave a sharp sob. What was it? "Get it out. Get it out of me!" She dug at her arms, but the ripple was gone, though she could feel it deep within.

"As you wish." Moving swiftly, the demon flicked its razor out, and Cleo scrambled madly on the seat as he trapped her beneath him, one hand locking beneath her jaw, squeezing her throat. "Stop fighting. This will all be over very soon."

It pinned her beneath its hard body, but it wasn't painful. "I would never hurt you," it whispered, stroking her hair. "You are my finest creation, Cleo. He never appreciated you."

What was it talking about? *Who?*

Another tender touch against her cheek. "Your father deserved everything he got. I wanted to kill him myself for planting such doubt in your heart, and for thinking to lock away your gifts. The trespass against me could be forgiven. He thought he could summon me to this plane and bind me to his will." It sneered. "I am not some immortal plaything for these puny humans. But you." Its hand softened against her jaw. "What he did to you was a crime."

"I don't want this!"

"Let me help you," the demon said. "Let me show you what you are."

Using the razor to slice the fleshy pad of its index finger, it let the blood well. Power shimmered over its skin, those dark eyes shining with pure energy.

"Bloom, my sweet daughter. Become what you are meant to be." It set its bloody fingertip to her forehead, even as she tried to squirm away, and painted a fiery rune there. Leaning closer, it kissed her cheek in a proud fashion as heat scored her veins. "Come forth, my queen."

Cleo screamed. There was something shifting beneath her skin. She felt like it was crawling up her throat, trying to force its way out. She couldn't breathe. Her eyes went wide, nostrils sucking in air, or trying to....

"Yes," said a dark voice within her. *"I've been patient enough."*

Blackness overwhelmed her, and there was no way to fight. No way to claw her way through it. An image came to mind, of herself in the Ouroboros mirror, dressed in black. Of her pale face staring malevolently at herself through the mirrors pane.

This thing inside her hated her, wanted to crush her up so very small....

"Rise," whispered the demon. "Take what you are owed, my daughter."

Cleo found herself in a small dark box, with a single light gleaming high above. She slammed her hands against invisible walls, trying to fight her way out. It wasn't enough. She was cold and alone, and her precious link to Sebastian was gone. "No!" she screamed silently, hammering on those walls.

They didn't break. They simply flexed beneath her palms.

"White queen in check," the demon whispered.

CHAPTER TWENTY-FIVE

"I NEED YOUR help," Sebastian said, bursting into Lady E's study.

The older woman looked up, and her female secretary moved away from her side abruptly, as if they'd been caught doing something they shouldn't have been.

"Have you ever heard of knocking?" Lady E asked, in the sort of tone he might have cringed at as a child.

"No time," he snapped. "It took Cleo."

And Bishop wasn't home, and Rathbourne Manor was miles away, and this was the closest place he could think of.... Panic rose like a choking tide. He had to find her.

"*What* took Cleo?" Lady E rose, leaning on her cane. The color drained from her face as her dark eyes flickered over him. "Where have you been? What happened? Where's Adrian?"

"The demon!" he burst out. "The demon took her!" And then the rest of the story was falling from his lips, and he could see it again... the look on her face when the demon hauled her out the door with the razor at her throat. "Please. I can't feel her. I know she's still alive—the soul-bond's still in place—but I can't find her, and I can't.... Everything's muted. She's not there."

It had been the bane of his existence from the first moment he woke after Cleo forced the soul-bond upon him in order to save his life. He hadn't realized how much he'd come to rely upon it. How much it terrified him to come so close to losing it, and her.

"Marie," Lady E said to her secretary, "fetch my scrying tray. You"—she stabbed a finger toward him—"lie down upon my sofa."

"Did you not hear me? The demon has *my wife*!"

"I heard you," she said firmly, dragging her small card table out of the way, and sweeping cushions off her sofa. "Did you not hear *me*? Do as you're told."

His hands shook as he made his way toward the sofa. It had been all he could do not to erupt as he summoned a hack and made his way here. *She needs me.* But he trusted Lady E, and wasn't that a revelation.

"Lie down." Lady E pressed her hand to his forehead as he did, her papery-thin skin soft upon his. "There are several ways one can mute a soul-bond. Husbands and wives in the past have realized they made a momentous mistake only too late, and there are ways to manage it. But the link doesn't vanish, not unless one—or both of them as often happens—dies. It's still there, and we can use the link to find her. Calm your racing heart."

Easy to say.... He dug his nails into his palms and tried to clear his mind the way Bishop had taught him.

"Place it right there," Lady E murmured, and he saw Marie set the tray beside her. Lady E's hand pressed him into the sofa. "Are you even trying?"

"It's not working."

"Fine." Lady E poured a liberal dash of whiskey into her teacup, and then reached for one of the small pots on the tray Marie had brought in. She scooped out a small teaspoon of powder and dumped it in the whiskey, giving it a stir before tapping the spoon on the rim of the cup. "Drink this."

He looked down. Then up. "What is it?"

"A relaxant." Lady E shoved the cup into his hand. "I want your sweet wife back as much as you do."

What other choice did he have? Sebastian downed the contents, gagging at the taste. Then Lady E pushed him back down.

A gentle lassitude swept through his muscles. He blinked. The world divided into two images of itself, until several Lady E's looked down into his face.

"Excellent. Close your eyes." She started muttering her personal power words under her breath, and he could feel heat sinking through her palms as she rested them upon his forehead. "Think of your wife. Picture her hair, her favorite dress, the scent of her perfume...."

Apricot-scented soap.

"Imagine her smile and what it does to you when you see it," Lady E's voice seemed to soften, or perhaps grow distant. "Think of the way her skin feels beneath your touch. Can you sense her?"

The bond seemed to glow in the darkness behind his closed eyes. An image of Cleo formed in his mind, turning to smile at him as she looked up from Quentin Farshaw's book. "Yes," he breathed.

"What color dress is she wearing?"

"Pink." The silk nightgown he so admired. He smiled, tempted to reach out and touch her.

"Sebastian, I want you to focus now." The words felt like they were coming through a thick pane of glass. "Reach out and try and grasp that bond."

Worry filled him. "I don't want to crush the light."

"You won't, my dear boy," she said, stroking his forehead lightly. "But I need you to reach for it. Can you do that?"

He felt like he closed his hand over the little glowing spark in his mind that represented his wife. Instantly the bond strengthened, and he gasped as he saw through her eyes. There was laughter. Flames. The taste of wine in her mouth.

Blood.

But Cleo herself felt so distant.... *"Help me. Please!"* she cried, as if sensing the light of their bond.

He could feel her banging on a wall as if trapped somewhere, and someone had put her in the fucking dark, but... but he was also seeing through her eyes, and there was a garden, and lights and he saw her black eyes turning his way—

"Oh, no you don't," said a darker version of Cleo's voice.

The bond evaporated, as if she'd sliced a razor through it. Still there, pulsing in the back of his mind, but quietly now. Quietly.

Sebastian's eyes jerked open, heart leaping wildly as he came back to the room. "She shut me out."

"*What?*"

Sebastian swung his legs over the sofa, the world spinning as he righted himself. "She... she cut through the bond somehow. Locked me out."

"*Cleo* did?" Lady E asked, as if to clarify.

Or did she?

Fear washed through him and he pushed to his feet, needing to feel the heat of the fire on his skin. No. No it couldn't be.

"I don't know what it wants from me."

"But now I think the black queen is also me."

What if the demon had taken her for a more specific reason than merely a hostage? What if it had succeeded in that reason?

"What is going through your mind right now?" Lady E whispered, following him in a swish of skirts. "You look like you're going to go toes-up at my feet."

He clutched the mantel, his voice hoarse. "She told me not to tell anyone."

"I am *not* simply anyone," Lady E said, in the loftiest tones he'd ever heard.

And he couldn't do this alone.

No matter what he'd promised her.

"Cleo had a dream," he said, meeting Lady E's eyes and silently begging her to understand. "Lord Tremayne summoned a demon into him the night Cleo was conceived. The demon inside Drake had something to do with her conception."

Lady E went pale.

CHAPTER
TWENTY-SIX

SEBASTIAN SLAMMED HIS fists into the sparring dummy, again and again. There was blood on his hands, and ice on the dummy. His mind felt numb, his heart working to pump blood through his veins, but nothing else. He was fighting through the rage, trying to overcome it, trying not to fall to his knees and cling desperately to the hollow ache where the bond had been. He felt like something was missing, amputated, leaving a ghostly echo behind.

All the light in his life was gone, all the laughter, and heat, and warmth was missing... and he couldn't think about what was happening to her. Couldn't think about Lady Beaumont's brutalized body. And Cleo's smile, the one that made his heart twist in his chest whenever he earned one of them.

She'd been wrapped around him like golden threads that pumped something vital into him, but now she was gone, and he had a horrible feeling the black queen had consumed her.

How long did he have to wait?

Lady E had rushed into motion the second he revealed Cleo's heritage and the truth about the black queen, insisting he prepare himself. And wait.

They needed the others, she'd told him, and he'd never seen Lady E—solid, unflappable Lady Eberhardt—look so flustered.

He couldn't simply do nothing. But what could he do by himself? Sebastian's arms finally failed him, and he slumped against the practice dummy in Bishop's dungeon-like cellar. Lady E insisted they gather there, and had sent out the call.

The door opened. Sebastian broke away from the dummy, turning with predatory intent, but it was a familiar figure.

Bishop stepped through, closing the door with a quiet snick. His brown eyes took in the state of the room, and the blood on Sebastian's knuckles. He cleared his throat. "Agatha told me what happened."

"I can't feel her." Sebastian looked away, the dense surge of hopelessness threatening to drag his head beneath the waters.

He couldn't give in. Rage poured through him. That was better than hopelessness. Guilt and shame flayed him raw, stripping the skin off his bones. He needed to make it hurt. It threatened to eat him alive, but he could work with pain. Cleo needed him.

Why had he ever let her leave with the demon?

"Where's Rathbourne?"

"On his way. Here," Bishop said, picking up one of the timber sparring staves. He tossed it toward Sebastian, who caught it, and began stripping his coat off. "Just give me a second."

The wood felt solid in his palm. "I thought I was supposed to meditate when I felt like this."

"Do you feel like meditating right now?"

"No." His breath steamed in the icy air. "I feel like punching something."

Bishop slicked his hair back with his palms, and then reached for the second stave. "That's why I'm here."

Sebastian faced him, the weight shifting off his shoulders. Hitting something was the only way he'd been able to still his mind, but having something hit back....

He needed this to clear his mind, or he'd go mad.

"You won't hurt me," Bishop said. "But you can try."

His voice felt raw. "Don't pull your blows. I want to feel it."

"I won't."

The first swing of the staff cut through the sheer weight of the anger riding him. Staff slammed against staff, and then he was shoving his brother back with raw strength, raw fury. Bishop's stave caught the edge of his ribs, and the lash of pain that swept through him cleared his mind. Sebastian swung back, the clack of timber bringing with it a sweet clarity of its own.

The fierce dance began to weave a magic of its own. No holding back. Bishop knew how to protect himself.

He pictured Cleo, laughing beneath him as he kissed his way down her throat. Took a knee to the ribs, and swung back, ducking beneath the wide hum of Bishop's stave. It hurt. It all hurt, but he needed this. Needed the pain.

Cleo, the knife to her throat. Sebastian took a blow to the shoulder that would have crippled him on a different day, but he simply plowed through it, feeling strangely numb, and scored a lucky strike. Bishop didn't wince, simply answered with a sweeping retaliation that made his ears ring.

Body against body. Blow against blow. It was physical and raw, driving all the thoughts from his head, but one.

Cleo. Telling him her heart was his.

The tide broke within him. A sob sounded in his throat. And Bishop slammed him back into the wall, smashing the stave aside, his arms dragging Sebastian to his chest. Sebastian swung an arm, but Bishop blocked it.

"No more. No more. We're done."

A fist curled in his hair, and he couldn't see. His face was buried in his brother's shoulder. One second they were fighting, and the next, his brother was dragging him into a hug.

"We'll get her back," Bishop whispered. "I promise you I will do anything—*anything*—to get her back safely."

Sebastian lifted his head, blinking through the haze. The words felt momentous. He didn't understand.

"Drake wouldn't want her to be hurt," Bishop said, meeting his eyes. "I know what he would tell me to do."

It struck him like a fist of iron. The one thing Bishop didn't want to do, the one thing he dreaded the most—

"You'd kill him?" he whispered hoarsely.

Bishop was offering to kill his father to stop the demon? To save Cleo? He could barely breathe.

"I know how I'd feel if that were Verity," Bishop murmured. "And you're my brother. My younger brother." His voice roughened. "I never understood that until now. Verity was right all along. We need to stick together."

Sebastian tried to clear his throat, choking on the emotion filling him. He didn't know what to say. A month ago this man had been a foe. "Thank you."

The words weren't enough, but Bishop nodded.

"Let's go find that demon and kill it."

CHAPTER TWENTY-SEVEN

'A well-spring bond is formed between two or more sorcerers when they wish to combine strength, however, one of them is in charge, and the others merely puppets.'
—*'Understanding the Divine'*, by Sir Antony Scott

"SO WHERE DID Lascher take her?" Lucien asked, leaning over the map of London that Bishop had produced.

Sebastian stared into the flames in the hearth. All of them had gathered there as evening fell. Lucien, Ianthe, Bishop, and Verity. Lady Eberhardt and Marie. Remington Cross and Eleanor, Drake's lover.

He hadn't understood until today. This wasn't just a war meeting, this was a family. Every single person here would fight to rescue Cleo, and not just because of duty, but because they loved her.

And he... he had a place here.

He cleared his throat, turning to face them. "I only caught a glimpse through the bond. There was light, a garden...." He fought to remember. "Flames in the background, and laughter. I'm sorry. I can't recall anything familiar, and it was so quick."

"Tomorrow night is the full moon," Lady Eberhardt grumbled, leaning on her cane. "It's a powerful time, especially if the demon is planning some great working."

"And?" Bishop asked.

Lady E circled the map. "If you'd allow me to finish.... A great working requires a certain phase of the moon. It also requires a certain place."

"A leyline," Ianthe said sharply, looking up. "It can draw the energy up through the earth."

"Somewhere consecrated," Lady E added. "Sorcerous power leaves an echo, and if the place is used often enough, it imbues the surrounding area with energy."

"One of the Order's ritual places, like the Hollow where the Ascension took place?" Verity chipped in.

Lady E began to draw faint lines across the enormous map with her finger, making them glow. "Here are the leylines within riding distance of London." She began to press her finger to points in the map. "And here are places that might hold power. We'll add Balthazar's Labyrinth to the list."

"And Seven Dials," Verity suggested. "My friends there haven't seen anything out of the usual, but it's full of curse workers."

The ladies began to highlight the map, arguing over this place or that, as Bishop made his way toward him. A crook of his finger at Lucien, and he indicated the three of them ought to seek a moment of quiet on the balcony.

"What is it?" Lucien asked.

"The prophecy is coming to a head," Bishop murmured. "We have all three brothers in place. We have the three Relics. This ends tomorrow, one way or another. We need to discuss a plan of attack."

Lucien slid his hands into his pockets. "Ianthe said you planned on killing him."

Bishop's lips thinned. "Only as a last resort. We have to make an attempt to wield the Relics Infernal against it, and try to exorcise Lascher from Drake's body."

Agreed. Sebastian tipped his head in a brief nod.

"If it doesn't work," Bishop said softly, "then... then I'll take care of matters."

"Ianthe and I have been reading through Drake's notes on the Relics," Lucien said. "Neither of us knew how they were created, but we found some of the more specific passages in his journal today. I don't quite understand all the theory yet, but there was something about Drake creating a spiritual echo of the Relics in another plane and tying them to the physical embodiment here. It's why they're so deadly to the demon. They exist here, and also in the dream-plane, or wherever it is that Cleo and Drake speak about. Demons can touch the dream-plane via the Shadow Dimensions, so the Relics have some sort of effect upon them."

"I've been to the dream plane," Sebastian said. "When I was trapped in my mother's dungeon, Drake brought me there to try and reach me."

"Tomorrow when we confront it," Lucien said, "we each need to funnel power through one of the Relics."

"I'll take the Chalice," Bishop said. "It's bound to the Grave Arts, so I doubt either of you will be able to wield it."

Lucien shrugged. "Ianthe and I have spent quite a bit of time with the Blade, considering she was the one who stole it from Drake. It makes sense—"

"No." Sebastian frowned. "I think I'm meant to have the Blade. Drake said something when he surfaced today. He said Cleo needed to stab him with it."

A moment of silence. Snowflakes fluttered out of the sky.

"You're linked to her," Bishop said slowly, "so it might work. Drake wouldn't have said it if it wasn't important."

"I'll take the Wand then. Have you looked over the spell to link the Relics?"

"Yes." Bishop turned, resting his hands on the balustrade. "It's complex. I'll go over it tonight with Sebastian." Dark eyes flashed toward him. "You'll have to master the chant. We can't afford a single error."

Done. He didn't care what it took. "I'll master it."

"Do you think you can withstand the raw energy we'll be dealing with?" Bishop asked, this time looking to Lucien.

Who hesitated. "I'm healing."

That wasn't an answer. A slither of dread made Sebastian's muscles tense. "This isn't going to work, is it? I have ridiculous power, but limited control. Lucien has years of experience and mastery, but can only handle a certain amount of sorcery without it feeling like a knife driving into his brain. And you.... You're the only one who might survive tomorrow." He laughed a little helplessly, and it took a moment to realize neither of his brothers was laughing with him.

Bishop looked up slowly, meeting Lucien's eyes.

"Hell," Lucien cursed, under his breath. "We're idiots. Three sons, three relics, three of... us. The key was there all along."

"Yes, excellent," Sebastian said. "You can count. What does any of that mean?"

Bishop remained frozen. "No," he said succinctly. "It wouldn't work."

"Why not?" Lucien pushed away from the balcony, brushing snowflakes off his sleeves. "Bonded sorcerers are always stronger than a single one. If we link—"

"I can think of a dozen reasons why it wouldn't work," Bishop countered. "Trust issues, for one. Who's going to be the Anchor?"

Sebastian looked between the two of them. "What the devil are you talking about? Anchor... for what?"

It was Bishop who answered, turning to the garden to stare into it as if it held all the answers. "He's talking about the three of us linking. It's something two or more sorcerers can do to combine strengths. The problem is: one of them has to lead it. One of them controls everything."

A trickle of ice went down Sebastian's spine. He'd been the demon's vessel for all of a day last month. It had been the ultimate loss of control, after a lifetime of being at the mercy of others. "No."

Not even to save Cleo?

That wasn't even a question, but could he do this? Could he physically hand over control of his will, body, and sorcery to another?

"Precisely," Bishop shot back, and pinched the bridge of his nose.

Lucien didn't seem quite as sanguine. He crossed his arms over his chest. "I don't know why you're so bothered," he told Bishop. "You'd be the one in control."

That earned him a savage glare, but Lucien met it with a faintly arched brow. "I'm stronger than you are— technically you're the weakest when one considers the amount of raw power one can wield. I'm barely beginning to regain mastery of myself, let alone two others. And Sebastian already has strength—what he needs is finesse."

"I don't want to control the link." Bishop replied. For the first time that Sebastian could recall, he actually saw doubt on Bishop's face.

Then he turned and walked back inside, leaving Lucien and Sebastian staring at each other.

"Why don't you want to be the Anchor?"

Sebastian found his brother in the billiards room, after Lucien joined the ladies. Bishop poured himself a generous glass of brandy, and then looked up when he entered the room and added another glass.

"Linking with another person is... quite a personal experience. There are only two people I've ever done it with." Bishop nudged the glass toward him.

"Verity and Agatha," he said, but he watched his brother's face. "And that's got little to do with it. Nice try."

Bishop's lips thinned.

"You promised me honesty," Sebastian said. "We don't have time for you to lie to us—or yourself."

There was a drawn-out moment of silence. Bishop sighed. "You're right. I demand honesty from you. I bet you're enjoying this moment."

"Somewhat," Sebastian admitted, and would have smiled if the circumstances were different.

"What do you know of the Grave Arts?"

"They're mostly necromancers." He glanced at Bishop. "Or Sicarii assassins, like you. Killing people gives them a rush of power that most couldn't imagine."

"It's addictive," Bishop said flatly. "We call it the *maladroise*, and it haunts my steps day and night. Little whispers in my mind—*how good it would feel, how easy it would be to take*...." He suddenly shook his head, as if casting off a sudden weight. "It usually ends with the afflicted sorcerer starting a lovely little murder spree that demands execution. I used to think there was no cure."

"Is there?"

"Yes." The way he said it made the word sound hollow.

Sebastian frowned. "Then what seems to be the problem?"

"From what I can gather from books, and my own personal experiments, I could use the Chalice to burn away my link to the Grave Arts. Instant relief."

"But?"

"But there is always a sacrifice when it comes to extreme acts of sorcery. I will possibly lose half of my power, or my ability to handle a certain amount of power," Bishop replied, and splayed his fingers wide on the billiards table. "And I cannot do that yet. Not until this is done and Cleo is safe."

"If you link with us—"

"Then there's a chance I would start to hear the whisper of the *maladroise*. Start to hear your heartbeats and the little song they sing to someone like me," Bishop whispered. "And your power.... Hell. All that power whispering along my nerves, like it could be mine for the taking. You'd be wide open to me if I were in control."

Completely vulnerable. He swallowed again. *Never.* "I thought you lived and breathed control."

"I do." Bishop looked away.

"It scares you," Sebastian said slowly, working his way through his tangled thoughts.

"And it should," Bishop replied. "The second I stop fearing it, is the second you need to send for an executioner."

They both fell silent.

"Then we do this individually," he said in a tired voice, downing the glass of brandy. "Where's that chant I need to learn?"

CHAPTER TWENTY-EIGHT

What would happen if anyone were to truly pierce the Veil to the Shadow Dimensions, and bring forth that ruinous host in the flesh, so to speak? A demon cannot do it from this side, as they are not truly here. But what if one of their vessels had the power to do so?

——Sidestep Through Time by Quentin Farshaw

"MALACHI GRAY'S ESTATE," Sebastian said, staring up at the enormous wrought iron gates. "Of course. This is the garden I saw through Cleo's eyes."

"And an incubus is a creature from the Shadow Dimensions." Bishop growled under his breath. "Lascher's probably been here the entire time."

"Plenty of blood and sex to feed it," he agreed, his nerves on edge. He was finally close to getting Cleo back.

Helping Verity down from the carriage, Sebastian surveyed the grounds. They'd have to walk. Who knew what they'd be bringing the horses into? He could feel something in the air, a certain sort of crispness, a waiting....

Eleanor Ross had insisted upon coming, despite her limp, and she stepped down from the second carriage, leaning upon her cane.

He was the reason for her limp, and the slack line of her left jaw. She'd been caught in the edge of an attack he'd thrown at his mother, and barely survived it.

That's enough, he told himself firmly. *She wouldn't be alive if you hadn't turned on your mother in that moment.*

Her presence had made Bishop uneasy; she wanted Drake back at all costs. Neither of them had the heart to tell her they'd have to kill him if they couldn't save him.

A hooded figure caught his eye as Remington stepped down from the second carriage. Morgana tripped in the snow and fell to her knees, a velvet hood over her face, and her hands bound with Bishop's golden spelled manacles. She'd been the cause of every major pain in his life, but he couldn't look at her for too long.

Not anymore.

The journal had given him the means to break free of Morgana's chains, but it had also had a far more unsettling effect upon him, coupled with the night Cleo sat and held his hand.

"Brush my hair for me?" Morgana whispered, handing him the ivory-handled brush that had once belonged to her mother. It was the only thing she'd ever had of his grandmother's, and it seemed far too big for his little hand.

But he tugged it gently through his mother's hair, enjoying the rare moment of kindness, and not knowing how soon those moments would vanish.

Execution was one thing. Giving her over to the demon, quite another. It would be easier if inconvenient memories didn't keep lodging in his mind. Damn Lady E for giving him that journal.

Taking up the leash around his mother's wrists, Sebastian stared down at her black hood. She was smaller than he remembered, or perhaps hunched over from her recent incarceration. "I wouldn't try anything, if I were you."

"Don't do thish," Morgana hissed around the gag she wore. "I'm your muver."

Even to the end, she sought to manipulate him. "And he's my father. He, at least, has earned my loyalty."

Tugging the leash, he dragged her forward.

"So it begins," Lucien said, tugging his gloves off as he stared up at the manor.

"Yes." Sebastian forced his mother's words away. He needed a clear mind for the coming event.

"No." Bishop strode ahead of them, his black cloak fluttering behind him. "Now it ends. Watch your backs. I doubt the demon's going to simply let us walk in here unmolested."

Torches lined the driveway as they walked through the snow. The gardens seemed far too silent, as if last night's snowfall muffled the sounds of the world. It was a hush filled with anticipation, for he couldn't escape the feeling he was being watched.

"Unless it's a trap," Lucien pointed out.

"It's a trap," Sebastian said, as the ladies fell in behind them. "But it won't spring shut until we get there. It wants us alive—for the moment—and it wants the Relics."

"And you're vringing it everyshing it wants," his mother hissed. "Are you inshane?"

"Shut up."

"Look at the clouds," Ianthe whispered, turning her face to the sky.

Thick white clouds boiled over the manor, tinged with hints of dark gray. It almost looked like they were going to birth some enormous monstrosity into the world, heavy and pregnant with portent.

"Cleo said the skies go dark when it all happens," he said, feeling an itch along his skin. "What is that hum?"

Bishop looked grim as they grew closer to the manor. "It's set up a major working. The spell must have been laid weeks ago, with the demon building the ritual day by day." His breath caught as a fluctuation in the energy suddenly burst through them all. "I've never seen anything like it. The complexity...."

"I have," Ianthe replied, her face serene and her emotions locked within as she picked her way through the snow. He'd missed the tearful goodbyes as she gave her daughter over into her apprentice's hands, and sent them north just in case this all went wrong, but Verity had mentioned it. No sign of turmoil on Ianthe's face now. This was a Prime, determined to right wrongs and face down a creature that threatened all those she was responsible for. "Drake created something like this years ago, when he was trying to set an elaborate trap for an incubus. This is merely the eye of the storm. It hasn't begun the final ritual."

If this was what it felt like before the ritual even began....

"There it is," Bishop said, as a figure in a red cloak moved onto the snowy lawns.

A ring of torches lit the stormy afternoon. The demon waited in the center of the torches, watching them come. It stood alone, but the hum of that seething magic began to pick up as they cleared the terrace. It pricked at Sebastian's skin, hungry for blood, tasting him and clearly liking what it found.

"Are you all right?" Ianthe murmured, as her husband flinched.

"The ritual's keyed to the three of us, I think," Lucien replied. "Unless you're feeling it too?"

"Drake's blood calling to yours," she muttered darkly.

"Three Relics, three brothers, three sacrifices." Bishop spoke of the long-ago prophecy that had set all this into place. "It must have used Drake's blood to set the spell into motion."

A bloodied hexagram was painted in the snow, with a discarded body at each point, their throats and wrists slit. Runes were painted around the hexagram, the kind of thing that made his vision waver every time he looked at them and tried to see what they were.

Nothing human. Nothing he could recognize. The heat shimmer of raw power hung in the air above each symbol, though the snow wasn't melting.

An enormous wooden cross in the shape of an X stood at each of three points. A man was crucified upon one of the crosses, his clothes fine and his body slack. A woman hung from the second, blood dripping from her empty eye sockets. Suddenly this felt real, and he looked for Cleo, both heartened and disheartened not to find her.

Only the third cross remained empty.

Foreboding crept up his spine.

"Well met," the demon called, guarded safely within the hexagram.

"Where is my wife?"

Its black eyes flickered to his. "Safe."

A demon couldn't lie, but there were always ways to bend the truth. "I want to see her."

"She will be joining us shortly. She's still preparing herself. Show me Morgana," the demon called, standing safely within the hexagram.

Sebastian reached for the black hood she wore. His mother's dark curls were in disarray as he dragged it from her head. The gag she wore cut into her mouth, and she glared at him. He tugged her gag down to hang loosely around her throat.

"It's time she paid her dues," the demon said.

"No," Morgana breathed, her face paling as she stared at the enormous crosses. She pulled against the spelled manacles she wore. "*No!*"

Sebastian felt sickened. It was one thing to want his mother dead—he hadn't even been able to look at her all morning—another to understand what the creature wanted with her. The single cross filled his vision, no matter where he looked. The demon needed three sacrifices to begin powering its spell.

They'd always thought the three sacrifices would be each of the brothers.

"Sebastian, please!" She gripped his sleeve, and for the first time he saw true fear in her eyes as she too gazed at the cross. "Don't do this. Don't do this! I'm your mother—"

"We brought the Relics," he said, turning toward the demon. "But I don't trust you. You're not getting my mother until I see my wife. Where's Cleo?"

The demon's black gaze cut to him. "She betrayed both of us, Sebastian. Morgana thought she could bring me into this world all those years ago, thinking to master me with these Relics." Its lip curled up. "She will pay the price of that with her life. This is a fitting end. This is justice."

"It's not justice." Even he knew that.

"Do you think she gave a damn about you, when she gave your control ring to those women?" The demon stalked closer, seeming curious. "Do you think she ever cared when she put a knife in your hand and pointed it at her enemies? Do you think, for one second, if you were the one in chains today, that she wouldn't hand you over to me."

No.

The words were barely audible in the crisp evening air. "*But I am not her.*"

"Pardon?"

He stared into those demonic eyes, his voice becoming a little stronger. "I am not her."

It seemed perplexed. Beside him, Morgana was sucking in panting gasps of relief, her hands clinging to his sleeve. "Thank you. Thank you."

"I'm not doing it for you," he said coldly.

"Morgana for Cleo. That is the deal," the demon said.

His lashes lowered and he nodded. "I will hand her over when my wife is at my side, and not before."

The demon turned, its cloak flaring behind it as it paced back to the safety of its hexagram, but he'd thrown it. It looked at him, and he remembered the little conversation they'd had about pressure points. "Place the Relics at each point that doesn't hold a cross. When your wife appears, you will hand over your mother."

It wasn't as though they had much choice, not until Cleo was safe. Bishop stalked slowly toward the furthest point, which also happened to be the one behind the demon, the Chalice in his hands. Lucien moved toward the northern point of the star with the Wand, which left Sebastian with the last.

He tugged the Blade from within its sheath, feeling the heavy weight of it in his palm. Last chance. He didn't want to let it go, but the demon held all the cards, and if he could distract it while Bishop got close...

Sebastian gently laid the Blade in the snow at the point.

The man on the cross beside him suddenly moaned, and he almost lashed out with his sorcery. *Sweet mercy.* He was still alive, still....

"Malachi Gray?" Sebastian breathed in horror, recognizing the face that had tormented him so when the incubus danced with his wife.

The incubus bared bloody teeth in a pained smile, sucking in breath. Blood dripped from his palms where the spikes had been driven in deep. "In the... flesh."

Jesus. Horror finally penetrated the cold mask he'd been wearing. He turned to face the demon, fighting to keep it off his face. "Do you treat all your allies this way?"

"Gray made the mistake of thinking he could break faith with me," the demon replied. "He tried to kidnap your wife, and remove her from my care."

Sebastian looked at Gray sharply.

"I don't know what he did to her, but she's not your wife anymore," the incubus rasped. "She wanted... to drink my blood. Whatever is in there right now... don't trust it."

Slowly he turned toward the demon, and it all became horribly clear. The demon had said he could have Cleo back in exchange for the Relics, but what if she refused? "What did you do to her?"

"All I did was unchain the girl's true self. She is more precious to me than you could ever know."

A demon sired me....

This demon?

A figure in black moved just behind Drake's shoulder. Bishop. Sebastian let his face blank of emotion. They had one chance left. He drew in enough power to prove a threat and keep its attention. *Watch me, you bastard.*

"Don't be foolish," the demon chided. "Don't do this, Sebastian. You're no match for me."

"I'm not leaving until I have what I came for."

The demon's eyes narrowed. "You're bluffing."

"No, he's not," Lucien called, drawing its attention. "We came for Cleo."

It looked between them, and sweat sprang down Sebastian's spine. He didn't dare look behind it, but out of the corner of his eyes he could see the demon's wards shimmering at the bottom, as Bishop set to work in sliding through them.

"I'm watching the wrong brothers," it whispered, as if it picked up on their intent somehow.

Blazing with sudden power, the demon spun toward the threat at its back, throwing a wave of force out.

Bishop's legs went out from under him, and he landed heavily in the snow with a grunt.

"Adrian!" Verity screamed.

"Move!" Lucien bellowed toward Ianthe and the others.

Everything happened so quickly. Sebastian stepped back toward the point where the Blade rested, swiftly unbuttoning his cufflinks. Drawing a small knife from his pocket, he sliced it across his finger, squeezing blood to the surface. It dripped onto the snow at his feet, some of it spattering on the Blade.

Sorcery whispered through his veins as the Blade of Altarrh woke. He could feel it hungering now for more blood, his mind connected to it, but they weren't quite ready.

"Bishop!" *Get up.*

"Do you truly think you could do it?" the demon taunted his fallen brother. "Kill your own father?"

Bishop staggered to his feet, forging a knife of raw matter in his hand, slicing his own finger and letting his blood drip into the Chalice. "Whatever it takes. Drake didn't want this."

"So be it." The demon hissed. "*Alshandra di lemos an scythios!*"

The star lit up. An enormous blaze of energy soared up through the earth, as if the leyline were suddenly unlocked. Heat and light soared toward the murky skies overhead, blinding Sebastian in the crossbeam. Morgana's startled scream echoed as the demon made a jerking motion, and yanked her through the air toward him.

"One more sacrifice," the demon promised, grabbing Morgana by the throat and slamming her back against the cross. It had a knife in its hand, though it paused to look in Sebastian's direction. "Remember this."

And it drove the knife through Morgana's throat, pinning her to the timber.

Energy had gushed into the sky as the star lit up, but now it came crashing back down, turning the lines of the hexagram molten. Little gold lines of spell work lit up all across the snow like a grid, as if Morgana's blood somehow activated the next phase of the spell.

Malachi Gray screamed, and the other woman on the cross—Odette?—threw her head back as if she were racked with new pain. All Sebastian could do was gape as Morgana's wide green eyes met his, choking, gurgling sounds coming from her throat. This wasn't meant to happen this way. And then her face softened, her body slumping forward, and the cross she was pinned to suddenly went up in white flames, as if her death powered some new aspect of the spell.

Dead. It felt like hollow drumbeat in his chest, but he didn't have time to think his way through the shock of it.

The demon moved with vicious intensity. It cut the blind Odette's throat, making her body jerk. A flash fire of white exploded up around her body, consuming her. A second hexagram began to glow inside the first.

"Oh, no you don't." He needed to stop this. Somehow.

Summoning his sorcery in a blaze of energy, he turned and sheared through the bottom half of the cross with exquisite skill, honed by Bishop's teaching. It fell backward, Malachi screaming, still pinned to the wood as the cross landed with a soft *whump* in the snow.

Sebastian skidded to his knees beside the incubus, reaching out to grip the steel spike driven through his palms.

"What are you doing?" Malachi gasped.

"Don't take it personally. It needs you dead. Hence, I'm going to save your life."

He yanked the spike free, and an utterly raw sound poured from Malachi's throat. The second spike was driven too deep. Their eyes met as Sebastian grabbed the bastard's wrist. There was no other way....

"Do it," Malachi panted.

He tore the incubus's hand from the spike, and Malachi screamed, curling into a pained ball on the snow.

"Sebastian," a woman's voice whispered through the bond. *"You're going to ruin everything. I can't allow that."*

"Cleo?" he rasped, looking around.

A shadow blurred. Bishop, trying again to break through this phenomenal ward. The second he hit the lines of the hexagram, he slammed into invisible walls of pure force that threw him back.

He hit the snow beside Sebastian, sliding several feet, his arm flung out to stop himself. The knife vanished. And then he didn't move.

"Bishop!" Sebastian sank to his knees beside his brother and shook him.

Glazed eyes met his, blood dripping from his brother's nose. "G-get... out... of here."

"Like hell." All around them the world spun into chaos as Ianthe and the others joined the fray in order to distract the demon.

Imps erupted from snowdrifts, proving the demon had never had any intention of seeing them leave. Mage globes exploded, and he could hear Lady E cursing under her breath, followed by sharp little detonations that showed she was probably causing the enemy one heck of a headache.

"You have to focus," Sebastian snarled, the words an echo of those his brother once said to him. "Get up. You don't get to just lie here, not now. Not like this."

But Bishop flopped like a deboned quail.

He couldn't do this without him. Despair licked along Sebastian's spine, but with it came the memory of lying in the dirt as his brother demanded he get up; a brutal month-long training program, but perhaps now he could understand Bishop's intention. Kid gloves would only have ended in his death. Bishop had known what was coming.

"If you give up now," Sebastian said coldly, "then Verity dies."

There. There was the spark of fire in his brother's eyes.

"I won't save her." Sebastian forced himself to continue. "I cannot save both Cleo and Verity, and if I have to make a choice...."

A fist curled in his collar, and Bishop yanked himself half upright with a snarl. Broken blood vessels in his eyes gave him a demonic appearance. "You little shit. Verity's the last person who'd bloody need saving."

"Aye." Sebastian winced, and tried to loosen the hold on his collar. "But if she sees you on your back, then she'll break protocol and she'll come in here to rescue you. Even if it means taking on the demon by herself. You know that."

It was the first time he'd ever seen his brother look beaten. "I don't know if I can... get to him."

"You know Drake's wards. You know a way through them."

"I've tried twice."

"Then try again." The problem wasn't in the wards, it was in the intent. Some part of his brother knew getting through those wards meant his father's death. This was the same sabotage Cleo had been doing to herself all month. "He begged you to save him. This is mercy, Bishop, not murder."

Bishop met his gaze. "And will you say the same when it's your black queen you have to put a knife in, and not your wife?"

They all had their weak spots.

"It's not going to get that far."

A red mage globe spun to life. Sebastian barely had time to notice it, before Bishop shoved him out of the way. They both went down in a snowdrift, and an explosion of red light behind them lit the world.

"Move!" Bishop screamed, scrambling to his feet and staggering.

Sebastian yanked him upright, slipping beneath his arm. "Lucien!"

"Here." Their eldest brother appeared out of the heart of a burning cloud. "We need to get inside the hexagram."

"How?" Another mage globe struck the brick of the wall beside them, and chunks of mortar blew out. Sebastian flung an arm over his face.

Something caught his attention.

A slender figure, dressed all in black, picking her way through the snow, moving slowly, as if in a dream. His blood ran cold. Cleo.

She wasn't even looking at him. She barely noticed the blood. Instead, she walked with deliberate purpose toward the star and crossed the line, bending to pick something up as she went. The Blade of Altarrh by the look of it. The demon held his hand out toward her, a satisfied smirk on its face.

Cleo took Lascher's gloved hand, her hair falling down her back in straight, silken sheets. Crow feathers capped her shoulders, and she wore a cloak of black velvet, her dress cut low in front to reveal the smooth slope of her breasts.

"Come, sweet child," the demon called. "Open the gates."

"We need one more sacrifice," she said.

"We have to stop her," Bishop told him, strain showing on his face. "If she opens those gates, we'll all die."

Cleo's eyes were blank. She took the Blade of Altarrh, and sliced it down her wrist. Not even a flinch betrayed her. Blood welled, and then she squeezed her tortured flesh, and it began to drip into the snow at the demon's feet.

This, then, was London's doom. This was how it would end, in a world full of blood and the screams of the dying as the Shadow Horde came through. She'd always seen him in the Vision. And herself.

But neither of them had ever realized which one of them would bring about the destruction.

One more sacrifice.... No. Not her. Cleo lifted the Blade, seeking his gaze as she angled it toward her chest. He shoved away from Bishop and staggered toward the inverted triangles.

"Don't!" Lucien cried, but it sounded so far away.

Sebastian slammed into the ward, but it didn't fling him back as it had done to Bishop. It melded around his skin, sound cutting off abruptly, and time seeming to slow around him as he passed through it. Mage globes exploded silently around him like fireworks, and he saw Remington slowly whirling and sending razor sharp ribbons of light from his fingers, cutting down a pair of imps who sought to leap upon Lady Eberhardt's back....

And then the world rushed past him again and Sebastian hit the ground inside the hexagram, rolling to his feet.

It was different in here. Sound muted, but no longer entirely silent. He saw two worlds beyond the invisible walls of the hexagram. The others were still fighting the pack of imps, though every movement seemed to have slowed down. Bishop turned, his knee lifting, and his leg stretching out into a painfully slow extension as an imp launched itself from the top of the garden wall, its lips peeling back in a hiss. His heel slammed into the imp's chin with a visible shudder, its face rippling from the impact. Ianthe and Lucien fought back to back, mage globes of red and blue whirling around the pair of them like a firestorm.

But if he stared past that world he could see another. Stars stretched from horizon to horizon, a black and white checkerboard flowing over the ground.

Two worlds.

Two planes.

And another one visible in the sky above them, fiery red lines boiling there impatiently, like a seamstress's ragged seam. The seam bulged, and he could see faces there, monstrous faces trying to push their way through. All it would take would be one pull and something would spill out....

"Do you see it now?" the demon whispered. "My world is dying. There are too many of us trapped within, and we have slowly torn each other to pieces. We need new prey. Something to feed this thirst."

"So you wish to destroy my world?" He turned back to them.

"There are many humans. What is the loss of a few million? You breed faster than we do."

"I won't let you have my world." He met the black queen's black eyes. "I won't let you have my wife."

Standing in front of the demon, she watched him come with a sultry expression, the Blade still angled toward her chest. "My king doesn't have a choice. He doesn't make my decisions for me."

Don't trust her, Malachi Gray had said.

She's no longer your wife.

"Cleo," he said hoarsely. He'd never seen her look like this, and it struck him how familiar her cross expression, exasperation, and glowing smiles had become. Cleo couldn't hide a damned thing, and yet this stranger—this black queen—held the same unblinking qualities as the demon. Whoever this was, it wasn't his wife. There was a stillness to her expression, a hungry eagerness that was unlike her.

But he could feel the real Cleo in the back of his mind, the bond between them pulsing a little brighter as he came into her sphere.

Cleo was still in there.

He just had to reach her.

The Blade in her hand flipped abruptly, the hilt falling into her palm. *One last sacrifice.* She hadn't meant herself.

Of course.

"You should have allowed me to kill the incubus," Lascher murmured. "I would have spared you, but the spell needs another death to power it. This is not personal."

"No!" A faint scream sounded through the bond. The real Cleo, hammering at her cell.

"Then wield the Blade yourself," he told it. She shouldn't have to watch this happen by her own hand.

"But I want to do it," said the black queen.

"She needs to be initiated," Lascher added. "Your blood will give her strength. And I can't touch the Blade."

The demon and the black queen parted, moving with predatory intensity around him. Sebastian opened himself to the flow of his sorcery. It buoyed him, offering strength, but he wasn't certain if he could face the demon and survive. And he *couldn't* hurt her. How to stop this then?

"I love you, and I would do anything to protect you, Sebastian."

A long ago night, Cleo's hand curling in his and offering comfort, but nothing more. *Love.* He'd never understood it, not truly.

The moment in Lady Beaumont's house came to mind, his father's face rippling as the demon finally threatened Sebastian. The threat had given Drake the strength to rise up and overtake it, even for a moment. His father had been driven by love, the one thing powerful enough to overcome the demon's stranglehold upon him.

This wasn't about fighting them. He couldn't win that way, and the pair of them were anticipating it. A month spent mastering himself was never going to be enough. Lady E had known that.

Could he gamble everything?

Upon love?

"You want a sacrifice?" His voice sounded hoarse, but he let the tide of power ebb from his body as he released it. He looked at his wife, forcing himself to see past those

382

black eyes, trying to find her somewhere within. "Then you have it."

He knelt on the wet lawn, unbuttoning his coat with swift fingers. Nerves fluttered in his stomach, but he cast the coat aside and looked up. Both of them blinked at him.

They're not human. The demon thinks it knows humanity, but it doesn't.

It couldn't see the trap.

"My life is yours, Cleo. It always has been." He started working on the buttons of his shirt, tearing it when his fingers fumbled, and jerking it open.

"Finish it," the demon said remotely, though he could see the bulge in its jaw as Drake fought to rise.

The black queen strode toward him, the Blade of Altarrh in her hands. His blood was already on the knife. He could feel it hungering for more.

Grabbing a handful of his hair, she yanked his head back, revealing his throat.

"The first time I ever met you," he said softly, "I wanted to hate you. I was terrified to see what sort of woman my mother had saddled me with. I knew your father, and so I wasn't hopeful of much. A forced marriage to Tremayne's daughter?" He laughed gently, free of the bitterness that had once chained him. "And yet, there you were, standing amidst your ducks. Feeding Sir Eiderdown and Lord Featherbottom, and Christ, you were babbling, but there was something about you I'd never seen before. And you were… beautiful. You were everything I think I'd never dared hope for."

She hesitated. Just a faint flicker of expression across that disdainful face, but it was there. He wasn't imagining it.

Could she hear him, deep in her prison? He swallowed hard. *"Fight her, Cleo."*

"The night I first kissed you, the frozen prison around my heart began to melt," he whispered. "You have been there at every step of the way, forcing me to be a better man. Holding me when I have weakened. And loving me, loving me no matter how much I loathed myself."

"Finish it," the demon hissed, sensing, perhaps, its doom.

"Cleo, I love you." Sebastian cupped the back of her calf through her dress. The soul-bond flared with the physical link. She was in there, he could feel her. Her light was small, but he cupped his hands around it and blew on the spark, trying to bring her back to life. "This is not your fault. I give you my heart, my death, if you want to take it. It's yours. My heart was always yours, and it always will be, no matter what. My life is yours. I love you."

The black queen shook her head, her skin rippling from beneath as if some hidden war was waged inside her.

"Fight her," he whispered, touching the link and feeling something brush against him.

Then her expression hardened.

"If you love me, then you're a fool," said the black queen, lifting the Blade of Altarrh in her hand.

CHAPTER TWENTY-NINE

A THOUSAND MOMENTS stretched out in that second.

And Cleo saw it all.

Sebastian on his knees in front of her. The knife in her hand, growing heavier by the second.

The knife descending toward his vulnerable throat.

No! She screamed it with her entire being.

With his hand touching her body, she was suddenly no longer alone, trapped in the dark. The bond between them swelled, and she *pushed* on the invisible walls trapping her in the dark, raging up within herself.

Sebastian looked up at her, his gaze unflinching. He refused to look at the descending knife. Refused to do anything but pour his emotions through the bond between them. *"My life is yours. I love you."*

Cleo screamed, the sound breaking from her lips as she fell heavily into her body. She could sense the shadow within her, fighting for control, but she had more power here, linked to him as she was.

The Blade fell harmlessly to her side.

And Cleo looked down into Sebastian's relieved face before closing her eyes. This was not done yet.

Whatever the demon had done to her, it had stripped all the veils from her eyes. The world seemed entirely different, a second plane of existence sitting almost on top of the real world. It was a simple matter to take that sidestep into another world. She opened her eyes and found herself in the dream-plane, the checkerboard tiles stretching from horizon to horizon, and the real world merely an echo.

A woman stood there, dressed all in black. She turned around, and Cleo stared into her mirror image, though she'd never worn an expression like that upon her face.

"I cast you out," she said softly, feeling the steadiness of Sebastian's hair beneath her hand in the real world.

"You cannot. I'm a part of you," said the black queen.

"I cast you out," she said, more firmly this time as she advanced. "You're nothing more than a parasite, and I am done with leeches trying to drain me."

The black queen threw everything she had at Cleo, twisting the dream world into a dark prison, reminiscent of the one she'd just been in. "Without me, you'll be alone. Trapped in here for all your years."

"I'm not alone," she said, taking another dangerous step forward. "My husband loves me. It is you who is alone."

The Blade in her hands shimmered, ethereal light streaming off its runes as it created light in the darkness. She finally understood how Drake, Morgana, and her father had created the Infernal Relics. They'd been crafted in the physical world, but it was here, in the plane between the mortal realm and the Shadow Dimensions, that the enchantments had been laid.

A weapon of both worlds, meant for a creature of both worlds.

"No," whispered the black queen, the dark heart of her.

"Yes. I cast you out." In the real world, she turned to look into the demon's horrified eyes. "You have your sacrifice."

Cleo drove the Blade into her own chest, shoving it down deep into her shadow self. The black queen screamed.

"Cleo!" Sebastian yelled, as she drove the Blade into her chest, sinking it up to the hilt. The demon bellowed in rage, sinking to its knees, its skin rippling violently.

No. He scrambled to catch her, to stem the blood, to save her, somehow... but those dark eyes were suddenly locking on his face as if she saw him again. *His* Cleo. Not the black queen.

And she drew the Blade of Altarrh from her chest, a thin line of blood suddenly flaring with golden power as the wound sealed itself. "It can't harm me in this place. I wasn't truly here. We're not truly in the real world."

A shuddering gasp escaped him. He traced his fingers down the center of her chest.

"She's gone," Cleo whispered. "I destroyed her."

"But... how?" No true wound from the Blade would ever heal. A single cut could kill a man, if he was unlucky.

"It's complicated. It's meant to kill a demon, which is not a physical entity, and... well... I'm not entirely human, or so it seems, and I was both here and on a different plane at the same time, so the wound was dealt on the dream plane, and dispatched the black queen—"

He didn't care. She was alive, and clearly not about to die. She was back, her eyes the same color as whiskey, and warm and lit from within with all the spark that made her what she was.

Sebastian captured her face and dragged her mouth to his. *"I thought you were about to die."* He shoved his hands into her hair, driving his tongue into her mouth, kissing her until neither of them could breathe. *"Don't ever leave me again."*

"I won't."

Cleo broke the kiss with a gasp, tears glistening in her eyes. "You came for me. You don't know what it felt like to be trapped inside her. Trapped"—her head turned toward the demon—"the way your father is trapped. We have to save him."

"The demon's too strong."

"No." Determination crossed her brow. Above them the skies were roiling, thick black clouds lit by the white light from the hexagram. "It's started the ritual, which is draining its strength. If the three of you distract it, I can get close to it. I know what to do now."

He stared down at the Blade in her hand. If the demon got its hands on her again....

"Start the spell!" Cleo snapped at him, turning to face the hexagram. "You need to trust me."

The demon saw her coming and hissed, driving to its feet. "You could have been great. You could have been mine. *My child.*"

"I am great," Cleo told it, her hair whipping back in the winds as the spell began to suck at the world around it. "And you have your sacrifice."

"You will pay for this." Then it smiled darkly and lifted its arms. "You will be the first to die, White Queen."

Sebastian lifted his arms at the eastern point, feeling Lucien take his place at the southern point of the star.

Verity helped Bishop stagger to the western point, her face pale, and Bishop's determined.

"Three sons," whispered the demon. "Three relics. Three sacrifices." It looked up, toward the black clouds. "And the perfect moment in time…. Can you feel it? How thin the Veil is right now?"

Heat shimmers bathed the air. The snow inside the triangle melted instantly, and Sebastian could feel immense power batter at him.

"Link!" Lucien yelled at him, and Sebastian saw golden light stream along the bloodied line between him and Bishop.

Bishop's power grew incrementally. He stretched out a hand—and the link—toward Sebastian.

He'd sworn once never to lose control of his body again. Never to be used. Never to trust.

One last chance to save Drake….

One last chance to save all of them, and stop this spell before the veil was torn open and the shadow horde appeared….

All he had to do was open himself up, wholly and completely, in a way he'd never dared before, and let his brother take over his puppet strings.

And he couldn't do it.

"Yes, you can," Cleo whispered through the bond.

He looked down at the two bloodied lines which led directly from his feet to Bishop and Lucien's. The two of them stared at him, Bishop gritting his teeth against the stream of power running through him. Bishop needed the lines to connect, so he could earth some of the energy.

It took everything within Sebastian to reach toward both Bishop and Lucien. It felt like he was pushing against some enormous iron doors in his mind; brushing against Bishop's psyche in a fumbling attempt to connect.

But Cleo believed in him.

And Bishop had been there for him, and Lucien, and all the others. This was family, the one thing he'd always craved.

And... there.

Bishop's metaphorical hand caught his own, just as he tumbled from the cliff in his mind.

"Got you." Bishop said along the link, and then power was roaring up through Sebastian's feet.

He was no longer in control. He was drunk on the feeling of it, Bishop angling the lines of power out toward Lucien.

"Got you," Lucien said, with a wince.

The triangle of light—one half of the hexagram—lit up, burning through the remaining snow. The demon in the center of the star looked down in surprise, clouds of darkness whipping past it, and the tear in the fabric of reality above it pausing. Sebastian could almost see its thought process. It turned toward Bishop, recognizing who held the triumvirate of power.

Who to kill.

"Now!" Ianthe yelled.

And the second triangle lit up as she, Verity, and Lady E took the remaining points of the star.

Ianthe was wielding the second triangle, and where the lines crossed the first, he could feel some sort of shiver of connection.

Bishop started chanting, binding the spell work into the ritual.

Sebastian ground his teeth together.

He'd spent all bloody night learning the words. It didn't truly matter what he said—the key was in the ritual, in his mind recognizing what he wanted to create—but the spell was complex enough that he'd stuck to memorizing

Bishop's spell. Words spilled from his lips, echoed by the other five.

The sheer amount of power Bishop was handling was incredible. Not even Drake's reserves could match it. But the demon was trying to fight, holding them at bay as they channeled energy through the three Relics Infernal.

A trembling hand rested on his forearm. He could barely feel it. The pain behind his right eye was intensifying. And then Eleanor stepped past, hobbling on her cane, her eyes locked on Drake.

They were betting everything on this moment. Eleanor's magic had not returned, not yet. She couldn't protect herself from the demon if it chose to annihilate her.

But there was someone who could.

Someone who could no more see harm done to his lover than he could harm her himself.

The demon's eyes lit up—just for a second—and then its face began to ripple again, horror filling its eyes. No, *Drake's* eyes. For just a second Sebastian saw the man he recognized as his father emerge from behind the demon's cool mask, stricken by the thought of harm coming to the woman he loved.

"Drake," Eleanor whispered, stepping inside the star with her hand outstretched. "Cast it out. Come home to me... *please.*"

Drake went down on one knee, his fingers curled into claws, and that horrible rippling still continuing beneath his skin.

Cleo moved toward him, the Blade in her hand, her skirts whipping behind her.

"Do it," Drake rasped, holding his hands wide.

"Begone," Cleo whispered, and grabbed a handful of his hair. "I cast you out, back to your world. You don't belong in this one."

And then she drove the Blade of Altarrh into Drake's chest.

The enormous six-pointed star of power flowed through Bishop, through the Blade, and smashed into Drake.

It felt like every last drop of energy was being wrung from him. Sebastian curled his hands into fists, wavering on his feet. He could see blood dripping from Lucien's nose, from Verity's. Cleo's face had drained of color, and her hair rippled around her face as all that power consumed her.

The hexagram exploded outwards, and Sebastian was lifted off his feet, his back and head slamming into the wall behind him.

CHAPTER THIRTY

THE CARNAGE WAS immense.

Sebastian rolled to his feet, his ears ringing and his vision wavering. Smoke billowed nearby; the corner of the manor had caught on fire during the explosion. Every glass window had blown out, flames licking at the window casings, and the black spray of ichor drenched the snow where dozens of imps had been obliterated.

He caught glimpses of it all; Lucien sitting with his head cradled in his hands, and Ianthe kneeling at his side to check on him; Drake cupping Eleanor's face in his hands as he tried to help her to stand; Cleo standing shakily, her black dress ripped and torn, and half her hair singed to her shoulders; and Bishop flat on his back, with Verity crouched over him.

"Are you all right?" Sebastian reached out to help Cleo to her feet.

"All right?" she looked around her in shock, one bedraggled crow feather melted into her hair.

No one had escaped unscathed, but he felt a buoyant surge of hope through the bond. Cleo's eyes shone with tears, and she'd never looked more beautiful. "I've never seen this far into the future. All my Visions stopped at London's doom."

But the evening skies were clearing, and there was no sign of the Gates to the Shadow Dimensions. And she was back. Back. He'd never take her presence for granted ever again.

"You came for me," she said, meeting his eyes.

"Always." Cleo threw her arms around his neck, and he dragged her into a hug. "I will always come for you."

Tears of happiness gleamed in her eyes, "We did it. The odds seemed so impossible at the time, and I was trapped in the dark for so long...." A shudder went through her. "But we're here now, and there's a whole future ahead of us."

"Help me," a voice begged, and the pair of them broke apart as reality began to intrude. They hadn't checked on everybody yet. Not everybody was guaranteed a future.

Sebastian found his brother in the snow, still unmoving. "Bishop."

"Someone help me! He's starting to fade." Verity stroked her husband's face, her expression stricken.

Drake crouched by Bishop's side. He pressed his fingertips to Bishop's chest, but it wasn't moving. "The fool.... He's drained himself dry." He looked up. "Ianthe?"

Ianthe staggered as she made her way toward them, her skirts ripped and her hair a mess. "I don't know how much I have left in me."

There was blood dripping from Lucien's nose, and he shook his head darkly. Nothing left in him either... indeed, it was a miracle he was still on his feet.

"Here, let me." And Sebastian knelt at his brother's side, and cupped Bishop's slack face in both hands. "I have more energy left in me than most."

His power had always been half curse, half promise. It had turned his mother from his side—but no, that was her bad luck, not his. Now it flooded through him from some deep well, and he reached out to hold Verity's hand so he could help her save his brother.

Or try to.

For the emptiness within his brother was dark and hungry. No matter how much energy he poured through their link, he could barely fill it.

"Come on, you stubborn bastard," Sebastian muttered beneath his breath. There was some sort of gaping hole in Bishop's aura, as if he'd burned some part of himself out.

"Come on," Verity whispered. "He was holding all that power. I felt it drag him under when he let the spell go."

Bishop suddenly sucked in a deep breath, startling them all. He grabbed Sebastian's wrist, and then relaxed back down when he saw whom it was. "What the hell—?"

Sebastian subsided, feeling empty and raw. "You're welcome."

"Thank you," Verity cried, and threw herself into her husband's arms.

Bishop groaned, wrapping a weary arm around his wife. "What... happened...? Where is... everybody?"

Sebastian grasped this brother's hand. "We did it," he said, repeating Cleo's words.

Drake clapped a gentle hand on his shoulder, and it was like looking up into a mirror. Or an older version of himself, at least, and it was rather uncanny. "It's good to finally meet you, face-to-face."

"Are you all right?" he asked, for he alone knew what it felt like to be a demon's vessel.

Drake shuddered. "I'm here. And I have all my sons safe before me. There will be time enough to forget... to forget everything it did with my body."

"You gave yourself up. For me," he whispered.

He'd wondered all this time why this man—a virtual stranger—had sacrificed himself for Sebastian.

He didn't wonder any more.

It was the same feeling that had made him share power with his unconscious brother; the same sensation that made him kneel at Cleo's feet even when she raised the knife and he thought she was going to kill him; the same stirring he felt when Lady Eberhardt kissed him on the cheek before she sent him into battle.

Love.

It all finally made sense now. And though his feelings for the others paled behind his feelings for Cleo, he would still stand between them and any sign of danger. Even, perhaps, die for them.

He'd lost so much over the course of his life. He'd endured so much pain. And yet it was all worth it—in some masochistic way—for the chance to stand here now, and to know these people.

Drake saw it all in his eyes, and gently offered him a hand to help him to his feet. "It was worth it. Even for the chance to see you like this, one more time. We have a great deal of missed time to make up for."

"Yes."

And then his father slowly dragged him into his arms in a hug.

And everything *was* all right.

Cleo picked her way through the snow while the others sat and recovered. The moon rose in the sky, gleaming brightly over what was left of the snow. There'd been a momentary panic when nobody could find Lady E for several minutes, but then she'd appeared around the corner of the garden folly, leaning heavily on Remington Cross's arm and cursing up a storm.

"Bloody imps," the old woman had spat. "We were trying to track the last of them down. Can't have that rabble gallivanting through London. The queen and Parliament would be up in arms."

"I take it you succeeded?" Drake had said dryly.

"Better than you, old friend." Lady E snorted, and poked Drake with her finger. "What the hell were you thinking? Letting a demon take possession of you?"

And there'd been an awkward moment when Sebastian looked up sharply, and Drake glanced down beneath his lashes.

"Some sacrifices are worth it," Drake murmured, and gently squeezed Sebastian's shoulder.

Cleo had left them there, needing a moment to herself. Premonition kept itching, but not the dangerous sort. There was something left unfinished.

She found Malachi Gray leaning against the wall, cradling his bloodied palms in his lap. Cleo flinched. She would never forgive herself.

"Hello," she called, wending her way toward him.

Malachi lifted that ageless face to hers intently, and for a moment it looked like he was going to flee. "You appear to be yourself again."

"Yes," she whispered. "What are you doing sitting here in the dark?"

His head slumped back against the wall. "It's where I belong." A faint mocking smile touched his lips. "You know what I am."

"Yes." She knelt beside him. "You're the man who knew I wasn't myself. The man who refused to... to take advantage of *her* advances."

Their eyes met.

"You weren't yourself," he repeated, looking away. "And I'm not interested in being a demon's meal."

"I think," she said quietly, "there is just enough chivalry within you, even though you try to hide it."

"There is nothing good within me, Cleo." He shifted angrily. "I'm an incubus. Touched by the Shadow Dimensions, twisted and unholy."

"And so am I," she told him.

He flinched from that.

"Are you trying to tell me there is nothing good within me either?"

"No." He slumped again. "Any fool can see there is goodness within you."

"Even after what I did?" She cupped his hands, drawing just enough power into herself to heal him. "I'm so, so sorry." Tears burned in her eyes as she saw her hand lift the hammer again, and drive the spike through his palm.

She hadn't been able to stop herself—or the black queen, to be honest, for she would bear the guilt for that creature's actions.

He hesitated. "It wasn't you."

"I couldn't stop her." The tears started flowing. "I could see everything she was doing, but my hands were not my own. I'm so sorry for your friend."

His mouth twisted. "Odette shouldn't have tried to protect me. And it was not your hand that struck her down. I'll lay that at the demon's feet."

"All the same, she was your friend." Cleo squeezed his hand. "I'm sorry for your loss."

"My loss." He looked up at her then, as if she'd said something utterly incomprehensible. "She was just an incubus, just...." And then he shook his head, as if even he couldn't believe the lies falling from his lips. "Odette mattered. To me."

"Yes," she said, dashing her tears from her cheeks. "You should join the others. They're going to rouse the carriages and return to town. There's nothing for you here."

"I don't think there is a place for me there either," he mused. "Your husband doesn't like me."

"I think he's forgiven you for stealing that kiss," she said. "He *did* save your life, after all. And he knows you tried to stop the demon from taking me. Those are points in your favor."

"What happens when she wakes?" he whispered hoarsely.

They were speaking of the girl in the glass coffin.

"I don't know. I didn't see that." Cleo squeezed his hand. "But I know she *will* wake, and perhaps the answer to that question is up to you. You're the one who makes your own choices, and you've been given a second chance now. What will she see when she wakes up? That choice is yours."

It clearly wasn't what he wanted to hear. Malachi's face shuttered, but he nodded. "I had best go bury Odette, or what is left of her." He hauled himself to his feet, scraping his hair back off his face before giving her a lingering look. "Good luck with your husband. You should know... I lied when I said he hadn't given you his heart. He had. He just didn't know it at the time."

A fist eased inside her. "Thank you."

Malachi pressed a gentle kiss to her cheek. "No. Thank you."

And then he was gone, disappearing into the dark as if it swallowed him whole.

"That was well done," said a voice behind her.

Cleo turned so swiftly she almost fell. Quentin Farshaw stepped out of the shadows, his dark hair tumbling in thick curls around his face.

"You were watching?" she demanded sharply.

He nodded slowly, his gaze settling on the still-burning pyres of the imps, and the smoldering star. "I saw it all. You chose the Light, and I was here to bear witness."

"I read your book. You were sired by a demon. Your gifts were demon-born too."

"Aye. There are several of us still out there. I could teach you. You could become one of us—"

"Us?"

"Travelers," he replied. "We watch the streams of time, protecting England—and the world—from all dangers from other planes."

"What is the point in watching?" Cleo demanded, thinking of all the death and pain that could have been avoided. "You had this knowledge, and you *did nothing* with it."

"You're young," Farshaw replied coldly. "You don't understand what it means to slip through time. A single conversation creates a million different possibilities in the time stream. To interfere is to interrupt—possibly even destroy—millions of futures. There are rules, and if the demons must play by them, then so must we. There is a pact in place. I couldn't break it. I did what I could."

His words took the heat from her anger as she remembered the book he'd given her. And a conversation in Balthazar's Labyrinth, so many days ago.

How many times had she tried to prevent what she saw in the future, only to have it twist in unpredictable ways?

"What rules?" she whispered. "What pact?"

"This isn't the first time a demon has been called into this world, or has broken free of its master's will. During the last black queen's rise, we were forced to forge a treaty with them, or there would have been no means to stop the plague."

"The Black Death?"

He nodded curtly.

"But that was before your time."

"Nothing is before my time."

What would it mean to be able to go back into the past and change the future? The thought of saving Sebastian from all the abuse he'd suffered sprang to mind, but she instantly knew it was wrong. Where would one stop? And what far-reaching implications would those choices have?

No. Far too dangerous. Far too tempting. Farshaw was right.

"The only way to interfere in the current game is to give your candidate knowledge," Farshaw said. "You were my white queen. I could only work through you, and even confronting you was a great risk."

Cleo raked a hand through her hair, turning away from him. "A bloody chess game."

"It is part of the pact," he admitted, taking several steps after her. "The game must be contained."

"It's not a game," she cried out. "These are people's lives you're playing with."

Farshaw tilted his head, and she realized he was so far outside time—the world—that he had no concept of the pieces he played with anymore. He didn't care about poor

Odette, who'd been swept up in a merciless war and paid the cost with her life. He didn't care about Drake, or Eleanor, or Bishop, or any of the others.

Not even her.

"Why are you here?" she asked suspiciously.

"Because you won the game," he replied. "You are a worthy successor to our ranks."

Cleo's breath caught. "You want me to join you?"

"I could teach you everything," he said. "How to time-walk; how to see the future in complete Visions; how to guard the world from the threat at our doorstep."

Away from Sebastian and her new family. Cleo shook her head. It wasn't even a consideration. "No. No thank you."

"The world is at risk," he said sharply. "You opened the Gates for the briefest of moments, and something came through. It's out there, even as we speak. You could stop it. You could help us hunt it down."

Cleo froze, haunted by what she'd done when she wasn't in control of her body. The guilt tempted her, where nothing else could....

But how could she fight something without Sebastian by her side? "I think... I think I am right where I am meant to be. You can't see every possibility. You can't see where every choice will take you. But this one? This one feels like the right one. Goodbye, Mr. Farshaw."

He looked taken aback. "You can't mean that."

"I do. I am more than a pawn in your immortal game. And so are my friends. And if there is indeed something out there, then I shall tell Ianthe and the others, and we will take care of it. Here. On this plane. In this time. Goodbye."

And then she turned her back on him, and went back to join her family.

EPILOGUE

Two years later....

HE WAS LATE. Sebastian snapped the pocket watch shut, cursing his brothers under his breath. He had a sparring appointment with Bishop every Monday morning, and Lucien had started joining in of late, now his full powers were finally starting to return.

Neither of them was any match for Bishop, of course, despite his vastly weakened state. He'd never truly regained his full strength after the battle with the demon, but he seemed at peace with it. The loss of power was a small price to pay for the loss of the *maladroise*, he claimed.

That didn't make him any less dangerous.

In spite of the drubbing Sebastian regularly took, it was enjoyable to meet with them, though he'd never admit that. Lucien's new baby, Adeline, took most of his attention these days, and Bishop could barely contain his enthusiasm over Verity's increasing state. They all had dinner once or twice a month, of course, for the ladies were firm friends—and dangerous allies when they all got together—and Drake enjoyed being able to host family dinners.

403

The carriage rattled as it hit a puddle. Cleo would be wondering where he was.

Sebastian collapsed back onto the carriage seat, trying to ignore his clammy great cloak. It would be a cold ride home, and to warm himself he thought of what waited for him there. A wife in every sense of the word. One who'd blindfolded him and pleasured him with her mouth and hands the night before. The thought of her summoned the little knot in his mind that was their link, and he couldn't help himself really. He reached through the link, the bond opening like a blooming flower until the sensation of her drenched him. Warmth cocooned her, and Cleo stirred sleepily, reaching out to touch the link on her side.

All of a sudden it was like staring directly at her. Thoughts swelled around him: her curiosity, her pleasure in having him reach out to her, and the simple state of happiness she relaxed within. She felt... sated.

"What are you doing?" he asked.

There was a pause. *"I'm in the bath. What are you doing?"*

Naked. Wet. All that glorious hair draped in a knot on top of her head. His mouth went dry. *"I'm on my way home. Doing what in the bath?"*

"Washing myself," she replied, with a wicked little laugh. *"What do you generally get up to when you're in the bath?"*

"You seem remarkably pleased with yourself," he pointed out. *"One wonders what you've been up to."*

After all, she was no longer quite so innocent.

"Wouldn't you like to know?"

The husky sensation of her thoughts made his cock harden. *"You've been fucking yourself with your fingers, haven't you?"*

The flush of embarrassment returned through the link, and any hints of Cleo as a seductress vanished. *"No! I was reading a book in the bath. I'm warm, relaxed, and it's an interesting book. Honestly, is that all you men think of?"*

These days, yes. *"What sort of book?"*

"Geraldine Hibbert's Thoughts on Time.*"*

More dry treatises on sorcery. He winced. *"Sounds interesting."*

"It is interesting," she replied, and he sensed her putting the book aside, where it wouldn't get wet. Water sloshed over her skin as she lay back, and he could almost feel the sensation on his own skin.

"Do you regret it?" he asked quietly, and her thoughts stilled as she followed the path of his own.

"Saying no to Quentin Farshaw? Of course not."

"You wouldn't have to resort to reading books by people with half your skills, or visiting with Madrigal Brown."

"And I wouldn't be happy either," she pointed out, *"or trying to seduce my husband."*

He smiled. *"Are you trying to seduce your husband?"*

"Well, I was, but he keeps distracting me."

"My apologies, my love. Are you using soap?" he sent, pressing his palm over his mouth, for the idea of her in the bath shook him. It was such a normal thing. A day-to-day thing.

"I have soap."

He pushed all the other overwhelming emotions out of the way. *"Do you? Tell me about your soap... and what you plan to do with it...."*

"Always giving me orders...." But it was not a complaint. He sensed her picking up the washcloth and lathering it. *"But since you like to be in control, what would you like me to do with the soap?"*

Her breasts obliterated his thoughts. *"Touch yourself,"* he whispered through their link.

"Where?" If she was here, he'd have been able to see the blush on her cheeks.

"Touch yourself," he sent again. *"Wash your breasts for me. Soap those pretty nipples."*

There was something to be said for telepathy. For a soul-bond. He shifted uncomfortably on the carriage seat, his cock straining against his trousers as he closed his eyes, all the better to feel what she was feeling.

Cleo dragged the washcloth over her chest, leaving a wake of suds. He could almost see through her eyes, and the sight made his cock pulse. She caressed her swollen nipples. *"They're clean. Where else would you like me to soap?"*

"You know where."

"Do I?"

"Part your legs," he breathed, *"and drag that cloth between them."*

Cleo's knees slowly sank against the sides of the bath. Her breath caught as she did as instructed, and he felt the slither of the cloth echo over his belly and cock. An odd sensation. Her flesh imprinted on his.

He caught a flash of image: a pale hand sliding down a woman's smooth stomach, delving beneath a mess of bubbles.

"How far away are you?" Cleo panted.

He flipped the blind up, recognizing the streets around him. *"A minute or two."* A smile broke across his mouth. *"Why?"*

"Because I don't know how long I can wait."

"Then don't," he replied. *"Come for me, Cleo. I want you to be wet and ready for when I get there."*

She felt him moving through the house like a brewing storm. Hunger itched within his skin, and anticipation swam through her. Drake had deeded them the town house, suggesting Sebastian and Cleo enjoy their time together with a small wink, and she delighted in having her own home. Everything she might have inherited from her father was deeded away through the male line—a distant cousin she could barely recall—but here they had a place of their own.

Hurrying out of the water, Cleo reached for her robe, dragging it over her shoulders just as the door opened. Sebastian appeared, a hard man dressed all in black. His eyes glittered as they raked over her, and she was suddenly aware of how tightly the silk clung to her wet body as he shut the door with a loud, controlled click.

"I—"

He stepped forward, pressing a finger to her mouth. Need clenched between her thighs at the relentless look in his eyes. She'd thought she was done, but desire flared back to life like a wildfire at the stroke of his finger.

She was restless enough that she turned her face to and fro, her wet mouth rasping against the press of his fingers. Those bird-of-prey eyes locked on her, and Sebastian pressed her back, her bottom biting into the vanity, one hand resting on her hip.

Nothing needed to be said. Cleo shivered as Sebastian slowly dragged that finger down her sensitive mouth and chin, and lower, down her throat. His gaze dipped, tracking the press of silk as he circled her nipple. The ache of it speared through her. She bit her lip, trying not to moan. Trying not to yield to the touch, though her knees wobbled.

Sebastian swooped down, his teeth biting into her throat in a sensation that made her jump. She captured his wrist in surprise, but everything else in her arched back, surrendering to the moment. He wasn't going to be sweet or tender tonight. She knew it.

And a restless part of her craved it.

"Fuck me." She wound her hands through his hair as he ravished her throat. *"Fill me."*

He was no longer hesitant in her bed, and she was not as naïve as she'd been once.

Sebastian's hands slid down the backs of her thighs, and he lifted her onto the vanity. Their eyes met, his stark and silver, and then he was shoving her thighs apart, forcing himself into the vee of them.

Cleo cried out, catching at his wet coat lapels. "Please—"

He captured her mouth, a hard, demanding kiss with no respite. No words. *No words.* And his hands slid down her robe, skating over her breasts, her nipples, even as his lips bruised hers. He fisted his fingers in her robe, tearing it apart.

Cleo's head swirled as they broke apart, and she gasped in air. Candlelight etched shadows beneath his cheekbones, giving him a predatory look.

But this was *her* predator. And she wanted to be consumed by him.

Hooking her fingers in his mouth, she snagged the tip of them on his teeth and hauled him back to her. Another kiss made of pure desire. It bruised her lip, and their teeth met, but she wasn't done yet. Capturing his hands, she pressed them to her naked breasts, moaning at the sensation of his touch. Any of her earlier shyness vanished. He wanted her. He wanted forever. And the darkness within her stretched and awoke, though it obeyed *her* now. She wanted to own him. Heart and soul.

"You already do," he rasped.

And then he was kissing his way down her body, hauling her hips to the edge of the vanity as his mouth locked over her nipple.

Ecstasy lanced through her. Cleo cried out, arching into his mouth and clinging to his hair. Teeth scored her delicate nipple. Then he turned to the other. It was far too overwhelming. She slumped back against the mirror as his hands bit into her thighs, hauling her against him.

The rasp of his trousers was such a foreign sensation between her thighs that she opened her eyes in shock. Sebastian never looked away from her as he thrust against her, a delicate sort of torture. Then he put one hand on her chest, forcing her to wilt back.

Dragging her hips off the vanity left her in a precarious position. The only thing holding her there was his hands, cupped beneath each thigh. Sebastian pressed a kiss directly between her breasts. Then lower, and Cleo's fingers curled into a fist in his hair as he kissed his way lower....

The wet lash of his tongue was enough to undo her. He kissed her sex with blunt possession, his tongue stabbing into her. The sensation lashed along her spine, erupting in little bumps all over her body.

"Sebastian!" she blurted, but she pressed his face closer to her, grinding her hips up. *Oh, merciful goddess*. Cleo arched her head back, carelessly trapping his head between her thighs.

The press of his mouth was indescribable. Inescapable. He'd been kind before. But not now. This was fierce and unstoppable, a flash fire burning through her veins. He consumed her with lips, and teeth, and tongue. She came with a loud cry, the explosion wracking through her.

"No more! No more!" she begged, and she could finally breathe again when he lifted his head.

Every inch of her body felt molten. She pressed the heel of her hand to her forehead, breathing hard. Moving seemed beyond her.

Ever again.

A soft kiss brushed against her hip. Then another a little higher, skating over her ribs. Cleo shivered. This wasn't done. Capturing his hand, she pressed a kiss to the back of it, and Sebastian glanced up from beneath those dangerous lashes, a faint, hawkish smile touching his swollen mouth, before he found her nipple. The hot clasp of his mouth was utterly sinful. She'd thought there was nothing left inside her, but a single touch and he fanned all the smoldering flames within her to life.

Cleo's heart nearly stopped as she cupped his face in her hands, lifting him to her mouth so she could claim another kiss. *I love you*. She knew he caught the edge of it, for a shudder went through his hard body.

A hand reached behind her, clutching at something. A towel. She caught a glimpse of it, as he folded it neatly beside her, over the edge of the timber.

"What are you—" *Oh*. The simple gesture—to protect her body from the hard edge of the vanity—touched her.

Flipping her over, he pressed her hips into the towel, his entire body molding to hers from behind. The fabric of his coat and trousers seemed rough against her sensitive skin, and there was something about the situation—about being practically naked, whilst he was still fully clothed— that made her inner muscles clench with need again. That wicked mouth scraped along her throat, his stubble sending a rasp of sensation through her. His hand covered her mouth, and she bit into his fingers as he slid the skirt of her robe up over her bottom, pressing a knee between her thighs.

"I love it when you scream my name," he whispered, reaching between them. He tugged at something, and then she felt the blunt edge of his cock brush up against her. The head of it dipped through the wet folds of her sex. "Scream it, Cleo. Scream it."

And she did as she was told as he thrust within her, sheathing his erection within her wetness, his hips slapping against her bottom.

"*Sebastian!*"

Another thrust. She bit his fingers, feeling like she was going to fracture. To fly apart into a million pieces.

"Scream it," he demanded, his hand delving down the front of her and cupping her firmly. Slow fingers moved through her wet folds, his index centering on that one particularly sensitive area, as if he knew exactly where it was. He pressed small circles there, pushing her inexorably toward the edge of another pleasure cliff.

The orgasm slammed through her, making her cry out. Her whole body shook, even as he thrust, hammering her against the vanity. Only the press of the towel he'd laid there cushioned her hips.

He hauled her close, turning her face to the side so he could kiss her again, frantic and furious. "Cleo. Cleo." The words tumbled from his lips in time to the thrust of his hips.

She reached out to him through the bond, desperate to share this moment. It bloomed to life within her heart, her mind.... Suddenly there was no Cleo. No Sebastian. They were one and whole, heartbeats locking into the same shocking rhythm. Pleasure surged up through him, and she wasn't certain which one of them cried out....

He came, thrusting hard within her, and suddenly she was back in her body again, feeling the wetness of his seed flood her within.

"I love you," he whispered, caressing her spine.

Afterwards, they lay entwined in the bed, snatching moments of sleep between movement. Sebastian woke sometime during the early evening, the stars gleaming through the window. His hand slid down Cleo's spine, and she stirred. Just enough to see the light from the grate reflect back off her dark eyes.

He rolled onto his side, sliding a hand over her faintly curved stomach. Cleo blinked sleepily at him. "What are you doing?"

"Can I feel the babe?" he whispered.

"Of course." She pressed his hand to the right area. Her body was barely beginning to show the signs of the child within her, but he could feel that little spark within, whispering against his psychic senses.

They hadn't told anyone yet. It was just their little secret, though he suspected Bishop knew. He was going through the same thing himself, and their children would play together in the future.

"Do you want to see her?" Cleo whispered.

Her? He met her dark eyes in shock. "It's going to be a daughter?"

Cleo rubbed her hand lazily over his. "Oh, yes. I predict many arguments in your future. She's going to be a hellion."

"Just like her mother."

"She's stubborn too, like her father." Cleo drew his hand to where the baby nestled. "Close your eyes."

He did, letting the soul-bond strengthen as Cleo opened herself up to her Visions. They'd returned slowly, as her belief in herself grew. And sometimes she let him see them.

Suddenly he was standing in his father's house, holding a child in his arms. The baby blinked up at him with enormous eyes, barely heavy enough to weigh him down, her tiny fingers reaching for him.

And then he blinked, and there was a little girl of about six running through the house, chasing a puppy. A little girl with hair just like her mother's, and Cleo's devastating smile.

But her eyes were pure gray, with thick smoky lashes, and there was a faint cleft in her chin, just like his.

Tears wet his eyes as he drew back from the Vision. "She's perfect," he said hoarsely. *"And she will never know what it feels like to be without her parents' affections."*

Cleo kissed him, dragging his body over hers. "No," she breathed. "All she will know is love."

COMING 2018

CURSEBOUND

BOOK ONE: THE DARK CURSE TRILOGY

Nobody knows the real Remington Cross. The stage magician is the perfect Master of Illusions; a charismatic sorcerer who hides a deep, dark secret. And when he finds the body of his magician's assistant—the first of many ritual deaths—he wonders if an ancient curse has returned to haunt him. With Scotland Yard hounding his every step, the only alibi Remy has is a young woman whose affections he once spurned.

Enter... Stage Right....

If it wasn't for murder, Thea Davies might enjoy holding the upper hand over the man who once broke her heart. Posing as Remy's stage assistant is the perfect cover to find out who—or what—is slaughtering her fellow sorcerers, and it's also an opportunity to get a taste of the passion that lingers between them.

The last thing Remy wants is to draw the innocent beauty into the twisted games his nemesis plays, but headstrong Thea is determined to uncover all his secrets. With a shadow looming over London, Remington must find the strength to break the curse... or risk losing Thea forever.

ACKNOWLEDGMENTS

Writing fast-paced, sexy, paranormal romance is the best fun imaginable, but as with every project I take on, I couldn't have done it without a lot of help from these amazing people:

I owe huge thanks to my editor Olivia from Hot Tree Editing for her work on this manuscript; to Mandy from Hot Tree Edits for the proofread; my wonderful cover artists from Damonza.com; and Marisa Shor from Cover Me Darling and Allyson Gottlieb for the print formatting.

To Keri, Jess, Robyn, Laurelle, Nicole and Kaye from the CVW Group, thanks for keeping me sane, and being my support group! Special thanks also go to my beta readers, Kylie Griffin and Jennie Kew—who ask me all of the hard questions, and support me on every step of this journey. And to my family for always supporting me on this journey. But the most thanks go to Byron, who has been my rock from the very beginning. I couldn't do what I do without his help.

Last, not certainly not least, to all of my readers who support me on this journey, and have been crazy vocal about their love for the London Steampunk series, and anything else I write!

ABOUT THE AUTHOR

Bec McMaster grew up on a steady diet of 80's fantasy movies like Ladyhawke, Labyrinth and The Princess Bride, and loves creating epic, fantasy-based worlds with heroes and heroines who must defeat all the odds to have their HEA. If you like sexy, dark, paranormal romance, try her Dark Arts series; for some kick-bustle ladies-saving-the-day steampunk romance then check out London Steampunk; and for rocket-fuelled post-apocalyptic romance with a twist on the werewolf theme, then see her Burned Lands series.

Bec has won a PRISM Award for Historical Fantasy with Hexbound (2016), been nominated for RT Reviews Best Steampunk Romance for Heart of Iron (2013), won RT Reviews Best Steampunk Romance with Of Silk And Steam (2015), and Forged By Desire was nominated for an RWA RITA award in 2015. The London Steampunk series has received starred reviews from Booklist, Publishers Weekly, and Library Journal, with Heart of Iron named one of their Best Romances of 2013.

She's also a dreamer. A travel addict. And an enthusiastic baker. If she's not sitting in front of the computer, she's probably plotting her next world trip. Bec lives in Australia, with her very own hero, Byron; a dog who will eat anything (even used teabags); and demanding chickens, Siggy and Lagertha.

For news on new releases, cover reveals, contests, and special promotions, join her mailing list at www.becmcmaster.com or follow her on Twitter @BecMcMaster, or www.facebook.com/BecMcMaster

91159464R00250

Made in the USA
Columbia, SC
13 March 2018